RAVES FOR
JAMES PATTERSON

"BEHIND ALL THE NOISE AND NUMBERS, WE SHOULDN'T FORGET THAT NO ONE GETS THIS BIG WITHOUT NATURAL STORY-TELLING TALENT—WHICH IS WHAT JAMES PATTERSON HAS, IN SPADES."
—Lee Child, #1 *New York Times* bestselling author of the Jack Reacher series

"EVERY ONCE IN A WHILE, A WRITER COMES ALONG AND FUNDAMENTALLY CHANGES THE WAY PEOPLE READ...WITH HIS MISSION STILL UNFOLDING, JAMES PATTERSON IS THE GOLD STANDARD BY WHICH ALL OTHERS ARE JUDGED."
—Steve Berry, #1 bestselling author of the Cotton Malone series

"JAMES PATTERSON IS THE BOSS. END OF."
—Ian Rankin, *New York Times* bestselling author of the Inspector Rebus series

For a complete list of books,
visit JamesPatterson.com.

THE CHEF

JAMES PATTERSON
AND MAX DiLALLO

GRAND CENTRAL
PUBLISHING

NEW YORK   BOSTON

Grand Central Publishing
Hachette Book Group
1290 Avenue of the Americas, New York, NY 10104
grandcentralpublishing.com
twitter.com/grandcentralpub

Originally published in hardcover and ebook by Little, Brown & Company in February 2019
First oversize mass market edition: April 2020

Grand Central Publishing is a division of Hachette Book Group, Inc. The Grand Central Publishing name and logo is a trademark of Hachette Book Group, Inc.

The publisher is not responsible for websites (or their content) that are not owned by the publisher.

The Hachette Speakers Bureau provides a wide range of authors for speaking events. To find out more, go to hachettespeakersbureau.com or call (866) 376-6591.

ISBNs: 978-1-5387-1490-4 (oversize mass market), 978-0-316-53000-2 (ebook)

Printed in the United States of America

OPM

10 9 8 7 6 5 4 3 2 1

To Suzie and Jack—
the chefs in our house

CHAPTER 1

"GIMME TWO scoops, three waddles, and a shake!"

Marlene is standing a few feet away from me, yelling out the next order because of the damn noise. Like the clanging of the manhole-sized skillet I'm using to sauté a fresh heap of diced onions, celery, and bell peppers. The popping and crackling of our deep fryer, louder than hail on a tin roof. The roar of the exhaust fan, straining to suck out all the smoke.

And that's just inside our sweltering little food truck.

Outside, a line of hungry customers stretching twice around the block is starting to get rowdy, yelling out encouragement and menu demands. Midday traffic with its engines and horns is rumbling up and down Canal Street, along with rattling trolley cars. And seemingly out of nowhere, a five-person roving brass jazz band has appeared on the corner, blaring a toe-tapping tune, causing some in line to snap photos with their phones to preserve yet another memory of their trip to this enchanted place.

A collision of food, music, history, passion, chaos... yep, that pretty much sums up New Orleans for you. "Nawlins," as us locals say it. NOLA. The Crescent City. The Big Easy. Different names for the same magical, one-of-a-kind place. My hometown of three-and-a-half decades. The capital of the world, as far as I'm concerned. A city where anything can happen, and nothing is *ever* as it seems.

Sometimes that's a good thing.

Other times—and I refuse to go there at the moment—it's a bad thing.

A very bad thing.

"Two scoops, three waddles, one shake!" I call back to Marlene, parroting the culinary shorthand we've developed running Killer Chef together these past few years. The work is grueling. Endless. Exhausting. But I love every second of it, doing something so simple yet so satisfying, providing great food at good prices to hungry and eager customers.

And with Marlene, I couldn't imagine having a better partner in crime, even though we've been divorced for years.

From the stack of empty paper serving boats beside me, I take six and fan them out along my prep space like a poker dealer flicking cards. From a plastic baggie sticking out of my back pocket, I grab an organic green jalapeño chili pepper and pop it into my mouth for a spicy pick-me-up. It's an unusual habit, I know, but better than a lot of *other* chefs' vices—trust me. Then I get to work.

I start with the "scoops." I fill two paper boats with mounds of fresh, piping-hot cheese grits. I top each with a healthy—well, *un*healthy—dollop of softened butter, followed by a huge scoop of *grillades*. That's a thick, fragrant Cajun stew made with seared veal medallions, onions, garlic, beef broth, and red wine.

Next come the "waddles." Into three serving boats go generous portions of "dirty rice," the grains the color of caramel, thanks to the spiced chicken giblets they're cooked with. Then, from the sizzling griddle in front of me, I add to each one a gator *boudin,* a succulent smoked sausage made with the meat of that legendary bayou predator. (The first time I ever cooked one for Marlene, years back, she said it tasted so fresh and juicy, she half-expected it to waddle off her plate. The name stuck.)

Last, I make the "shake." I dump a batch of twisted strips of raw dough into the metal deep-fryer basket, then plunge them into the scalding vat of oil. Once they're golden brown and perfectly flaky, I slide them into a serving boat and dust them with precisely six shakes of powdered sugar. Most New Orleans joints serve *beignets,* a similar, more common regional pastry. But I've always preferred these, known as angel wings. And I've never been one to follow the crowd, either here or in my other career.

"Order up!" I cry, sliding the six steaming paper boats over to Marlene.

She grabs them without looking, bundling each with napkins and plastic cutlery. Then she hands them down through the service window to a gaggle of attractive women, already tipsy despite the early hour, each wearing a bright sash over their shoulders and tiaras in their hair. A bachelorette party, if I had to guess, which is about as common in this city as air.

"Thanks, Killer Chef," one of the ladies says to me, twirling her colorful beaded necklaces around her finger. She adds with a coy giggle, "It sure looks… *yummy.*"

Most of our customers come to us for the incredible food. Can I help it if a few also want to flirt? And truth is, all sweaty, covered with food stains and smelling of cooking oil, I love the attention.

But before I can respond, Marlene answers for me—with a blatant eye roll.

"Oh, honey," she says, her voice dripping with experience and sarcasm. "Don't let Caleb's two hundred pounds of hunkiness fool you. That man's a lot like the sun. Plenty hot when he shines on you, but try to get close and he'll burn you to a crisp. Believe me. I know."

Good old Marlene. Opening this truck with her was one of the best decisions I ever made. But walking down the aisle with her? Eh, not so much.

I'm just about to tell these gals how my ex-wife is a lot like a lemon—sweet-looking but truly bitter—when something outside catches my eye.

And chills me, despite the sweltering heat inside my truck.

Down the block, four white boys in their midtwenties are leaning against the hood of a black SUV, a Ford Explorer with new, shiny chrome rims. They're passing around a bottle of liquor in a paper bag. Whispering among themselves. Watching the traffic go by. Watching the morning tourists stroll past.

But most of all, watching me.

I don't recognize their faces, but I do recognize their clothes. Each is wearing something yellow. A yellow bandana. A yellow baseball cap. A yellow hoodie.

Gang colors.

They're part of the Franklin Avenue Soldiers, an up-and-coming crew based out of the St. Roch neighborhood, a good four miles from here. I wasn't expecting to see any of them this far from their turf. In fact, I was hoping that working this busy brunch shift would distract me, would help keep all that bullshit out of my brain for a few hours.

I should have known they'd find me.

Especially today.

"Hey, fall asleep at the stove again?" Marlene barks, jolting me back to reality. "I need four waddles, two shakes, and three scoops!"

And so goes the rest of our morning. I try to stay focused on cooking our food. On pleasing our customers. On flashing a devilish grin at the pretty ones. But every time I glance through the service window, those gang-bangers are still out there. Glaring at me. Waiting for me to make my next move. Waiting for me to step out and away from all these potential witnesses lined up at my truck.

"And that's the last of 'em," Marlene finally says long minutes later, as the last two happy customers stroll away, leaving the sidewalk clear before us. She wipes her hands on her apron. It's stained with so many different colors, it looks like some kind of abstract painting.

I've already untied my own apron—and stripped off my sweaty black T-shirt with the Killer Chef logo as well. I wet a clean towel with cold water and rub down my chest, belly, and arms, trying to get most of the sweat off. I reach for a black duffel bag in the corner of the truck. I unzip it and start rummaging inside. Marlene clicks her tongue, annoyed.

"You're really not gonna stick around and help me prep for lunch, huh? Slacker."

"Trust me, Mar, I'd much rather keep slaving away over a hot stove than get dragged over the hot coals that are waiting for me down the way," I say, taking out a stick of deodorant that I liberally apply to each underarm. "Even if it means listening to you yammer on while I do it."

My ex-wife snickers. We're just busting each other's

chops. The truth is, I *would* rather do just about anything right now over what I'm about to. And she knows it, too.

"Caleb," she says softly, putting her hand on my bare chest. "Good luck."

"Thanks," I answer. Then I remove from the duffel bag a folded blue dress shirt, along with a plastic ID card dangling from a cloth lanyard.

It reads: *ROONEY, CALEB J.—DETECTIVE—NEW ORLEANS POLICE DEPARTMENT.*

I have a badge, too. I swear. And a gun.

But currently, they're not in my possession.

Long story.

I slip on the collared shirt, stuff my ID into my pocket, then look one more time through the service window at those gangbangers.

To my surprise, they're gone.

I should be relieved, but I'm not.

I know at the time and place of their choosing, they'll be back.

And they won't be lining up for my famous food.

CHAPTER 2

I STEP out of the food truck and suck in a deep breath of fresh air from the sidewalk.

The temperature probably topped triple digits inside that metal sardine can, but out here it's balmy and delightful. Folks are walking around in shorts and T-shirts. The palm trees lining Canal Street are gently swaying from the slight breeze. Anytime is a perfect time to visit New Orleans, if you ask me, but February can't be beat, especially if you're from some frozen place like Maine or Minnesota.

I start walking north away from my truck and ex-wife. After a few steps, I hear a metallic screeching and clattering coming up behind me. Turning back, I see a distinctive red and yellow vintage streetcar slowing down as it nears its next stop. If I broke into a jog, I could probably catch it. I'm going in that direction anyway. But I decide not to. I'm in no rush. Besides, I want to use the mile-and-a-half walk to do some thinking.

And ponder that visit from the Franklin Avenue Soldiers.

So I keep strolling, taking in all the sights and sounds. Preparations are well under way for Carnival, the two wild weeks leading up to Mardi Gras, the single greatest party on the entire planet—at least in my totally biased opinion.

It kicks off tonight and you can feel it in the air, see it everywhere you look. Shopkeepers have started hanging up purple, green, and gold streamers, flags, and other decorations in their windows. Eager, excited tourists have already begun trickling in. And at various key intersections around the city, the NOPD has started placing Delta barriers—big, white, mechanical traffic barricades that keep cars off designated parade routes and pedestrian paths. Things can get pretty crazy when the festivities are in full swing, but law, order, and safety are always top priorities.

Right now, I'm thinking about my own safety.

In more ways than one.

As I keep moving, scanning the streets for any lurking Franklin Avenue boys, I mentally rehearse how this whole thing is going to play out in just a short while.

I know what I saw. I know I did the right thing. And I know what I want to say.

So why do I still feel like I'm walking the plank?

Soon I'm hooking a left onto South Broad Avenue. I keep going until I cross Tulane—the thoroughfare, not the university. Up ahead is the Orleans Parish criminal court, one of the ugliest buildings in this otherwise beautiful city, a hideous concrete fortress surrounded by barbed-wire fences.

After I cross Gravier Street, my destination comes into view. Set back from the road by a wide courtyard, it's a place I've spent hundreds of hours of my life and been a part of some extraordinary investigations. But today, the New Orleans Police Department headquarters feels different. Strange. Foreboding. Uninviting.

I consider whether to enter through one of its side

doors, or maybe via the staff parking garage. Both would avoid a possible scene.

But that would also make it look like I had something to hide.

Screw that.

I take a final moment to compose myself. Then I march straight through the courtyard and up to the main entrance. As I expected, a flock of reporters is there waiting. They spot me, and the feeding frenzy begins. They'd all showed up at Killer Chef earlier, but Marlene screamed that she'd ban them from the truck forever if they didn't leave us alone. That took care of them.

"Detective Rooney, Detective Rooney!" they yell. "Any last words before you—"

"Last words?" I ask wryly. "This isn't an execution. Just a firing squad."

A shout comes from the rear of the journalist scrum. "Is it true you've waived your right to have a police union official or other counsel represent you?"

"You're looking at an innocent man," I firmly say.

I've nearly reached the glass front doors. I'm almost inside. So the questions come even faster, in a frantic jumble, like they're desperately trying to trip me up.

"What outcome are you expecting this afternoon, Detective?"

"How do you respond to critics who claim this whole proceeding is a sham?"

"Do you regret any of your actions?"

"Do you have anything to say to the victim's family?"

Grasping the metal door handle, I turn back and face the thick throng of reporters, some I know intimately from investigations past. You'd think they'd show me some courtesy, some consideration, not be part of a baying pack eager to bring me down.

But you'd be wrong.

To them, I'm a story now. Strictly business. Nothing personal.

The reporters finally quiet down, waiting, their cameras and phones ready and rolling.

I want to say plenty. To everyone involved.

But not here. Not now.

I give the crowd a nod and head inside, knowing that when I eventually leave this huge building with so many memories, I won't be the same man who came in.

Which both frightens and exhilarates me.

CHAPTER 3

TYPICALLY, THE NOPD Use of Force Review Board hearings are handled internally on the third floor, inside a stuffy conference room furnished with a beat-up oval table and a bunch of uncomfortable chairs. I know this because over the course of my fourteen-year career with the department, I've testified in three such proceedings on behalf of fellow cops.

But in this, my fourth appearance before the Board, I'm the focus.

Not a great feeling.

Usually the hearings are kept confidential and closed to the public, except in cases where the department is looking to make an example of someone and try and look good to the public.

Like this one.

I'm kept waiting for nearly twenty minutes in the hallway outside the spacious ground-floor briefing room co-opted for today's event. The uniformed officer acting as the hearing's sergeant-at-arms—a kid barely out of the academy, with a face so pink and boyish I bet he gets carded at R-rated movies—tells me the committee must first address some "administrative matters."

"Sounds like a bullshit excuse," he adds under his breath. He's clearly trying to buddy up to me, gain some macho props. "This whole *thing's* bullshit, if you want the truth, Rooney. Everybody knows it, too. Your shot was cleaner than a nun's ass."

I pity-chuckle at the officer's attempt at humor, but smile with genuine thanks for the support. I couldn't agree with this kid more. Every police shooting should be investigated thoroughly, but what the department's making me go through is ridiculous. It's all politics. Pure PR.

But that's the job. Sometimes it's your turn to be "made an example of," and my number just came up.

It pisses me off so much that some nights I can't sleep, just replaying the events over and over again in my mind: the chase, the gunshot, the aftermath.

Each time I think it through, I know I made the right choice.

But facts aren't going to matter today.

Appearances will.

Finally, the young officer opens the door to the briefing room and I walk in. Five NOPD brass are seated behind a polished wooden table up at the front. They range in rank from lieutenant to the big cheese, Deputy Superintendent of Field Operations Charles Bossett, a burly African-American man whose mere presence projects authority.

About two dozen people are crammed into the gallery. As I take my seat by myself at a separate table, I give the crowd a scan. It's a mix of spectators, reporters, a few department colleagues and police union reps, as well as the friends and family of the late Larry Grant.

His death last month by my use of a department-issued sidearm—which is currently being kept inside a locked steel cage deep in this building's evidence room, alongside my silver badge—is why we're all here today.

"For the record," Deputy Superintendent Bossett begins with a stern voice, "Detective Caleb James Rooney has joined the proceedings."

"Good afternoon," I respond with a respectful nod.

Bossett continues. "We now return to the matter of the detective's use of lethal force in the line of duty against Lawrence Christopher Grant, age twenty-nine, at approximately 11:43 p.m. on the night of January 10, 2018—an episode, we are all aware, that has been the subject of ample media coverage, both local and national."

No shit, I think. *That's* why the department is making such a big spectacle out of this. Not because of the facts of the shooting, which was about as by-the-book as could be. But to try to regain some shred of public respect after all the negative press over the past years.

Grant had been on my radar for a couple months. He was a mid-level Franklin Avenue Soldier and well-known drug dealer. But he was also a devoted husband who coached his little cousin's youth basketball team and took night classes at nearby Delgado Community College. Not exactly your typical criminal lowlife.

And I'm not exactly your typical police, either. Just try to find another major crimes detective anywhere in the country who moonlights as an award-winning chef and runs a popular food truck in his spare time.

The blogs and papers had a field day with that. The story spread far and wide. The headlines practically wrote themselves. KILLER CHEF TURNS KILLER COP. NOPD IN BOILING WATER AFTER FOODIE FLATFOOT FIRES FIRST. PUBLIC TO CITY: 'COOKING COP MUST FRY.'

I've never tried to keep my double life hidden from

anybody. Not from the community, not from my superiors. Killer Chef even catered the policemen's ball three years running, and the wedding of my chief's niece. I understand police use-of-force policies are being put under a fresh microscopic examination across the nation. So overnight in my hometown of New Orleans, I'd become an embarrassment to the entire department. A liability. Any support I might have gotten from my fellow cops and senior officers dried right up.

So here we are.

"This board has had the opportunity to read your official statement regarding the events of that evening, Detective," Bossett says. "Before we begin our questioning, is there anything you'd like to add to your story? Now is your chance."

My *story*. Like I was a suspect hauled in for questioning!

What a shit-show. What a *betrayal*.

But I know if I ever want to get my gun and badge back, I have no choice but to play along.

I take a breath, knowing everything—my life, my future, my dual careers, hell, even the possibility of a prison term—rests on what I'm about to say.

CHAPTER 4

"THANK YOU, sir," I reply, grabbing the armrests of my chair to try to control my building anger. "I stand by *my story* one hundred percent. But yes, there is something I'd like to say before we get started."

The room grows pin-drop quiet, everyone anxiously waiting to hear the accused speak.

I swivel in my seat so I can address Grant's family, who are sitting off to the side in the front row. Among them I recognize his soft-spoken widow, Crystal, her eyes puffy from crying. Next to her is Grant's younger brother, Ty, his face clenched in a tight scowl. It's no coincidence he's wearing a pale-yellow dress shirt and a mustard-yellow tie, a symbol of his Franklin Avenue affiliation. A warning—like I needed one after seeing that SUV earlier today—that the gang is watching me.

"Larry Grant may have made some poor choices in his life," I calmly say. "Like selling crack cocaine. Like pulling a handgun on a police officer. Still, his untimely death is a tragedy, for both his family and our city. My sincere hope is that his memory lives on, and that the legacy of the good he did for his family and community serves as an inspiration to others. Thank you."

The crowd reacts with murmurs of pleasant surprise. Even Crystal and Ty look taken aback. I don't feel I owe an apology to anyone for following protocol and taking out a dangerous would-be gunman. But of course I mourn the man's death. I'm a human being. Unfortunately, that's rare to hear any cop publicly admit in this day and age.

"Very well, Detective," Bossett says, looking a bit distracted from my statement. He shuffles some papers. "To begin…can you please explain why you chose to continue chasing suspect Grant, despite the situation meeting multiple criteria for *terminating* a foot pursuit as set forth in Section 458.3 of the NOPD policy handbook? Among them: you had been separated from the rest of your unit, and as you informed the radio dispatcher, you were unaware of both Grant's exact location as well as your own. Do I have that correct?"

Now *I'm* the one caught off guard. Bossett is hitting me hard right out of the gate. I wasn't expecting this hearing to be a breeze, but I didn't think I'd get grilled like this, either.

"You do, sir," I reply. "But I believe the exact wording of Section 458.3 lists guidelines for an officer to *consider* terminating a foot pursuit. Doing so is still up to his or her discretion."

Bossett frowns. We both know I've got my facts right.

"So even though you were all alone, in the pitch dark, in an unfamiliar part of the city…"

I cut him off. "Actually, sir, I had been on a team surveilling suspect Grant all over his St. Roch neighborhood for the past week. I felt I knew my way around well enough. And there were multiple streetlights and porch lights on that night. A full moon, too."

"*I* have a question, Detective Rooney," says Major Deborah Katz, the sole female on today's board, a compact woman whose bun is tied so tightly, her hair looks as flat and shiny as glass. "Your report says you pursued the suspect with your sidearm in hand. Which is also against department guidelines. Some might say, having your weapon out and ready like that would make you…more likely to use it."

I give the major a polite smile. "Was that a question, ma'am?"

She gives it right back to me. "Do you have an *answer,* Detective?"

"My Glock was out, yes—because I'd drawn it moments earlier. Me and my fellow officers had just moved on the suspect and his accomplices after observing them selling narcotics in an abandoned lot off Touro Street. When Grant ran, I chose not to waste even one second re-holstering my weapon. I also knew I might have to use it, too."

Major Katz's eyes grow perceptibly wider. "So you admit you *were* predisposed to firing your sidearm that night?"

I grit my teeth. I'm starting to lose my patience with these grandstanders.

"I admit I did my *homework*. Grant was a Franklin Avenue enforcer. Known to be armed and dangerous—which, as seems to have gotten lost in today's hearing, he *was*."

Bossett interjects, "Yes, about that handgun allegedly recovered at the scene…"

Allegedly? No way. He's not about to suggest I *planted* it, is he?

"A number of witnesses have come forward to say they saw you placing the weapon near the suspect following the shooting," he continues. "How do you respond?"

Okay, this is beyond ridiculous now. It's downright insulting. And another thought about my future is starting to demand attention.

"With respect, sir, that's absurd," I reply, working to keep my voice calm and level. "Those witnesses are all fellow gang members. And not one has offered a single photo or frame of video to back that story up."

I feel myself picking up steam so I keep going with it.

"And let's talk about the weapon itself for a minute," my voice rising. "Earlier I'd learned from an informant that Grant was rumored to pack a golden, personalized piece. It's in my field paperwork from two days *before* the shooting. And that's exactly what was recovered at the scene: a gold-plated 9mm Heckler & Koch, engraved with the letters *L-C-G*. The gun he pulled on me before I fired two shots of my own."

I'm right at the brink of losing my cool and I know I should back down, but I can't help myself. This isn't a hearing. It's a ceremony of a human sacrifice, a good cop being put down to ease the anger of others.

"Is this committee *really* suggesting that forty-eight hours earlier, I somehow tracked down a golden handgun, engraved Larry Grant's initials into it, then jammed it into his dead hand without one single bystander taking out their phone to film it…all to justify my shooting some random drug dealer I'd never even met before?"

I let that question hang in the air for a moment. Then I make my final statement.

"I want all of you to think about that," I say. "Then I want you to consider my fourteen-year record. Then consider who I am. What I do in my off time. And ask yourselves, if I was just another average cop, would any of this charade be happening?"

My little monologue leaves me practically winded but also leaves Bossett and the other committee members briefly speechless. They lean in and whisper among themselves for a few seconds. Then the deputy superintendent clears his throat. I think I even detect a bit of contrition in his voice as he says, "Detective Rooney, this board has no further questions."

I get out of my chair, wanting to feel triumphant, but only feeling relief it's over.

CHAPTER 5

I WALK out of the hearing room about two inches taller than I walked in as Ty leaps to his feet and shouts, "Shit, Rooney, you're good as dead!"

I try to ignore the commotion that breaks out as I exit, Bossett struggling to maintain order, raising his voice. I also ignore the subtle offer of a fist bump from that smirking young officer posted at the door.

Look, a man is dead. Passions are running high on both sides of the blue line. And the press is having a field day because I happen to love food as well as justice. I get all that. I do. But none of that is any excuse for the way my department has treated me. Which I think—I *hope*—I just made clear in there.

I'm confident the review board will rule my use of force was justified. Until they release their final recommendation, however, letting me get my gun and badge back, technically I'm still on administrative leave.

But even with the hearing over, there's one more thing I have to do. To my surprise, the decision came to me as I was walking out of that chamber, leaving behind the shouts, curses, and insults.

As I walk through the building's central ground-floor hallway toward the elevators, I exchange greetings with the many officers, detectives, and administrators I pass. Each one tries to act casual, but I can tell they're a little spooked to see me. They all know my hearing was today. And watching a colleague catch heat is never easy. I feel like I have some sort of contagion that they want to avoid catching.

I ride the elevator to the fourth floor, then turn left and head for the bull pen of the Major Crimes Unit. I reach my desk—which is usually covered with bulging folders and stacks of papers, but today is eerily clean—and keep going toward the corner office.

Lots of memories in that crowded bull pen come to me, of long days and longer nights, endless phone calls and data searches, interviews with grieving family members and sullen suspects, working to serve and protect the city I love and its citizens.

Through the open door of the corner office, Chief of Detectives Brian Cunningham is inside, sitting behind his desk, barking into the phone. This smart, driven, paunchy, balding middle-aged cop has been my boss for the past six years. A good one, too. He's got a passion for cracking cases and keeping this city safe that rivals my own. The moment Cunningham sees me, he hangs up the phone with a heavy *slam* and beckons me in.

"Caleb!" he calls out. "Come in, come in. You're out of the hearing already? How'd it go?"

"You could've seen it yourself," I answer. "It would've been nice to have my chief in the stands cheering me on."

"Jesus, don't start," Cunningham says, popping a fistful of Tums into his mouth like candy. "I submitted my supporting statement. Spoke to Bossett. Having a CO show up at one of his guys' review panels—it's just not done. It's poor form. It could hurt rather than help, Caleb."

I shake my head in disbelief.

"Know what else is poor form?" I ask. "Turning that panel into a circus. Putting a top detective through the wringer, making him a scapegoat just for doing his job. This department's changing, Chief. I barely recognize it. And I don't like it."

"I know, I know," Cunningham says, his voice tired. "Me neither. But to do what we do, that's the system we have. What else can we do?"

I consider his words for a moment, and feel something brewing inside me, something that's been haunting me for weeks ever since the shooting. I take my detective ID badge out of my pocket.

"I can think of something," I say.

I toss the plastic card and lanyard at Cunningham, who fumbles to catch it.

"What the hell is this?" he asks in disbelief.

"You already have my Glock and shield," I say. "Keep 'em."

Cunningham's jaw goes slack, his eyes wide with disbelief.

"Jesus Christ, Rooney! Hang on…you—you're not really—"

"I am," I say, my voice thick. "It's been a good run, Chief, but I'm done with all this horseshit. I'm out."

I turn and walk out, dust from somewhere suddenly collecting in my eyes.

CHAPTER 6

AFTER THEY leave the force, most cops I've known like to hit the links. Or the bottle. Or maybe get a little place on the Gulf Coast, do some fishing, take it easy.

Me? I got rid of my NOPD uniform shirt, threw on a fresh black T-shirt and apron, and went straight back to work.

Marlene moved the truck after the lunch shift, and this evening Killer Chef is parked on Elysian Fields Avenue, a main drag through the heart of the Marigny, a colorful neighborhood known for its legendary jazz clubs and bumping nightlife. Today is no exception. It's barely dusk when I arrive and the party is already in full swing.

Though I'm not looking forward to this conversation, I was hoping to pull Marlene aside for a minute or two before dinner service to fill her in on what happened. But since a line of hungry customers is already winding around the block, I see she's decided to open up the truck a little early.

Tossing a few jalapeños into my mouth, I jump right in and give her a hand.

I spend the next four hours grilling up slabs of juicy, rum-glazed pork belly. Deep-frying heaps of Cajun-battered shrimp and oysters. Stirring a giant, simmering vat of kidney beans and spiced ham that's so thick and rich, I worry my arm might fall off.

The shift is exhausting. Endless. But like always, it's pretty damn exhilarating. And after a day like today, it's just the distraction I need.

Once we've closed down for the night, Marlene and I finally have a chance to talk. Mopping the sweat from my brow, I tell her all about my review board hearing earlier that day. About how shitty I was treated. About my heart-to-heart with Chief Cunningham. About my decision to throw in the towel as a cop. Recounting all of it, I feel a whole range of emotions, from worry to relief, just like I did when it was happening. But I try to keep my story as matter-of-fact as possible.

Usually chatty, my ex-wife listens in total silence. When I'm finally finished, she turns to me, squints a bit, and asks, "So what are you going to do now?"

"That's easy," I reply. "You're looking at it. I'm gonna keep cooking up a storm with *you*. I was thinking I'd man the grill in here full time. I want to work on a couple new recipes for us, too. Mess around a bit with the menu. Maybe even—"

"I meant *now*," Marlene interrupts, bringing me down to earth. "Are you going to sanitize the prep counters first or scour the gumbo pot? This truck ain't going to clean itself, pal."

I shake my head and laugh. So does Marlene. When we were married, this woman drove me nuts. But lately, she's the only one who keeps me sane.

"But seriously, I think that all sounds like a great plan," she says as we get back to work. Marlene tears off some sheets of plastic wrap and covers our metal food-prep bins, filled with chopped garlic, onions, peppers, and celery. I give the food-splattered stove top a few sprays of cleaning solution and start scrubbing it down.

"And especially with Mardi Gras around the corner," she continues, "Lord knows I'll be glad to have the extra help. Things are going to get real crazy, real fast."

That's putting it mildly. These next two weeks here in the Big Easy? They're going to make New Year's Eve in Times Square look calmer than a knitting circle.

"I'm proud of you, Caleb," she says. "I know it wasn't easy doing what you did. Standing up for what's right. That takes some real balls. And you got 'em."

"I guess you would know," I say with a little smirk. "From personal experience."

She pretends to gag. "Ugh, don't remind me!"

When the last of our leftover food has been put away, the fridge reorganized, every surface wiped down, and each pot and pan and utensil washed and dried, I turn off all the inside lights and appliances and padlock the rear doors.

Marlene, meanwhile, heads around to the front and gets behind the wheel. She starts up the engine, which makes the truck growl and shudder.

"Want a ride back to that filthy bachelor pad you call a home?" she asks.

"No, thanks," I answer. "It's a beautiful night. I'm gonna walk. Do some thinking."

"*That'll* be a first," she says. "Oh, well. Catch you later, Killer Chef."

She puts the truck into gear and sputters down Elysian Fields Avenue.

I take a moment to soak in the scene—the people, the music, the energy—then turn and head in the opposite direction. I'm about to start crossing Royal Street—

When a car cuts me off, nearly running me over.

"Hey!" I exclaim, leaping backward. "Watch where you're—"

Only then do I recognize the speeding vehicle. It's the same black Ford Explorer with the shiny chrome rims I saw earlier in the day.

The driver is a guy in a yellow knit cap.

The front-seat passenger has got on a baggy yellow tank top.

And in the back, still wearing his yellow shirt and tie from the review board meeting this afternoon, is Ty Grant.

With an icy glare, he mimes a handgun with his index finger and thumb, then "shoots" me through the open window as the SUV roars on.

By instinct, I reach for my *real* gun holstered on my belt—but of course it's not there.

All I can do is watch as the vehicle picks up speed, rounds the next corner, and disappears into the night, with one angry gangbanger who's vowed revenge against me.

Now what?

I take a breath and cross the street, just like I had planned.

CHAPTER 7

THE FRENCH Quarter. Plenty of native New Orleanians would rather be caught soliciting a hooker on North Claiborne Avenue than taking a stroll through this infamous tourist trap.

But yours truly isn't one of 'em.

From Lakeview to Lake Saint Catherine, I love every square inch of this city. And the *Vieux Carré,* as it's also known, is its oldest neighborhood, located right in the heart. Especially on a gorgeous afternoon like this, there's nowhere in the world I'd rather be.

Especially after enduring the circus-like interrogation of the review board, telling my boss that I was through being an NOPD detective, and then being threatened by Ty Grant in public and on the streets.

Yeah, it was a day, all right.

"Can I get you anything else, chef?"

I'm just finishing a cup of chicory coffee and an extraordinary slice of *doberge* cake—a multilayered masterpiece of silky chocolate fudge and rich lemon pudding encased in a thick fondant shell—here on the open-air, second-floor balcony of Chez Mélanie, a superb French Quarter café. Despite its authentic décor and historic feel, the place has only been around for about a year. And its owner, Melanie Rosenbaum, is actually a thirty-something virtuoso pastry chef…from Toronto, Canada.

As she explained to me after-hours a few months ago on this very same balcony, over a congratulatory bottle I gifted her of Châteauneuf-du-Pape, her adorable brunette curls bouncing with every word, she'd been enchanted by creole food and culture her entire life. So one day, she decided to hop on a plane, accent her name, and open up a boulangerie of her own. She was nervous at first, but the place became a runaway success almost overnight. For good reason.

And here she is now, standing beside me, her springy brown curls—along with the rest of her—looking just as cute as I remember.

"As a matter of fact, Mel, you *can,*" I say, gesturing to my empty, icing-smeared plate. "How about the recipe for this little slice of heaven?"

Melanie smiles and swats the air.

"Keep dreaming, Caleb. A girl has to have *some* secrets."

"Fair enough. I'll just take the check then."

"It's on the house," she replies. "I insist. Just promise me: if Killer Chef ever starts selling pastries, you'll let me take first crack at creating them."

"Are you serious?" I ask. "I'd be honored."

I exit the café by trotting down an outside metal stairway and turn down narrow Dumaine Street. The French Quarter is always brimming with bodies, but today the place is packed more than usual. And the air is practically buzzing with excitement and anticipation. In just over an hour, the first official "krewe parade" of the season is going to be passing through. Organized by the Krewe of Cork, a parade group social club of revelers with a particular fondness for food and wine, it promises to be a boozy, boisterous event.

As I get closer to Bourbon Street, I can see spectators already lining up along the sidewalk, jostling for the best views. Lots of them are obviously tourists, their cheeks already rosy from guzzling all those awful, over-priced fluorescent-blue hurricanes, beads around their fleshy necks.

But I also see plenty of locals, especially parents with young children. Fathers in Saints jerseys hoisting toddlers onto their shoulders. Mothers setting up homemade wooden Mardi Gras ladders—painted crazy colors and decorated with streamers and glitter, a fun, popular craft—to give bigger kids a seated perch.

If you ask me, *that's* what makes this celebration—and this city—so special. Mardi Gras is a whole lot more than just the debauchery you see in the movies. It's a rich cultural tradition that's fun for the whole family.

Then all thoughts of fun melt away—like an ice cube dropped on the sidewalk—when from the corner of my eye, I see a man dressed in black, carrying an automatic rifle, shoving his way among the happy and clueless civilians.

CHAPTER 8

I SPIN and take in a full view, and then relax my fists—where did *they* come from?

It's just an NOPD cop, who's joined by another emerging from the crowd.

I don't know them personally, but they're members of the department's elite tactical unit, the NOPD SWAT team.

They've each got a military-grade M4 assault rifle slung over their shoulders. And they're dressed in full tactical gear: fatigues, Kevlar vests, combat boots, even ballistic helmets.

Normally these guys work high-risk warrants. VIP protection. Riot control.

Seeing a pair of them strolling down the street is both concerning and confusing. I've never seen anything like it during Carnival time.

Are they just on routine patrol? Or is something else going on?

"Excuse me, officers," I say as they approach. "Was there some kind of critical incident in the area we should be aware of? I'm wondering why you—"

"No, sir," the near one says, eyes looking over the crowd. "Please move along now."

Neither one even slows down as they stroll by. Normally I'd flash my badge and ID myself, but of course that's not an option anymore. Right now I'm just an ordinary citizen, being treated like one.

"Wait a minute," the second SWAT officer says, turning around and lowering his sunglasses. "Aren't you Detective Rooney with major crimes?"

Finally, a little recognition, a little respect.

"I used to be," I reply. "Now I'm just letting the *bon temps rouler*."

"Oh, yeah, that's right," the near one says, nodding. "The review board sure bent you over bad before kicking you to the curb. That sucks."

I appreciate his sympathy, but I have something else on my mind.

"It was a little more complicated than that," I say. "But what's with all the battle rattle on Bourbon Street? Something going on?"

The officers look at each other, then both just shrug.

The second officer says, "Our lieutenant put the whole platoon on double-overtime, said we're doing foot patrols and random sweeps around the clock for the next two weeks. Looking for anything unusual."

His partner laughs. "Yeah. Unusual on Bourbon Street. That'd be something noteworthy, eh?"

"But why?"

"You think they tell us shit?" the other officer says. "Run it up the chain, Detective. Something's spooked somebody. Some of our guys are even undercover, mingling with the civilians. Making sure everybody stays happy and safe. Look, we gotta keep moving. Take care of yourself."

The two officers continue heading down the bustling

street. There's so much noise and celebration all around, hardly anyone seems to notice them.

But I do.

I stand still and let my gaze wander.

There.

And there.

Two partygoers, man and woman, about fifty feet from each other, with bright clothes and wearing beads around their muscular necks. One leaning against a lamppost, one standing in front of a bar with rock music roaring out. Sipping something I'm sure is not alcoholic, because they're not here to have fun.

They both have hard cop eyes I instantly recognize, and like the two heavily armed cops I talked to earlier, they are definitely checking out the crowd.

A hint of regret whispers to me, of having resigned. Even on admin leave, I could find out what's suddenly spooked the higher-ups, maybe even lend a hand.

But I'm not a cop anymore.

Times like this, with something dangerous going on in the city I love, I hate reminding myself of that sorry fact.

CHAPTER 9

"NO HAY sustituciones. Aucune substitutions. Keine Substitutionen!"

It's a day later and I'm back behind the stove, sautéing a trio of spicy creole duck breasts, still seeing those cops—in battle rattle *and* undercover—working Bourbon Street. But interrupting my thoughts and over all the clanging and sizzling of my cooking, I think I hear Marlene...speaking in tongues?

I look over and see she's in the middle of a heated exchange through the service window with a red-faced male customer around twenty years old.

I notice a few other young patrons in line behind him have taken out their phones to record the action.

"No substitutions, sir," Marlene insists. "I'm sorry, but it says so right there on the sign, in six different languages. Do I have to tell you in Pig Latin?"

Oh, boy.

I've had enough arguments with my ex-wife over the years to know when she's about to blow her top. That's the last thing our business needs right now. I turn down the flame and hurry over to play peacemaker.

I stand next to Marlene and call down to the line

outside. "Okay, everybody, are we having some kind of little issue here?"

"Da-damn right you…I mean, *we* are!" the man slurs.

It's starting to get dark out, but I can see he's wearing a sweat-soaked blue polo shirt, a crumpled masquerade mask on his forehead, a single muddy flip-flop, and I can smell the booze on his breath from inside the truck.

"I said I wanted an egg sandwich, okay?" he slurs out in a loud voice. "None of that seafood crap. But this old bitch said y'all don't do that. Didn't you ever hear of 'the customer is always right'?"

I give Marlene a sympathetic look. The vast majority of the people we feed—even the drunk ones—are usually pretty cool. But like every business, once in a while we get a bad apple. Normally I'd politely but firmly turn a belligerent fellow like this away, then physically escort him off the premises myself if I had to.

But seeing so many phones recording, and worried that he's gearing up for a fistfight, I get another idea.

"Sir, I'll tell you what," I say, turning back to him. "You seem like such an upstanding young man, just relax, give me two minutes, and I'll make you the best egg sandwich you ever had. Deal?"

Before Marlene can stop me, I scurry back to the stove.

I spoon some glistening duck fat into a fresh frying pan, then drop in some onions for a quick sauté. Next I crack in a pair of eggs, add a splash of cream, sprinkle liberally with my homemade blend of Cajun seasonings, then whisk and fold until everything is cooked through.

When the eggs are done, I slide them onto a freshly toasted baguette, top with a handful of diced scallions, then wrap the sandwich in wax paper.

"Order up!" I say, handing my unique creation down through the service window to the waiting man, who somehow seems to have gotten even tipsier and angrier in the past few minutes. "One Cajun-style duck-fat scrambled-egg po'boy. Enjoy."

The man grunts thanks, then suspiciously unwraps the sandwich and takes a bite. Instantly, his eyes widen in ecstasy.

"Ohmph ghhhd thygt ghrhd!" he exclaims, spewing chunks of chewed egg and bread everywhere. He swallows hard then says again: "Oh, my God, that's good!"

The other customers in line—their phones capturing the whole thing—start to cheer and applaud.

"Kill-er Chef!" someone starts to chant. "Kill-er Chef!"

Others quickly join in. "Kill-er Chef! Kill-er Chef! Kill-er Chef!"

I look over at Marlene, expecting a grateful smile, maybe even a high five.

Instead she's angrily folding her arms.

"Way to go, Caleb," she says, her angry voice grinding out at me. "Are you going to be making special meals for *every* drunk asshole who calls me names from now on?"

"Come on, Mar, don't be like that," I say. "Would you rather a video go viral of me getting into a brawl with a college student? Or one that shows Killer Chef keeping the peace with great food instead?"

She shakes her head. "Just get back behind the stove and let *me* handle customer service, all right?"

I give my feisty ex-wife a mock salute and I'm about to return to cooking, when I hear commotion outside.

I move closer to the service window, look out.

In the middle of a triangular half-block patch of public park known as Bienville Place, two people are having a physical altercation as others look on, not doing a thing.

One of them is a big lug of a man.

The other is a petite woman.

And she's screaming in terror.

CHAPTER 10

THE SIGHT of an innocent person in trouble triggers something deep inside of me. It flips a switch, flushes a wave of adrenaline, instantly putting me on alert. I can't resist it even if I wanted to.

"Caleb, wait—" Marlene calls to me.

But I don't hear anything more from Marlene as I throw open the rear truck doors and burst outside into the cool evening.

Still wearing my apron, I shove my way through the confused crowds ambling up and down Decatur Street and run toward the screaming woman.

Just before I get to her, I see her assailant—he's wearing a bandana over his nose and mouth—yank her pocketbook out of her hands, knock her down, and take off running.

I'm itching to pursue that brazen son of a bitch, but first I want to make sure she's okay. I skid to a halt and kneel down beside the victim, a twenty-something African-American woman with a few strands of plastic beads around her neck. Her peach-colored blouse has a giant tear down the side. She's shaken and crying but otherwise looks unharmed.

"Ma'am, I'm a po—*former* police officer, are you hurt?" I ask.

"I don't think so…but he took my bag!" she sobs to me. "With my phone, my wallet, everything!"

I point to the nearest gawking bystanders I see, a middle-aged husband and wife, watching wide-eyed. From their socks and sandals, I deduce they're European tourists.

"Hey, you guys speak English?" I call out.

"We *are* English," the man says with a crisp accent.

"Do you know what 911 is?" I ask. "Okay, great. Stay with this woman and dial it now!"

Satisfied the victim is out of harm's way, I stand up and look for her attacker, scanning the busy sidewalk until I spot him darting right, onto Conti Street.

"Stop!" I shout. But of course he ignores me.

I am *not* going to lose him, so I break into a sprint and follow him down Conti, seeing him pushing his way through the throngs. Whether he knows it or not, he's heading straight toward a massive, four-story white marble building: the Supreme Court of the State of Louisiana. Seriously! There are CCTV cameras all over the French Quarter, but the old court building, surrounded by a high fence, is guarded by even more security. What an idiot.

Sure enough, the man sees what's ahead of him, backtracks and hooks a left down Exchange Place, a narrow alleyway between two buildings painted salmon-pink and canary-yellow.

I stay on his tail the whole time. This little passageway finally spits us out onto Iberville Street, a more bustling thoroughfare jammed with noisy revelers, zooming bicyclists, and not one, but two, roving jazz brass bands.

He steals a quick glance back at me as we keep weaving through the crowds toward Royal Street. Which is when my lungs start burning and my legs start going wobbly. No, I can't lose him, I won't...

But the next thing I know, he's gone!

Damnit!

I frantically survey the busy intersection, looking for any sign of him.

Nothing.

I need a better view.

With no hesitation, I step up onto a fire hydrant, take a second to get my balance, then leap up and grab the bottom bar of a metal fence lining the second-floor balcony of a private apartment building. Grunting and straining, using every ounce of upper-body strength I've got, I slowly pull my way up and over.

Using these few seconds to catch my breath as well, I look out from this elevated position on the masses below, scanning all of them like a hawk hunting for his prey.

There he is!

Running down Royal Street. I scurry along the balcony as far as it goes...then jump across to the next metal balcony nearly abutting it...and then another.

When I run out of balconies, I have no choice but to take a leap of faith. Literally. I spot a green plastic awning and jump down onto it, hoping to use it like a giant slide to ease my fall.

No luck.

I crash right through the tarp and tumble onto the pavement, hard.

It hurts like hell, but I pick myself right back up and keep going, as the crowd backs away, camera flashes nearly blinding me as my long chase is recorded.

Ahead of me the suspect finally begins to slow down as he starts running out of steam. So I push myself a little bit more, with my chance to tackle the perp coming up.

I'm only a few yards away from him when he makes a sharp left into the covered driveway of a parking garage. I follow him, thinking maybe he has a car or truck parked inside.

He heads up the darkened ramp then comes to a stop up against a gated partition. There's nowhere left for him to run.

"Put your hands where I can see them!" I shout, slowly stepping toward him.

I sure do wish I had my old gun and badge on me right about now—instead of just an apron with a meat thermometer tucked in the pocket. Or even a radio so I could call for backup. "Put down the purse, get on your knees, and—"

I feel a sharp *whack* against the back of my skull, which sends me tumbling forward.

I grunt as I hit the garage floor, and grunt again as another impact strikes me on my right ribs. I hear a crunch, and the pain comes sharp and hot and steals the breath right out of me.

Moaning in agony, I roll to my side and look up. My vision is a little blurry, but I can make out three figures standing over me.

Franklin Avenue Soldiers. Each one, even inside the poorly lit parking garage, is clearly wearing a yellow article of clothing. One is holding a metal baseball bat: Ty Grant.

"'Put your hands where I can see 'em,'" he parrots. "Shit, Rooney…is that what you say to every gangbanger before you shoot 'em? Including my brother?"

He takes another swing at me, straight for my head. I flinch and reflexively block it with my left hand—which almost goes numb from the impact.

"Jesus Christ, Ty!" I yell. "Are you crazy? You're gonna kill a cop in the middle of the French Quarter during Carnival?"

Ty laughs, snorts, then hocks a wad of spit and mucus right at my face.

"I ain't gonna kill you," he says, smiling. "But you ain't a cop no more, neither."

He gives my unprotected gut one final, brutal blow. Then he nods to his goons, and the four of them—including the alleged purse-snatcher—scram.

As I watch them scuttle down the ramp and back outside on the street, my pain peaks and then throbs away as I black out.

CHAPTER 11

"AND ARE we celebrating anything this evening, *monsieur et madame?*" the voice says.

I'm sitting at a table with a crisp white tablecloth and clusters of plates, silverware, and glassware. Marlene is sitting next to me, and turns to the stuffy maître d', whose head is as round and bald as a ping-pong ball, and gives him a mischievous smirk.

"I guess you could say so," she says, the sarcasm in her voice seemingly dipped in syrup. "My ex-husband here survived being lured into a dark building and viciously attacked three nights ago. Then again, if he'd actually *died,* I'd probably be drunk on champagne right now, dancing topless on a bar in Cancun."

The prim and proper host forces an awkward smile, takes a pace back, like he's afraid of being touched with whatever madness might be infecting my ex-wife.

"Bon," he says, pursing his lips. "Why don't I send over the sommelier to take you through our wine list?"

Once the poor man is out of earshot, I say, "Jeez, Mar, you're terrible, you know that?"

She smiles. "You still figuring that out?"

"Not me," I say. "But hey, I'm glad you can find humor in my misery."

"*Your* misery?" she says, her smile wavering, her voice rising. "Who stayed by your bed all night in the ER? Who cooked you all your meals? Wrapped your bandages in food-grade plastic so you could take a shower? Did all the ingredient prep and handled four full shifts at the truck by herself? All because *you* had to play hero."

There's a burning feeling in my guts as her voice rises with each sentence, her anger growing, her disappointment in me strengthening, all winding up to the same conclusion reached years ago: we aren't made to be husband and wife.

"I wasn't playing," I say. "For fourteen years I've been a cop. It's in my blood. It always will be. And when I see someone in trouble, I'm going to respond."

"Oh, please," she says. "Don't gimme that I'll-always-be-a-hero crap. Look what the department did for you. Why should you risk your life anymore? Call 911 next time, okay?"

I tap out two Tylenol onto the white tablecloth, then down them with a slug of sparkling spring water. Marlene has a point, but I'm not going to get into this with her, not now. Too many old battles and old arguments should stay good and buried.

So instead I say, "You look really pretty tonight. I haven't seen you out of your kitchen garb in so long. If I didn't know you, I might actually find you attractive."

Marlene's mood lightens up and her smile returns. But it's true. She's tamed her normally frizzy curls into a loose, wavy up-do. She's painted her face with care, coating her eyelids with a dramatic shade of green. And she's wearing a tasteful LBD—little black dress—that shows off her figure.

Which is appropriate, since we're *in* LBD.

That's the name of this chic, new creole-Asian fusion spot in the Garden District owned by hotshot Miami restaurateur Lucas Bryant Dodd. When he heard about my little mishap in the parking garage—like thousands of other New Orleans residents who read the next day's *Times-Picayune* or caught the morning news on one of our four local TV stations—he reached out and invited me and Marlene to visit his famed restaurant, on the house.

Apparently, he felt an ex-cop with a nearly fractured rib, a bruised spleen, a busted hand, and a minor concussion could go for a fancy four-course meal.

Sure.

Plus he was insistent on me saying yes, which is typical for restaurant kings like Lucas Dodd. Like everyone else who owns high-class establishments in the Big Easy, he and others love to sprinkle movie stars, athletes, and newsmakers in the dining crowd, to get good news coverage and keep a buzz going.

So I eventually said yes, which also gave me a chance to put on a nice suit and tie and take my business partner out on the town. I figured, why not?

Marlene sees me sneak the Tylenol and says, "Have any to spare for an aching lady?"

"Damn, I'm sorry, I don't," I say. "What's hurting you, Mar?"

She takes a sip of her water. "Ah, you know what it is. Standing on your feet all day, moving your arms back and forth, chopping and cutting. Some days you slide by, other days, you don't."

I reach over and touch the back of her near hand, noticing her muscular forearms marked with scratches and small burn marks from splattering hot oil. All part of the glamour of working in a famous food truck.

"Plus it hurts more when you have to work harder because your business partner is flat on his butt at Tulane Medical Center," I say.

Before Marlene can reply, another man's voice is heard behind us, confident and smooth. "Ah, Mr. Rooney, Ms. DiPietra. I'm so glad you could join us this evening. I trust you're feeling better?"

Dodd is a short man of about forty-five. His salt-and-pepper hair is slicked back like a helmet. He's got on a light-blue designer sport coat over a cheap white thrift-shop tee. And his permanently tanned skin somehow looks at once glowing and prematurely wrinkled.

"I sure am, thanks," I say, shaking his silky-soft hand. Dodd may be a successful restaurant owner, but I can tell he's never worked a day in a *real* kitchen in his life. "And thanks for inviting us. We're looking forward to trying everything. I'm famished."

"Then I'll send your food out right away," he says, gently touching my left shoulder. "Have any arrests been made in connection with your brutal attack?"

"Yes," I say. "The cops got one of them." That would be Ty Grant. From my bed in the ER, I ID'd him to the officer who took my statement, but who clearly wanted nothing to do with me. "The other two are still on the loose. I'm sure they'll find them."

"Well, that's good news. I'll bet they'll find the others soon. If you'll excuse me."

He strolls away and goes to the kitchen on the other side of the dining room, and I hear his raised and impatient voice, and in less than a minute, flustered waiters emerge bearing trays.

I'll admit I had my doubts about blending Southern flavors with Far East ones, but I have to say, LBD makes it work. Our appetizer is a pan-fried creole-shrimp egg roll, the perfect mix of crunchy and zesty. Our first course is grilled crawfish, with a tangy ginger glaze laced with smoky-spicy Szechuan peppercorns. Next comes a Thai curry crab étouffée, a rich, fragrant stew served over a bed of jasmine rice. Finally, it's time for dessert: warm, gooey bread pudding drenched in sweet sake and topped with a scoop of green tea ice cream.

I've just taken the last bite when Dodd appears next to our table, accompanied by a guy with a goatee dressed in black trousers and white shirt, carrying a Nikon camera.

"Would you mind if I take my photo with you, Caleb? Something to hang up in our foyer?"

Marlene sticks her tongue out and reluctantly I say, "Sure, I guess so."

He pulls a chair over, sits down next to me, and after a few bright flashes from the Nikon, he leans in and eagerly says, "Well, what did you think?"

Marlene jumps in and answers for both of us.

"It was delicious, Lucas," she says. "And so inventive. My mouth feels like it's just taken a six-week tour of Asia without ever leaving New Orleans."

Dodd clasps his hands in delight.

"I'm so glad to hear that. Now what about the restaurant?"

I glance around the spacious dining room. Antique chandeliers hang from the ceiling, while the walls and tables are mostly glass and polished metal. It's an interesting blend, I tell Dodd, of classic elegance and contemporary minimalism. I say I also love the open-plan industrial kitchen at the other side of the room: big, bright, modern, and brimming with stainless steel, it looks like a dream to cook in.

"How's that?" he asks.

"Well, you know what I mean," I say. "There's a lot to be said about being able to walk more than four paces in any direction from your hot stove."

"And have a place to take a break," Marlene says.

"And a bathroom to use when you need, instead of going across the street to a gas station or drugstore."

Marlene grins. "And have more than just one crazy ex-husband to work with."

I give it right back to her. "Or a grumpy ex-wife, too."

Dodd's head goes back and forth during our repartee, like an audience member during a tennis match.

"So that would be a dream," he says, smiling at me.

"Yeah, I guess so."

Dodd flashes a wide grin, revealing his perfectly straight, perfectly white teeth.

"Caleb, let me ask you this: what if I could make that dream a reality?"

CHAPTER 12

EVEN WITH the outside noise of New Orleans and the cheerful conversation inside among our fellow diners, it seems very quiet and still at our table.

I look at Dodd, astonished and confused. "You want me to come and work *here*?"

LBD is a nice spot for a unique dinner, but it's definitely not my cup of tea, and under the table, I get a gentle kick from Marlene.

"No, no, no," Dodd replies, waving his hands around wildly like a conductor at the climax of a symphony. "But imagine if you two had a place like this of your own."

I now look to Marlene and she returns my gaze. This just went from "no way" to "do tell us more."

"You mean, a Killer Chef restaurant?" Marlene asks.

"Exactly!" Dodd says. "Your truck is a modern culinary institution in this city. I'm talking the same great menu. The same great food. The same great owners. But instead of waiting in line in the hot sun for an hour, your patrons can sit back and relax in a comfortable, classy establishment just steps from Bourbon Street."

Marlene and I share a look. It's an intriguing idea,

no doubt about it. But I'm not about to say yes straight away.

Then Dodd gently touches my hand and then Marlene's, and ups the ante. "You two are great. Talented. Skilled. But none of us are getting any younger, are we? With comfort for the patrons, there'd be something for you. Air-conditioning. Additional kitchen help. The latest in stoves and fryers. And like you both said, room to move around, a place to take a break. And your own restroom!"

Now he's in full salesman mode, and I'm still being cautious. But the thought of working in a cool environment, without smoke billowing around my face, constantly bumping into Marlene, getting splattered by hot grease, well, it's beginning to sound better and better.

I take a breath, keep my gaze on Marlene, my partner.

"A lot of what we serve, as I'm sure you know, is casual fare," I say. "Po'boys and fries. That kind of thing. That's what our customers love. Do you really see that working in a fancy place like this?"

"That's a good point," Dodd says. "I'm sure your customers would follow you anywhere. But with a new setting, a staff, and better kitchen gear, I'm sure you'd agree that a few modifications in what you serve would make sense."

Okay, I feel the brakes kicking in. "So it *wouldn't* be the 'same great menu' then, would it?"

"Of course it would be the same great menu," Dodd says. "It would be expanded some, with just a few minor…upgrades."

Marlene is keeping quiet, which is quite unusual. I shift in my seat and think of something just as important as our menu.

"How might financing work?" I ask as Marlene picks up her wineglass. "We're making a comfortable profit running the truck, but we're not getting rich. I assume you'd help fund this brick-and-mortar venture?"

"Certainly," Dodd assures us. "Typically, when I partner with a chef or existing brand, I provide up to fifty percent capitalization for a sixty-six percent company stake."

Marlene nearly snorts red wine through her nose.

"Whoa, whoa, whoa," she says, putting her glass down. "You'd only be ponying up half the cash, but walking away with two-thirds of the profits?"

Dodd's reply is a bit condescending. "A joint venture with the Dodd Restaurant Group offers enormous opportunities for growth and exposure. I think the deal structure is more than fair."

Yeah, right. Marlene's eyes look like they're ready to start shooting lightning bolts at our smooth and gracious host.

"Well, let us think about it," I say, blotting my mouth with my napkin, even though I know full well Marlene and I have zero intention of going into business with this guy. I remember a line from one of my high school English classes, how Satan once said he'd rather reign in Hell than serve in Heaven. I'm no Satan, but I'd rather rule from my steamy hot food truck than serve with this guy in air-conditioned comfort.

"Of course," he says, still all smiles and oozing politeness. "Please take as much time as you'd like. Here's my business card. That's my personal number. Feel free to call with any other questions. Or stop in anytime if you'd like to—"

A sudden crash of plates and glasses echoes from across the restaurant.

Dodd swivels his head to the source. And in an instant, his cheery if slippery demeanor transforms into rage.

"For God's sake!" he yells, storming over to the poor server, who's on her hands and knees picking up broken pieces of china and glass.

I can't hear exactly what he's saying to her, but from his expression and body language, he's clearly tearing her apart. Over a simple accident! He jabs his finger in her face. Then he kicks a shard of a broken dish against the wall, smashing it further. Damn, if me and Marlene acted this way to each other any time we broke a plate or serving dish, we'd never get any cooking done.

Other diners have started to watch with horror. The server has started to cry. The whole thing has turned into quite an ugly scene...

Until another woman hurries over and gently pulls Dodd aside. She looks to be about thirty, has long, flowing blond hair, and is wearing a tight, blue satin dress printed with pink and white lotus flowers.

She is also stunningly, jaw-droppingly beautiful.

"Let's get outta here," Marlene says, pushing her chair back and standing up, "before that nut job goes postal on *us*."

Of course, my ex is right. But I can't tear my eyes away from that statuesque creature with the blond hair and blue dress whispering soothingly to Dodd and stroking his chest. Watching her calm the beast like that makes her even more appealing.

To get my attention, Marlene tugs on my bandaged arm. I yelp in pain, but reluctantly follow her out.

But before we leave the restaurant, I steal one more look at that alluring beauty. I'm not a fan of Dodd's, but I'd love to get to know his colleague.

I know I'll never go into business with him, but all the same, I'm thinking that a follow-up meeting with Dodd—with his female companion nearby—would be a wonderful thing.

Just to be polite, of course.

CHAPTER 13

I'M STANDING with Marlene at the valet station waiting for the attendant to bring around my car. With my unhurt hand, I'm fishing through my wallet, looking for a few bills to tip him with, when I hear a voice call to me.

"Mr. Rooney, wait!"

I turn to face this unknown woman coming out of the LBD front door—and I practically do a double take.

It's the blonde in the blue dress.

She knows me? And wants to talk to me?

"Mr. Rooney," she says again, now standing at my side, a bit out of breath. "I'm so sorry you had to witness that. Lucas can be…a bit of a perfectionist. I hope it didn't ruin your evening."

"Are you kidding?" Marlene interrupts. "We got a free dinner *and* a show."

I subtly elbow my ex-wife to get her to keep quiet and let *me* do the flirting.

"Not at all," I say. "The food was exceptional."

"Thank you," she says. "And Lucas…he appreciates culinary talent. And he likes to nurture it. I know he talked to you two about possibly going into business."

Interesting, I think. She knows about the business proposal, so she must work for Lucas in some sort of management or business capacity. Earlier, like the typical dumb male, I thought that with her stunning good looks she was possibly a hostess or something similar. Yeah, dumb indeed.

"Well, it certainly is an interesting proposal," I say. "There's a lot to consider, but I tell you, I might have to come back here to discuss it with him further, to get some additional details."

I hope this lovely woman doesn't hear the exasperated sigh coming from Marlene, because my business partner knows I'm talking straight-up bullshit. But she knows what kind of flirtatious fellow I can be, so she's letting me yammer on.

"Oh, I'm glad you're considering it," the woman says, relief in her voice. "We really hope you and your partner find your way to working with us. We're all such huge fans of Killer Chef."

My eyes flick down to the woman's left hand. Seeing no engagement ring, I decide to take things up a notch.

"Is that so?" I ask. "I'm usually there working the grill. And I always like to…keep an eye on our customers. But I don't remember seeing you around. I'm sure I'd remember."

The woman blushes a bit. It's adorable. Marlene is impatient and sighs again.

"You caught me," she says, smiling. "Lucas has a team of assistants who scour the city for interesting food and bring it back to us. I'd love to visit your truck sometime, but I'm usually cooped up in the back office. Handling the books, dealing with payroll, haggling with suppliers, that sort of thing. It's not exactly what I thought I'd be doing with a master's degree in Renaissance art history but"—and her cheerful voice slides into a regretful tone—"life doesn't always go the way you think it will, does it?"

"No, it certainly doesn't," I answer. I stare deeply into her enchanting brown pupils and her gaze stays with me. "Although sometimes, life has a way of pleasantly surprising you."

We share a little smile, a fleeting moment of connection—which is interrupted by the toot of a horn. I turn to see the valet pulling my silver Impala up to the curb.

"I don't think I got your name," I say to the woman, knowing I wasn't about to leave without that little fact.

"Vanessa," she answers. "Vanessa McKeon."

We shake hands. It's professional, but I swear she holds on a second too long.

"It was a pleasure meeting you, Vanessa," I say, my hand feeling warm from her touch. "Despite the drama, we had a wonderful evening."

"I'm really glad to hear that, Caleb. And I hope you take my husband's offer seriously. He knows what he likes, and he's very good at spotting special talent."

Ugh. Hang on. That asshole Lucas Dodd is this angel Vanessa McKeon's *husband*? I'm so disappointed I can practically taste it.

"Well, with you as his wife, I congratulate him on his talent-spotting skills," I say. "Good night, now."

I hand the young valet a few dollars, then slide into my car with its engine running and slump behind the wheel. Marlene gets in beside me, chuckling and singing out loud: *"Caleb and Vanessa, sittin' in a tree..."*

"Very funny, Marlene. Very mature, too."

"Oh, lighten up. So you can't sleep with every hot piece of ass in New Orleans—just *most* of them. It's still early. Plenty of time to go to a bar and pick some-body up."

I check my watch. She's right. It's not even nine o'clock. I *could* go out. Or, if we opened up Killer Chef right now, we could still serve a ton of customers.

"Nah, there's something else I feel like doing instead. Let's go cook."

"Caleb?" she says, lowering the window on her side to bring in some fresh air.

"Yes?" I say, following her lead on my side, feeling the warm night air slide in.

I slowly drive out and stop at the intersection with St. Charles Avenue. Long lines of tourists stream across the crosswalk in front of us.

Marlene says, "Please take this in the spirit in which it's offered, dear ex-husband of mine, but you're being an idiot."

"Marlene…"

"I know you think you're indestructible, but you've got bumps, bruises, aches and pains, and a bandaged hand. You just got out of the hospital. You nearly had what little brains you have smashed out on the ground by those gangbangers."

"Marlene…"

"And I don't mind that you're not at a hundred percent, but if you go start cooking tonight, you'll be sloppy, you'll make mistakes, and you'll drop stuff. And that means you, and you alone, will be disap-pointing our customers. And hurting our business. And I'm not going to let that happen. So, big hand-some fella, the only thing you're doing is dropping me at home, and getting your sorry and aching ass to bed for another good night's sleep. I'll see you in the truck tomorrow."

The way is clear ahead of me, and I just have to shake my head. Hate to admit it, but my ex is right.

I start to ease out onto St. Charles Avenue, and then a low roaring noise catches my attention.

I suddenly brake and lean my head outside, looking up.

There.

One, and then two, Black Hawk military helicopters are flying overhead, slowly passing over the Garden District, at a low altitude.

Marlene is looking as well. "Those belong to the police?"

I ease my way back into my car. A horn impatiently sounds behind me.

"No," I say. "The NOPD doesn't have helicopters, and the state police use Bells. Those are Black Hawk. National Guard or Army."

I make a left-hand turn, thinking of what those SWAT cops said the other night.

Something's spooked somebody.

"Must be a drill, huh?" Marlene asks.

"Must be," I say, though I know deep down that no, something bad is out there in my Crescent City, scaring both the locals and the military.

And I can't do a damn thing about it.

CHAPTER 14

THE NIGHT after our gourmet meal and amateur WrestleMania hour back at LBD, Marlene and I park our truck on the corner of Orleans Avenue and Salcedo Street, right in the heart of Bayou St. John—a leafy, tranquil residential neighborhood, far removed from all the hubbub of the French Quarter. Since we didn't have much time to prep ingredients that evening and will be doing most of it on the fly, I'm hoping for a relatively slow shift.

Fat chance.

Fifteen minutes after we open, there's a line stretching down the block. After thirty minutes, it's snaked around the corner. I deliberately didn't post our location to any of our Killer Chef social media accounts, which have a combined following of more than two hundred thousand people, but I should have known word would spread. Not that I'm complaining. When you're running a business, popularity is a great problem to have.

It's also an exhausting one.

And sometimes, a potentially dangerous one.

As I'm finishing up two orders, Marlene comes next to me and says, "Looks like three of your friends are in line tonight."

"Really?" I say, pleased at what she just said. Since I've left the force—hell, even after my beatdown four nights ago—I haven't heard one word from any of my buds on the force, not a one. I realize it's the tone of the time and politics, that nobody out there wants to be seen with someone accused of killing an "innocent" civilian, but it's still a lonely feeling.

I wipe my hands on my apron, move over to the side, look out the serving window at the long line of customers, trying to see which detective or cop or if even my old boss, Cunningham, is waiting in line, but I don't see a familiar face.

But I do see three guys, dressed in yellow sweats and yellow hoodies, staring right at me with hate.

I go back to my station, slide the food over. "Order up!"

The night goes on. With the three gangbangers getting closer and closer as happy customers slide away with their orders, Marlene says, "Whaddaya gonna do?"

"I might spit in their food," I say, "but just my luck, a health inspector might be out there in line, too."

"Caleb, shouldn't you make a call?"

I get back to the stove. "To report what? Three men standing quietly in line wearing yellow? Those guys weren't in the crew that was with Ty and his baseball bat."

"Fine," she says, digging through her pockets, taking out her phone and putting it on a shelf, between a stack of paper boats. "One of those yellow jerks does so much as lift their voice, I'm calling 911."

"I love it when you stick up for me," I say.

"Up yours, Caleb, I'm protecting Killer Chef."

I feel better getting back to work. That's my Marlene.

The three guys come closer and closer, and even the other customers in line can sense something is off about them. The gangbangers aren't saying anything, aren't making any threatening moves, aren't doing a damn thing.

Which is out of place. Everybody else in line is slightly buzzed, or talking loudly, or taking photos of the line or selfies, some dancing in place to music from a nearby nightclub. But these members of the Franklin Avenue crew are stoic and hard-looking, just patiently moving forward with the rest of the line, and customers in front of and behind them are giving them lots of space.

Even if they don't know what's going on, these hungry folks in line are smart enough to stay as far away as they can from potential trouble.

I focus on chopping, cooking, plating, sliding the food over, and then there are four customers in front of them, then three, then one, and—

They just stand there.

"Help you fellas?" Marlene asks, as harried and friendly as ever.

No answer.

"Guys?"

Their faces are determined, humorless, and I stand next to Marlene, making sure the three of them can see the knife in my hand.

I say, "Good evening, gents, what's your pleasure tonight?"

The lead one slowly lifts up his hand, makes a pointing gesture at me with his finger, waving it back and forth, back and forth, and says, "Shit, man, our pleasure is gonna be any night we choose."

The other two laugh, and then they walk away.

I go back to my station.

Marlene remains her take-charge self. "Next!"

After another hour of frantically toasting baguettes, slicing up chuck roast, and flash-frying shrimp, my apron is soaked through with sweat. Plus I've run out of raw jalapeños, my lifeblood when I'm cooking, and our food stocks are just about gone, too.

The gangbangers haven't come back, which is fine.

They were here to send a message, and their message was certainly received.

"That's all she wrote, folks!" I call to the dozen or so customers still waiting, who let out a collective groan. "I know, I know. Life is so unfair sometimes. But I'll make a deal with you. If the sun rises in the morning, Killer Chef will reopen. Sound good?"

The crowd starts to disperse, and Marlene and I begin to clean up. We're nearly finished when I hear a *knock-knock-knock* against the closed service window.

"Sorry," I say, loudly, without looking over. "Truck's closed for the night."

But the tapping continues.

"I admire your determination, I really do, but—"

It's quiet.

Then there's insistent knocking on the rear door.

"We're closed!" Marlene yells.

The knocking doesn't give up.

Marlene reaches up, takes down her phone, her thumb over the keypad to dial 911 if need be.

I guess I could stay here until the knocking goes away, but suppose it doesn't? And what if it's not a couple of drunk bachelorettes looking to score some angel wings pastries before stumbling off to bed?

I go to the door, picking up one of my large, sharp

Korin Gyutou knives along the way. At home I have a backup piece, a 9mm Smith & Wesson M&P, and that pistol should be here where it could do some good, not home, gathering dust.

I grab the handle, give it a turn, and shove the door open.

CHAPTER 15

AND NEARLY hit Vanessa McKeon straight in her gorgeous, flawless face.

She laughs and skips back, and says, "Boy, when you say you're closed, you really mean it!"

I feel foolish holding the knife and hide it behind my tired butt, but in truth, after all the work tonight and the disappointment of not seeing friends in line and the unsettling view of the three gangbangers making a threat, it's a sweet treat seeing Vanessa standing there before me. From the soft glow of a nearby streetlamp, her blond hair and light-pink floral-print dress look almost radiant.

I'm not as tired anymore.

I turn and Marlene makes a teasing kiss-kiss face, and then she shoves her phone back in her pocket, starts wiping down the near counter again.

"Of all the po'boy joints in all the towns in all the world, you walk up to mine," I say with a grin, stepping back for a second to put the Korin Gyutou down, then stepping out of the truck. "To what do I owe the pleasure?"

"I was hoping for some *culinary* pleasure," she replies, smiling. "I had to work through our staff meal at the restaurant earlier tonight, and I didn't feel like sticking around and eating leftovers. So I thought I'd swing by Killer Chef for one of your legendary sandwiches. But I see you're closed. Maybe another time."

"Don't be ridiculous," I say. "That time is now."

"Are you sure? Really?"

Biting her bottom lip, Vanessa excitedly scans the chalkboard menu hanging on the front of the truck. She looks so cute doing it, I hate to stop her.

"That list won't help you much," I say. "We ran out of just about everything on it. But if you tell me what you're in the mood for…"

"Hmm," she says, nodding. "In that case, I'll make it a chef's choice. Rumor is, he's pretty talented." Another sweet smile my way. "But I don't believe everything I hear. Just what I taste."

With an idea already taking shape in my mind, I hop back into the rear of the truck. I drop a pat of butter into a frying pan and fire up the freshly cleaned stove.

Marlene exhales loudly and puts her hands on her hips.

"Seriously, Caleb?" she says. "After we just finished scrubbing this whole place down?"

"Relax. I'll *re*-scrub it," I say, moving the frying pan around in smooth circles so the butter will evenly spread. "It'll be spotless before we reopen tomorrow, I promise. Cut me a little slack, would you? And cut me some onions and green peppers, too."

From the fridge I remove a catfish filet and lay it into the sizzling pan. I sprinkle it with salt and pepper, then baste it with an improvised glaze of honey, cayenne, and cardamom. Once the fish has been blackened on both sides, I set the steaming filet onto a toasted baguette, dress it with some sautéed peppers and onions, and top it off with a few strategically placed dabs of horseradish. Along the way Marlene is muttering under her breath about having to work late, messing up the truck after it's been cleaned, and doing all this to help her dumb ex-husband get laid.

I ignore her with a grin and focus on the food, and I wrap the whole thing in wax paper and step outside to serve it personally to tonight's guest of honor.

"It smells incredible," Vanessa says, gently breathing in the fresh scent while holding the sandwich in her petite hands. "Can you tell me about it?"

"Well, I'd say it's a very interesting creation. It's sweet on the outside. And very appealing. But it's sharp, too. A little spicy. Surprising. And *very* tempting."

Vanessa gives me a look. Then takes a big bite—and lets out a little moan.

"*Mmmm.* I didn't know it before now, but this is *exactly* what I wanted."

"I know the feeling," I reply.

Vanessa smiles coyly. She's about to take another bite, but instead she hesitates, then starts rewrapping the sandwich.

"I'm sorry to run," she says softly. "But I told Lucas I was on my way home. I don't want him to get worried...or, well, you know."

Oh, right. For a minute there, I forgot Vanessa was married. To a total jerk. A wealthy jerk that could probably buy six of these food trucks with change found under his living room couch cushions.

"Hey, no problem," I say. "I'm glad you stopped by to see me. Maybe we can—"

"I stopped by for a *sandwich,* Caleb," she says briskly, her attitude turning chilly. "Nothing more, nothing less. Have a good night…and tell your partner I appreciate her working late."

Vanessa turns and walks away, her slim shoulders slumped. I watch her for a moment, hoping she'll glance back. Hoping she'll give me a sign she's interested in more than just my food.

But she doesn't.

CHAPTER 16

I AM nothing if not a man of my word. I promised Marlene I'd clean our truck again, so that's precisely what I do—and *then* some.

My grumpy ex-wife heads home a few minutes after Vanessa leaves, with one parting shot: "Poor big hand-some Caleb. Thought his last-minute meal would save the princess. But the princess is going back to her troll, and you're going to be stuck doing the dishes."

I know she's on the money—which I refuse to admit out loud—and I spend another hour wiping down the stove again, rewashing the pans and utensils, and re-sanitizing our prep station.

The next morning, I get up a whole hour early—still stiff and sore with my one-sided fight with a baseball bat—to give Killer Chef a good scrub on the *outside,* too. Since you can't exactly drive a giant food truck through an automatic car wash, I park her on the curb in front of my colorful ranch house in Tremé—a funky, historic part of the city I just adore—to do it by hand. I fill an empty plastic trash can with soapy water, grab a long-handled mop, and get to it.

Soon the truck is dripping with suds, top to bottom. I'm dripping, too. This is harder work than it looks, but the predawn morning is cool and quiet, and I'm enjoying the solitude. A couple of the neighborhood kids who are also up early peer at me and give me big waves, and I wave back. When Killer Chef and his magical truck started parking here, I made a point of passing along leftovers to area families I knew were going through rough times.

But I did it right. I gave them my food with a slip of paper, saying I was doing test runs in my kitchen, and having their written reviews would help me out. It still works today, and you know what? They and their kids watch out for my truck, and not once has it ever been spray-painted, or broken into, or had the tires slashed.

I uncoil my garden hose and start spraying Killer Chef's shrimp-and-crossbones logo with water, washing off the last of the soapy suds, when a couple of the kids across the street yell out, "Hey, mister, watch out! Watch out!"

I turn, and a man pops up from the other side of the truck, and I nearly turn the hose on his face full-force—thinking at least the cold blast of water would knock him back—but then I lower the hose and say, "Shit, you've *got* to be kidding me."

It's not Ty Grant, nor anyone from his posse, nor anybody wearing yellow, or even a reporter from the *Times-Picayune* or a TV crew looking for an ambush interview.

It's my former boss, Chief of Detectives Brian Cunningham.

I lower the hose and he steps forward, saying, "Sorry, I didn't mean to scare you."

Trying to save some face, I reply, "That's not why I said 'shit,' Chief. Shit is what you *look* like."

I hate to admit it, but it's true. His eyes are red and

droopy. His hair is all mussed up. His striped blue tie is stained and lying askew across his belly. And his dress shirt is so wrinkled it looks like a white raisin, and there are stains along his gray slacks legs. Even when we've worked some vicious and shocking murder cases in the past, going "balls to the wall" for days, I've never seen him like this.

"A week without sleep will do that," he says. "Look, Caleb, I need to talk to you."

I give my old boss a brisk shake of my head. "Don't bother, Chief. I'm over it."

While I'll always resent the way he left me hanging during the whole shooting investigation, I have too much respect for the man to hear him grovel. I'm sure he heard about my baseball bat meeting with Ty Grant and wants to make late amends. I go back to spraying down my truck, the water pinging loudly off the metal siding.

"Caleb, I'm not here to—"

"It's too late for an apology," I tell him. "Official or otherwise. I'm not interested. Besides, handing in my resignation was the best decision I ever made."

"Would you please just—"

"Do I miss my old job?" I ask. "Sure. But my life is good now, Chief. I'm cooking around the clock. I bet the Franklin Avenue knuckleheads eventually stop following me around and go back to selling dope and making money. And I feel happier than I have in a very long—"

"Damnit, Rooney, can you shut off that water and listen?"

I worked for him for six years and never once heard him raise his voice to me. Something's wrong. I lower my hose and turn off the spigot.

He wipes his face with his right hand, lets out a deep sigh. "During a staff meeting of senior department heads a week ago, we got an unexpected visitor who made everyone sit up at attention."

He grasps the lapels of his jacket and flips them back and forth. "From the feds. Dressed in a much nicer suit than mine."

I drop the hose on the pavement, try to find a dry piece of my T-shirt to wipe my soaked hands, and fail.

"Who was he?"

"Special Agent Marcus Morgan, with the FBI's Counterterrorism Division. He was paying us a courtesy call. To let us poor peasants know that he and his team had come here to investigate a high-level terrorist threat alert against New Orleans. One that's both credible *and* imminent."

"Shit," I say. "Now it makes sense. A week ago I was on Bourbon Street, saw two undercover cops scoping the crowd along with two tactical unit guys in full battle rattle. They wouldn't say why they were out and about, only that some higher-ups were spooked."

He nods. "Spooked. Yeah. How about scared shitless?"

There's a spreading puddle of water from my hose going across the pavement. "Marlene and I also spotted two Black Hawk helicopters flying low and slow near the Garden District the other night. Part of the alert?"

He nods and says, "You may think you're just cooking there, Chef Caleb, but you sure as hell are staying alert."

"Did the feds say when we might get hit?"

He holds out his hands. "When else? During Mardi Gras. Nine days away. And we're not talking one nut or two like the Orlando nightclub shooting or the Boston

Marathon bombing. This? We could be dealing with an entire cell of professional, stone-cold killers who want to do as much death and destruction as possible."

My God. Out here on the quiet morning streets of my dear Tremé, it seems like I'm in one of those nightmares where you see something dangerous and violent approaching you, and your legs can't move, freezing you in place.

"Any indication how?"

He shrugs. "Take your pick. Suicide vests, IEDs, snipers, biological weapons like anthrax…the thing is, terrorist bastards are always one step ahead, weaponizing stuff that's usually innocuous. Like box cutters, or razor blades, or sneakers, like that shoe bomber asshole in 2001. It's all due to him that thousands of folks have to take their shoes off every day at airports."

I say, "What's our…I mean, besides the higher alert and more guys on the street, what's the department's action plan?"

"Plan?" he says. "Jesus, Caleb, we didn't have time for any planning after Morgan briefed us. Every cop in that room started yelling out offers to help, however they could. Anything the feds needed, the NOPD would give 'em. Resources, manpower, equipment, intel, you name it. And that's why you've seen those additional faces on the street."

Up the street two young girls are jumping rope, their cheery little voices reaching us here, these two older and wiser men talking about hundreds—hell, maybe thousands!—dead in just over a week. Those little girls. My friends. Neighbors. The tourists coming here, looking for a good time.

Now they're all just targets.

"And what else?" I ask.

"Hah," he says, weaving back on his heels. "That's an excellent question. 'What else?' Everyone in that room with a crescent badge demanded that we do more, flood the streets, start cracking down on our street sources and other informants to see what we could squeeze out. But you know what happened, right?"

Right, I thought, remembering my senior year in high school, right after 9/11, and learning later that the information and intelligence *was* out there about the impending attack, but bureaucratic inertia and turf battles let al-Qaeda proceed unmolested, sending nearly three thousand innocents to their graves.

"They said screw you, stay out of our way."

Another sigh from my overwhelmed and overworked former boss. "That's about it. Morgan said we should keep our damn mouths shut and stay the hell out of it. Let *them* handle the situation."

"Christ, that doesn't make any sense, Chief," I say. "The FBI always coordinates with the locals with something like this. We know the city better than anybody. What's different this time?"

"Way above our pay grades, Caleb," he says. "Some big-time meetings are taking place in DC. Apparently, there's international security implications, too. Unbelievable, isn't it?"

He shakes his head with disgust and dread, and right now, I'm so angry I feel like punching a hole into the side of my truck.

"After the agent and his team cleared out," he continues, "Superintendent Fontaine took the floor. Everyone—and I mean everyone!—thought he was going to say to hell with the feds, that we have to save our city, and do what has to be done. Instead, the ass-kissing bastard doubled down on Morgan's orders. You can imagine the response that got…but he wouldn't say anything different. Even said that under threat of immediate termination, everyone in the department would follow the FBI's lead. Or else."

I'm disgusted but not surprised. "Sure, from Fontaine's perspective, doing that makes sense," I say. "He follows the FBI's lead and nothing happens, he's gained a lot of favors with the feds. And if something does happen, well, his hands are clean. How could a department like us win out against the big bad feds from DC?"

"Shit, yeah, right to the point as always, Rooney."

"Then again…maybe the feds are overreacting. Getting jumpy. Maybe their intel stinks, and they don't want to look embarrassed if they're wrong."

"But what if their intel *isn't* wrong?" he says. "Doesn't mean we have to follow their lead, now, does it. But here we are, with our collective thumbs up our asses."

I see the little girls still jumping rope and turn away so I don't have to see their innocence and, yes, vulnerability. I say, "Yep, that sounds like the dysfunctional New Orleans Police Department I used to know and love."

"The one and only," he says.

I go to grab my hose to roll it up and put it away.

"No offense, Chief, I'm sure glad I'm no longer part of it."

He narrows his eyes and gives me a cryptic look that stops me in place.

"Me, too," he says. "That's why I'm here."

"How's that?"

"Rooney, we need your help."

CHAPTER 17

I'VE SEEN my former commanding officer make that face before. It used to mean he was about to give me an order he knew I wasn't going to like. But now that he's not my boss anymore, I don't know *what* the hell it means.

"Hold on, Chief," I start, but he cuts me off.

"Do I have to remind you what happened the *last* time the feds showed up to 'help' us through a major crisis?" he says, shaking his head in disgust. "How the hell did that work out for the Big Easy? Am I right?"

Of course he's talking about Katrina. A brutal once-in-a-century hurricane that battered our city and changed it forever, leaving behind waterlogged corpses in the streets, thousands of destroyed homes and dreams, and neighborhoods that more than a decade later are still ghost towns. When it was all over, nearly two thousand New Orleanians had lost their lives, many of them women and children, and there are some who think that number is still too low. I remember drinking in a Bourbon Street bar one night, years ago during an anniversary event of Katrina, and one old-timer saying to the other, "You know what the difference is between New Orleans now and Nazi Germany in 1945? Back in '45, the Americans treated Germany's cities better after it was all over."

Yeah, so there's not much of a reservoir of trust and good feelings toward the feds.

But now, a major terrorist attack during Mardi Gras? The body count could dwarf the Katrina stats, make the memories of that killer storm seem pleasant in comparison.

"You don't have to convince me," I say. "But what kind of help are you talking about?"

He nods. "No one's counting on a couple carpetbagging suits from DC to keep us safe. Least of all me. Like you said, Rooney, no one cares more about this place—or knows it better—than the people who call it home. But no one's willing to touch this thing. Not with the FBI up our ass and the superintendent rolling over like a dog. Everybody's hands are tied."

He pauses a moment, and I know what he's going to say next, and I beat him to it.

"Except for mine, right?"

"That's right."

I shake my head in disbelief.

"Chief, you want me to interfere with a federal terrorism investigation? As a *civilian*?"

"I want your *help,* Rooney. I want your eyes. Your ears. I want you to knock on doors. Knock around a couple heads if you have to. I need someone on the outside. A man I can trust. A good cop who gives a real damn about this city—"

"I'm *not* a cop, Chief. Not anymore."

"Tell that to the gangbanger you chased down the other day," he says. "You couldn't stop yourself from going after a *purse snatcher*. Are you really going to sit on the sidelines *now*? Bullshit. I know you, Rooney. It's who you are."

I try to keep my expression calm and composed. But

I'd be lying if I said his words weren't touching a nerve in me.

"Look, even if I wanted to...I used to work major crimes," I say. "My beat was homicide, gangs, drugs. We're talking a terrorist cell infiltrating the city, setting up...whatever the hell they're planning. Where would I even start?"

He glances down at his shoes, like he's ashamed at what he's going to say next.

"I wish I could tell you. Agent Morgan and his team wouldn't say a peep after that shit-ass briefing. They're keeping their leads and intel close to the vest. I've spent the last week poring over hundreds of *our* old case files, looking for any terrorist links. I got nothing."

Great. So this isn't just the biggest case I've ever tackled. It's also the coldest.

"There's always *something,* Chief. Maybe you've been sitting behind a desk for too long."

"Let's hope you haven't been standing behind a *stove* too long," he shoots back, lightening our collective mood just a bit as we both smile.

He extends his hand. "Thanks, Rooney."

"Don't thank me yet. I haven't done a thing."

"No," he says with confidence. "But you will. I know you too well."

We shake, affirming our secret pact. Then Cunningham turns to go, and something comes to me.

"Chief..." I say. "You showing up like this—why the whole fedora-and-trench-coat routine? Why not save yourself a trip and just give me a call?"

He turns back and speaks plainly. "Because if the feds are any good...and I pray to God that they are...they're listening. To both the good guys *and* the bad guys."

CHAPTER 18

CUNNINGHAM'S WORDS leave me in a dark place that morning, thinking and re-thinking, pondering and trying to come up with avenues of approach to grab an investigative thread—any thread—and start pulling. During the entire busy brunch shift, as the customers line up, I get a sick feeling to my stomach looking at this line of innocents, knowing at this moment, there are probably a group of men in this city who would love to see them dead, shattered, bleeding, wounded, and screaming in pain and horror.

My old chief is right. This city's been to hell and back once before. I can't leave its fate in the hands of a bunch of outsiders. I have to step up and help.

But how?

My head is swirling so much, I botch not one, but two, food orders that morning. I even nick the tip of my index finger with my chef's knife, an amateur accident I've not had in years.

My ex-wife easily notices that something's on my mind. But in typical Marlene fashion, her "support" comes in the form of sarcastic scolding.

"Hey, quit fantasizing about that married broad and focus on our food!"

Of course I can't tell her the truth. That I'm not day-dreaming about Vanessa.

I'm trying to figure out how to prevent a *nightmare*.

It does leave a bad taste in my mouth, not being able to tell Marlene what's really bothering me, but I need to keep focused, and I can't bring her into what I'm doing.

I've done it before when I was active-duty in major crimes, but it still doesn't make it feel any better.

When the morning shift finally ends, I hang up my apron and bid Marlene adieu. Then I hop the Rampart Street streetcar and ride it to the end of the line. From there it's a short walk to my destination: the central business district. A lot of folks think New Orleans is all old, narrow roads and balconied town houses. But this "downtown" part of the city has wide, traffic-snarled avenues running between tall, glistening office towers.

It's also packed with people. Especially lots of *children,* everywhere I look. Which isn't typical, but today is the first Sunday of Carnival season—"Family Sunday," as it's known—and the procession passing through here this afternoon promises to be a lot tamer and more kid-friendly than most others. At least by New Orleans standards.

I slip in among the throngs of people all waiting to get a glimpse of the approaching procession. This one is sponsored by the famous Krewe of King Arthur and Merlin. Within a few minutes, before I see the actual parade, I *hear* it. The buzzy blare of trumpets and trombones. The *rat-a-tat-tat* of a drum corps. All around me, kids and their parents are brimming with excitement.

Deep inside I know I'm wasting time, that I should be out and doing *something,* but that something has yet to come to mind.

Finally, a high school marching band comes into view around the corner. They're wearing vibrant purple and orange uniforms and playing a funky brass-band rendition of Beyoncé's "Crazy in Love." They're followed by the lead float. Decorated like a tropical island, it's carrying women dressed as mermaids and men as pirates, all of whom are tossing beads down at the cheering crowds.

The scene is noisy and wild and jubilant. The joy is practically infectious.

But I'm not here to have fun.

I've come to this parade to do recon.

With no leads, no clues, and no suspects, I've decided to start my off-the-books investigation by trying to get inside the bad guys' heads. I ask myself: If *I* were a smart and resourceful terrorist, hell-bent on causing the most chaos and carnage possible, what would *I* do? If I can figure out *how* these bastards plan to wreak havoc on Mardi Gras, it might help me figure out who they are—and how to stop them.

It sounds like a stretch, I know. But for now, it's the only thing I've got.

First, I glance around at all the spectators. I'm trying to spot the most obvious security holes that could be exploited the most readily.

But I quickly realize there are too damn many to count.

The crowd numbers well into the thousands, and almost everybody's carrying an unscreened backpack or purse that could easily be hiding explosives.

And if something were detonated, good luck trying to flee. We're all penned in by metal barricades. And most of the side streets—possible escape routes—are blocked off, too. I do see a handful of uniformed cops stationed here and there, but after long days of working double shifts, they look bored and exhausted. Seeing them doesn't inspire much confidence.

Next I turn my attention to the parade itself, and beyond.

Which is even worse.

Hundreds of performers are wearing billowy costumes. Any one of them could be concealing a suicide vest with C-4 plastic explosive and ball bearings, ready to scythe through the families laughing and clapping nearby.

There are dozens of giant floats. Any could be hiding a massive car bomb, with chunks of metal, screws, and nails, all designed to shred flesh and break bone.

And stuffed into any marching band member's hollow instrument could be an atomized chemical or biological agent, drifting out in an invisible yet deadly cloud, ready to start killing hundreds within minutes.

On any rooftop, a trained sniper could be crouching, ready to fire into the crowd.

A sniper wouldn't even *have* to be trained! Any fool with a few minutes of experience with a military-style assault rifle with piles of cartridge-filled magazines up on top of one of those roofs could kill hundreds just aiming down and pulling the trigger, over and over again, just firing into the screaming crowd.

Hell, the dusted sugar on any plate of beignets could be *anthrax!*

God almighty. I shiver at the endless, chilling possibilities. With the right equipment, the proper planning, and enough dedication, a determined band of evil men could cause enormous casualties at an event like this in seconds.

And like Cunningham observed earlier, hard-core terrorists are always thinking ahead, looking to use common, everyday objects and turn them into weapons of killing and destruction. Like plastic explosives in shoes, to be detonated aboard an aircraft, right above the fuel tanks!

What could these bastards be planning that no one's ever thought of before?

I close my eyes and pinch the bridge of my nose. What the hell was I thinking coming to this parade in the first place? What did I really think I'd learn? All it's done is show me how vulnerable Mardi Gras really is. And make me even more worried.

Then it hits me.

Literally.

I feel something strike the top of my head and skitter to the ground. I open my eyes—and realize it was just a necklace of plastic beads. It was tossed at me by a man wearing a colorful court jester costume in a passing float, doing a silly little jig.

"Be merry, good sir!" he calls in an awful English accent. "Here cometh the king!"

He's pointing behind him to an approaching float: the biggest and most elaborate of all, decorated to look like a giant castle. On a "throne" toward the rear is a matronly looking woman wearing a large white robe, a dazzling gold crown, and giant reflective sunglasses. She's "King Arthur," the parade's star—even though that "real" legendary monarch probably wasn't a middle-aged lady in aviator sunglasses.

But that's part of the fun of Mardi Gras, I think, as I politely push my way back through the crowds to leave. Anybody can be anyone. Nothing is as it seems.

And unless I do something to stop it, anything horrific can happen.

CHAPTER 19

I PARK on Freret Street and cut the engine. Used to be, this was a strip of shuttered storefronts and abandoned buildings. You didn't dare come near here after sundown—unless you were in the market for a new wallet and phone with few questions asked.

But today it's an up-and-coming dining hot spot. That's thanks largely to Beatrice St. Ville, a local chef who opened Bea's Café on this block a few years ago, jump-starting the area's revival. I don't know Beatrice personally, but she has a reputation for being extremely liberal—with her Cajun seasoning *and* her politics. The food at her new joint was plenty good. But what really put it on the map was her policy of hiring cooks, servers, and other staff exclusively from disadvantaged backgrounds. Like undocumented immigrants. Recovering addicts. Even ex-cons.

Which is all well and good with me.

Except when one of them might be a terrorist.

Ibrahim Farzat, a thirty-year-old Syrian refugee, moved to New Orleans with his wife about a year ago and got a job at Bea's as a dishwasher. I remember him showing up on the NOPD's radar last summer when he was arrested for disorderly conduct and resisting arrest.

After he was booked, detectives took a gander at his online activity. A conservative Muslim, Farzat posted frequently about his religious devotion, and he followed some pro-Islam accounts that looked edgy.

But there were no immediate terrorist red flags, and the charges against him were eventually dropped. Still, we passed the info on to Homeland Security, just to be safe. They got back to us quick. The Farzats, we were told, had been thoroughly vetted and weren't considered a terrorist threat.

Looking back, maybe Homeland got back to us a little *too* quick.

If there's one thing I've learned about the feds, they like to take their sweet time. DC isn't a swamp; it's an ocean full of quicksand. Why was DHS so lightning-fast to dismiss our concerns *that* time? What didn't they want the NOPD to know?

I swung by Farzat's last known address earlier this afternoon to try to find out. But his rented home in Dixon was dark and empty. Neighbors told me they hadn't seen him or his wife around in weeks. One gave me Farzat's cell number, but when I called, a cheery recorded voice told me it was no longer in service.

It's not a crime to move houses or change numbers or follow people on Twitter. And maybe I'm going down a dead end here. But given what I know about Farzat, I just want to find the guy, ask him a few questions, and rule him out.

I exit my car and unlock the trunk. Bea's Café doesn't open for another hour, and since I don't have a badge to flash anymore, I probably won't get anybody to talk to me much about Farzat. Especially not this close to dinner service.

So I have another idea.

I remove a freshly washed, white chef's apron and slip it on. Then I head into the alley behind the restaurant. When I reach the café's rear service entrance, I see it's propped open with an empty wooden vegetable crate, and so I head inside.

Like most professional kitchens, this one is a swirl of heat, noise, and chaos. Prep cooks and sous chefs in a rainbow of skin tones are chopping and dicing — and sweating buckets in the process. I wend my way through, keeping my head down and acting like I belong there, hoping I can spot the fellow I've come to see — if he even still works there, that is.

But after reaching the end of the kitchen, I don't. So it's time to open my mouth.

"You're trimming those pork chops real nice," I say to one of the prep cooks nearest me. He's African American, looks about twenty-five, and wears a red, black, and green bandana over his thick mane of dreadlocks.

He makes a quizzical expression and grunts, "Thanks."

"Hey, lemme ask you, does a guy named Ibrahim Farzat still work here? Mid-thirties, black hair, beard, accent. He washed dishes. Maybe he—"

"Naw, man. And I got work to do."

I can't tell if this guy really doesn't know Farzat, if he's too busy to talk to a stranger, or if he's hiding something. I decide to try someone else.

"'Scuse me," I say to a tough-looking Hispanic fellow in his forties, julienning a pile of carrots. "Do you know a dishwasher who works here named Ibrahim Farzat?"

Without stopping cutting, he flashes me a suspicious look.

"You a cop or something?"

"More like a private eye."

"Is Abe in some kinda trouble?"

"No, nothing like that. But I really have to speak to him. It's a family emergency."

The man shrugs, ignoring me.

"Look, I don't want any trouble," I say. "I just want to talk to him. When's the last time you saw him here? Does anybody have an address, or a number I can—"

"You don't want any trouble, huh?" the cook says, his voice thickening with menace. He finally stops his chopping, but tightens his grip on his knife. "You come in here in your little chef costume, start bothering people, asking questions. Get out."

I glance around the kitchen. A few other sous chefs nearby have stopped their work, too, to watch this brewing confrontation. They also seem to be readying their blades. It's been decades since I worked in a brick-and-mortar restaurant like this and I forgot how strong the brotherly bonds among kitchen staff can be.

"You're making a mistake here," I insist. "The man you used to know might be—"

"Luis said get out," says another sous chef on my left. He takes a step toward me, holding his cleaver just above waist level. I see it's damp with fresh cow's blood.

This whole thing is going south *fast*.

I really wish I had my sidearm right now, and I think of grabbing one of the knives or cleavers and beating a hasty yet armed retreat.

But I don't want to make a scene, I don't want any violence, and most of all, at this point and as a fellow chef, I don't want to screw up the prep work for Bea's hardworking and loyal crew.

So I hold my hands out and say, "Sorry to disturb you guys. Have a great night, okay?"

Then I get the hell out of there.

Back to my car, I'm pissed I didn't get any info on Farzat, but then again, maybe there was no info to get from that crew of cooks and sous chefs.

At this point, I just don't know.

I strip off my chef's apron in disgust, open up the trunk of the car, and toss it in with a well-earned swear word.

My first attempt at getting a lead on this threatened terrorist attack on my hometown has just failed. I'm glad Cunningham wasn't around to witness it.

I slam the trunk.

But I'll be damned if I'm giving up.

I speak into the darkness.

"I don't know who you are or where you are," I say. "But I'm coming after you."

CHAPTER 20

THE NEXT morning I slide into work with the muscle-memory of hundreds of cooking shifts, but my mind is elsewhere after last night's failed attempt to get information out of Bea's cooking staff. As I cut, chop, and prep, I run through last night's events, wondering if I should have tried something else, like talking to Bea herself instead of the suspicious kitchen staff.

Marlene speaks to me twice and on the third time, she kicks me in the shin.

"Hey!" I yell out.

"Hey, yourself," she says, wiping her hands on a cloth. "What's going on with you?"

"Nothing, I'm working here. What's going on with you?"

"I tried to tell you twice…and you just grunted back at me. So what's up? Still thinking about that married blonde?"

"No," I say. "Just trying to get the prep work done. Sorry. What were you saying?"

She slaps me on my butt. "Fool. Just told you that don't forget, we're doing brunch…so don't prep so many veggies, okay?"

I go back to work.

And at some point, I notice the obnoxious growl of a passing sports car. All morning it's been vrooming up and down Loyola Avenue, the six-lane boulevard where we parked the truck today. This is the fourth time in the last hour. The first three times, I just ignored it. But I can't any longer. It takes a special kind of asshole to rev his V10 engine like that again and again, to ruin an otherwise lovely day for no reason.

But then I start to wonder: Does it have something to do with *me*?

A Franklin Avenue gangbanger could never afford wheels like that—unless they were lifted. Maybe the driver is trying to send me a message. A warning. Just like the other night with those three gangbangers standing quietly and deadly in line.

I crane my head to look through the service window as the vehicle tears past. I get just a glimpse of it, a shiny blue Lamborghini Huracán—not the best name of a car to be driving through New Orleans, if you ask me. It's a convertible with the top down, but I can't make out the driver.

What can be done?

Nothing.

A line starts to form outside, and I go back to work.

Once my shift ends and our last customer is fed, I start wiping down the stove and scouring my pans and utensils as fast as I can. I'm anxious to get back out on the streets, and I'm thinking maybe I shouldn't have come to work today. These hours of chopping, frying, and sautéing are hours I should have been out on the streets, helping out Cunningham and the NOPD as quietly as I can.

But how could I have done that without tipping off Marlene that something's up?

"Hey," I say to her as I take off my apron. "I've got a couple of errands to run, Mar, so the rest of the day is yours."

"Really?" she shoots back. "Will your pants be coming off during any of these errands?"

I ignore her and get ready to leave when she says, "Wow, talk about coincidences, hot stuff. Looks like your quote, errand, unquote, is already here."

I look out the window.

It's Vanessa.

She's dressed casually in dark jeans and a red blouse, and gives me a friendly wave. Once again, her presence is a total surprise. A pleasant one, but still…

I step out of the truck. "Hey," I say. "You sure have a knack for timing."

"Is now not good?"

"I just wish you'd shown up ten minutes earlier. We're closed again. And I can't really stick around right now."

Her cheery expression fades a bit, like she's used to being disappointed by the men in her life. "Oh. Sorry. I understand."

"But what's up?"

"I guess I should have called first, but, I was hoping…"

She trails off, hesitant and a little uneasy. She absently twirls the fringe of her crimson blouse. Despite what I *need* to do right now, I'm curious.

"You were hoping what?"

"I was hoping…we could take a little walk."

Shit.

I check my watch. Two minutes. I'll give her two minutes.

"Okay, let's go for a walk."

Soon we're strolling down Loyola Avenue. It's a

busy commercial strip, and we pass throngs of people. Most are office workers dressed in suits and ties, but plenty are tourists and Carnival revelers wearing costumes and masquerade masks.

But how safe will they be in just a few days?

"You grew up here, right?" she asks. "So this is all...normal to you?"

"Born and raised, so yeah, somewhat normal," I answer. "You a transplant?"

"I've lived here for a couple years so I'm still getting used to it," she says. "I'm originally from a little town on Long Island, Glen Cove."

"Really?" I ask. "Then how come you don't have one of those funny 'Lonk I-land' accents?"

"A New Orleanian making fun of an accent?" She smiles and shakes her head. "But wear me out—when I get tired you'll start to hear it."

"Oh, sure. Your husband would *love* it if I did that."

I meant it as a flirty joke, of course. But her smile fades fast.

"You didn't see him today, did you?"

"Lucas? No. Why?"

Her eyes flicker down to her wedding ring. Its massive diamond glitters in the midday sun like a disco ball. For some reason—unlike the night we first met—she's wearing it.

"We...had a stupid fight this morning," she says. "I told him how I'd stopped by your truck the other night. How you made me that amazing sandwich. Well, Lucas blew a gasket. He started yelling, calling me names. Told me I could never eat at Killer Chef again."

"Gosh," I say, with fake innocence. "I guess that means I don't need to call him back and officially say no to his offer."

That makes her laugh, but just for a moment. I want to say more but I bite my tongue. I'd love to see her leave that son of a bitch, but their marriage isn't any of my business.

She goes on. "I told him he was acting crazy. That I could do whatever I wanted. That maybe I'd stop by your truck again today—out of spite. He actually threatened to drive around it in circles all morning if he had to. Can you believe that? In his stupid new Lamborghini, too. Sounds like a jet taking off. And he said if he saw me…"

One mystery solved, I think, as she trails off.

But seeing her face tighten with emotion, I decide to keep that thought to myself. I offer her a sympathetic shrug, along with the only kernel of romantic wisdom I absolutely know to be true.

"Marriage ain't easy," I say. "Believe me. I've been there."

We cross Gravier Street and reach an entrance to Duncan Plaza. It's a nice little park, an island of pleasant shade and open green space in this sea of office buildings. Inside the park, a group of rowdy schoolchildren are on a field trip, and a thirty-something father is gently throwing a foam football to his adorable toddler, playing catch, even though the foam toy bounces off the toddler's giggling face.

"Want to walk through?" I ask. "And maybe toss that pigskin around?"

She grins at the cute scene, but hesitates.

"I should be getting back to LBD. We have our all-hands Monday meeting in an hour. Then I'm interviewing some new hostess candidates, there's our new spring cocktail menu to approve—"

"Hey, I get it. You co-run a sixty-seat fine dining

restaurant. I can barely handle a two-person food truck."

"Don't sell yourself short, Killer Chef," she says. "I think that place is pretty special."

She turns to face me. She tucks a strand of blond hair behind her ear.

Then she leans in and pecks me on the cheek.

As she bashfully pulls away, I ask, "What was that for?"

"It was just a kiss, Caleb. Nothing more, nothing less."

She smiles, spins, and heads back the way we came.

I stand still as I watch her go, my feet planted firmly on the sidewalk.

But I swear it almost feels like I'm floating.

Then I check my watch.

My two minutes has slid into fifteen.

I'm no longer floating.

I've got to get to work.

CHAPTER 21

THINK COOKING in the back of a truck can feel cramped? Try whipping up some grub in the front seat of a car.

I've been sitting behind the wheel of my car all day. My legs are tingling, my back is aching, and my stomach is growling something fierce. I forgot how much a stakeout could suck, especially when you're doing it alone.

But now, it's finally time for a delicious dinner. Have I earned it? *Hell,* yes.

I open the small red cooler sitting on the passenger seat, which I packed earlier with everything I need to assemble a legendary Killer Chef sloppy roast beef po'boy—or at least a close approximation. When I was a cop, younger and dumber, plastic-wrapped sandwiches from a gas station would take care of my hunger, but times—and my life—have changed.

First things first, I fire up my "stove," a portable mini hotplate that plugs into my dashboard's power jack.

As it heats up, I dump a scoopful of cooked, cooled, shredded roast beef into a small camping skillet. I sauté the meat in its own fat until it gets warm and juicy. My car soon fills with the tantalizing scent of garlic, onion, and Cajun spices. Once the beef is heated through, I carefully stack it onto a baguette. Then I drown the meat with "debris gravy"—made from simmered beef scraps—kept warm in a Thermos. Lastly, the fixings: sliced tomatoes, chopped cabbage, diced pickles.

The first bite of my creation is...*divine*. So is the second, the third, the fourth. I swear the sandwich is as good as if I made it in the truck. Although maybe after ten hours of boring, fruitless waiting, my mind—and tongue—are starting to play tricks on me.

I take another bite, wondering how Marlene did today with the truck. I chickened out and texted her early this morning, telling her that my old aches and pains were still throbbing from my earlier baseball-bat-related injuries, and that I was taking the day off.

Poor Marlene.

I glance back down the road at the modest red-brick bungalow I've been keeping my eye on all day. After my quick, sweet meeting with Vanessa, I spent most of the day working the phones, talking to old reliable sources and even some private investigators who owe me favors. Eventually my work paid off, and last night I managed to get a hold of the Farzats' former landlord. After telling him I was from an insurance company, looking to pass on a settlement check to the family— making him eligible for a finder's fee—he gave me their latest mailing address.

So here I am. But thus far, I haven't seen a sign of either of them.

And I know it's insane to focus all of my attention on him, but without any added info from Cunningham, for now, Farzat is all I got. And if I'm going to seriously surveil Farzat, tracking his comings and goings, map-ping his network of associates, obviously I need to *find* the guy first.

Back when I was on the force, we used to hide motion-activated GPS sensors under the bumpers of suspects' cars. That let us keep an eye on their movements from the comfort of, well, anywhere. Today, I don't have that luxury. I can't even pull up the state DMV records, so I have no way of knowing which of the beat-up cars parked on this quiet street are his.

So it's back to basics. Putting in some quality "ass time," as we used to call it. Waiting and watching. Twiddling my thumbs and crossing my fingers.

Hoping my silent phone eventually rings with something, anything, from Cunningham.

As I finish my sandwich, licking the sweet gravy off my fingers, I notice some movement. Not from the house. Behind me. A black SUV with tinted windows is cruising along, coming this way, headlights off. It slows ever so slightly as it passes Farzat's home.

Holy shit.

I can't see the plates, but I'd bet they're government-issued. Could the FBI be out here tonight, too? Chasing Farzat just like I am?

I don't have much time to think on that, because all of a sudden, I see *more* movement.

This time, from inside the house.

Then the outside light over the front door flicks on.

I snatch my Nikon D3400 camera from the console. I hurriedly focus its high-powered lens and hold my breath.

The bungalow's front door slowly opens...and there they are, where they've been in that tiny home for as long as I've been sitting out here. Farzat and his wife, Rima. Both stepping out onto the porch. He's carrying a large, lumpy black duffel bag. She's berating him about something, dabbing her eyes, clearly upset.

I hold down the shutter button and take a flurry of digital pictures of the unhappy couple. I'd kill to have a long-range shotgun mic right about now—or the foresight to have hidden a tiny wireless bug somewhere on the Farzats' porch.

Eventually, Rima gives up her pleading. She goes back into the house and slams the door. Farzat heads to one of the old rust buckets parked on the street. *Bingo*. He unlocks the trunk and places his duffel bag inside.

I pull out a tiny voice recorder—smaller than a pack of gum—that's been resting in my shirt pocket. I press the little red button, slip it back inside my pocket, and speak: "White Ford Taurus, late nineties. License plate: Sierra Victor Hotel eight five two."

If I had a partner with me, she'd be scribbling down these details while I kept watch. But tonight, I've got to do double duty. I've seen a lot of cops use the built-in voice memo function on their phones for stuff like this, but my trusty digital voice recorder has never let me down.

I keep snapping photos as Farzat gets behind the wheel. He looks different from the last time I saw him. His beard is longer. His curly hair is flecked with gray. He looks quite a bit older than his thirty years. And haggard. *Haunted*.

I can only imagine why.

When he starts his engine and drives off down the street, I start my own engine, but keep my headlights off.

As I put my car into gear and get ready to follow, I look up the road for that FBI vehicle that passed, but I don't see it. Interesting. Maybe it wasn't the feds after all, then.

Maybe—no, *probably*—it's just me out here.

All alone.

Fine.

I'll gladly take on the job.

CHAPTER 22

NORMALLY, "MOVING surveillance" like this is done in teams of at least five. The "point" detective sits on the suspect's home, then alerts his colleagues, all parked nearby and already facing different directions on the bad guy's route. The appropriate car starts to follow, while the others fall behind, providing extra cover and driving along parallel streets, all to keep the surveillance as secret as possible. For real high-value targets, the NOPD can sometimes call in air assets from the state police, like a helicopter, or even a drone.

Pursuing a suspected terrorist with just one car and driver would be insane. It would never be done.

But that's what I'm doing tonight.

I wait a few seconds until Farzat cruises down the block. Then I pull onto the road behind him, keeping as much distance between us as I can, just like I was trained.

He first turns onto Downman Road, a main artery through this quiet neighborhood, heading north. That's a strange move, since there's not much that way except Lakefront Airport, a regional public airfield with mostly short-range private charter flights and notori-

ously lax security. Not much more than a couple rent-a-
cops and some ancient chain-link fencing.

I grip the steering wheel a little tighter and keep following.

Thankfully, Farzat makes a turn a few blocks *before* the airport—then, even more strangely, pulls
up to the drive-thru window of a twenty-four-hour
McDonald's.

I idle on the curb a half-block away and watch
through a small pair of binoculars as he pays cash for
three greasy bags of food and six cups of coffee in two
cardboard holders. It's possible Farzat is just going to
a nightshift job and is picking up a meal for his
buddies—not feeding a group of fundamentalists. I
pray that's the case. We'll see.

Back on the road, Farzat heads south on Mayo
Boulevard. He passes the I-10—then suddenly makes a
squealing U-turn and starts speeding back the way he
came.

Damnit, did he spot me?

No way I can pull that same move without blowing
my cover. So instead, I cut onto the closest side street
and quickly turn around. I'm about to turn back onto
Mayo again when Farzat's car zooms past—going
south again.

Huh?

Whatever. I pull out and keep following.

I continue tailing Farzat for a few more minutes
onto Almonaster Avenue. Running parallel to a wide
shipping channel, this two-lane road is badly potholed
and eerily desolate. I pass some abandoned industrial
sites on my left that are obscured by overgrown thickets
of shrubs and trees. On my right is nothing but acres
and acres of dark, eerie swamp.

Finally, Farzat's car slows and pulls into a hidden driveway, which is blocked off by a rusty iron gate. I brake a ways before and ease onto the gravelly shoulder, take out my binoculars again.

I watch as Farzat gets out of his Ford, unlocks the metal gate, then gets back in and drives inside. As he does, his headlights briefly illuminate a faded metal sign that reads: GUILLORY & SONS AUTO SALVAGE.

Like I said, Farzat *could* have a completely legitimate reason for being here at this hour. Maybe he's the junkyard's graveyard shift security guard. Maybe he's friends with the owner. Or maybe...maybe...

Bullshit. Who am I kidding?

This looks pretty damn bad.

And yeah, there's another advantage to doing a multi-unit surveillance.

Backup is just one radio message away.

You're never out alone with the bad guys.

Like I am now.

CHAPTER 23

BUT WHAT'S my next move?

Normally I'd have a whole team with me. Detectives on my flank, officers securing a perimeter, a chopper overhead, a SWAT team standing by.

But tonight, it's just me.

I'm dying to know what's happening on the other side of that gate. Who else is part of the meeting. Who's in charge. What they're saying. I consider getting the 9mm Smith & Wesson M&P out of my locked glove box, hopping the fence, and taking a look for myself. But realistically, without backup and support, that might be a one-way kamikaze mission.

Instead, I decide to sit tight. Even though Farzat stopped for a couple of Big Macs or whatever, I'm hoping he's not the last one to arrive, and that more late-night attendees show up any minute. If I can grab their license plate numbers, that would go a long way in helping me map out Farzat's contacts and associates.

Sure enough, barely five minutes later, a pair of headlights appear in my side-view mirror. I slink down in my seat as a beat-up, mud-splattered, maroon Jeep Cherokee passes by...and turns into the junkyard driveway.

I raise my binoculars again as I speak the license plate letters and numbers into my voice recorder.

Moments later, a third car appears and I repeat my action. This one is a shiny silver Audi, driven by a man in a jacket and tie. And as it disappears into the scrapyard, I spot the silhouette of a man in the backseat.

I feel my hands getting clammy with anticipation. Who could these people be? And what kind of terrorist gets driven by a chauffeur to a sleeper cell meeting?

With all these thoughts bouncing around my head, I pick up my camera and think about sneaking over the fence to see if I can grab some photos of the participants and—

Smash!

My driver's-side window shatters.

I flinch and squeeze my eyes shut as glass shards pelt me like hail.

I hear someone reach in and unlock my door.

When I open my eyes, I see a pair of knobby hands coming straight for me.

Instantly, my years of defensive training kick in: "ArCon," short for "arrest and control," a mishmash of jujitsu and wrestling holds that all law enforcement officers are taught and drilled in.

But it's a system designed for subduing and handcuffing suspects while on your feet, not defending against an ambush inside your own car. I barely get my hands around my attacker's wrist and start to twist— when his other hand encircles my neck.

I gag and gurgle, struggle and writhe. But it's no use. My throat is beginning to burn. My lungs are starting to tighten. I'm feeling light-headed. My vision is tunneling.

Finally, relief—as I'm yanked out of my car and

hurled onto the pavement, my bulky camera tumbling onto the road along with me.

Still coughing like mad, I turn onto my side to protect myself from further assault. As every cop knows, the most dangerous position to be in is on your back.

"What the hell are you doin' here?" the man demands, his voice low and husky.

I turn my head slightly to try to get a glimpse of him. But in the faint glow from my car's dome light, all I can see are his dirty leather work boots. I brace for a kick...that doesn't come.

But I do get hit with something even worse: the sight of a pair of grubby old Converse sneakers next to him, as well as a pair of green rubber Wellington boots.

Shit. I'm alone. Effectively unarmed. And outnumbered, three to one.

The man snarls again, louder, "I *said,* what the hell are—"

"What are *you?*" I demand. "And how stupid can you all be?"

Then I bluff, hoping they'll back off.

"The cops are onto your little plot, believe me," I say. "They know everything. Do you all really want to spend the rest of your lives in a six-by-ten cell in a federal supermax? Just walk away. While you still can."

The three men briefly tense. All share a nervous glance. But just as quickly, their expressions harden. And each takes a step closer to me.

"You're full of shit," the second one says—accompanied by the faint metallic *flick* of a butterfly knife being opened. Which complements the crowbar the third man has.

I feel my pulse rising and my adrenaline starting to kick in. I just know they're going to attack any second.

No way do I have the time to scramble and unlock my glove box and get my gun. So instead, I decide to strike first. And hard.

I twist onto my hands and knees, grab the only weapon I've got—my Nikon—then spring to my feet and start swinging.

Using it like a cudgel, I bash the first man square in the nose with it, then sweep his legs out with a kick.

The man with the crowbar lunges at me and swings. I slip and avoid the brunt of the blow, but the side of my head still gets dinged. He winds up and swings again—which, this time, I block with the camera. Its casing shatters but the lens is still intact, so I drop into a crouch and strike him right in the groin with it. A cheap shot, but an effective one.

Now it's just me versus the man with the knife. He starts swiping at me wildly, frantically, but I keep moving and parrying and dodging. At last I manage to pummel the underside of his chin like an uppercut. I feel a few of his teeth crack as his legs buckle.

All three assailants—scruffy swamp men, two white, one black—are writhing and moaning on the street. I take a step back and try to catch my breath. I feel like total shit, but also pretty damn exhilarated, too. There's nothing like escaping death to make a man feel alive.

But I'm practically drowning in confusion. Who *are* these goons? Are they just hired muscle to keep guard, or are they part of the terrorist cell themselves?

My head is spinning—and not just from the mystery. The spot that crowbar clocked me is throbbing. My ears are ringing, too. It almost sounds like police sirens.

Wait…shit. Those *are* sirens. Who the hell called the cops?

I have a thousand and one questions for these ass-holes. But I can't be here when the fuzz arrives. It would ruin everything. At least I have the...

No, my camera's destroyed, I *don't* have the photos I took of Farzat and the others! And a peek inside my breast pocket reveals my voice recorder was smashed in the melee as well. Goddamnit! I can definitely try to reconstruct what I've seen and observed, but it'll be a damn challenge.

With the sirens getting closer, I hop back into my Impala and speed off. Back on the road, I take stock. Despite the setbacks, I did stumble on what looked to be a secret terrorist meeting spot. Saw some additional suspects. And learned a whole lot.

I'm just not sure what.

CHAPTER 24

ARRIVING HOME, I open my front door and practically collapse right there in the entryway. With the adrenaline surge from the fight long over, the full agony of its aftermath is starting to hit me, hard.

I stumble into my bathroom and peel off my torn, bloody T-shirt. My chest and arms are a patchwork of cuts and bruises. That includes a long but shallow scrape across my shoulder. Must have been from the attacker's knife. In the heat of battle, I guess I didn't even notice it. I douse the wound with disinfectant, which feels like I'm bathing in acid, and it makes me groan.

But the real doozy is the welt on my temple from that crowbar. I inspect the plump, crimson mound in the mirror, then head into the kitchen and wrap a few ice cubes in a dish towel. Sagging onto a creaky wooden stool by the counter, I hold the cold compress against my head, and let out a long, jagged sigh.

I try to think back to the many men I encountered tonight. It was hard to see faces, fighting in the dark, but still, I'm trying to burn the images of their mugs into my brain. With my camera and its memory card destroyed, that's the only record of them I have.

But then, *another* face pops into my mind.

Vanessa—which is a very welcome distraction. I honestly don't know what it is about this woman that's affected me so much. Sure, she's smart and poised, driven and charming, with piercing eyes and a dazzling smile. But she's also aloof. Enigmatic. Not to mention *married,* for God's sake. To a less-than-stellar guy, sure. And I've been called a lady-killer once or twice in my day. But I'm no home-wrecker.

Shaking Vanessa from my mind, I rise and pad into my bedroom. I'm sweaty and grimy and caked with dried blood, but I just don't have the strength right now to shower. Instead, I strip to my boxers and flop down on my bed...

When there's a pounding at my front door.

Shit. I'm instantly alert again. My entire body stiffens with the rush of adrenaline.

Did somebody from the junkyard follow me home? Are they here to finish the job?

I quietly creep out back into the kitchen, still in just my underwear. With my phone in one hand, ready to dial 911, and a long carving knife in the other, I approach my front door as the forceful knocking continues. Damnit, I have a pistol, but it's in the car.

"Caleb Rooney?" booms a voice on the other side. "FBI. Open the damn door."

The feds? Here? Now?

Not taking any chances, I peer through the peephole. Sure enough, I spy a phalanx of men and women in dark suits standing like statues. Unbelievable.

At least they don't have a warrant. If they did, they wouldn't be knocking *on* my door, they'd be knocking it *down.* I have the right to tell them to shove off. But that's probably not the smartest move. Word to the wise: When a team of federal law enforcement agents shows up at your doorstep unannounced in the middle of the night, it's probably best to at least hear what they have to say.

I plaster on a polite smile, set the knife and phone on the counter, and open the door.

"Evening, Agent," I say. "To what do I owe the pleasure?"

I'm standing face to face with a muscular, imposing African-American man of about forty-five. His head is as smooth as a cue ball, but a bristly black beard covers his sunken cheeks and chin. He flashes his FBI badge and glares at me. No, *through* me.

"Special Agent Marcus Morgan, Counterterrorism," he nearly barks at me. "Let's talk inside."

I nod and step aside for the agent and his five-member team to enter.

"Welcome to New Orleans, by the way," I say as I lead them all into the living room. Though there's plenty of seating, they all remain on their feet. "But I'm guessing you're not here for my restaurant recommendations?"

"Do you have any goddamn idea what you did tonight?" Morgan growls, hands on his hips.

"I'm afraid I don't know what you're—"

"Your hanging around the house, then your little stunt at the junkyard? You set our investigation back *weeks,* Rooney. That's time we don't have to waste."

Just as I thought. The FBI *was* out there tonight. Even worse, agents just stood by and watched as I got my ass handed to me. Unbelievable.

"I *warned* you people," he continues, "to stay away from this thing. And this is exactly why!"

I shake my head in disgust.

"First of all, I'm *not* 'you people,'" I point out. "I'm

just your average Joe Citizen trying to protect the place I love most. And in just one afternoon, I made more progress than you have in—"

"We'd been casing that yard for *months,*" he interrupts. "Had it bugged top to bottom. If you hadn't rolled up playing cops and robbers, spooked the whole lot of them, we'd…"

He trails off. The frustration in his eyes is real. But so is the concern. The fear. So much so, it starts to rub off on *me*.

"I had no idea you guys had gotten there before me," I reply gently. "Who were those guys? What were they—"

"*Stop,* Rooney," he insists. "Just—stop. Go back to flipping burgers or whatever the hell you now do. There's more at play here than you could ever imagine."

"So read me into it!" I demand. "I'm not interested in a pissing contest, Agent Morgan. Let me help you. I know this city and its players and—"

"You really want to help us? Then stay the hell away."

He steps forward. His gaze bores into me. I return it in kind and don't flinch. But neither does he.

At last he asks, "Am I clear, Detective? Or should it be *chef*?"

Swallowing my fury, I answer, "Perfectly, either way."

He signals to his team that it's time to leave. They stream out as silently as they entered, heads bowed like monks. After locking and bolting the front door, I listen to their caravan of black SUVs roar away into the night.

Gently, I touch the welt on the side of my head. It

still hurts, but already the swelling and pain are starting to go away. I hope it heals quickly.

I also hope he bought my performance just now.

Because there's no way in hell I am backing down. Knowing how close I came tonight, and what's at stake, I'm just getting warmed up.

CHAPTER 25

THE NEXT morning, I arrive at Killer Chef to find Marlene outside, leaning over an ice-filled trough and filling it with plastic bottles of Big Shot.

"Huh," she says, as she shoves in another bottle. "Wouldja look at what the catfish dragged in."

If you're not from the Big Easy, you've probably never heard of Big Shot. But if you are, you know it's a locally made soda, beloved for its funky flavors like red crème and pineapple blue bayou. It's fun and fizzy and the opposite of fancy. Which is why it's the only beverage we sell.

"I thought you'd be happier to see me," I say, shambling toward my ex. I'm still feeling stiff and achy from last night's brawl, on top of my wounds from the assault in the parking garage. Getting attacked with a baseball bat and a crowbar inside of a week will have you moving slower than usual. "An extra pair of hands and all."

"*Extra?* Caleb, we're partners—not in matrimony anymore, thank God, but in this little endeavor we call Killer Chef. Or have you forgotten? Lately, that's how it feels."

"Marlene, I—"

Then she gives me a good look and is startled, gently

touching the fresh welt on the side of my head that my hair doesn't fully cover.

"What the hell happened to you?" she asks. "Run into blondie's angry husband?"

"Nope," I say, walking away from her and entering the rear of the truck, as she follows me.

"You gonna tell me what happened to that thick head of yours? You've already had one concussion this week. Are you okay? Was it the Franklin Avenue crew?"

I wish, I think. That would be a nice change of pace.

I shrug, grab a knife from the counter, get ready to start the morning's food prep. "It wasn't the Franklin Avenue boys."

"Caleb…"

I say, "Look, Mar, I can talk or start working. I'd rather start working before the line starts heading down the street."

She mutters something in anger and joins me in getting ready for the day.

Marlene is right to be angry, and to her point, I *had* been planning to bail on my brunch shift again this morning so I can continue my investigation. But after Morgan tore me a new one last night, I figured I should at least make it *look* like I was backing off. If he's smart, he posted a plainclothes agent outside my house this morning to make sure I was keeping my word. At least that's what *I* would do.

After tossing a few jalapeños down my gullet, I set about chopping veggies for the busy morning ahead. But my mind is a million miles away. I turn over the events of last night for the umpteenth time, searching for any clue I might have missed, groping for any lead I can follow up next.

There's no way I can ever get that close to Farzat again without the feds taking me down. And who were those three goons who attacked me last night? I don't have a clue.

But maybe that's the silver lining in all this. Farzat's not some untraceable lone wolf after all. He's working with a group. And one thing I learned from years of doing battle with gangs: The more people who know a secret, the higher the chance one of them will spill it.

I'm jolted out of my thoughts by the thunderous revving of a car engine, and the angry *beep-beep-beep-beeeeeep* of a horn.

I shake my head. Is Lucas Dodd seriously driving circles around my truck *again*? What a petty, pathetic little man — who definitely doesn't deserve such a wonderful wife.

I try to ignore this automotive distraction and refocus on my food prep. But when it continues for a solid thirty seconds, I angrily set my knife down and step out of the rear of the truck. It's time I gave this dude a piece of my mind. And maybe my fists, too.

But when I get outside, I don't see a blue Lamborghini at all. Instead, the noise is coming from an older-model white Lexus with shiny chrome rims idling across the street. And inside are four guys in yellow T-shirts, hoodies, hats.

Well, well.

My old friends are back.

After lying low these past few days, they've returned. In broad daylight. And they're here to send me a very clear warning: A gangbanger never forgets.

Great. As if I didn't already have enough shit to deal with.

I stand there on the sidewalk glowering back at these knuckleheads. I want to send them a clear message, too. They don't scare me. And never will.

Finally, my one-way staring contest ends. They start to whoop and holler, flash a mix of gang signs and one-finger salutes my way, then peel out.

"I see your fanboys have returned," Marlene says as I reenter the truck. "Why didn't you go over and drop off something for them? Like a cup of hot grease?"

I ignore her violent yet attractive suggestion and check my watch.

"Why don't we open up a little early. I've got some more…errands to run this afternoon," I say.

Marlene says, "You gonna tell me what's going on?"

I say, "Can you keep a secret?"

"Of course I can," she says.

"Good for you," I reply, and she tries to kick me like yesterday, and I jump back.

Sure enough, our first few hungry patrons soon appear—locals who share social media notes and texts when our truck is spotted—and are delighted to find us already open. The shift gets busy, fast—until about twenty minutes before closing time, when I notice Marlene has stopped calling out orders and buttering corn bread. Instead, she's having a little chitchat with someone outside, who I can't see.

"Hey, Mar," I call out teasingly, "more slathering, less blathering!"

"Oh, excuse me," she sasses back. "*You're* allowed to flirt with Miss McKeon, but I'm not?"

Hang on. Is Marlene really talking to Vanessa? My ex-wife chatting with a woman who's grabbed my attention, and more?

I step back from the stove to get a better look.

Yep, there she is. Wearing an aquamarine dress, chunky tortoiseshell sunglasses, and her trademark luminous smile.

For one very brief moment, all is right again in the world.

CHAPTER 26

WIPING MY hands on a dishrag, I join Marlene at the service window and flash our visitor a tired but happy grin.

"Vanessa, what's wrong?" I ask. "You're here while we're actually still open."

"Ha ha ha," she says, looking up at me. "Everyone's just fine, thank you. Now let's see...I think I'll have the crab gumbo with grits...and the crawfish boudin with dirty rice."

She plucks two Big Shots from the cooler: one cola, one watermelon.

"And these, too, please."

"Two entrees, two drinks," I say curiously. "Who's your lucky dining companion?"

Marlene jabs her elbow into my ribs.

"You don't interrogate customers, Caleb," she reminds me. "You cook for them. Now chop, chop!"

With a smirk, I obey—and put a little extra love into the order, too. I ladle the gumbo from the very bottom of the pot so it's chock-full of crab meat. And I keep a close eye on grilling the crawfish sausage, making sure its char marks are perfect.

"On the house," I say to Marlene as I pass her Vanessa's food.

"On your dime," she corrects me.

I'd love to watch Vanessa's expression when she takes her first bite, but taking care of a few more orders won't give me that chance.

When our last customer has been served, I duck out of the truck and scan the crowd. I expect to see her and a friend polishing off the last of their lunch, but instead I see Vanessa sitting patiently on a bench. Alone, her food untouched, her two Big Shots unopened.

"Oh, no," I say, walking up to her. "Did your lunch date stand you up?"

"Quite the opposite," she answers cheerily. "So, I'll admit I had a taste of both dishes. The crawfish is amazing. But that gumbo, Caleb? *Heavenly*."

She picks up the two bottles of soda and holds them out to me.

"But I'll be nice and let you pick your drink."

Which is when I realize her lunch date is…*me*. I can't suppress the smile that blooms across my face, even though part of me is a bit uneasy.

"What about Lucas?"

She says, "My husband is in Metairie all day, scouting locations for a new bistro he wants to open. I'm supposed to be running LBD. But I guess you could say I got a little cabin fever—*kitchen* fever—and wanted to stretch my legs. But if you're busy again…"

I am. Terribly.

"Wait—what happened to your head?" she asks.

"Kitchen accident. Occupational hazard!" I say. I don't want to lie—but I can't tell her the truth.

But something comes to me that I'm ashamed to

admit. Being with Vanessa for the next few minutes might help convince whatever FBI surveillance is out there that I'm being a good little chef after last night's visit from Special Agent Morgan.

Plus I get to spend some time with this gorgeous and intriguing woman.

A win-win all around.

"Let's walk and talk," I say. "I know another spot not too far from here that's pure New Orleans. Just as long as you're not afraid of ghosts."

She seems to perk up at the idea.

"Lead the way, Killer Chef," she says. "I'm not scared of *nothin'*."

Digging into our food and sipping our sodas, we stroll together down St. Claude Avenue, the main drag of this cozy neighborhood of the same name. It's lined with an eclectic mix of shops, cafés, and detached houses painted vibrant colors like lime, blueberry, and tangerine. Our conversation is mostly small talk: how busy work's been; how mild the weather's been, how much fun Carnival's been.

I wish I could share with her and anyone else what I'm working on, the burden of knowing that right now, scores of federal agents are scouring this city, looking for terrorists who want to strike during our high holy day, Mardi Gras.

But I can't.

We hook a right on Desire Street. The irony of the name isn't lost on me and I wonder if she picks up on it as well. Soon we arrive at two long brick walls on opposite sides of the street. Both are painted perfectly pristine white, with black wrought-iron gates facing each other. Lettering across the top reads, ST. VINCENT DEPAUL NO. 1 AND NO. 2.

"A graveyard?" she asks dubiously. "This is pure New Orleans?"

"Just trust me, okay?" I say. "Here, take my arm. And stay close."

We toss our trash in a receptacle near one of the gates, then link elbows and enter this quiet, other-worldly place.

Hundreds of granite and marble mausoleums, many more than a century and a half old, branch out in every direction like a creepy, mind-bending maze. It's a window back in time. Haunting, but also calming. And eerily beautiful.

"Oh, wow," she whispers. She grasps my arm a little tighter as we amble through together, taking it all in.

"Some people feel sad when they visit a cemetery," I say. "Like they're surrounded by death. But to me, a place like this is a reminder. That each of us only gets one life. So we damn better live it to the fullest, every single day."

She nods, contemplating that. "It's a stretch, but seeing these tombs…it reminds me some of the medieval cathedrals. Exquisite pieces of architecture and art, celebrating our life here and our life afterward, when—"

Her phone rings, and instantly she grows frantic, rummaging for it through her purse.

"Shit, I'm sorry, that could be Lucas. I have to get it. If I don't, he—"

"Hey, no problem," I assure her as she finally finds her phone. I notice her hands are practically trembling as she puts it to her ear.

She turns her back to me. I take a few steps farther away to give her extra privacy. Still, I can make out snippets of what is obviously an unpleasant conversation.

"I swear I'm at the restaurant…you know I would never lie to you…can you please stop screaming at me? Of course I love you!"

When the call finally ends, she gives me a sullen, embarrassed look.

"I should probably get going," she says. "But thanks for a great lunch, Caleb. And another lovely walk."

"Vanessa," I say, taking her arm again. "Look. I realize I barely know you. And it's none of my business. But if Lucas is treating you half as bad as it sounds like—"

"You're right," she answers brusquely. "It's none of your damn business."

I drop both her arm and the issue and lead her out of the cemetery in silence. Back on the sidewalk, she doesn't kiss my cheek. She barely even says good-bye.

I hope any FBI surveillance watching me is happy now, because I'm not.

Time to get back to work, and I *don't* head to the Killer Chef truck.

CHAPTER 27

I THOUGHT I'd pass through the gates of hell before I walked through these doors again. But here I am.

The musty, glass-walled lobby of NOPD headquarters.

It's been ten days since I stormed out of this place in a blaze of glory. But it might as well be years because it kind of feels like I'm visiting my old junior high school. The place seems smaller than I remember. Claustrophobic, even. Everything looks familiar, but feels a little strange.

Trying not to dwell on the memories crowding their way in, I make my way through the midday hustle and bustle. Past a plainclothes narcotics detective I vaguely recognize talking on his phone in heated Spanish. Past a two-bit defense lawyer in a rumpled gray suit conferring with his voluptuous female client, who I'd bet was caught turning tricks on Chartres Street. Past a pair of uniformed officers escorting a handcuffed drunk in a bloodied LSU hoodie, who's thrashing about and rambling incoherently. What a zoo.

I reach the desk officer on duty, a ruddy guy whose

uniform is at least one size too small for his portly frame. He's the station's gatekeeper.

"Help you?" he huffs, keeping an eye on the activity in the rest of the lobby.

I act casual, barely slowing down. "Just heading up to major crimes," I say.

"Hang on. You got an appointment?"

"They're expecting me."

He holds up a hand and picks up his desk phone. "*Who's* expecting you?"

I hesitate. I'm here to see Cunningham, who decidedly *isn't* expecting me. In fact, he made it quite clear I should lay low and keep my distance. If this kid tips him off I'm here, my ex-chief won't just refuse to meet me. He'll blow a fuse. And toss me out. And short-circuit whatever progress I've made.

"Look, I used to be on the job," I say. "Retired last week. I just want to—"

The officer scowls at me. "I know who you are. But you're not getting by without a good reason."

I consider backing away and just hanging around the lobby until Cunningham inevitably passes through. But that could take hours, precious time I can't afford to waste. So instead, I decide to answer straight up. If my old chief gets pissed off that I'm here and turns me away, that's on *him*. But before I do...

"Rooney?" says a deep voice behind me.

I turn around and see Sergeant Kevin Spearman waddling over. Years ago, when I first joined the force, he was a SWAT platoon leader, as cocky as he was fit—until a training injury landed him behind a desk for good. Since then, he's put on at least seventy pounds, but hasn't lost one ounce of arrogance.

"I didn't think you'd have the balls to step foot in

here again," he says, giving me a locker room–style tap on the ass. "Unless it was to beg for your pension back. On your knees."

"That reminds me, Kev," I shoot back. "How's your wife doing?"

Spearman briefly sets his jaw in anger, then forces a laugh. "Funny guy."

"I'm trying to get upstairs to see my old CO," I say. "Can you get me inside?"

Spearman hesitates for a moment, and then whatever good nature that still exists in that flabby mind rises to the occasion. He nods, first at me, then the desk officer, who lets me pass.

I take the elevator to the fourth floor, like I've done hundreds of times before. Trying to keep a low profile, I stalk through the major crimes bull pen, exchanging only the briefest of hellos with the handful of surprised former colleagues who notice me. I also take the long way to Cunningham's office, bypassing my old desk. The only thing worse than seeing it bare would be seeing somebody else sitting at it.

Cunningham's door is open, but he's sipping coffee from a paper cup and has his head buried deep in a stack of papers. I give the frame a firm knock. My old chief looks up—and practically spits out his steaming beverage in furious disbelief.

I step inside and shut the door, just as he swallows, wipes his mouth, and stammers, "Are you kidding me, Rooney?"

"Nice to see you too, Chief," I say, sitting down in front of him. "We need to talk, and there's no kidding involved."

CHAPTER 28

CUNNINGHAM RISES from his desk and starts pacing around his office like he wants to step out and leave me and my problems behind.

"Whatever this is about, it better be worth the risk you took," he says. "If Morgan finds out that you barged in here, if he suspects you're sniffing around his case—"

"He already knows," I say, leaning back in the chair, my folded hands across my belly.

He places a hand to his forehead, sits down heavily in his chair.

"Christ, Caleb!" he says, practically moaning. "I told you to be…I thought you knew what you were doing!"

"I do know what I'm doing, Chief," I say. "That's *why* he knows. Yesterday I tracked down a guy that's come up on our radar before."

"Who's that?"

"Ibrahim Farzat," I say. "A Syrian refugee we arrested last year for disorderly conduct and resisting arrest."

"Wait a sec," he says. "The guy that worked as a dishwasher at Bea's?"

"Yeah," I say. "That's the one. He posted some nasty

jihad stuff online and we passed it on to Homeland Security, and they basically said, don't worry, be happy. But I didn't have anything else to work with so I tailed him last night."

"Good," he says. "What happened?"

"I followed him from his house to some kind of secret meet-up at a scrapyard near the Industrial Canal, along with a few other apparent fellow travelers. He even double-backed to avoid being tailed but I managed to keep up with him. Then things got interesting."

"Interesting how?"

I brush away a lock of hair to reveal the welt on the side of my head from that crowbar strike, still red and swollen. He winces.

"An hour later, Morgan was at my door. Apparently, the feds were at the scrapyard, watching as well. Morgan practically threatened to beat my ass himself if I tried to get close to Farzat again."

"So what's Farzat up to?" he asks. "Is he the sleeper cell leader? The mastermind behind the attack?"

I shake my head.

"My gut says he's low-level, Chief," I say. "A pawn. During my tail last night, he stopped at a Mickey D's to make a food run. That's not what a mastermind does. Farzat is low-level and if the FBI is tailing him, then I need something else, something new."

"Christ, Caleb, I wish I could help," he says. "I already gave you everything I know."

I jerk my thumb behind me, toward the bull pen.

"What about what *they* know?" I ask. "There's gotta be some new intel off the streets in the past seventy-two hours in the I & A's, even if it doesn't stand out."

That would be "incident and arrest reports."

Detailed records of department call-ups, witness statements, officer observations. A treasure trove of data, if you know what you're looking for.

"I went through them this morning," he says. "Not much stood out, but I'll take another look."

He starts flipping through a stack of papers—without a whole lot of enthusiasm.

"A series of small explosions were reported in a parking lot in Versailles," he says. "Officers found remnants of what appeared to be firecrackers, but forensics is running tests. An attempted break-in at a gun shop in Gentilly. A smashed window, but no firearms were stolen, referred to ATF. Early yesterday morning, an employee reported a man in a suspicious black vehicle casing a riverside industrial park in Pines Village, but the suspect had left the scene when officers arrived. And last night, a unit responded to reports of yelling in the courtyard of a mosque in the South Seventh Ward. But the imam refused the officers entry, saying the situation was being handled internally."

He leans back in his chair, resigned. Any one of those incidents could be related to the Mardi Gras attack. Or none of them. *Jesus, this is infuriating!*

"I suggest you get back out there, Rooney. Keep doing whatever it is you—"

"Wait," I interrupt.

My mind has been turning over the litany of crimes, desperate to find even a shred of a possible new lead in one of them. And maybe I just did.

"The third one you said. The Pines Village industrial park. What's the address?"

Skeptically, he flips back through the file.

"6200 Lewis Road."

"Neptune Premium Seafood?"

My former boss looks taken aback.

"You know it?"

"They're a gourmet shrimp and crawfish processor," I say. "I'm a gourmet chef who's gotta be familiar with all my local supply options. Thanks for the tip, boss."

I get up out of the chair and open the door, start hauling ass out of his office.

"What the hell does a *seafood plant* have to do with this?" he calls out as I'm nearly halfway across the bull pen.

Honestly, I'm not sure yet.

But I'm going to find out.

CHAPTER 29

THE DINNER shift has barely started and there's already a line down the block.

Thankfully, this isn't the queue for Killer Chef. I'm back in the Garden District—the home of LBD, Lucas Dodd, and the hauntingly beautiful Vanessa McKeon. Gorgeous stately mansions line every street, hidden behind lush oak trees swaying gently in the evening breeze. When folks say New Orleans has a hint of old-world magic in the air, this is what they mean.

I make my way to the front of the line and enter Petite Amie, an upscale but laid-back creole fine dining spot inside an old saloon—formerly of ill repute—painted the color of lemon meringue pie. The scene inside is elegant but lively. Servers haul food on silver platters to tables full of NOLA's rich and fashionable. Antique crystal chandeliers dangle from the ceiling. In the corner, a brass jazz quartet plays a raucous and happy tune.

And I catch a glimpse through the swinging doors of the restaurant's wiry, forty-six-year-old owner, Billy Needham, moving around like a ballet dancer performing before an appreciative audience. He opened this place a few years ago and it's already become an institution.

Among the antique and contemporary prints in the foyer are photos of Billy with a number of celebrities, and a few aerial shots of New Orleans and the Garden District, and even a couple showing Billy in the cockpit of a small aircraft, wearing aviator sunglasses and radio earphones, grinning and giving a thumbs-up.

I step up to the charming young hostess dressed in black slacks and a black sleeveless blouse and preempt everything she's about to say.

"I know," I say. "I don't have a reservation and you're all booked up until Christmas. But I'm not here tonight to eat. I just want a few words with Billy."

The hostess's smile doesn't waver, but she's clearly thrown by my request.

"I'm afraid Mr. Needham is rather occupied at the moment. Can I pass along a message?"

"No, that's all right," I say. "I'll be hanging out right over here until he's free. Thank you."

Before the hostess can stop me, I step into a nook near the entrance. And wait.

One glance around his flagship establishment and it's clear that Billy Needham is an exceptional chef and owner. But that isn't surprising. It's in his blood. For generations, the extended Needham family has had a hand in a staggering number of eateries all across the city. Exact stats are hard to come by, but something like one in five New Orleans restaurants is either owned or partially financed by someone with that surname. For years, rumors have swirled about discord and family drama behind the scenes, which has apparently been getting worse. But no one in the food world can figure out why. By all accounts, the Needham family business is booming.

To kill some time before I speak to Billy, I take

out my phone to see if one of my private investigator friends—Gordon Andrews—has gotten back to me yet. I called him when I left the police station this afternoon and asked him to do a little digging for me on a whole host of topics. Gordon is one of the best PIs in Crescent City and definitely the most educated, with two master's degrees: criminal psychology from LSU and French literature from Tulane. I check my voicemail and refresh my e-mail, hoping I've gotten a response. But nothing.

"Excuse me, Mr. Rooney? Your table is ready."

I look up at the hostess, who is somehow smiling even bigger than before. I'm not surprised someone on staff recognized me. But giving me a table?

"That's very kind of you, but like I said, I'm not here to—"

"Please. Mr. Needham insists. This way, sir."

They're really rolling out the red carpet for me. *All right then,* I think. Let's play along, see where this goes.

I follow the hostess as she leads me to a spacious four-top in the most desirable corner of the restaurant with the best view of all the action. I've barely pulled my chair in when a French-born sommelier appears beside me, brandishing some bubbly.

"Welcome to Petite Amie, Monsieur Rooney. May I offer you a glass of 2004 Veuve Clicquot Grande Dame Rosé to start?"

That's a full pour from a three-hundred-dollar bottle of champagne. Knowing resistance is futile, I shrug and accept it.

"What about an amuse-bouche?" asks a server. "Gulf oyster–enriched grass-fed veal cheek, topped with organic rhubarb aioli."

Again, I acquiesce. So he places a large plate in front

of me containing a small oyster shell. Inside is what looks like the world's tiniest grilled steak, drizzled with pink mayonnaise and flecked with diced green onion.

"This really isn't necessary, guys," I say. "But thank you both."

"Enjoy," they say in unison, then depart.

I really did just come here to ask Billy a few questions related to the investigation, not get a comped drink and app while I waited.

But as it turns out, this is only the beginning. Over the next ninety minutes, despite my constant protests and insistence that I simply want to see the owner, dish after scrumptious dish is set in front of me.

Entrees like sugarcane rum–braised Kobe beef, which tastes sweeter than candy, atop a bed of curried collards and mashed yams. Truffle-braised scallops with an orange-saffron vinaigrette, a delightful blend of savory and tangy. And a cast-iron-seared duck breast finished with an absinthe glaze, a unique blend of fowl and licorice flavors I've never tasted. And of course, each dish is paired with an exceptional glass of red or white wine, with a palette-cleansing sorbet in between.

Try as I might to stop them, the servers and sommelier just won't listen.

When the desserts finally arrive—a heavenly creole-style bread pudding drowning in praline sauce, and a slice of pistachio cream pie topped with candied pecans—my belly is full and my mind is a little hazy. I hate to admit it, but if Billy was trying to show off and impress me, it's certainly worked.

I'm sipping a demitasse of hickory-infused espresso when I notice the evening's last seating of patrons has started to trickle out. The restaurant is growing quieter. Dinner service is nearly complete. I get the attention of a passing waiter and say firmly, "Excuse me. I'd like to order one final thing for the table, please. *The owner*."

The server nods and disappears into the kitchen. But Billy keeps me waiting a solid ten minutes more before finally emerging, arms spread and smiling wide, like we're old friends. In fact, we've only met a few times over the years. But I play along.

"There he is!" I say, rising and pulling him into a bear hug. "Billy, you outdid yourself. Thank you. Your food is incredible. Fresh, complex, inventive... wow."

"I'm very glad to hear that, Caleb. I hope my team took good care of you. It's not every day a *celebrity food truck owner* walks through our door."

I ignore that little dig and reply, "I have good reason. Got a few minutes to talk?"

He scrunches his face. "Maybe another time. I'll have my assistant call you, we'll set something up. Sometime after Mardi Gras, of course. You know how busy—"

"*Enough,* Billy," I say, gripping his shoulder with menace. "No more games. Please. Sit. I insist."

And he does just that.

CHAPTER 30

LOOKING INSULTED yet intrigued, Billy complies. Once we're seated, I pull my chair a bit closer and lean in. It's a classic interrogation technique. A way to build trust.

With a possible suspect.

"How do you and your family find the energy?" I ask. "Seems like every time I look, one of you is opening another eatery."

"My one and only sister, Emily, maybe," he says. "Our cousin David for sure. *My* main focus is Petite Amie and taking flying lessons when I can. Those two are the ones who keep pushing to expand the family empire."

"And not just brick-and-mortar restaurants," I say. "The food blogs have been saying your family's been getting into the vertical integration game lately. Investing in an organic beet farm in Paulina. A cruelty-free chicken hatchery in Hammond. A seafood processing plant in Pines Village. Do I have that right?"

I watch his reaction closely. But he doesn't betray a thing.

He says, "Sure. The more you can control your

supply chain, the more you can control quality. And your bottom line. At least that's how *they* see it."

"It sounds like you disagree."

"Me?" he says. "Look around. I'm a foodie at heart. Not a corporate raider. So if that's what you wanted to talk about, Caleb, sorry. Looks like you picked the wrong Needham."

"So just to be clear," I say, "that farm, that hatchery, that seafood plant—you're telling me you don't have a financial stake in any of them?"

He says, "I don't think so. But I wish I could say for sure."

I give him a quizzical look. What kind of successful business owner doesn't know what's in his own portfolio?

"What I'm telling you," he says, talking like an elementary school teacher explaining an atom to a dull student, "it is *possible* I own some tiny piece of them. The Needham family's finances are complicated. Eighty-five years in the food business in this city. Four generations. Dozens of children, cousins, spouses, *ex*-spouses—who haven't always seen eye to eye. I've lost count of all the lawsuits and arbitrations and settlements we've been through. Our money's tied up in more joint trusts and 'portable fiduciary instruments' than there are crawfish in the Gulf."

I see what he's getting at. "I bet that makes for some awkward conversations at Thanksgiving."

"I wish," he says, shaking his head. "It's gotten so bad, a lot of us can't even be in the same room together. Forget sitting down at the same table at the holidays."

I touch his arm in sympathy. Another interrogation trick.

"I've heard rumors to that effect," I say. "I'm sorry to learn they're true."

He lowers his voice and somberly shakes his head.

"If you knew the half of it, Caleb...you'd be *more* than sorry. You'd be worried. You might even be telling some of your police buddies."

Oh? My ears prick up at that. I try not to show it, but I've subtly moved to the edge of my seat.

"What do you mean?"

"Over the years...I've heard some of my relatives accuse one another of theft. Embezzlement. Money laundering. Bribes. Some have even...tossed around *threats of violence*."

"Violence?" I ask. "Okay, now I *am* getting a little worried, Billy."

He's about to say something, but stops himself. And backpedals, like he's realized he's admitted too much.

"Look, you used to be a cop," he says, sounding distressed. "You know what people are like. David says stupid things in the heat of the moment. Things he doesn't mean. If I thought for one second anybody in my family would ever actually *act* on their words..."

His tone suddenly changes from rueful to cheerful.

"But enough about our dirty laundry," he says, sitting up. "I'm sure this is boring you to death."

Quite the opposite, of course. But it's clear he wants to drop the subject. So I don't press it. I've already learned plenty.

"I know you need to get back to the kitchen," I say, "so I won't keep you. Just one more question. How well do you know Beatrice St. Ville?"

"Bea? I've met her a few times. Why?"

"The other day," I reply, "I swung by her café on Freret Street."

I didn't bother telling him my real reason for stopping by.

"What'd you think?" he asks.

"She does a great black-bottom pecan pie with pistachio à la mode," I answer. "Your pistachio cream pie with candied pecans made me think of it. It's worth a try."

His smile grows wider.

"Where do you think I got the idea?" he asks. "I've eaten there with Emily a bunch of times. Bea's whole social justice mission—hiring ex-cons to be cooks, recovered drug addicts to be servers—my sister loved it. She was one of the café's first investors. Even got David to open his wallet up, too."

Interesting. I still only have a few dots. But slowly, it seems like they're starting to connect. At least I sure as hell hope so.

"Thanks again for the great meal, Billy," I say, standing and shaking his hand.

"Anytime. Hopefully we'll be seeing more of each other, Caleb."

I firmly grip his palm.

"Something tells me we will," I say.

CHAPTER 31

A COINCIDENCE in a police investigation is like an honest man in politics.

They're pretty damn rare.

I'd heard the Needhams had invested in Neptune Premium Seafood a couple years ago. There's not much inside worth stealing except pallets of dead fish, so the incident report Cunningham shared with me—a man in a black car outside, in the middle of the night—sounded less like a thief casing the place and more like a fed checking it out.

I had no idea, until Billy told me, that members of the Needham family had ever made threats of violence against anyone.

And I *definitely* didn't know some were part-owners of the restaurant where Farzat used to work.

Could all this be a crazy coincidence leading me down a dead end?

Absolutely.

Or, maybe not. The only way to find out…is to find out.

And maybe—thankfully!—Special Agent Morgan and the rest of the feds are wrong. Maybe this isn't an upcoming terrorist attack on Mardi Gras. Maybe it's a familial civil war, one branch of the Needham family finally settling old grudges and scores with a shattering act of violence.

I'm up before dawn the next morning, with only a minor hangover from all the wine and champagne I had at Petite Amie. But I can't leave Marlene entirely in the lurch. She's probably still asleep, so I shoot her a text as I'm walking to my car. I'll be "running errands" all day, I tell her, using our code phrase for "don't ask." But I explain I'm heading to the truck extra early to do food prep for the day's brunch, lunch, and dinner shifts. Hopefully she'll understand. If not, well…it's not like she can divorce me twice.

The sun is just peeking above the horizon when I turn onto Canal Street, heading southeast. It's usually a busy thoroughfare, but I'm practically the only car on the road. I keep following it toward the French Quarter, passing a few temporary, ominous police barricades as I get closer. In just a few hours, this whole area will be bumping with music and tourists and the day's extravagant parades. But right now, it's almost eerily quiet. Gutters are clogged with colorful beads and empty plastic cups. Streamers drift down sidewalks like tumbleweed. I guess even the craziest party animals on the planet have to sleep *sometime*.

I make a left onto Burgundy Street and start looking for a parking spot. The truck is parked just a few blocks away. Just as I find one, my phone rings. *Great*. Marlene's about to ream me out for ditching her all day *and* for waking her up early. Putting my car in Reverse and backing into the space, I answer my phone on speaker.

"Mar, I'm sorry, but there's a lot going on right now and I need you to—"

"Caleb?" comes a man's voice. "It's Gordon. Did I wake you?"

Oops. Gordon Andrews, the charming, skilled, and very intelligent private investigator I called yesterday, the one with two master's degrees.

"Oh, hi," I say. "No, you didn't. What's up?"

"I'm calling with a bit of news. Thought you'd want to hear it."

I most certainly do. I glance at my dashboard clock. It's 6:33 a.m.

"You sure don't let the grass grow, Gordon. Thanks for getting back to me so quick. What have you learned?"

"I know you asked me to look into Lucas Dodd. I'm still digging. But that other fellow you mentioned…"

He means Farzat. Whose name he's smart enough not to mention over an open phone line.

"I heard over the scanner that the police just caught him."

"That's great!" I say. "Thanks, Andrews. That's the best news I could have heard. What station are they booking him at?"

"No, Caleb," he says. "You don't understand. They caught his *body*. Homicide."

CHAPTER 32

IT TAKES a few seconds for Gordon's words to sink in.

The lead suspect in my investigation just turned up dead.

Normally I wouldn't much mourn the passing of a would-be terrorist. But in this case, there's nothing good about it at all. If Farzat had been killed, say, in a shootout with federal agents, that would be one thing. A positive sign that Morgan's team was closing in, tightening the noose. If he accidentally blew himself up constructing a bomb, that would be even better news. An indication the guy was an amateur, not an expert.

Instead, Farzat's body has been found fully intact. And is currently in the custody of the New Orleans PD. Which means, somehow, the FBI lost his trail.

Then somebody else found him first.

And decided to shut him up.

But who? And why?

I throw my car back into Drive and speed to the address Gordon gave me, on Tricou Street in the Lower Ninth Ward. It's only a twelve-minute ride from the French Quarter, but the place might as well be another planet. This is the neighborhood made famous—*infamous*—for bearing the brunt of that bitch Katrina. When the levees broke, water surged into this low-lying area, swallowing up whole blocks. Its recovery has been miraculous, but imperfect. Today, a dozen years later, the Lower Ninth is still pocked with crumbling homes and abandoned lots. Residents complain of stubborn blight and lingering crime. Murders aren't common, but they're not unheard of.

Let's see what I can learn from *this* one.

As I near the scene, I see flashing red-and-blue bubble lights. Turning onto Tricou, there's an NOPD cruiser parked diagonally in the middle of the road, blocking further access. Beyond it, yellow crime-scene tape hangs between trees and lampposts like limp clothesline. It rings a small, decrepit house with boarded-up windows and a rotting roof that looks like it could collapse at any second.

I park and step out—and start looking for my way in.

I see a few uniformed cops and plainclothes detectives milling around the perimeter. Thankfully, I don't spot any black SUVs or suited federal agents on the scene. Which means the feds haven't taken it over yet. But they will. Trust me. Morgan is probably on his way here at this very moment. If I have any chance whatsoever of getting a look inside that house, I've got to move fast.

Approaching the building from the side, I get as close as I can before the officer, her brown hair pinned in a tight bun, spots me and holds up her hand.

"Sir, I'm gonna need you to step back, please."

"I'm a licensed private investigator," I lie. "Who's OIC this morning?"

That would be the scene's "officer in charge."

Typically, the primary responding detective, he or she is the one with full discretion over who has access to the premises. There's a decent chance I might know the guy, and could ask a favor.

Instead, the cop replies firmly, "*Sir,* I told you to step back."

No dice. Swallowing my resentment, I walk around to a different part of the crime scene perimeter. As I near the home's sagging front porch, I spot my opportunity.

Exiting the front door is a bespectacled African-American man who could pass for James Earl Jones's fraternal twin. He's wearing a navy jumpsuit, orange felt booties over snakeskin loafers, and an irritated expression. Behind him are two similarly dressed assistants wheeling a stretcher with a body bag on it. An *empty* body bag.

"Morning, Quincy," I call out to him.

The man's face registers pleasant surprise. Dr. Quincy Johnson, the Orleans Parish deputy coroner, is an old friend I've worked dozens of crime scenes with over the years. He pivots and heads my way.

"Rooney!" he calls out with a booming voice. "I thought you'd gotten out of the murder business," he says, ducking under the yellow tape. He peels off his latex gloves and extends a hand.

"Old habits die hard," I answer.

Quincy darkens and replies somberly: "Not as hard as the vic in there."

His words fill me with dread. Here's a man who's handled hundreds of grisly homicides over multiple decades. He's truly seen it all. That he's even the slightest bit rattled by whatever is inside that house is a very, very bad sign.

"Too early to move the body?" I ask, gesturing to his assistants loading the empty stretcher into a white van parked on the curb. "Forensics hasn't released the scene?"

Quincy shakes his head. "Not their call anymore. Word just came down. This one's gone federal. I can't move a hair on his head until they say so. A real mess, too."

I lean in a bit and say quietly, "Between us, Quincy, I'm working an angle on this one. I'm trying to clean that mess up, too. Any chance I could get a peek?"

Quincy raises a skeptical eyebrow above the frames of his tortoiseshell glasses. I continue pleading my case.

"Just for a minute," I say. "You know I wouldn't ask if it wasn't important. Very important."

Quincy purses his lips. "What did you have for breakfast, Killer Chef?"

Breakfast? His bizarre question throws me.

"Nothing," I say. "Why? I came straight here as soon as I got word. But now that you mention it, I'm starving."

Quincy glances around, then lifts up a section of crime-scene tape and beckons me underneath.

"You won't be for long."

CHAPTER 33

TOGETHER WE walk up the porch's rickety wooden steps. Before crossing the threshold, Quincy hands me a paper face mask, disposable gloves, and a pair of felt booties. He doesn't have to say a word; I remember the drill well. I slip them on, nod, and we enter.

I'm hit right away with the stench of stale urine. Padding through the dim entryway, I see soiled clothes and moldy fast-food containers strewn all around. Plenty of drug paraphernalia, too. Blackened spoons, charred crack pipes, dirty needles. This house might have been abandoned, but clearly, certain people still called it home.

When we step into the living room, I detect a different aroma. One I encountered plenty of times in my career, but hoped I'd never smell again.

The putrid tang of a rotting human corpse.

The small living room feels even more cramped since it's packed with people, forensic equipment, and activity. Set up in each corner are portable three-legged fluorescent lamps that cast harsh light across the room's stained walls and filthy carpet. Yellow plastic evidence markers have been placed all around the floor. One forensic tech is snapping pictures. A second is dusting a grimy glass coffee table for prints.

Two other techs are examining and taking swabs of Farzat's body. Their own bodies are blocking my view, but his corpse appears to be lying in an old recliner. His bare feet are dangling over the footrest at a stiff, unnatural angle.

Quincy calls to the pair, "Bryant, De Soto, give us a look?"

The two techs step away from the body—to reveal a stomach-churning sight.

Farzat isn't just lying in the recliner. He's *lashed* to it, naked, his bare arms and legs wrapped multiple times with thick strips of silver duct tape, resembling an unfinished mummy. The chair's upholstery is stained black-brown, soaked through with his blood. Strange circular wounds the size of quarters—and deep enough to expose muscle and bone—pockmark his torso and extremities. His head hangs limply to one side. His face is frozen in a visage of sheer terror. And his lips and bearded chin are covered with dried blood, like the snout of a wild animal that's just fed on fresh meat.

This was no ordinary murder.

Farzat was abducted. Held against his will, for God knows how long.

And tortured. Horrifically. Until his dying breath.

Whatever information his captors were trying to get out of him, it had to be pretty damn important. And *they* had to be pretty damn cruel.

"Told you it was a mess," Quincy says softly.

I swallow hard, and slowly step closer to Farzat's body to get a better look. It takes everything I've got to fight the temptation to turn away, lift my mask, and retch.

"Where did these round wounds come from?" I ask, puzzled.

Quincy answers dryly, "You've heard of a contract killer? Try a killer contractor."

I follow his gaze to a blood-dappled electric drill lying nearby, with a circular, serrated metal bit about an inch long. It's a tool normally used to bore holes in drywall.

Or in this case, human flesh. I step back. My breathing quickens, my eyes water.

"Have an approximate time of death yet?" I ask.

"Based on his body temp and state of decomp, our current estimate is between six and nine hours ago."

"Any idea how long he was tortured?"

Quincy slowly shrugs, like the weight of the whole parish is on his shoulders. "What I want to know is," he asks, "how did they expect to get *any* information out of him if . . . he couldn't speak?"

Confused, I step in again and peer closer at Farzat's bloody mouth. One of the forensic techs shines a flashlight inside—illuminating a shredded stump where the victim's tongue once was. The bastards must have stuck the drill bit in his mouth and pulled the trigger.

"Bet you wish you had more *customers* like that," Quincy says. "Sure, they can't taste your food. But they can't complain about it, either."

Gallows humor. That's Quincy for you.

But I don't shoot a joke back. At a time like this, I don't feel like laughing.

And unless I find out who killed Farzat, and fast, in a few days there won't be much laughter in New Orleans at all.

CHAPTER 34

QUINCY WAS right. I don't have any appetite left. But that's not going to stop me from going where I need to go next.

One of the fanciest, most exclusive restaurants in all of New Orleans.

Rosella sits on a leafy street in the Garden District, inside a meticulously renovated plantation-style mansion. It's actually not far from LBD—Lucas Dodd's eatery, where I first met Vanessa—but right now, that's the *last* thing on my mind.

Even a light meal at Rosella will set you back a few hundred bucks. It's where celebrities, athletes, and politicians chow when they're in town. A couple of paparazzi, cameras in hand, always seem to be hanging around outside, chain-smoking. The eccentric owner, David Needham, Billy Needham's older cousin, once tried to push an ordinance through the city council forbidding that—then changed his mind and lobbied to have it fail. His critics said it was all a publicity stunt. A "humblebrag" to trumpet his restaurant's popularity. An attempt to have it both ways.

Which is very much in character. David Needham is a man known for his contradictions—even though few people seem to know him well. He's staggeringly wealthy but notoriously cheap. He's a hurricane of creativity in the kitchen but a fastidious and cutthroat investor. He serves ludicrously fattening meals and desserts but is a lifelong holistic health nut. He wears five-thousand-dollar Brioni suits with beat-up tennis shoes. He craves fame and adulation but shuns the spotlight like a hermit.

It's one thing to be a little odd, a bit kooky. But could David Needham really be connected somehow to a terrorist plot against Mardi Gras?

A few days ago, I would have said that was preposterous.

Until his cousin said he'd made threats of violence.

Until an industrial site he recently purchased was surveilled by the FBI.

Until a possible terrorist suspect turned out to work at a café he'd invested in, and said suspect ended up tortured and killed.

Let's just say, David Needham has a few questions to answer.

And I'm hoping, praying, that what's going on is *not* a possible terrorist action, but something simpler and more prosaic: a family feud escalating from threats to actual violence.

I exit my car and after a few brisk steps, walk inside the ritz and glitz that is Rosella. It's about midway into lunch service and the elegant dining room is packed. Walking through the gold-paneled entryway, scanning the crowd, I spot two city council members, the Louisiana state attorney general, the assistant head coach of the Saints, and a handsome Hollywood A-lister known to have deep affection for our fine city.

I stride past the hostess stand into the dining room,

bound for the kitchen—when a firm hand grabs my elbow. Like a ninja, the maître d' slides in front of my path.

"Are you lost, my friend?" he demands, in a vaguely Eastern European accent.

Not to be cruel, but despite the fitted tuxedo he's wearing, this is one unattractive fellow. He's fifty-ish, short, bald with splotchy skin, with a patchy moustache nestled under a crooked nose. But I give the guy credit. He does know how to project authority.

"Not at all," I answer. Then I bluff: "I actually *am* a friend. Of David's. He's just getting settled in the back office. He's expecting me."

Keeping his hand on my elbow, the maître d' laughs in my face.

"Really? If that were the case, sir, you would know that Mr. Needham won't be arriving at the restaurant until later this evening."

I lock eyes with the maître d', refusing to back down.

"If *that* were the case, why did I see his Town Car show up ten minutes ago?"

That's another interesting fact about David Needham. Whether it's a phobia of the road, a fear of another DUI like the one he got in his twenties, or just a rich man's affectation, he doesn't drive. Hasn't in years. He has a black Town Car and chauffeur that takes him wherever he wants to go. David has also constructed a discreet, covered rear entrance for Rosella's more famous diners to use—which I spied his vehicle pulling up to just minutes ago. I'd parked my own car down the block and had been eyeballing the place for the past few hours.

The maître d' frowns but keeps blocking me from going any farther.

"I don't know what you're doing here, sir," he says. "But I strongly suggest you leave."

He tightens his grip on my elbow — with alarming strength for a man his size and age — applying painful pressure directly to the tendon. I try to keep my face composed from the increasing pain and I can't do it.

And then it dawns on me. His accent isn't Eastern European. It's Israeli. This man might indeed be the maître d'…but before memorizing menus and wine lists, I bet he used to be Mossad. Maybe now he doubles as the restaurant's undercover security chief. Which makes sense, given Rosella's exclusive clientele and David's paranoid eccentricities. And that bulge in the maître d's side pocket *could* be the master wine list. Or, a concealed Jericho 941 9mm semiautomatic, developed by the Israeli army.

My arm is growing painfully tingly. And I'm not about to get into a brawl in the middle of a busy restaurant. That wouldn't do anyone any good. Least of all me.

"Good day then," I simply reply, jerking my arm from the ex-soldier's iron grip.

I turn and stride out the way I came. Thwarted, but undeterred. That a former Israeli commando just stopped me from interviewing my newest person of interest worked for the moment.

But it's only made me more determined to confront David Needham about what he's up to.

CHAPTER 35

SO IT'S back to the waiting game. Back to basics. More ass time in the car. More hours to maddeningly while away—as the start of Mardi Gras creeps closer.

But I have to admit, I also know I'm very near LBD and its owner's wife, Vanessa, and while the cool and professional part of me is looking out for David Needham, the base part of me—so attracted to Vanessa, her look, her shape, her scent—is also keeping an eye out for her familiar and enticing form.

A contradiction, I know, but I can't help it. Even with what's going on with my investigation, the dead-end leads, the building suspicion of what violence might be planned out there for my city, I can't keep her out of my mind.

Thankfully, today's stakeout is a short one.

It's a little after 3 p.m. when the black Town Car I glimpsed David riding in earlier pulls out from behind his restaurant.

This is my chance.

But I have to move quickly.

I start my engine and reverse backward down Rosella's quiet street. I pull a half "J-turn," just like I learned in the defensive driving unit at the academy. I brake and jerk the wheel as I reach the first intersection, positioning my car in the middle of the road, blocking it completely. I flip on my hazards, then jump out and crouch behind a mailbox on the sidewalk, like a predator waiting for its prey.

A few moments later, David's car slows to a stop behind my vehicle. Through the tinted rear passenger window, I see him look up and say something to his driver, confused and irritated by the roadblock.

With both men distracted, I make my move.

I race over to the car, open the unlocked rear door, and slide inside.

"What the—who do you—" David stammers, surprised and scared.

If his chauffeur were also ex–Israeli Special Forces, he'd already have a silenced pistol trained right between my eyes. Instead, the guy sits there, frozen, his hands still on the wheel. Guess he's just a driver. *Phew*.

"Mr. Needham, relax," I say. "I'm Caleb Rooney. I only want to talk for a moment."

His expression slides from concern to conceit.

"Wait a minute, I know who you are," he says sharply. "You're that cop who thinks he's a chef. You serve up second-rate slop from the back of a *truck*."

I smile flatly, not taking the bait.

"But my customers say it's very tasty second-rate slop."

He now looks furious. "How dare you jump into my car like this!"

"Sorry," I say. "Couldn't be avoided. It's vitally important."

"Concerning me?" he asks, nearly laughing. "Get out. I'm very, very busy."

I shake my head.

"Your whole *family* seems pretty busy," I say. "But I've heard you don't always get along. You've accused some of them of lying to you over the years. Of *stealing* from you. Of bribery and blackmail, too. Am I right?"

He swears at me. "Get out. Why should I answer you?"

"Because a lot of questions are out there about you, David. Some circulating among law enforcement. Maybe I could make them go away if you tell me the truth, how you and your family don't get along."

"That's nonsense," he says. "I love and trust all of my relatives. We have our disagreements now and then, sure, but—"

I break his chain of thought, trying to get him frazzled. "Tell me about Ibrahim Farzat. What did he know that was so damn important to you?"

"Ibrahim who?" he asks. "I've never heard that name before in my—"

"Look," I say, interrupting him again. "I get it, David. We're talking tens of millions of dollars here. Not to mention betrayal from those closest to you. Of course you'd want to get even. *Publicly,* too. Really stick it to them. Maybe by torching one of your cousin's restaurants. Bombing a street fair where they'd set up a tasting booth. And with the kind of ex-military folks on your payroll, you certainly have the means. Am I getting warm?"

My suspect's expression now turns to outraged indignation.

"What in the hell are you talking about? Are you honestly accusing me of—"

I grab him by the scruff of his stained chef's whites.

"What are you planning, David?" I demand. "Why

are all roads leading back to you? What the hell is going to happen on—"

Ch-chink.

The unmistakable sound of a pistol being cocked.

I turn to the driver, who's holding a jet-black Jericho 941 inches from my face.

"You will remove your hands from Mr. Needham and exit the vehicle at once," he says calmly, speaking in a now-familiar Middle Eastern accent.

I guess he was more than just a driver after all.

With no other choice, I obey. I let go of David's collar and keep my hands raised.

But I'm not leaving without an earnest plea.

"You're a New Orleans native," I say to him softly. "Just think about what you're doing. What it will do to our city. *Please.*"

If my words have any impact on this man, he certainly doesn't show it. His eyes shoot daggers at me as I open the car door and step out.

Without waiting for me to close it, the driver peels out in reverse, back down this quiet, tree-lined street. He pulls a full J-turn, much more smoothly than I did, then disappears around the next corner.

I exhale and rub the back of my weary head.

Because what I just saw in David Needham's eyes was a glint of real *fear*. I've interrogated enough guilty bastards in my day to recognize it.

So I know I'm getting closer.

I just wish to God I knew closer to *what*.

CHAPTER 36

THE STORY of Islam in the Big Easy is a rich and complicated one. Thanks to the city's great diversity and history of tolerance, its Muslim population is larger than many might think, especially for the South. There's even a handful of gorgeous old mosques around the region, with ornate crescent archways and soaring minarets.

But this isn't one of them.

I'm standing across the street from a much more modest Islamic house of worship in scruffy East New Orleans. It's the closest one to Farzat's last address, which I had checked out earlier and found empty. By now his wife, Rima, has surely heard the news of his death—and I'm desperate to have a few words with her. With her not home, I'm trying my luck here. Is it the most respectful thing in the world to corner a grieving widow just hours after she learned her husband died a horrible, violent death?

Of course not. But hours might be all I have.

Damnit, I just don't know.

The sun is slipping below the horizon and evening prayer service is just letting out. Muslim men and women are walking out of the white clapboard building from separate entrances, but I'm keeping my eye on the latter group. Just like our city, there's a wide range of diversity here. Many female worshippers are wearing full-body *abayas,* long robe-like dresses, with flowing *hijabs* obscuring all but the front of their faces. Others are in street clothes, with nothing covering their heads or hair at all.

At last I spot Rima. She's wearing a conservative black blouse and a modest black veil, and is being comforted by a group of friends. Even in the twilight and from this far away, I can tell her eyes are raw from crying.

This is going to be rough. But here goes. I go to her.

"Excuse me, Mrs. Farzat?" I say as tenderly as I can.

"Are you police?" she snaps, suddenly suspicious. "The press? What do you want from me?"

"I'm just a man looking for some answers. May I have a moment of your time?"

My habit would be to introduce myself and extend my right hand to shake. Instead, I say nothing, and place my right hand over my heart, a sign of courtesy toward a practicing Muslim woman. This seems to surprise Rima in a positive way, and earn me the tiniest shred of her trust. So I go on.

"My sincerest condolences over the loss of your husband," I say. "From everything I've heard, he seems to have loved you very much."

Rima's face turns hard as granite.

"You seem to be misinformed," she says sharply. "Ibrahim was a good man. A hard worker. A devout believer. But he was *not* a loving husband."

"Every marriage has its difficulties," I reply. "Take it from someone who knows."

Her eyes flicker down to my left hand.

"You speak the truth, I see. You no longer wear

the ring. A woman such as myself does not have that luxury."

"That sounds incredibly hard. I'm very sorry. If I may ask, what *made* your union so rocky? Were there things Ibrahim did, people he associated with, places he went that you didn't approve? For example…two nights ago?"

Rima gives her group of friends a subtle look. They exchange some words in hushed Arabic, then take a few steps away so she and I can speak more privately.

"I already told the police everything I could."

"Which was?"

"*Nothing*. My faith teaches total loyalty to one's husband. Absolute obedience. In life as well as in death."

"Mrs. Farzat, that's a noble ideal," I say. "But I have very good reason to believe your husband was involved in a matter of grave national security."

She looks like she's about to spit on the cracked sidewalk. "You Americans and your 'national security.' As if those two words are magic that allows you to do whatever you please! For three terrible years we were trapped in Aleppo. Then three more we lived in a camp in Jordan before we could come here. All because of your precious national security. What about *our* security?"

"Mrs. Farzat, please…"

"What about my *husband's* security?" she says, her voice getting sharper. "He is dead. Dead! And for what?!"

Rima is getting pretty worked up. I try to stay calm and steer her back on track.

"That's exactly what I'm trying to find out," I say, keeping my voice soft and level. "I can help find the men who hurt him, if you'd just tell me—"

"What little I know of my husband's affairs…I

will go to my *own* grave with before I say one word to you pigs."

Now she spits on the ground, angrily turns, and starts off. Without thinking, I reach for her shoulder to stop her.

"Mrs. Farzat—"

"Do not touch me!" she exclaims, jerking away from me as if my fingers were a hot iron. "Leave me alone!"

I'm really trying to keep my cool here. But she's not making it easy.

"There are lives at stake," I say. "Do you understand that? Hundreds, maybe thousands. What about *their* security? If they die, their blood is on *your* hands!"

Finally, Rima stops. And hangs her head. Keeping her back to me, she seems to unzip her purse and rummage through it.

"Fine," she says at last. "I do have something that might help."

Rima spins back around—and sprays a brownish mist at my face.

"Aargh!" I exclaim as I duck and jerk backward, avoiding a direct hit. But plenty of the pepper spray still reaches my eyes, scorching them like an open flame.

Rima hurries to rejoin her friends. I lean over, rest my hands on my knees, and rapidly blink and squint and sniffle, the searing pain intensifying.

After what seems like several agonizing minutes—but is probably just a few seconds—I manage to get back to my car, where I pour some bottled water over my eyes to try and stop the stinging. I even manage to forget about my throbbing head and busted arms and fractured rib. Eventually, the last few days catch up with me, and I fall asleep.

*　　*　　*

When I wake up, it's pitch black, and I feel my phone vibrate in my pocket. I take it out, manage to tap the right spot on the touchscreen to answer, and place it to my ear.

It's Marlene.

Who sounds more scared than I've ever heard her before.

"Caleb…" she says, voice shaking. "Oh, Caleb…get here…get here now!"

CHAPTER 37

I'M STILL too blinded from the pepper spray to safely drive, so I step into the street and frantically wave down the first orange city cab I see.

The driver is a middle-aged woman with thick dreadlocks cascading down her back like a waterfall. It briefly crosses my mind that I can't remember the last time, if ever, I had a female taxi driver—until my thoughts immediately shift back to Marlene.

Christ, what have I dragged that poor woman into?

Tossing a wad of bills at the driver as we arrive, I don't even wait for her to completely stop the vehicle before I fling open the rear door and leap out.

Two NOPD cruisers and an NOFD ambulance are idling beside the Killer Chef truck, which is parked on a quiet side street off Esplanade Avenue in Marigny.

And our beloved truck has been brutalized.

The windshield and side windows have all been shattered. The outside metal siding has been battered and dented. The tires have been slashed. Even the shrimp-and-crossbones Killer Chef logo has been sprayed with ugly black graffiti. Not to mention the inside, which has been completely trashed, too.

It's a stunning, heartbreaking sight.

I feel like I've been punched in my stomach.

But the worst is yet to come.

"Marlene?!" I yell out, as I hurry around to the ambulance's rear.

She's sitting on the rear bumper, as two cops stand by, one with a clipboard in his hands, scribbling away, probably having just taken her statement. I don't recognize either of them. There are two EMTs, one finishing bandaging her left forearm, the other stepping back after having used a penlight to inspect her pupils.

My ex-wife appears rattled and more than a little roughed up—but also as strong and sassy as ever.

"Marlene," I say again, breathlessly rushing toward her. "Are you okay?"

She gives me one look—then starts to crack up.

"Our Father who art in Heaven, I never thought I'd see the day," she starts on me. "The unflappable Caleb James Rooney actually shedding a tear?"

I smile, flooded with relief—along with a few other feelings I haven't felt for this woman in years. I wipe at my still-raw pepper-sprayed eyes.

"Don't flatter yourself," I answer. "I had a little run-in right before you called. It doesn't matter. Tell me what happened."

Marlene takes a deep breath and starts talking.

It was dark and she was inside the truck, cleaning up after dinner service, when she heard the back door open. She thought it was me and didn't bother turning around—when someone grabbed her from behind, shoved her to the floor, and gave her a few sharp kicks, before turning his attention to wrecking the kitchen.

Marlene didn't get a good look at the guy, but if she had to guess, he was in his thirties or forties, strong and fit, ethnicity unknown. As she was still being assaulted, she heard glass shattering outside and tires hissing. Which means there was at least a second attacker. Maybe more. After a minute or two, the men stopped and ran off. Since it was so late, the streets were fairly empty, and most people who were out probably assumed the noise was just some pre–Mardi Gras revelry—or were too drunk to notice anything.

Pulling herself together, Marlene dialed 911, then called me—right as I was still recovering from a face full of pepper spray.

Marlene tells her story stoically, but hearing it leaves *me* practically shaking with rage at the monsters who did this—and with shame that I might be partly responsible.

"Do either of y'all have any enemies?" asks one of the police officers, a middle-aged fellow with a thick bayou accent.

"Officer," I answer, "don't pretend you don't know who I am. I've been on the job for years. Take a look through my case files. I've got *plenty* of enemies."

And that doesn't include all the ones I've made *recently*.

Like the Franklin Avenue gang, or Lucas Dodd, or David Needham, or those goons who whooped me outside the scrapyard the other night, coming by to finish what they started.

Damn. That list is growing longer than the Mississippi. Where would I even start?

After the paramedics finish their examination and treatment of Marlene's minor scrapes and cuts, and the officers give us the earnest but empty promise—which I unfortunately know so very well—to "do everything they can to find the folks who did this," the first responders get back in their respective vehicles and drive off.

Now it's just me, my ex-wife, our damaged truck... and our even more damaged relationship. It's awkward. Tense. Silent. Finally, I break the silence, hesitantly.

"Mar...I'm so sorry," I begin. "This is my fault. And I really do promise to find the sons of bitches who did this to you. Whoever it was, they made a damn big mistake."

"Oh, Caleb," she huffs, "just zip it, would you? I told you to be careful! Whatever you've been running around this past week doing...*that's* the damn big mistake."

I bite my tongue. I've been running around working to keep terror from raining down on this city. But in the process, I brought it into my home.

Now I'll just have to work even harder, smarter, and be ready to give them back tenfold what they've done to Marlene.

CHAPTER 38

SWEEPING UP broken glass. Scrubbing off ugly spray paint. Sifting through mangled belongings. Struggling with a swirl of emotions.

Marlene and I did all this once before. Twelve years ago. After Katrina, when floodwater ravaged the ground floor of our old Tremé town house, back when we were husband and wife, young, and full of laughs and dreams.

Now we're doing it again by the morning light. Separated, older, still with dreams and laughs. But this time, we're cleaning up after a disaster that can't be blamed on random nature, but on a specific evil.

"A flatbed's en route," my ex-wife announces, limping back into the truck, phone in hand.

I nod. "Good job, Mar. Let's check out the stove."

I go back into our poor mangled truck, get on my hands and knees, and use a flashlight to inspect our mobile kitchen's most important — and most expensive — piece of equipment.

"Looks like those assholes didn't rupture any gas lines," I say, flicking the beam of light around the complex guts of pipes and wires. "But I want a second opinion from a pro before I fire it up."

"That's a good idea," Marlene says from behind me. "Not that I wouldn't enjoy watching you go down in a literal blaze of glory…"

I chuckle as I stand and dust off my hands. Then, under the glare of a hanging industrial flood lamp—since all the interior lights were smashed—I survey our poor kitchen. After only a few hours of work, it's already showing signs of life. But it's still a pitiable mess. And a long way from being functional again.

"I need a little air," I mutter, brushing past Marlene to head outside.

It's cooler out here in the morning breeze than inside the stuffy truck, but not by much. I grab a lemon-lime Big Shot bobbing in the pool of chilly water in our ice cooler. I crack it open and guzzle the soda so fast, I feel half of it dribble down my unshaven chin and trickle onto my sweat-soaked undershirt. I don't even want to think about how unattractive I must look right about now.

"Oh, my God, it's really true!" I hear a woman behind me cry out.

I turn around. Just my luck. It's Vanessa. Of *course* it is.

"Are you guys okay?" she says, hurrying up to me.

I swallow my mouthful of fizzy sugar water and wipe my lips on my forearm.

"Marlene's the one to ask," I say. "But she's fine, thank God. They don't make 'em any tougher than her. She can handle anything. Our truck on the other hand…"

She cuts me off by slinging her arms over my shoulders and pulling me in for a long hug. I'm caught off guard by the tender gesture, and by how much I appreciate it…and enjoy it.

"How did you hear?" I ask.

She slowly lets me go and steps back, brushing back her hair. "I checked Twitter to see where Killer Chef was going to be for brunch. But every mention showed pictures of the trashed truck."

I turn and take another sorry look at the flat tires, the spray-painted exterior, and the hammered metal sides. "Look at that," I say. "Sometimes, the things you read online are true."

She approaches the vehicle and gently strokes one of the dents in the metal sheeting as if it were a wounded animal.

"How sick do you have to be to do something like this?" she says quietly, shaking her head.

"Not sick," I say. "Determined. Hard. Here to send a message, hurt Mar and our business."

"Still…" She steps back. It looks like her eyes are getting watery.

Emotion for seeing this vandalism, or emotion at seeing how distressed I am?

I say, "Vanessa, having you come by…it means a lot. Especially after how we left things at the cemetery. I gotta admit, I was worried I wouldn't be seeing you for a while."

She looks away from our ruined truck, gives me a wide smile that makes me forget the damaged truck, all my aches and pains, and my smelly and sweat-stained clothes.

"I'm sorry I snapped at you, Caleb," she says. "You don't need to be a star detective to figure out things with me and Lucas are…complicated. But lately…"

She trails off as she looks back at the truck, her face pale with concern.

I know exactly what she's thinking, too. Because just a few hours earlier, I had the same thought myself.

"There's *no way* your husband could have done this," I assure her—even though I know full well it's completely possible. Maybe even probable.

And on some level, she probably does, too. But she seems to appreciate my words anyway. So much so that she claps her hands, instantly brightening up.

"You guys are probably starving!" she says. "Let me order you and Marlene some breakfast. From anywhere in the city. My treat."

"That's really nice of you," I say. "But we actually have more food right now than we know what to do with. Everything that was in our prep fridge—if we don't eat it in the next day or two, it'll go bad."

She deflates and I feel like kicking myself. A wonderful, beautiful, and complicated woman wants to do me and my ex-wife a favor, to show her concern and appreciation, and I just answered like a cold-hearted accountant, measuring the worth of prepped food and how it shouldn't be wasted.

Idiot.

She seems to shake off her disappointment and steps closer to me.

"Well, maybe another night," she says. "And maybe… just the two of us?"

I'm about to respond with an unqualified affirmative—and even a dig or two at Lucas's expense—when I hear the grumble of a diesel engine and the hiss of a set of air brakes. The flatbed tow truck Marlene called is turning onto our street.

Sometimes, after misfortune strikes, it's hard to see the silver lining.

But other times, it's literally standing right in front of you.

"Another night, just the two of us," I repeat, warmly. "It's a date."

And I love the confirming smile she sends in my direction.

CHAPTER 39

ORDINARILY, I'D be out for blood.

After what happened to Marlene and our truck, I'd be turning over every stone. Leaning on old informants. Paying visits to old nemeses. Dropping everything else until I found the sons of bitches that dared lay a finger on the two things I hold dearest.

Then I'd make them pay.

But these aren't ordinary times. Right now, my priorities are guided by simple arithmetic. The fact is, getting revenge against a *few* has to take a backseat to stopping an attack against *many*.

So here I am, one hundred miles northeast of New Orleans' city limits, speeding along an empty rural highway in the middle of nowhere.

"In one hundred feet, you will arrive at your destination," chirps my GPS.

But I have a hunch that's premature. Sure enough, when I reach the address I've plugged in, I see nothing but a hidden country road marked PRIVATE. I turn onto it and keep going, down an endless gravel pathway lined with weeping willows.

Finally, my actual destination comes into view: a breathtaking plantation-style mansion, ringed by a spiked iron fence, surrounded by endless green fields and stables both near and far.

I drive up to the imposing metal gate. On the video callbox is a single button labeled *BEAUDETTE* in fancy cursive. I press it. I smile into the camera. I wait.

After a moment, the gate automatically opens inward.

As I pull up to the magnificent house, I see a handsome middle-aged woman with long brown hair standing by the front door, hands on her hips. Her fair skin has that glow that fabulously rich peoples' skin tends to have. And she's dressed in full equestrian getup: white blouse, navy riding jacket with tails, leather boots. The whole scene looks like something out of a high-end catalog spread.

Her name is Emily Beaudette. She's Billy Needham's half-sister. David Needham's cousin. Fellow family investor.

And she may be my last hope for learning the truth about her messed-up family.

"You're early, Detective," she snaps as I get out of my car.

"How can I be early, Ms. Beaudette?" I cheerily answer. "You told me not to come at all."

I give her a friendly grin. Not surprisingly, it doesn't change the pinched expression on her face.

"Exactly," she says, voice determined. "My lawyer said I shouldn't say one word to you people. That I have nothing to gain and everything to lose. Not that I have anything to hide, of course. It's just that—"

"Hang on," I say, stepping up onto her wraparound front porch. "Us *people*? You mean the cops already tried to talk to you?"

"It wasn't the police," she says. "It was the FBI.

They drove their parade of black SUVs right up to my front gate yesterday, just like you did. I turned them away."

"And yet," I say with another wry smile, "you buzzed me through. Why?"

She seems to stand a bit taller and answers, "You *asked* for my help. They showed up unannounced and demanded it. Then started making threats. If I didn't turn over my corporation's complete financial records, I could expect a lifetime of audits. Or worse."

Interesting. So the feds *have* been sniffing around the Needham family properties and finances, just like I thought. I'm dying to know what they were looking for. And what Emily—and her company ledgers—might reveal.

My hundred-mile road trip looks like it just might pay off.

"I'm really sorry they came after you like that," I say.

Then I step closer to this woman and speak more firmly.

"But I'm *not* asking for your help anymore, Ms. Beaudette," I say. "I'm begging for it. There are lives at stake here. More than you can imagine. I don't give a damn about catching tax evaders. I'm trying to stop another kind of bad guy—one that starts with a 'T.'"

Her eyes subtly widen, in either concern or defiance. I can't tell.

"Oh, please," she whispers. "But…I'm just a hospitality industry financier."

She spreads her arms, gesturing to her sprawling property.

"And a horse sanctuary owner. I don't see how I could possibly help. No, Detective Rooney. I—I'm sorry, but no."

Shaken, she takes a step backward and starts to head inside.

I'm losing her; my window here is closing. How can I possibly get her to change her mind and open up?

Then I get an idea.

"Let *me* be the judge of that, Ms. Beaudette, on what kind of help you can provide."

She stops. "You want to judge me and my family, then?"

"No," I say. "I'm just looking for some kind of evidence. A trace. Hint of something untoward."

She stares at me.

"You're asking me for a lot."

I answer her truthfully. "I know."

"And what can you...give me for this exchange?"

Give to her? Good question. Money? Yeah, right. A lifetime free meal ticket for Killer Chef? While she might enjoy the food, she's not the type to stand in line under the hot sun with tourists and scruffy locals.

Then, seeing her stables once again, it comes to me.

"How about an afternoon of amusing entertainment?"

That seems to intrigue her. A smile appears—and then disappears.

"Amusing entertainment?" she asks. "I certainly could use something to lighten up my spirits. What do you have in mind?"

"The two of us go on a horseback ride, and I ask a couple of questions. Deal?"

"What's so amusing about that?"

"You'll quickly find out."

That appearing and disappearing smile returns.

"Tell me, then, Detective Rooney," she asks. "Have you ever ridden a horse before?"

"Sure," I say. "But only if a carousel counts."

The smile comes back and stays.

"Perhaps it does," she says. "Let's find out."

Yes, I want to shout.

This should be…*interesting,* because I've never ridden a real horse in my life.

But if I have to take my first ride on a horse to get more information, I'll happily take the risk.

CHAPTER 40

THE STABLES on Emily's property are as impressive as her home. Together, we enter a soaring U-shaped wooden structure containing dozens of horses and twice as many trainers and staff. I try to keep my nerves at bay as she leads me to a freshly hayed corner stall that holds a beautiful mocha-colored mare.

"This is Gladys," she says. "One of our older residents. A little slow, but gentle as a lamb. Do you prefer English style or Western, Detective Rooney?"

Uh...there are styles? Who knew.

"Dealer's choice," I answer.

A few minutes later a Hispanic stableman is holding Gladys steady as I struggle to heave myself up into her saddle. With a grunt, I finally manage to do so, muscles and tendons I didn't know I had straining from the effort. I'm still squirming and fidgeting, trying to get comfortable and balanced, when she *clip-clops* over on her horse of choice for the afternoon, a beautiful white stallion she tells me is named Cooper.

"Ready to ride?" she asks.

Without waiting for my response, she gives her animal a squeeze with her heels and starts trotting out toward the fields. I hear a low roar of engines and off to the right, see two workers each riding a four-wheeled ATV, heading to a fence line.

"Yah!" I urge Gladys and give her reins a gentle tug. She jerks and bucks, nearly tossing me off. But then, thank goodness, she seems to sense that she has a pure tenderfoot on her mature back, and she starts heading into the right direction.

Soon I've caught up to Emily and Cooper, who start, quite literally, running circles around us on the smooth green pasture, moving with elegance and grace. As for me, Gladys is ambling along in a straight line and I'm still holding on for dear life with the reins, resisting the temptation to lean forward and wrap my arms around her long neck.

"Your carousel riding has obviously served you well," she observes with a smile.

I feel like at any moment gravity is going to tug me to the ground. "Hey, I'd like to see you try to make a pot of sous vide ham hock jambalaya sometime."

"I hire and fire cooks, Detective Rooney," she replies, with the confident tone of one always being in charge. "I never claimed to be one."

Fair enough. For a woman who grew up in one of New Orleans' biggest foodie families, she is on record as saying she can barely boil water. She's a money person. An "epicurean entrepreneur," as she's put it, with only a casual interest in fine dining. While her relatives studied at Cordon Bleu, she went to Columbia Business School. Today, she splits her time between managing the finances of the restaurants and food distributors she co-owns, and overseeing this nonprofit horse farm.

By now we're riding parallel, though I can sense that she wishes she could let Cooper run free to the horizon, instead of plodding along with a first-timer like myself. We're away from the main stables by the house, though there are two other low-slung wooden buildings off to the right, several hundred feet away, even larger than the stables we exited, and one of them has a large antenna set to the rear. Near the buildings are two tall, empty flagpoles.

"Tell me about David," I say.

Which makes her snicker.

"My cousin?" she says. "He's a character. At least from what I remember."

"Oh?"

"You've probably heard the rumors," she says, her voice regretful. "We Needhams don't really speak much anymore. And when we do...let's just say, it's not exactly rainbows and sunshine. David especially. He's a great chef, I'll give him that. But if we were standing together on the rim of the Grand Canyon, I wouldn't be surprised if he gave me a little push."

"You're saying he's dangerous?"

"Of course not," she sharply replies. "I'm saying I don't really know the man. At least not anymore. Sure, I've heard him spew some crazy things over the years..."

"Like what?"

She gives Cooper another heel-squeeze, making him twirl and neigh, and she fixes her gaze on me.

"When it's been just the two of us, it's mostly political ranting. Against taxes, regulation, the government. When we're all together, as a family..."

She reins Cooper in and takes a moment to collect her thoughts, like the memories are just too painful.

"Greed is an ugly, ugly thing, Detective," she says. "We have so much. I try to give back as often as I can. But the others are never satisfied. They always want more. Including Billy, who's no Mother Teresa himself and who seems to have his head up in the air lately, ever since he took up flying. But David is the worst. I manage most of the family's portfolio through my holding corporation—and even with my Columbia MBA, I can't keep track of all the joint shell companies and offshore accounts he's set up."

"For the feds, all that financial activity is like dangling raw meat in front of a lion," I say. "No wonder they want to look at your books."

She nods.

"My lawyer told me the only reason they asked was because they couldn't get a warrant. *Yet*. But he thinks they'll have one by Monday, maybe earlier."

"When it comes to getting an IRS refund or standing in line at the DMV, government can move as slow as a sloth taking cough syrup," I say. "But when they scent something funny going on with money, watch out."

She shakes her head.

"What does the government think we're hiding? What do they think David's up to?"

"I don't know," I say. She seems generally upset, and concerned. I sense an opening and go on.

"But if you give me a peek, I might be able to give you and your lawyer a tip-off, before the feds return in their black SUVs with a freshly printed search warrant."

She gives Cooper a gentle squeeze and starts moving, and my trustworthy Gladys keeps pace. I have to take a moment to admire the pasture we're riding on—the land is firm and flat, and the grass has been closely cropped, like the place was getting ready to be turned into a golf course.

"You're asking me to turn over thousands of pages

of highly sensitive financial records to a total stranger, who isn't even a cop anymore?"

I tug firmly on my horse's reins, making Gladys stop completely. She snorts and stomps as I give her a sharp, demanding look.

"Ms. Beaudette," I start, "are you aware that your cousin employs numerous armed ex–Israeli commandos as his personal bodyguards? And that your half-brother Billy has heard him make threats of violence?"

She starts to speak and then stops, trying to absorb what I've just told her. By her troubled expression, it looks like the answer to both questions is "No."

"I think I have to speak with my lawyer again," she mumbles.

Then she makes a *click-click* sound with her tongue, and Cooper bursts into a brisk canter back toward the stables.

"Ms. Beaudette, wait!" I call out.

But her horse doesn't slow. And its rider doesn't look back.

Gladys lets out a long whinny and takes a few shaky steps backward.

"Easy, girl," I say, patting her muscular shoulders. "I know. I'm scared, too."

CHAPTER 41

THE DRIVE back to the city takes nearly twice as long as the ride out. Traffic along I-12 is crawling, and the Lake Pontchartrain Causeway might as well be a twenty-three-mile-long parking lot. Not that I'm surprised. Mardi Gras is just around the corner and hundreds of thousands of folks are streaming in from all around the country to take part in this wonderful event.

If only they knew the hell that might be waiting for them.

Stuck in gridlock just past the I-610 interchange, I shut my eyes and give them a good rub. I'm finally making some real headway in my investigation, but I'm still miles away from any solid answers—or actionable details. And it's starting to drive me nuts. I feel like I've got the pieces of a jigsaw puzzle and I can feel them…but I can't see them, because I'm in a pitch-black room. I can try to guess the shapes and forms, but I also have no idea what other puzzle pieces might be out there, waiting for me in the dark.

My search for the bastards who messed up my truck and hurt Marlene is stuck in the mud, too. Just thinking about it now makes me burn with rage all over again.

But hey, at least I got a date with Vanessa out of it. Which reminds me...

I whip out my phone and dial. On the fourth ring, Gordon Andrews picks up.

"Caleb, you're a mind reader," he says, with a hearty chuckle.

"I wish," I say. "It would make this whole private eye thing a hell of a lot easier. I don't know how you can stand to do it, hour after hour, day after day."

He says, "Well, this particular PI leaves enough time each day for something fine to eat, and something even finer to drink. But to get back to the point...I was about to phone you in a bit."

"What's going on?" I ask.

"I finally had a chance to look into that Lucas Dodd fellow and his wife," he says, with a smooth and cultured voice. "And, hoo boy, let me tell you, with friends like that..."

My ears perk up. I sit a little taller in my seat, wincing from long-dormant muscles that are loudly complaining about my first horse ride and the two beatings I've taken. Around this part of the gridlocked exchange are lots of trees and small homes and businesses. The sky is overcast, nearly melding in with the far gray horizon.

"Lucas," I blurt, "is *not* my friend."

Quite the understatement. I've been sneaking around behind his back with his beautiful wife now for more than a week.

"So what do you know, Gordon?" I add.

"I just want to be clear," he says. "At this point, it's only a rumor. But like my granddaddy used to say, if it fights like a gator, if it bites like a gator..."

"I get it. Rumor. Okay. Just spit it out."

I lean forward slightly in anticipation and grip my phone a bit tighter as he shares with me what he's dug up on Mr. and Mrs. Dodd.

The details are sketchy, but the broad strokes are shocking. And quite troubling.

But if what he's saying is true, it would explain a lot—not least why Vanessa seems trapped in a failing marriage that so clearly makes her miserable.

He is in the middle of a sentence when I hear a faint *beep-beep* sound interrupting us on the line. Another call is coming in. Right now? Really?

I glance at my screen. "Gordon, sorry, I'll call you back." It's a number I don't recognize, with a 318 area code. That's central Louisiana. Where Emily Beaudette's horse farm is. I wonder…

Before I've finished saying "hello," she cuts me off.

"Detective?" she says strongly. "I want you to know that, against my lawyer's very insistent advice…I instructed my accountant to send you something you might find helpful. At least I hope you do. Check your e-mail."

I follow her command. In my inbox is a new message with a tantalizing little paper clip icon beside it. I tap the screen to open the e-mail. The attachment appears to be a spreadsheet, a whopping half-gigabyte in size, titled KB CORP—MASTER FIN REPS, FY 2007-17.

"Is this what I think it is?" I ask, struggling to control my joy at having convinced her to share this with me.

"My holding company's comprehensive financial reports," she says. "Going back ten fiscal years. Don't you dare tell the feds you have them. And definitely don't tell my crazy family. But do tell me if you need anything else."

"I…yes, I will," I say. "Thank you, Ms. Beaudette."

"But remember what you offered earlier," she points out. "If you find anything…out of the ordinary that you believe the federal authorities might be interested in, you will notify my attorney and myself. Am I clear?"

"Absolutely," I say, and then I realize I'm talking into thin air.

She's disconnected the call. No matter.

I've just made a major step forward, documents that might help me get a handle on what's going on with the Needhams, records that just might shed some light on—

A rising chorus of sirens snap me out of my rapid thoughts, and I glance up at the rearview mirror, seeing the flashing blue lights. With the other drivers, I pull over as far as I can, no mean feat in this gridlock.

But a narrow path does open.

I glance up again, expecting to see an NOPD cruiser or two, perhaps an ambulance, or maybe a state police cruiser.

But not what's coming our way.

A convoy of National Guard Humvees and trucks with trailers behind them, being led by three Humvees with a flashing red-blue light bar just above the windshield.

I count twenty of the vehicles as they pass me and head into the heart of New Orleans.

I'm not happy anymore.

I'm terrified of what's going to happen in the few days before Mardi Gras, and terrified that even with this welcome gift of information, I'll be too late.

With a honk of my horn, I get back into the gridlock, stuck again.

CHAPTER 42

WHO KNEW hundreds of pages of accounting records could be so riveting?

As soon as I walk through the door, I pop open a ninety-dollar bottle of Côtes du Rhône I've been saving for a special occasion. I pour myself a glass. Then I plop down at my kitchen table, fire up my laptop, and set about poring over the numbers.

Let me be clear: I am *not* a forensic accountant. Not even close.

Still, I know what a professional restaurant ledger is supposed to look like. I have a decent sense of wholesale food prices, reasonable service wages, average industry profit margins.

Which is why, three hours and as many glasses of wine later, I'm feeling pretty damn discouraged. I've scrutinized every line. Recalculated every column. And everything is adding up perfectly. Nothing is jumping out at me at all.

If David—or Billy or Emily or anyone else in the extended Needham family, for that matter—is padding their business expenses, siphoning even a few bucks a month to some terrorist organization, I can't see it in their books.

With disgust and a fresh glass of vino, I click on the tab in the Excel file detailing the Needhams' extensive IRS-reported charitable giving.

As I expected, the payout structure of many of the donations is highly complicated. A few years ago, I assisted the Louisiana State Police with a major embezzlement case, so I know this type of payout is simply done for tax purposes, and is perfectly legal.

But other times, it's a technique that can be used by white-collar criminals to hide questionable transactions or launder illicit funds.

So I dive in, painstakingly triple-checking the complex math. This takes me another solid two hours. But here, too, everything seems squeaky clean. *Damnit*.

Knowing there must be *something* here, I return to the top of this section and comb through the list of charities themselves, looking for any that might stand out in a suspicious manner.

According to the records, dozens of nonprofits have been the beneficiaries of the Needhams' generosity over the past decade. And not just local soup kitchens and food banks, like you'd expect from a family of New Orleans restaurateurs. Also on the list is an organization that provides free computer programming classes to area veterans. One that promotes childhood literacy in the city's public schools. And also one that, based on the name, "Crescent Care," I assume offers subsidized medical or other assistance to low-income residents of the Crescent City.

Unless...

I look the group up online.

And my insides feel queasy with dread.

According to their homepage, the "crescent" in their title is a nod to New Orleans' nickname *and* a reference to a symbol of Islam. And their stated mission is to "provide material help and spiritual guidance to the city's underserved Muslim population, with a special focus on struggling immigrants and vulnerable refugees."

Now, look. I don't want to jump to conclusions here. Or rely on ugly stereotypes. But given everything else I know, this "charity" that's been receiving generous annual gifts from David Needham through Emily's primary corporate holding company for the past three years sounds at least a little suspect.

I have to find out more. Ideally from Needham himself, up close and personal.

But how the hell am I supposed to do that? Our last meeting ended with one of his Mossad-trained bodyguards aiming a pistol at me.

Feeling both encouraged and doubtful, I stand and stretch my legs. I pace around the kitchen table, then slam a hand on it in frustration. I slosh some more booze down my throat—not wine, but a slug of Kentucky bourbon, straight from the bottle.

I pick up my phone from the counter and see it's nearly midnight. But I also have a text. So focused on the Needhams' financial records, I didn't hear it chime.

I tap the screen and open it. It was sent about an hour ago.

By Vanessa.

HOPE THE TRUCK IS ON THE MEND, it reads. SO WHEN AM I BUYING YOU DINNER? ;)

Despite these dark times, that little string of words is a big ray of light. And that coy winking face brings a childish grin to my own.

It gives me a risky idea, too, of a two-birds-one-stone kind.

I'm usually loath to mix unofficial business with potential pleasure. But this might be the only real chance I'll get to see David Needham. It could also backfire spectacularly. It could ruin my chances of stopping the Mardi Gras attack *and* of getting with Vanessa. But isn't it worth a shot?

My thumbs hover over the keypad for a moment, twitching.

Before I can change my mind, I tap back: THANKS! HOW ABOUT TOMORROW? I KNOW JUST THE SPOT.

CHAPTER 43

VANESSA IS waiting for me in front of the restaurant. She's wearing a vibrant red dress, and stands out from the dinnertime crowd like a lighthouse on a stormy night.

Her outfit is classy and flirty, serious and fun—just like her. And it definitely flatters her body.

When she spots me approaching, her sweet and attractive face breaks into laughter.

"Caleb, what in God's name is on your face?"

"Mais non, mademoiselle," I say in my most ridiculous Pepé Le Pew accent. "My name iz Maurice La Fondue. And to be your dining partner for zee evening will be *un grand plaisir!"*

She puts her hands on her hips. "I wish you'd told me to come in costume."

"Nonsense, *mademoiselle*. You are always in costume: a beauty queen!"

I take her gently by the arm and lead her inside.

In most places, a grown man waltzing into an upscale eatery wearing a gold masquerade mask with a crown of rainbow feathers would raise eyebrows. But this is New Orleans during Carnival. A whole different set of rules applies.

And the restaurant is Soûlard, which serves high-class

food in a funky, low-class setting. Located near the French Quarter, it's also blocks from where the insanely lavish Mystic Krewe of Morpheus parade has just ended. The dining room is packed with costumed marchers and spectators, all stopping in for an extraordinary bite.

Amazingly, I'm one of the more conservatively dressed people here.

"Hello, we have a reservation for two at eight o'clock," Vanessa says to the maître d'. "It's under the name 'Mrs. Lucas Dodd.'"

Before you judge her too harshly for that, know that using her restaurateur husband's name to snag us this last-minute plum reservation was *my* idea.

We're led through the dining room. It's filled with kitschy décor, like vintage Louisiana license plates from the 1940s and a plastic skeleton wearing a Saints jersey.

As we settle into our cozy corner table, she asks, "Are you seriously going to keep that mask on all night?"

"Of course. It's part of the fun of this place, isn't it?"

"Okay," she says, "I shouldn't admit this. But part of the fun of having dinner with you, Caleb…is getting to look at you. The *real* you…"

Her compliment makes me blush. I'm even tempted to take my silly mask off right now.

But I can't. Not yet.

Doing so now would be way too big a risk, and I can't afford any more risks tonight.

A tall, redheaded waiter arrives at our table. "Good evening and welcome to Soûlard," he says. "May I offer you two our wine and cocktail list?"

"No, thank you," she replies. "Just club soda and lime for me."

"Really?" I ask her, tilting my head in surprise. "Are you sure?"

This place is known for its fanciful concoctions. Hell, the word *soûlard* means "drunk."

"I'm very sure," she answers. "I'm not drinking."

"As in…not drinking *tonight*? Or ever?"

There's an edge to her tone as she says: "Can we just drop it?"

Now I feel like a dope. I'm pretty sure I know what's going on, but don't press the issue. At least not yet. I ask our waiter to make it two club sodas with lime.

After a brief discussion with my dining partner, we order our food. We decide to share two appetizers: fried tempura zucchini patties drizzled with velvety crab remoulade, and shrimp dumplings with tomato concassé (a snooty culinary way of saying "crushed"). Our mains will be a citrus-glazed swordfish amandine that promises to be tangy, flaky, and crunchy all at once, and a succulent lamb chop Clemenceau on a garlicky bed of mushrooms, peas, and diced potatoes.

The food, as I expected, is incredible.

But the company is even better.

There's an easy playfulness to her tonight that I've never seen. Our conversation flows easily. She tells me about her master's degree from NYU in Renaissance art history. Her thesis—big surprise—explored the use of food and drink imagery in the work of Michelangelo. We talk about our childhoods, hers in a wealthy suburb on Long Island, mine in a crumbling row house practically down the street. We share memories of our most memorable vacations. Our most delicious meals. Our favorite bad movies. And on and on.

Through it all, I keep her smiling and laughing, prodding her to open up more and more. As we pass a dinner plate back and forth, our hands briefly touch.

Later, no food involved, our hands touch a few more times. And linger for longer.

After our dessert course is cleared away—a roasted fig-infused sweet pudding called a blancmange, and a molten chocolate "blackout" cake so gooey it makes my teeth stick together—I say to her, "All right, *now* I'll give you what you came for."

With a dramatic flourish, I remove my masquerade mask.

"Oh, my God, you're hideous!" she exclaims, cringing and shielding her eyes. "This dinner is ruined. I think I'm going to be sick!"

I pretend to be crushed. "Sorry," I say. "That's the way God made me. Can you forgive me?"

I reach over and stroke her forearm. I shamelessly make puppy-dog eyes at her, too.

She does not, however, have my *undivided* attention.

All night, I've also been keeping an eye on a muscular, suit-clad man with vaguely Middle Eastern features slowly pacing around the dining room.

And it looks like, now with the mask off he's spotted me.

He's speaking into his wrist mic now. Probably alerting the rest of his security team—likely made of fellow ex-Mossad agents—to my presence.

At least I *hope* he is.

Oh, I forgot to mention: Soûlard is one of the restaurants run by David Needham.

The man I'm desperate to talk to again in connection with the pending attack.

Right now, I just need to sit back, wait, and let him come to *me*.

While keeping my date none the wiser.

CHAPTER 44

OUR WAITER sets the check down on our table. I reach for it, but Vanessa whisks it away so fast, I feel a small breeze.

"Nuh-uh," she teases. "A deal's a deal, Caleb. Think of all the delicious food you've been treating *me* to lately."

"Not fair," I say. "That was a couple sandwiches and a few scoops of grits. This is an expensive three-course extravaganza."

But she insists. She puts down a credit card and says, "Anyway, I'm expensing this. I'm going to make my *husband* pay."

As the waiter returns with her receipt, I notice the security guard is now standing by the swinging kitchen doors. He's watching me carefully, like a sniper lining up a shot.

I recognize the stone-faced man next to him, too, whispering into his ear. It's David Needham's chauffeur. The same Israeli asshole that stuck a pistol in my face in the backseat of his Town Car two days ago.

This means David has recently arrived.

Excellent. Just as I'd hoped.

"I have to run to the little boys' for a minute," I tell her. "Meet you out front?"

We stand and part ways. I head toward the restrooms, until I see her exit the restaurant. Then I change course for David's bodyguards.

"Hello, gentlemen," I say. "I believe your boss is expecting…"

Oooohhfff! With one swift move, the chauffeur sucker-punches me in the gut.

I hunch over. Gasping for breath. Anticipating another strike.

"You know he was *not* expecting you, Mr. Rooney," he says, voice strong and in control. "But he does wish to see you."

The two men lead me through the bustling kitchen and into a cramped, dim storage pantry. As they take their posts just outside the door, I see David Needham standing inside, next to a pyramid of bottled béarnaise sauce.

"You're a real snake, Rooney," he says darkly.

"Well, you're a real hard person to get an audience with," I say, struggling to catch my breath and not to hurl the lovely meal I just consumed onto the floor. "I assume you got the messages I left at your office last night, this morning, and this afternoon?"

"I did," he says, folding his arms. "So you're threatening to leak fake financial records to the *Times-Picayune* that link me to a murdered *terrorist*? Give me a goddamn break. That's the most ridiculous and insulting thing I've ever—"

"And yet you came running over here to see me as soon as I popped up in one of your restaurants," I say. "Listen, David. The records are real. We wouldn't be having this conversation if they weren't. And if you didn't have something to hide."

His pasty face tightens—with either nerves or rage. Or both.

"I do *not*. But a libelous news story like that—think of the damage it would do to my restaurants. You of all people should know how a trial-by-tabloid will sink a career."

I take a step toward him and say, "I'm not interested in bringing down your business. I'm trying to bring down a terrorist cell before it's too late. So tell me why a rich, conservative, paranoid foodie with a security team fit for a crown prince has been funneling money to an inner-city Islamic charity for Muslim refugees."

He looks confused.

"An Islamic charity? What are you talking about?"

"Don't bullshit me, David," I say. "You've given twelve thousand dollars to Crescent Care through four different shell companies. That's enough to buy hundreds of pounds of fertilizer. Cases of gunpowder. Dozens of pressure cookers. Or God knows what else. This is your one chance to come clean and stop this thing before it goes any further."

I take another step forward. But he doesn't flinch.

Instead, he starts to smile.

"I think the exhaust fumes from cooking inside that jalopy of yours are messing with your head," he says softly. "Do you have any idea how many charities I've supported in my lifetime? This 'Crescent' one you mentioned—I've never heard of it. But if I've given them money, I'm sure the work they do is upstanding. *And* completely legal."

He takes a breath. And smirks.

"You made it sound like you had a smoking gun," he says. "You don't even have a water pistol. Now take your mask and your lies and get the hell out of my restaurant."

My instincts tell me this bastard is lying. He's such a goddamn control freak, I bet he knows the thread count of the napkins on every one of his tables. The brand of urinal cakes in every men's room. He definitely knows where his money goes.

I feel an urge to wring his neck until I get the truth…if there weren't two armed ex-commandos standing five feet away from me.

"Don't worry," I answer. "I won't be coming back here."

I can't help but add: "The zucchini was too salty and my lamb chop was dry."

He smiles.

"Thanks for the feedback, Killer Chef. Maybe someday I'll be good enough to ladle dog shit out of the back of a truck."

He pauses, then says, "Or go after another man's wife."

My fists tighten. Now I *really* want to wring his neck. Or worse.

But I keep my cool. Barely. I turn and exit the pantry. With an escort from his two security goons, we retrace our steps back through the kitchen.

This time, however, they lead me to the rear "staff only" exit.

The door opens up into a dark, quiet alley.

Realizing this, I spin around. I raise my hands, bracing for a beatdown.

But the two Israelis just stare at me. Then they slam the heavy door in my face.

Slowly, I lower my fists in relief.

Alone now, I have two thoughts.

One: I'm even more worried than ever before.

Two: The zucchini and lamb chop were actually perfect.

CHAPTER 45

"SORRY FOR the wait," I say to Vanessa as I return to the front of the restaurant.

She's standing with her back to me. But I notice the mist of her breath is visible.

How strange. It's February, but this is New Orleans. The temperature tonight is a balmy sixty-one degrees.

Then I see why: she flicks a cigarette butt to the sidewalk.

If that rumor Gordon Andrews shared with me is true, she's someone who should *definitely* kick the habit. But it's obviously not my place to mention that.

So instead, I smile and say, "You're just full of contradictions, aren't you? An art historian in the food biz. A Big Apple girl in the Big Easy. Sober, but a smoker."

She grimaces. "I picked it up in grad school. What can I say? The flesh is weak. All my doctors keep begging me to quit."

"'*All* your doctors'?" I ask. "What's that mean?"

Now, that's not a "gotcha" question. I'm just testing to see how much she cares to reveal about herself. A classic interrogation technique, repurposed for romance.

"I meant, um…anytime I see a doctor, they—not that I see them often, just—"

"No explanation necessary," I reassure her.

I step closer and put my hand on her shoulder.

"Besides," I continue, "where there's smoke…there's probably something burning on a stainless-steel, six-burner professional stove."

She rolls her eyes at my cheesy line. Then she smiles. "Thanks for tonight, Caleb. I had a wonderful time."

"'Had'? Are you saying the evening's over?"

She gives me a look. "Are you saying it's not?"

To be honest, I *was* planning to say good night to her at this point. To end our night on a high note. After my confrontation with David, I'm dying to dive back into my investigation. To find out what the hell he's hiding and why.

But standing so close to her, soaking in her beauty under the hazy orange glow of the streetlamps, I can't help myself. My flesh is *very* weak.

"I was thinking of taking a stroll through the French Quarter to walk off some of that meal," I say. "I'd love it if you joined me."

She smiles. "Consider yourself joined."

We start heading east down St. Charles Avenue, along one of the final stretches of tonight's parade. The procession ended hours ago, but the narrow street is still thick with spectators. Nearly every one of them has beads around their necks and drinks in their hands.

As we make our way, she and I are jostled by a group of drunk college kids. We have to step around them, and for a few, brief seconds we're separated.

When we reconnect, I exclaim: "*Phew,* there you are! Did you miss me?"

She laughs. "Desperately, Caleb. And so it doesn't happen again…"

She slips her small, soft hand into mine and gives it a gentle squeeze.

It's a simple gesture that catches me by surprise—and fills me with delight.

Hand in hand, we turn right onto Canal Street and head into the French Quarter.

I notice lots of metal police barricades set up along the sidewalks. Crowd control. I see some officers, too. A few Louisiana State Troopers on foot patrol. A pair of NOPD mounted cops keeping watch. I'm sure there are undercover cops here as well, and having seen that National Guard convoy earlier, I'm sure they are quartered somewhere close, as a QRF—Quick Reaction Force—to respond instantly in case something breaks out.

Having them all here is better than nothing. But Christ, in the case of an actual emergency…

"Why the long face, mister?" she asks. "Everything okay?"

I brush aside my doomsday-scenario fears and force a smile.

"Right here, right now…everything is just *perfect*."

After a few more blocks, we reach Bourbon Street, a stretch of road whose name is synonymous with debauchery. Sure enough, it's teeming with loud, rowdy partiers. Loud whoops and yells. Frat boys with matching jerseys jostling and screaming up at the balconies, clustered with hard-core drinkers, dangling beads in their hands. Little squads of bachelorette parties—pretty, innocent women wearing sashes and tiaras—stumbling by in their high heels, careful not to take a tumble or spill their drinks. The flashes of phones taking photos of ladies exposing their breasts for the privilege of receiving strings of worthless plastic beads.

Dueling bands and DJs send waves of music among the crowds from the open doors and windows of bars.

"I don't think I have the strength for this tonight," she says, stopping at a street corner. "Sorry. It's getting late. Can we start heading back?"

We've reached a crossroads. In more ways than one. An invitation back to my place is on the tip of my tongue. But with Vanessa, I don't want to rush things. It's a delicate balance, with her being married and my attention already so divided.

"That's probably a good idea," I reluctantly answer.

"Right. Yeah. It is. *Unless...*" Her lips curl into a hint of a smile. "Do you want to come over for a nightcap? I make a mean club soda with lime."

This part of Bourbon Street is raucous, loud, and overwhelming.

But through some miracle of science or affection, I've heard her words loud and clear.

We squeeze hands and walk away.

CHAPTER 46

WE DRIVE separately to her and Lucas's home in the Lower Garden District. It's a classic terraced town house, with a beige façade and periwinkle shutters. The way its paint scheme reflects the moonlight, it looks like, well, something magical out of a fantasy movie, one involving wizards, elves, beautiful maidens, and heroic warrior/chefs.

I park in front and take a moment to collect myself before I go inside.

Since my divorce from Marlene, this is the first time I've felt this good about another woman. I can even imagine a real future with her.

But at the same time, I'm thinking, *what the hell am I doing?* Our timing is terrible. Our circumstances are even worse. For God's sake, she's *married*.

I wish things were different. Desperately. But this is the hand I've been dealt.

I know if I don't try to play it…I might regret it forever.

Vanessa greets me at the front door with a "Hi," and a tender kiss on the cheek.

She leads me into the living room, which is decorated in an eclectic Southern style: a Victorian love seat, antique French cast-iron chairs. The lights are dim, and some tinkling Art Tatum piano jazz is wafting from an actual record player in the corner.

"Take a seat," she says. "I'll be right back."

I oblige, easing myself into an overstuffed green sofa. Then I take some deep breaths. I'm practically jittery with anticipation, like a high schooler being alone with his prom date, recently crowned Prom Queen.

Vanessa returns carrying two tumblers of club soda on the rocks with fresh lime wedges perched on the rims. She hands me a glass, then lifts hers to toast.

"To...Miami," she declares.

I wrinkle my nose. "Um, okay. It's a great city and all, but why—"

"It's where Lucas is. All this week, at least. Checking out locations for a new Cuban-fusion restaurant. I hope it takes him a *long* time to find one."

"I'll be happy as long as he doesn't come home *tonight*."

We chuckle and clink glasses. Then she leans back on the couch. She coils her legs beneath her like a cat and rests a hand on my knee.

"You should know, Caleb, this feels a little strange to me."

"Something wrong with my knee?"

She playfully slaps it.

"I don't normally do this kind of thing. And by 'I don't normally,' I mean...'I've never done anything like this before, ever.' Not since Lucas and I were married."

"Then we can take things slowly," I reply. "Or, stop altogether if you think that's best."

She bites her lip, considering. "What do *you* think?"

I set down my club soda, take both of her hands, and look into her eyes.

"I'll tell you something I learned after all my years as a cop: You never know what life has in store for you. So when you see something you want…you should go for it."

She glances away. Then she looks back at me. We lock eyes.

The tension between us is building. I lean toward her slightly. I tuck a lock of hair behind her ear. I stroke her soft, rosy cheek with my thumb.

She leans in toward me now. Closer. And at last…

We kiss.

Tentatively at first. But things heat up fast. Our hands begin to wander and explore. Buttons are opened. Zippers are undone.

Suddenly, she stops.

"Wait. Let's…let's…"

I pause, worried I've moved too fast. Concerned she's having second thoughts.

She continues: "Let's move this into the bedroom."

Giggling and stealing kisses as we go, we stumble down the hall and into the master bedroom. As I guide her onto the bed, I glance down at her bare torso—and see a jagged L-shaped scar on her right side.

Confirming what Gordon told me earlier is true.

I try to be subtle about it. But I guess she notices me noticing. She covers the scar with her hand, self-conscious.

"Looking at my ugly battle wound?"

"Not at all," I say.

I lean into her and nuzzle her neck.

"Everything I see is beautiful!"

CHAPTER 47

I WAKE up the next morning around dawn.

Not that we did much sleeping.

I slide out of bed and into my clothes as quietly as I can. Vanessa is snoring softly beside me. I don't want to wake her, but I don't want to sneak out without saying good-bye. I used to pull that move with women I didn't want to see again.

Not one I'm falling for, hard.

I walk to her side of the bed and gaze down at this stunning woman. Her tousled hair. Her smattering of freckles. Her back, gently rising and falling.

I hate to disturb her—and thankfully, I don't have to. As if sensing I'm watching her, she opens her eyes and groggily smiles.

"Morning," she murmurs. "Leaving already?"

"I don't want to," I reply. "Believe me. But I've got work to do."

"Oh, come on," she teases. "You'd really choose food prep over *me?*"

"The truck's in the shop for a few more days," I say. "In the meantime…I'm doing a favor for my old boss in the police department. Checking up on something sensitive that he can't approach."

"It can't be *that* urgent…"

If only she knew.

As she playfully reaches for my belt buckle, images from our walk last night in the French Quarter flash through my mind. Tens of thousands of innocent people. Completely unaware that they might soon be in unimaginable danger.

Very reluctantly, I take her hand, stopping her, then kiss the top of it.

"I had a wonderful time last night," I say. "Let's do it again soon."

She nods, a sleepy smile on her face. I kiss her forehead, then her lips.

Then I leave, not wanting to look back, knowing that in my weakness, I just might do a U-turn and tumble back into bed with her.

Driving back to my place at this early hour takes less than ten minutes. I'm one of the only cars on the road, and I'm yawning from the lack of sleep—no complaints there!—and an early-morning lack of caffeine.

But as I turn left onto my block, I spot a vehicle that instantly wakes me up.

A few hundred feet from my home is a black, government SUV.

The goddamn feds again. Waiting for me to show up so they can no doubt give me another dressing down, with Agent Morgan tearing me a new one for "getting in his way"—when I'm doing his job better than he is!

I found Farzat first. Got the Needhams' financial records. Uncovered what I think is David's money-laundering scheme and turned up the heat on him, all on my own.

I'm *this close* to cracking this case wide open. The FBI has to know that. They're fools to keep me at arm's length when I can be so useful to them. I still don't know why they're doing it. But it doesn't matter. The last thing I need right now is some G-man reaming me out and slowing me down. Or tailing me and getting in *my* way.

I'd wanted to stop home for a shower and change of clothes. Instead, I blow right past my house and keep going.

I have a new destination in mind. And some new people I want to talk to.

Although I have a dark feeling they won't be all that chatty.

No matter. With the stakes this high, I have ways of being…*persuasive*.

CHAPTER 48

AN HOUR later I pull up to a grim, red-brick commercial building. Its paint is peeling. Its windows are cracked. Its walls are marred with graffiti.

But it's still the nicest building on the block.

I'm in Mid-City, a scruffy part of New Orleans most tourists never visit. It's mostly working-class, very diverse, with low rents and a fast-growing immigrant population.

The perfect place for an Islamic charity to set up shop to help the community.

Or, to set up a front. For *other* purposes.

Crescent Care doesn't list their physical address on their website or Facebook page. To find this address, I had to go back to the financial records from Emily Beaudette. Scanning the building now, there's no signage, either. This could all be for legitimate security reasons. They may not want the attention.

Or, it could be part of a ruse. Because the group has a lot to hide.

It's still pretty early, not even eight thirty. And there are no lights on inside the building. So I decide to wait it out, see if anybody shows up, which—unfortunately—could be a while.

Fortunately, I swung by a fantastic but lesser-known local eatery on the way over: Hoang Pham Café & Bakery, makers of the most mouthwatering Vietnamese pastries this side of Hanoi. I hungrily tuck into a flaky, savory meat pie known as *bánh pa tê sô,* and a few *chè trôi nước,* sugary jellied rice balls sprinkled with sesame seeds. I pair it with a Vietnamese-style iced coffee, sweet and creamy and packing a powerful caffeine punch.

I'm dusting off my hands when I see an older, paunchy man limping up to the building's front door. He looks Middle Eastern, has a bushy white beard, and wears an olive-green *taqiyah*—religious skullcap—white slacks, and a short black jacket. When he starts unlocking the door, I nod with satisfaction. He's an employee. Probably a very solid source of intel.

Before I get out and confront him, I unlock my glove box and grab my 9mm Smith & Wesson M&P. I stuff the black pistol into my jeans and cover it with my shirt.

Yes, the man looks older, slow, and all alone.

But I'm not taking any chances.

And I'm not playing any more games.

"As-salaam-alaikum," I say, using a respectful Arabic greeting as I approach.

"Wa-alaikum-salaam," he replies with a wary look. "May I help you?"

"This is the headquarters of Crescent Care, yes?" I ask. "I'm Greg Cole, a reporter with NOLA-News dot com. I'm writing a piece on your organization and had a few questions."

"Ah, I'm sorry, I'm just the office manager," he says. "You need to speak to my boss."

"No problem," I say, flashing him my best smile, trying to put him at ease. "How can I reach him?"

"He is…out of the country," he says. "But he is returning in a few weeks."

A few weeks, huh? How suspiciously convenient. So I go with my gut.

"That would be Saleel el-Sharif, right?"

That's the name of the charity's point person listed in the Needhams' financial records.

The man in front of me doesn't say a word, but his nervous eyes tell me a lot.

I step forward and say, "Why do I get the feeling… I'm staring right at him?"

He says, "Then your feeling would be wrong."

"Really? I doubt that, since I saw a photo of Saleel el-Sharif after doing a very extensive internet search. And the photo I saw matches you, right down to your bushy white beard. Which means you're Saleel el-Sharif, or his twin. Which is it?"

The man's expression subtly changes into one I've seen a thousand times before in my career. A suspect who's just been caught.

Even though he doesn't know I'm bullshitting him. As far as I know, there's not a single photo of Saleel el-Sharif on the internet.

But this fellow obviously doesn't know that.

"You have clearly done your research," he says. "Very good. What would you like to know?"

"Everything," I say.

And I subtly lift my shirt, exposing my concealed handgun.

His eyes widen in shock. He glances up and down the block. A few cars are driving by, but we're the only people out on the street.

"Let's go inside," I say. "Nice and slow."

CHAPTER 49

EL-SHARIF nervously leads me into the reception area, limping more and bumping into a few piled cardboard boxes. At the wall, he flips up a few light switches and overhead fluorescent lights *click-click-click* into life. It's a pretty depressing space. A few folding chairs arranged along the walls. Some old flyers and photographs on a bulletin board. The only other decoration, a large and faded poster of the Great Mosque of Mecca, tacked on a far wall.

I was a detective long enough to know this is a phony operation.

"We...we have no money here," he stammers. "Please. We are a humble charity. We simply help our Muslim brothers and sisters who are new to this country—"

"I think you *launder* money, Saleel," I say. "You help *terrorists*."

His nervousness ebbs into quiet anger.

"I should have known," he says, his voice growing louder with anger. "Stupid American. How dare you accuse us of—"

Thinking of the thousands of innocents I was with just hours ago, my own impatient rage gets the better of me. I push him against the thin plaster wall, knocking the bulletin board to the ground.

"An unhinged multimillionaire is funneling thousands of dollars through you!" I demand. "Why? What the hell is going to happen on Mardi Gras?"

"Nothing that I know of," he shoots back. "As Allah is my witness." Then he adds, spitting on the floor in disgust, "Except a full day of obscenity and blasphemy that is a complete disgrace to Islam."

"What about Ibrahim Farzat?" I demand. "*He* was a Muslim refugee who struggled to adjust to his new life. The exact kind of person your group 'helps.' Or should I say, *'recruits'*?"

"I know of no man by that name," he says with contempt. "And the only cause I have ever 'recruited' for is peace."

I'm getting to the end of my rope with this guy.

"Who did Farzat associate with? What are you planning?"

He hesitates—so I release my grip on him…and draw my weapon.

"Please, I swear to you," his voice softens. "I am not a violent man. I am not a terrorist. Whatever you are trying to find out, I do not know. Perhaps others here do but—"

"Exactly," I say, holding my weapon so he can easily see it. "Which is why I'm going to need documents. The name of everybody who's ever walked through these doors. Their numbers, addresses, e-mails. Your group's tax and financial records, too. Paper, digital, everything you've got. Now!"

He swallows. Then nods, resigned.

"All of that is stored in the back office. You may wait here, or come with me."

I scoff. "Let's take a walk."

Without lowering my weapon, we walk along together down a narrow corridor with some open doors on either side, revealing their interiors. One is a dim, barren conference room with a few copies of the Koran scattered around the table. Another looks like a prayer room, with colorful woven rugs rolled up and stacked in the corner. A third is some sort of daycare room, with Legos, dolls, and other toys strewn about the grubby carpet.

We arrive at the last door at the far end of the hall.

He unlocks it and we step inside this dark, dusty office. He turns on the lights—revealing an absolute mess. Piles of papers everywhere. Metal cabinets that look decades old. A beige PC on the desk that can't be much younger.

"I should start with the computer," he says. "It will take a minute to boot up."

"I don't need it turned on," I say. "Just give me the whole thing."

"Very well."

He moves behind the desk and starts pulling cords.

"David Needham," I say. "Tell me everything you know about him."

"I do not know that name, either," he says. "Who is he?"

I shake my head in frustration. Again my instinct says he's bullshitting me. I really don't want to have to hurt him to get the truth. But will I have a choice?

As he finishes disconnecting the computer, I glance around at the mountains of paper, looking for any of value. But most are written in Arabic. Damn.

"I need your phone, too," I say, turning away for a moment. "And any other computers and tablets. Your texts, e-mails, phone records, anything else that could possibly—"

CHOCK-CHICK!

That's a sound I've heard more times than I care to count.

A shell being chambered in a pump-action shotgun.

CHAPTER 50

INSTINCTIVELY I hit the deck, just as—*BLAM!*—buckshot roars over my head.

I lift my pistol and—

POP-POP-POP!

I fire three rounds at el-Sharif—hidden behind two filing cabinets—and desperately look around for cover.

CHOCK-CHICK!

My only real option is the office doorway behind me.

I scramble backward toward the doorframe and slip behind it just in time.

BLAM!

I get hit—but only by plaster dust that's been shot loose from the wall.

POP-POP! POP-POP!

I return fire again, and then from my knees sneak a peek into the office.

The room was already dark. Now it's filled with hazy smoke. Zero visibility.

I hear rustling inside. I see his shadow darting around. But I can't get a clear shot. Not that I'm sure I want to take it. Damnit! Am I really going to have to shoot my only living suspect?!

"Saleel, just talk to me!" I yell. "Help me. And I can help *you*."

CHOCK-CHICK...BLAM!

CHOCK-CHICK...BLAM!

Two more shotgun blasts keep me pinned down. I stay perfectly still and listen...until I don't hear any more motion coming from inside the office.

So I make my move.

I burst inside, gun trained...and see the place is empty.

I spot a back door. Hidden behind one of the filing cabinets he's been using to hide from me. It's slightly ajar.

He must have slipped out.

I kick it open and carefully step through, holding out my pistol, using two trash bins as cover. The open door leads to an empty parking lot and alleyway behind the office building.

Both are empty. No sign of him.

I kick the nearest trash bin and loudly swear, and then I shut up and listen again, trying to determine which direction he ran.

But all I can hear are distant police sirens.

Could those be...for *me*? This fast?

I turn back into the office to try to gather up whatever evidence I can, and immediately go to the computer on the desk. Shit! It's been shot through with buckshot.

Then I see a landline phone, lying off the hook on the floor, and hear the operator, "Are you safe? Can you talk? What is your emergency?"

He dialed 911 on his way out.

So those sirens *are* for me. Great.

I really gotta go...but refuse to have come all this

way to leave empty-handed. I give some of the filing cabinet drawers a tug, but every one of them is locked. I don't have the tools—or time—to crack them open.

I slam my pistol against a cabinet in rage. Then I scurry back down the hallway the direction I came, back into the drab reception area.

Those police sirens are getting louder. I can't let the cops find me here. I know my time is running out. I'm almost out the door...

When I glimpse something on the ground that makes me stop short.

The bulletin board I knocked off the wall has a number of photographs pinned to it. They seem to be highlights of some of Crescent Care's recent community outreach programs. In one, a group of bearded Muslim men are cleaning up a local park. In another, Muslim women are mugging for the camera in headscarves and 10K race bibs.

And in another picture, a group of people—some Muslim, some not—are posing with their arms around one another at a cookout along the shore of Lake Pontchartrain.

One of the men is Ibrahim Farzat.

Another is David Needham.

For a moment I stand frozen, not believing what I'm seeing.

But the police sirens around the corner snap me back to life.

I kneel down and rip that picture off the board. I stuff it into my pocket and bolt outside, running and then jumping into my Impala, starting up the engine before closing the door. Slam my foot down on the accelerator. Take off down Orleans Avenue.

I can feel the adrenaline leaving my body as my heart rate slows and I start calming down. But my shock at my discovery is only growing.

I might have screwed up and let el-Sharif get away.

But I got something else of even more value. Finally. *Proof.*

CHAPTER 51

I'M SPEEDING down Bienville Street, heading back toward the heart of the city.

But my mind is racing even faster than my car.

The crinkled photo in my pocket isn't enough to get a warrant for David Needham's arrest. Or even a search warrant for his home or restaurants.

But my God. It's incriminating. Overwhelmingly so.

The photo shows him linking arms with a man suspected by the FBI of terrorism. A man who, just days ago, was found brutally tortured and killed.

It also proves my hunch that David was lying to me. He *was* secretly funneling money to a shady Islamist extremist front after all. And no wonder I ended up dodging shotgun blasts when I tried to learn more.

But damnit, I'm still short on details though I'm more sure than ever that David, Farzat, and el-Sharif's group are all involved in the Mardi Gras attack in a major way.

At least that's what I think. Until…I start to have some doubts.

And with thickening traffic up ahead, I slow the car, and my rapid thoughts ease as well.

All right, then.

If David really is bankrolling the group's attack, why the hell would he let himself be seen at one of their charity events? He used multiple shell companies to hide his tracks. He lied to my face when I confronted him. But after all that, he posed for a group photo?

That doesn't make sense.

The back of my head starts throbbing. All the stress from the past week—including the lack of sleep from last night's stimulating activities—is finally getting to me.

Coming to a stop at a traffic light, I shut my eyes and rub my temples. All I want to do is head home, take a hot shower, change my clothes. But with so many lives hanging in the balance, I feel guilty for even thinking about myself at all.

And *furious* when I remember that black SUV waiting for me.

What arrogance by the FBI to box out local law enforcement like this! Especially on a case this serious. It's reckless. It's foolish. It's downright disgusting.

I know Cunningham ordered me to lay low and steer clear of the NOPD while I was consulting on this one. Plausible deniability and all that. But screw it. There's way too much on the line now. I'm done playing politics. I'm done playing nice.

I take out my phone, intending to give my old chief a ring. I see I have a new text from Vanessa. Sent about twenty minutes ago. Which means that while el-Sharif was firing a gun at me, Cupid was shooting an arrow.

LAST NIGHT WAS DELICIOUS, it says. DINNER WASN'T BAD EITHER ;) HAVE TIME 4 A PICNIC LUNCH IN JACKSON SQUARE? U BRING THE SANDWICHES, I'LL BRING...DESSERT.

Reading her words makes my face flush. Her offer is wildly tempting. But as always, our timing is terrible. I hate to put off a second date after our first went so well. But after this is all over, she'll understand. At least, I hope she will.

I fire off a reply—pleading for a rain check—then dial Cunningham's cell.

He picks up on the third ring. "Rooney?" he growls.

Great. I haven't spoken a word and already he's pissed at me.

"I know what you're going to say, Chief," I cut in. "But just listen. I'm getting close. Really close. I followed the money. Found the source *and* the means. But I've hit another dead end. And time really isn't on our side here. Is there *anything* more you can give me? Got any new leads at all?"

Silence. Then, I hear rustling on the other end. Followed by a long sigh. I can picture him perfectly right now. Shaking his head. Drumming his stubby fingers on his round belly. Wiping away the spit bubble forming in the corner of his mouth. It used to happen every time he got irritated by my past "antics," as he called them.

But he'd always come around, because he knew my antics worked.

Lowering his voice, he says, "*They're* getting really close, too. Word is, the sleeper cell is squatting in abandoned buildings all around town. But the bastards keep moving before the feds can get there. Changing addresses all the time."

"Wait, Agent Morgan actually *told* you this?" I ask. "The FBI's sharing intel now?"

"Please," he says. "They wouldn't tell me the *time* if I asked. But the rumor checks out. In the last seventy-two hours, there's been a surge in 311 complaints about middle-of-the-night 'police raids' all over the city.

Except, *we're* not the ones doing them. I even got an angry call the other day from the Grant family."

"*That* Grant family?"

As in…the relatives of Larry Grant.

The gang member I shot in the line of duty and quit my job over.

"The one and only," Cunningham says. "So there you have it. Everything new I know. It's all the help I can give you, Rooney. Wish I had more, but—"

"Chief? Thanks. You just gave me *plenty*."

Immediately I pull a screeching U-turn and head to my new destination: St. Roch. It's the rough neighborhood where the Grants live. From all the surveillance I did there, I know it like the back of my food truck.

It's also teeming with Franklin Avenue gangbangers, who want me dead.

I swore I'd never step foot there again. But if that's where a secret FBI raid recently went down, I might be able to find the spot they hit. Learn more about the cell they're looking for. Who's in it. Where the bad guys went next. How to catch them.

I know it's a long shot. But right now, it's the only one I've got.

I take a deep breath and say a little prayer.

"Dear God, please let me make it the hell out of there alive."

And then, remembering a documentary I saw last year about America's first flight into space, I remember the astronaut's prayer, supposedly uttered by Alan Shepard:

"And, dear God, please don't let me screw up."

CHAPTER 52

I EXIT the I-10 onto the western border of St. Roch: Elysian Fields Avenue.

Elysian. A synonym for "heaven." Yeah, right. This place is *far* from heavenly.

Other parts of the city, just a few miles away, are packed with tourists and partygoers. Booze is bubbling. Business is booming. Life is good. Really good.

Here, not so much.

The streets are quiet. Eerie. Grim. Colorful but ramshackle shotgun houses line every block. Some lawns are trimmed. Most are choked by weeds and cast-off children's toys, rusting bicycles, and car tires.

In front of one overgrown yard, I see two men lounging on a filthy leather sofa. They're passing around a glass pipe in broad daylight.

I turn onto North Derbigny Street and see a bold, purple mural painted on a wooden fence proclaiming BAPTIZED WHEN THE LEVEES BROKE. In front of it, two homeless men are screaming at each other over a shopping cart full of soda cans.

Driving deeper into the neighborhood, I see clusters of people loitering on street corners. Playing dice. Staking territory. Dealing dope. More than a few are wearing yellow T-shirts, yellow shorts, yellow bandanas.

Franklin Avenue gang colors.

I tilt the brim of the Pelicans cap I've got on a little lower over my sunglasses, and sink down into my seat. I grip the steering wheel tighter with my left hand, resting my right on the Smith & Wesson tucked in the waist of my jeans.

I'm not looking for trouble. But I'm ready if trouble finds me.

I make a left onto Spain Street—and feel my chest tighten. This is where Larry Grant used to live. He shared a little gray bungalow down the road with his wife. His mom and grandmother still live in the light-blue house on the corner.

If one of them phoned Cunningham to complain about a disruptive late-night "police" raid nearby, the abandoned building the FBI hit must be close.

I slow down as I cruise along their block. I keep my eyes peeled for a home or garage roped off by yellow crime-scene tape.

Nothing.

I make a turn. Then another. I drive up and down a few other streets.

Still nothing.

Damn. Maybe coming here was both dangerous *and* a waste of time.

Then it dawns on me. If the FBI has been hitting a bunch of suspected addresses all over the city, they've been acting on tips and hunches, like a manhunt team going door to door to find an escaped fugitive. With their resources already stretched so thin, I bet they don't have search warrants and aren't processing every building they raid, sealing the scenes with tape.

Which means I won't be able to spot their target here in St. Roch from the comfort and safety of a moving car. I'm going to have to look a little closer.

On foot.

Great. I'm about to take a stroll through a warzone.

What could possibly go wrong?

CHAPTER 53

CIRCLING BACK around, I see plenty of open spots on Spain Street.

But no way am I going to park on the block of the man I killed.

That's not just disrespectful. It's suicidal.

So I hook a right onto Prieur Street and pull over at the edge of St. Roch Park, a small oasis of green space in this concrete desert. I notice a group of guys playing a rough game of pickup basketball. Many are dressed in yellow. *Wonderful*.

Before I exit my car, I check to make sure my pistol is fully loaded, even though I know it is. Just one of those last-minute reassuring good luck charms, and I'm going to need all of the good luck I can scrape together.

Carefully sliding it into the back of my jeans, I take a deep breath and step out. Keeping my back to the basketball players, I turn and casually walk toward Spain Street.

So far, so good.

I scan each abandoned building I pass, looking for recent signs of police entry. Like a doorframe splintered by a battering ram. A discarded pin from a stun grenade on a walkway. A tactical glove dropped on the lawn or something similar.

But it's tough to tell which homes even *are* abandoned, and which are occupied. One house might look run-down, but will have lights on inside, or a child's tricycle in the driveway. Another might be in okay shape, but its windows are covered by rotting two-by-fours, or its front door is spray-painted with a big red X.

Soon I reach Spain Street—and feel my skin tingle.

This isn't where Grant and I exchanged gunfire. But it's where I staked him out and started chasing him on the night that changed my life—and ended his.

Pushing my unease aside, I continue walking down the sidewalk, inspecting every structure I pass for telltale signs.

Nothing.

I'm almost at the end of the block when I do finally notice something.

With my nose.

The sweet, musky aroma of creole-style barbecued shrimp. *Mmmm.*

Someone must be grilling nearby. Someone who really knows what they're doing, too. The mix of spices smells pretty unusual.

The cop in me wants to move on, but the chef in me wants to know more, especially if the home cook lives nearby and saw the FBI raid. If I can bond with this potential witness over food, maybe I can walk away with a new recipe *and* some new intelligence.

Sniffing the air like a human bloodhound, I follow the scent onto Galvez Street, and spot tufts of gray smoke coming from a backyard three homes down. I make my way over. I quietly and carefully walk down the driveway and behind the house.

An old African-American woman is working the grill. She's flipping skewers of shrimp, peppers, and onions while humming what sounds like a church hymn. A boy, maybe three or four, is playing with blocks on the brown grass behind her.

"Hi there, good morning," I say, as friendly as possible.

The woman stops humming and eyes me with suspicion. "You lost, child?"

"No, ma'am. I was just walking by when I smelled your *amazing* creole-style prawns. I'm dying to know what's in your spice rub. Is that cardamom? Allspice?"

The woman glares at me, even more skeptical.

"I smell somethin' too," she says. "Somethin' *fishy*. I'm gonna give you to the count of three to remove yourself from my property, before I call the damn pol—"

"Ma'am, you've certainly got a good sense of smell and an even sharper pair of eyes," I interrupt. "I used to *be* police, but not anymore. I'm in private business now, trying to find out if the police recently raided an abandoned house nearby."

The barbecue sizzles and spits. She just stares at me with the well-deserved suspicion that this and many other neighborhoods have of a white stranger coming onto their property.

"Please," I say. "Do you remember seeing anything like that? Probably late at night? It's really, *really* important."

The woman scrunches her lips. "The police are *always* up in here. Botherin' us. Or worse. One of my neighbors? Lost her son to a cop's bullet not long ago. Shame."

I freeze—and try to maintain my poker face as best I can. Am I caught?

"But now that you mention it," she continues, "the police *were* here on Thursday. Around two o'clock in the morning. Their sirens and shoutin' woke me up. I was mad as hell…until I saw they were finally takin' care of that crack house on Johnson Street."

"'Finally'?" I ask.

"I called 'em about it a few times. Damn thing seemed to pop up out of nowhere. One day it's an empty old shack. The next, mean-lookin' folks are comin' and goin' like it's a Winn-Dixie the day before Thanksgivin'.'"

Jackpot! If what Cunningham told me is true—that the sleeper cell keeps setting up new locations at the drop of a hat—this woman's story makes sense.

"What do you mean by 'mean-looking'?" I ask. "Were they Arab?"

The woman cracks a sassy smile. "Child," she says, "they looked like *you*. A couple were talkin' in Spanish. But most? They were white folks."

White? All right, so much for a jackpot. Maybe it's a bust. Damnit.

"The leader was this blond man," she goes on. "With a tattoo on his arm. Circle with a cross in it. My nephew told me what it means. Not somethin' you see around here too often."

No kidding. It sounds like she's describing a Celtic cross. A common symbol among white supremacists.

"You said this place was on Johnson Street, right?" She nods.

I thank the woman and start to head off.

"One more thing," she calls to me. "I put ground nutmeg on my shrimp. Some curry powder for heat. And for sweetness, a splash of 7 Up. You surprised?"

"Ma'am?" I say. "You have no idea how surprised I am."

CHAPTER 54

I'VE NEVER been so jazzed to check out a former crack house.

I walk back along Galvez Street the same way I came, then turn right at the next corner. I wouldn't say there's an actual spring in my step, but I'm feeling a little bounce.

When I reach Johnson Street, I slow down and keep my eyes open.

Which isn't so easy to do right now. Even though it's February, the Louisiana sun has me sweating. By habit, I start to remove my cap and sunglasses to mop my brow—but I catch myself.

I forgot. I'm in "disguise." Showing my face around here could be a death sentence.

At the next intersection, I spot a derelict, single-story house with a detached garage. Both are the color of rotted eggshell, the paint flaking off in big chunks. All the doors and windows are boarded up. The foundation is crumbling. The front yard looks as lush and wild as a bayou swamp.

This has got to be the place the woman was talking about.

But was it really a terrorist safe house raided by the FBI?

I step over a sagging section of the rusty chain-link fence surrounding the property. Then I go to the front door. More accurately, I go to the giant piece of plywood *covering* the front door.

Getting closer, I realize this wood is much newer than the rotting two-by-fours covering the windows—like it was recently installed. The nails holding it in place are also shiny. And the doorframe is badly cracked on one side, as if the lock had been bashed in with a tactical battering ram.

Yep. The BBQ chef back there definitely got it right.

Earlier I put an eight-inch metal pry bar into my pocket and now I take it out, get to work, jamming one end into the tight crevice between the plywood and doorframe, jimmying them apart.

By the time I get the goddamn board off my pants and shirt are soaked through with sweat. I set the plywood aside and peer into the house.

It's dark and dusty, like the entrance to an abandoned mineshaft.

Double-checking that my pistol is still tucked in my waistband, I switch on my pocket flashlight and enter.

I've searched many a drug den in my day, yet they never cease to make my skin crawl. This one is no exception.

As soon as I cross the threshold, I'm hit with a stale, musty smell. Wrinkling my nose, I step farther inside and slowly start moving from room to room.

In the den, I see a few pieces of stained, mismatched furniture. Littering the floor are old newspapers and some Popeyes fried chicken wrappers. Books, too. Including some in Spanish, others in Arabic.

In the kitchen, dirty plates and glasses are stacked on the counters. The fridge is open, the inside speckled with mold.

I enter the bedroom and see two queen-sized mattresses squatting on the grungy carpet. Some lumpy pillows and sleeping bags are draped over them.

My light falls on a *tiny human form* lying in the corner and I step back with a lurch.

Holy shit! With dread, I look closer, and then relax.

It's just a plastic doll. How did *that* get in here? And why?

But I've got much bigger questions. Who all was crashing here? And why? What the hell is the sleeper cell planning and where did they go next?

I kick a brittle wall in anger and frustration, denting it with my foot.

After I prowled around this disgusting—and dangerous—neighborhood, located this safe house, and searched every room, it looks like all I'm leaving with is a new barbecue shrimp recipe.

Damnit!

Wait. Something comes to me.

The garage. I forgot about the garage.

CHAPTER 55

I EXIT the house and stride across the overgrown lawn.

The garage's side entrance is boarded up with another new piece of plywood. But the main door is only secured at the bottom, with a single rusty padlock.

I lean down and position the short end of my pry bar underneath the latch. I stomp down on the long end—hard—and the old lock pops right off.

I yank the door open. The garage floods with sunlight, exposing a space crammed with all kinds of junk. Shelves are lined with paint cans, cardboard boxes, scrap metal, spools of wire, tools.

How strange. The house was practically empty. But the garage looks like it's been used recently...as a *workshop?*

I step inside for a closer look—when I'm hit by another smell, sharp and intense.

Ammonia. Or maybe chlorine. Whatever it is, it's much stronger than any household cleaning agent, that's for sure. Industrial strength.

Those kinds of chemicals aren't used to make meth or cut coke.

They're used to build bombs.

I really wish now I was still on the force. Or at least had access to some of my old resources. I'd have a forensics team dust this place for prints, fibers, DNA, top to bottom. Swab and analyze every chemical trace in here. Cross-reference everything with the ATF's databases to search for any bomb-maker signatures.

I pray the FBI is doing all that.

But by the looks of the place, untouched, I have my doubts.

I'm stewing with real frustration now. I'm getting so close! But I'm still one step behind. The bastards are building bombs. Great. *Where are they going to—*

I notice something on the grimy garage floor, stop with the internal questions.

Tire tracks.

But weird ones.

The back-wheel tracks look thick and wide-set. The front ones are narrower and set closer together. No car on the planet that I've ever seen is built like that.

But *tractors* are.

And tractors are what pull Mardi Gras floats.

My knees feel weak. My scariest theory seems to be proving true.

These bastards are going to strike one of the final day's parades. By hiding a bomb inside a tractor pulling a float.

But which parade? There are still a dozen left. And which float? There are hundreds! And who says it's going to be just one?

Jesus Christ!

I snap a few pictures of the garage and tractor tracks with my phone. My hand is practically shaking.

I suppose it *was* worthwhile for me to trek all the way out here and search this property. There's still so much I don't know. But at least now I *know* what I don't know.

And that shakes me to my very core.

CHAPTER 56

"BABY," I say, beaming, "you sure are a sight for sore eyes."

No, I'm not talking to Vanessa.

I'm looking at our food truck. Fully repaired. Back and better than ever.

New tires, a new windshield, all the damage to the body fixed, a fresh paint job. Even a tune-up and oil change for good measure.

Just in time for Mardi Gras, too.

Although after what I found in that garage yesterday, I'm not so sure that's a good thing.

I can see Marlene through our new, crystal-clear plastic service window, bustling around inside like a busy little worker bee.

I call out to her. "I thought it wasn't going to be ready till next week."

"The shop told me a couple of their mechanics love our grub," she answers. "They put in some extra hours to make it happen. I told 'em we've got free sandwiches with their names on 'em."

I climb into the back of the truck and check out the interior. *Wow*. Given the awful state I saw it in last time, I'm stunned by how good it looks.

"Free sandwiches?" I say in disbelief. "We owe them a nine-course dinner!"

Marlene texted me while I was still in St. Roch that she'd picked up the truck ahead of schedule. Told me the unusual part of town she decided to park it in. And ordered me—not asked, *ordered me*—to make sure my butt was here as quick as possible to help her get Killer Chef up and running again. I decided not to argue with her.

Of course I have some bigger fish to fry. But I also have some alligator sausages to sauté and some cheese grits to simmer. If David Needham can find the time to run five gourmet restaurants across the city *and* plot a terrorist attack, I can squeeze in a couple hours in my food truck—and still stop that bastard before it goes down.

Still, I am concerned over what I found back at that garage, and I'm tempted to e-mail the photo of the tire tracks over to Cunningham at NOPD along with a detailed e-mail. But suppose the FBI is monitoring his e-mail? Not only would he be in instant trouble, the FBI would also know I was still poking around.

Which is another good reason to be at Killer Chef right now. If the FBI and its strained resources are following Killer Chef and its famous cook, seeing me at work for a couple of hours just might convince them to leave me alone, and leave me free to keep on working my *other* job.

Today Marlene has parked us a stone's throw from the Tulane campus, on a leafy block lined with fraternity houses, which strikes me as strange.

"How come you picked Broadway Street for our grand reopening, Mar?" I ask. "The only people you hate more than drunk tourists are drunk college kids."

She stops restocking the napkins and paper plates and says, "So we can iron out any kinks without anybody noticing. Let's say our stove isn't working right. Our new fridge conks out. Our food isn't up to our usual standards. You think a bunch of wasted frat boys on the day before Mardi Gras are gonna care? We could feed 'em cat food and they'd love it."

I nod and smile. As always, my ex-wife makes an excellent point.

I grab my trusty apron and loop it around my neck, pop a tingly-hot jalapeño into my mouth, and get to work.

My mind is churning. Going over all the evidence I've gathered. Trying—and failing—to decide my next move. But I soon lose myself in the familiar ritual of food prep: peeling shrimp, chopping onions, seasoning duck breast, mincing garlic.

I'm glad for the mental break. Damn, do I need it.

About forty minutes later, a line starts to form along the sidewalk. We don't open for another hour; we haven't even tweeted our location yet. But, as always, word spread on social media. I guess after a few days without Killer Chef, our fans have worked up a real appetite.

Then I hear something. The grumbling engine of a souped-up sports car.

It sounds like the racket I heard just last week. When Lucas drove back and forth past my truck, paranoid that Vanessa might stop by for lunch.

Unbelievable. He's the kind of guy who gives assholes a bad name.

I ignore the noise and focus on my food. But it keeps getting louder. And closer.

Then I glimpse the blue Lamborghini screech to a stop right across the street.

No. It can't be. Didn't Vanessa say he was in Miami all week? *Oh, boy.*

"Rooney, you son of a bitch!" comes an arrogant shout.

Lucas slams the door and marches up to the truck, wearing white pants and a bright-orange polo shirt. I turn down my burners and step outside to confront him. And hopefully keep him cool.

Too late. His fists are balled. His jaw is clenched. A vein across his forehead looks like it's about to burst. I'm half-expecting steam to start coming out of his ears.

"You're a real piece of shit, know that?" he shouts. "You want to go around banging every bimbo in the Big Easy? Fine. But stay the hell away from my wife!"

"Vanessa?" I reply. "I haven't seen her since that night at LBD."

"You're a lousy cook, and an even lousier liar," he keeps going. "I know about you two. I know everything. I'm only going to say this once. Tell me now— *swear* it, Rooney—that things are over with the two of you. Or I'll make sure *both* of you regret it!"

I stare Lucas dead in the eye. Torn, I consider fibbing, telling him what he wants to hear. To protect the wife he doesn't deserve. But I also want to tell him the truth: that I'm falling hard for that incredible woman, and she won't be his for long.

But now isn't the time to make trouble. So I play it right down the line.

"Lucas, I have a policy," I say. "I never make a promise I can't keep."

Lucas's nostrils flare. His face turns redder than a boiled crawfish. My customers in line are staring in awe at this man's roadside show.

"You just made the biggest mistake of your life," he snarls. "Her, too!"

Then he marches back to his Lamborghini, climbs in, and peels out, its V10 engine roaring and echoing along the street.

As I watch him go, I shake my head in amusement. What a ridiculous, clichéd, empty threat.

Then again, I've heard rumors about what that man's capable of.

Maybe it's not so empty after all.

I look to my line of customers.

"Hope you enjoyed the show," I call out. "Ready to eat?"

The happy shouts of encouragement lift my spirits as I go back to Killer Chef.

CHAPTER 57

ASIDE FROM the husband of the woman I'm falling in love with showing up and threatening to ruin my life, the first brunch shift in our new-and-improved truck goes off without a hitch. It's the only one we'll work today, as we're still a day away from being fully stocked and up and running.

But it's a good shift: Our equipment holds up. Our food turns out great. Our customers all go home happy. What more could you ask?

But about midway through, I start feeling antsy.

I'm champing at the bit to get out there again. To dive back into my investigation. To keep putting together the pieces before it's too late.

So after I swear to Marlene I'll make it up to her, she agrees to do the cleanup alone. The minute our last po'boy is served, I jump into my car and hit the road.

My destination is Lake Terrace. An exclusive neighborhood nestled along Lake Pontchartrain.

More specifically, I'm heading to the tacky McMansion on Oriole Street that David Needham calls home.

There's not a shred of doubt in my mind that man knows a hell of a lot more than he let on. He wouldn't talk to me in his restaurant, surrounded by bodyguards. But tonight, I'm going to give him one more chance. *To confess*.

Am I counting on it? Of course not. But this time, I'm bringing a lot more to the party than just a hunch.

I have that photo of him and Farzat at the Crescent Care event.

The pictures I took of the bomb-making workshop in the garage.

And my Smith & Wesson, which is never leaving my side again.

I merge onto the I-10…and only get about a quarter of a mile before I realize that was a stupid idea. It's still early, but the highway is crawling with traffic.

I sigh and lean my exhausted head against the back of my seat.

At least I'm not in a hurry. David's probably working late at one of his restaurants tonight. I'll have to stake his place out for a few hours until he comes home. Good thing I have a Killer Chef specialty—a blackened catfish sandwich with duck-fat fries—a fully loaded iPod, and my memories of last night with Vanessa to tide me over.

I've barely moved an inch in this bumper-to-bumper nightmare when my phone rings.

Speak of the devil. It's Vanessa.

I wonder if she's talked to Lucas. If she knows her husband is onto us, and came by my place of business to threaten me. If she knows *how* he knows—which, come to think of it, I'm curious about myself.

I answer the phone and put it on speaker.

"Hey, Vanessa," I say happily. "What's up?"

"Caleb," she says in a frantic whisper, "oh, my God, help!"

I bolt upright in my seat. There's fear in her voice. Real and visceral.

"Vanessa?" I ask, holding the phone close to my face. "Are you okay?"

"No—definitely—*not!*"

Her words are clipped and urgent, spit out between sharp breaths.

"Where are you? What's going on?"

"I'm in—Central City, I think. They followed me. Rammed my car. Made me crash! I managed to run away. Now I'm hiding—in a gas station bathroom. They're going to kill me!"

"Whoa, whoa, slow down," I plead. "Followed you? *Kill* you? Where are you right now?"

She sniffles. On the verge of tears.

"I'm at Claiborne and Felicity. I think they're really close, hurry!"

I take a quick, sweeping glance at the traffic jam I'm in.

"Vanessa, just stay calm. I'm calling the police—"

"No!" she shouts. "Don't. No cops. Just you. Come fast, Caleb, please!"

No cops. Just me?

If *your* life was in danger, wouldn't you want the police to come as quick as they could—not your retired-detective lover, all by himself?

Vanessa's call is so weird, so scary, so out of character, I wonder if someone's forcing her to make it against her will.

Maybe it's Lucas…or David…or a Franklin Avenue gang leader…or somebody else. Holding her at gunpoint. Using this damsel-in-distress ploy to lure me into a trap.

God, what the hell have I gotten us into?

But what choice do I have?

Ruse or not, she's in real danger.

"Okay, I'm on my way," I say. "No cops. Just me, as fast as I can."

She doesn't say anything.

"Vanessa? You still there?"

But the line's dead.

CHAPTER 58

ON THE other end is silence. Total, chilling silence.

Did Vanessa just hang up? Or did one of her attackers *make* her hang up?

A wave of panic crashes over me, forcing me to focus on staying calm, stable, not wildly reacting. Even though my pulse is racing, time seems to be slowing down.

I don't care if this is some kind of trap. A woman I'm falling in love with is in danger. And she's only a few miles away from here.

I've got to get to her. Find out what the hell is going on.

And if what she's saying is true, save her life.

But my first goddamn problem is finding a way out of this slow-moving stream of traffic.

Instinctively I reach for the center of my dashboard to flip on my lights and sirens—when I realize, *shit*, of course, I don't have those anymore.

Instead, I lay on the horn. Cut the wheel sharply. And start lurching my way across all three lanes. Gas, brake, gas, brake. Other drivers honk at me. Curse. Flash every rude gesture in the book. But I ignore every one of them and stay focused.

Once I make it onto the gravel shoulder, I floor it.

I can eventually see that there's a major accident—looks like every cop in Louisiana is on the scene. I take the first exit, Howard Avenue, then pull a screeching right turn onto Jefferson Davis Parkway. It's named after the former head of the Confederacy—a stark reminder that as progressive and free-spirited as New Orleans tries to be today, it still has a ways to go.

Traffic is okay for a few blocks, so I zoom right along. Things get hairier when I hit Washington Avenue (named after, well, *you* know). But I refuse to slow down. I honk and swerve, weaving in and out of cars and trucks, driving as if I were pursuing a suspect. Like they taught me in the Academy, I keep my hands gripped low on the steering wheel for better control, and my eyes straight ahead.

At the major intersection of Washington and Broad, the light turns yellow. I accelerate—but there's no way I'm going to make it. I slam the pedal even harder. I pound my horn like a maniac and blast through the red. *"Thank you,"* I whisper, that I make it past without an accident—lucky for me, all the cops are otherwise occupied and I don't have to lead them on a high-speed chase to get to Vanessa, because I'm not slowing down for *anybody*.

Traffic is starting to get heavy again, so I decide to turn off this main road and zip along some side streets as I near the heart of Central City. Not far from here is the Southern Food and Beverage Museum, a kitschy collection of exhibits about a topic dear to my heart. Close by, too, is the famous Leidenheimer Baking Company, makers of bread so addictive, the stuff ought to be a controlled substance.

But Central City is also a neighborhood known

for homelessness, blight, and heavy drug use among its residents and transients looking to hook up for a quick score. Not to mention murders and other crimes. Forget locking herself in a gas station bathroom. What was Vanessa doing here in the first place?

I continue zooming along potholed residential roads. Past tumbledown houses and abandoned lots, a blur of poverty and neglect. Finally, I turn onto Claiborne Avenue and keep my eyes open for that rundown gas station. I'm almost there.

I see one, a Shell, but it looks pretty clean and fairly busy.

A block later, I spot another one, a Valero, but it's also doing brisk business.

Once I cross Felicity, I think I've found the place: An old, shabby Gasco.

It looks closed, but whether for the day or for good, I can't tell. Two cars are parked sloppily in front of it. One is a maroon Jeep Cherokee that has a badly dented bumper. Maybe the vehicle that rammed Vanessa, forcing her off the road?

Then I remember: a maroon Jeep Cherokee drove into that scrapyard last week, to that sleeper cell meeting, when I was tailing Farzat.

I hate coincidences.

And then I see it: Vanessa's Lexus, turned sideways half a block from the Gasco—that must be where they rammed her, and she escaped on foot.

Jesus Christ.

As I drive closer, four shady-looking guys are at the shabby-looking gas station. Two of them are keeping lookout by the Jeep. Two others are at the restroom door, angrily pounding on it.

None seem dumb enough to have drawn a weapon in broad daylight…but I do see some telltale bulges on their hips.

My own 9mm is still at my side—but this is *not* the time or place to use it. If I get into a four-on-one, close-range shootout with these guys, I'll be pumped full of lead in seconds.

I scan the gas station, wracking my brain for possible options, desperate to come up with something to scare these assholes off and free Vanessa.

What can I do?

Then, I get an idea. A risky one.

No, a crazy one.

But it could work. If it doesn't burn me alive first.

CHAPTER 59

SWALLOWING MY fear before I choke on it, I turn into the gas station and pull up to a pump. I choose one close to the action.

Before I even shut off my engine, I see the near two men, standing guard, tense up and exchange words. I assume they're debating how to handle my unexpected arrival.

I rummage through the junk in my center console— paper clips, napkins, sugar packets, a pen, a Bic lighter, loose change, old receipts—and take what I need.

Then I casually exit and turn to the pump. Out of the corner of my eye, I see one of the men approaching.

My palms are starting to get clammy, but I keep my cool. I remove my wallet and dip a credit card into the slot. I lift and squeeze the nozzle's handle, starting the flow of fuel, then I flip the little latch that locks it in place.

"*Hey,*" the man grunts. "Y'all can't be here. We're closed."

"What was that?" I ask with a friendly nonchalance.

And without being too conspicuous, I give the guy a once-over: Caucasian, mid-thirties, shaved head, scraggly black beard, a few missing teeth, his neck a tapestry of tattoos. Not the kind of guy you hope takes your daughter to prom.

"I said we're closed," he repeats. "Get outta here."

"I'm just getting some gas," I say, keeping my back to him.

"You're not hearing me, pal," he says. "Get back in your car and *go*. Now."

"Just a second. I'm almost done."

"I said *now*. If I gotta tell you again, there's gonna be...*what the hell?*"

The man looks down at his feet—and sees he's just stepped in a stream of fast-moving amber liquid: *gas*.

I haven't been filling my tank at all.

I've been letting the fuel flow onto the concrete.

I've also been crumpling up all the stray paper I found in my car—napkins, receipts, sugar packets—into a tight, combustible wad.

I drop the still-gushing nozzle to the ground and spin around.

I'm holding the bundle of papers in one hand.

And the Bic in the other.

CHAPTER 60

"OKAY, ALL of *you* get on your knees with your hands on your heads!" I shout. "Right now! Or this whole place goes up in flames!"

The man freezes as he realizes what's happening. His eyes dart around, watching the gasoline spreading around him and toward his accomplices.

"Aw, shit," he mutters, and gropes for his gun.

"Bad idea," I say. "The spark from one shot could blow it all up…that is, if I don't light the liquid first myself."

A look of confusion and terror spreads across the man's face.

"Whoa, okay, take it easy," he pleads, and holds up his empty hands. He stumbles backward toward his friends, calling to them: "Hey, uh, we got a problem!"

The other three catch on fast—especially when they notice the river of fuel streaming their way.

One of the men standing by the bathroom door, a wiry middle-aged fellow in a grimy trucker hat, draws out a dirty-looking revolver.

I light my paper bundle and hold it out like a torch.

"Angus, don't shoot!" the first man screams,

waving his arms in the air like a driver of a disabled vehicle, desperately seeking help.

"You heard him!" I shout back. "Now I'm gonna count to three! One! Two!"

The men share some words I can't make out. They're clearly starting to panic. They think I'm crazy. Which is exactly the point.

It doesn't take much longer for them to decide to run like hell.

Cursing under their breath, none of them do what I ask. Two of them make a dash for their cars. The other two—including the trucker-hat man with the gun—take off on foot, in the opposite direction.

Once they're gone, I relax, and toss the fiery wad of paper to the ground. It lands right in the fuel...and sizzles out, completely harmlessly.

Those idiots, I think, ecstatic my little ruse worked. They clearly grew up watching action movies. But in real life, it's almost impossible to light gasoline like that, despite the Hollywood cliché. I picked diesel fuel, too. Even less combustible.

But my celebration doesn't last long. I sprint over to the bathroom door and drum my hands against it. "Vanessa? It's Caleb! Are you okay?"

Silence. I keep banging on the door. I keep calling her name. Still nothing.

My stomach starts to feel heavy with dread. Is she even in there?

Is she still alive?

After what feels like a week, I hear the lock click.

I slowly open the door.

She's there. Cowering like a scared animal. Her cheeks are lined with rivulets of tears and mascara. She's terrified, but looks unharmed.

I don't say another word. Choked up, I'm not sure if I could.

I crouch down and wrap her in my arms. It's the tightest, most protective embrace I've ever given anyone. I'm flooded with relief…and then with anger.

I *need* to catch one of those sons of bitches and make them pay—*especially* if they're connected in any way whatsoever to the Mardi Gras attack!

"Get in my car, lock the doors, and call 911," I tell her, thrusting my keys and phone at her. When she seems to hesitate, I bark, "Just do it! It's okay to call the cops now. You're *safe* now. I'll be back, I promise."

Before she can say anything that might change my mind, I leap to my feet again and start running, splashing through the diesel fuel and back onto the sidewalk. I look left, right. The vehicles are long gone. That skinhead has disappeared, too.

But I do get a glimpse of the trucker-hat man, the one called Angus. He's only a couple blocks away. He's moving pretty fast—but it looks like he has an injury: a limp.

Poor baby.

Like a lion picking out the slowest gazelle in the herd, I spring into pursuit. I race across the street, just narrowly avoiding being hit by a delivery van. Then I really start to pick up speed. I shove some pedestrians out of my way. I dodge not one, not two, but three teenagers zooming past on Razor scooters.

I'm gaining on him—who glances backward and only then realizes I'm chasing him. Suddenly afraid, he tries to run faster. His hat flies off in the process, revealing a tangled mane of blond hair, but his leg is still holding him back.

He starts to pull out his revolver again…but I'm practically on his heels.

I pounce. Lunging at him, I throw both my arms around his waist. I tackle him, flinging him down onto the rock-hard sidewalk. His gun skitters out of his hand as we land with a bone-crunching *thud*.

If I were still a cop, I'd already be pulling his arms behind his back, slapping on a pair of cuffs, and reminding him of his rights.

Instead, I *twist* one of his arms—and shove his face hard into the cement.

"Who the hell are you?" I demand. "And who told you to hurt Vanessa?"

He doesn't answer. Maybe it's because he's panting like a dog.

Or maybe he needs a little more…*encouragement*.

I twist his arm harder until he groans in pain. I notice that his hand is mottled with fresh burns of some kind. And his forearms are a tapestry of faded prison tattoos—among them, a black cross inside a black circle.

Oh, my God. That woman I met, the one barbecuing shrimp near the safe house in St. Roch—she told me she saw a blond man hanging around there with this exact white nationalist symbol on his arm. There's a pretty good chance that this is the same guy.

"If I were you, Angus," I snarl, "I'd start talking."

And at last, he does: "Screw you!"

I take a deep breath. Gotta stay calm. Especially since a small crowd of onlookers is starting to gather on the sidewalk. I'm sure one of them is going to start filming this with their phone at any second. So I have to be fast.

"What happened to your nose, Angus?" I ask. "Is it broken?"

"Huh?" he says, and turns his head slightly to face me.

I slam the heel of my palm into his nostrils. Cartilage crunches. Blood spews.

"How about *now*?"

CHAPTER 61

"LE PETIT filet for the mademoiselle. And le grand rib eye for the monsieur."

The waiter sets down two thick, juicy slabs of prime beef in front of Marlene and me. I straighten the cloth napkin in my lap in anticipation.

"And for the other mademoiselle, a Caesar salad."

He places a pile of romaine lettuce, croutons, and Parmesan cheese—a perfectly fine dish, but let's be honest, not nearly as mouthwatering—in front of Vanessa.

"Bon appetit."

The three of us are sitting in the wood-paneled dining room of Mr. John's Steakhouse. Tucked away in the Lower Garden District, this classy spot serves some of the best steaks this side of the Mississippi in a relaxing, elegant setting. Nothing trendy, nothing flashy. Just quiet perfection.

After a day like today, that's exactly what all of us need.

I feel like I'm a thousand miles away from the violent men, decaying gas station, and blighted neighborhood of Central City, and I'm hoping—*praying*—that Vanessa feels the same way.

"I feel a little silly ordering a salad at a steak house," says Vanessa, picking at her food while Marlene and I dig in. "I guess I don't have much of an appetite tonight."

I reach across the table and place my hand on hers. I'm careful to avoid her bandaged thumb, one of her few minor injuries from her car crash and foot chase earlier today. It's a damn miracle she walked away with only cuts and bruises. Her face has been scrubbed clean as well of the tear marks and smeared mascara, and she looks younger, even more vulnerable.

"You could order off the kids' menu tonight for all I care," I say. "I'm just glad you're safe. And if your appetite happens to come back, you're welcome to some of mine."

"She *is?*" Marlene exclaims. "I think I might faint. Did Caleb Rooney just offer to share his precious steak? Back when we were married, I used to have to beg him just to get a bite. This woman must be pretty special."

I smile broadly.

"You both are special," I say. "You know that. That's why I wanted us to have dinner together. I figured we could all use a night out."

"Thanks again for the invitation," Vanessa says. She turns to Marlene. "I'm glad you're here, Marlene. It means a lot. If Lucas asked me to join *him* for a meal with one of *his* girlfriends, I think I'd jump in front of a streetcar before I said yes."

"Hmm," Marlene says. "About that. Can I be honest here for a minute?"

Uh-oh. Believe me, that is never the way you want your ex-wife to start a sentence. I open my mouth to try to stop her, but Vanessa answers first.

"Of course you can," she says. "Always."

"When I first realized that Caleb was seeing a married woman, it didn't sit right with me," Marlene says, choosing her words well. "Not for any moral reasons. I just don't want to see my business partner get hurt—unless *I'm* the one doing it. Sure, he's tough. Especially when it comes to the fairer sex. But you can dent a cast-iron skillet if you hit it hard enough. Get me?"

Marlene spears a piece of steak on her fork and jabs it in the air for emphasis.

"You've proven me wrong, Vanessa," my ex-wife says. "Whatever happens between you two is none of my business...but y'all have something really nice. I'm happy for you."

For a moment, I'm speechless. And a little touched.

"That was lovely, Mar," I say. "I don't think I've ever heard you be so...nice."

"Yeah, well, don't get used it."

We all share a little laugh, our first of many this evening.

As dinner continues, I'm pleasantly surprised by how well the three of us are getting along. How charming Vanessa is, given her harrowing ordeal today. How gracious Marlene is, given that...well, she's Marlene. The two most important women in my life discover a ton of shared interests to bond over, everything from country music out of Nashville, to the New York Yankees, to trashy reality TV like *The Real Housewives of Atlanta*. By the end of the meal, any tension there might have been between them has vanished.

Once I've settled the check, we head outside to the valet stand to wait for our cars. Mine and Marlene's, that is. Vanessa's Lexus is in the shop, thanks to today's violent activities.

"What's that building over there?" Vanessa asks. "I've never noticed it before."

She's pointing across the street to an unusual steel and glass structure with a long, plank-like entryway and a triangular trellised metal roof. The architectural style sticks out like Vanessa's sore thumb from the genteel buildings all around it.

"Oh, that?" I answer with a smile. "It's the Eiffel Tower."

"Very funny," she says. "Look, I know I'm not local, but don't tease me. Really, what is it?"

Marlene sighs. "Actually, honey, he's telling the truth."

Vanessa corkscrews her pretty face, mystified.

"Straight from Paris, France," I explain. "It used to be a restaurant at the top of the tower. Picasso, Charlie Chaplin, even Hitler—everyone ate there. When it closed in the 1980s, they took it apart, piece by piece. Shipped it over here. Rebuilt it. Now it's a museum and event space called the Eiffel Society. We should check it out sometime."

Vanessa shakes her head in awe as she sticks a cigarette between her lips.

"This city never ceases to amaze me."

"It just goes to show," I say, plucking the unlit smoke with my thumb and index finger, "that no matter where you come from, or what your past is, you can come to New Orleans and have a second chance. You can be accepted. For who you are."

I lock eyes with her and hold her gaze.

"Hey, lovebirds, our cars are here," Marlene calls out, breaking the connection.

"I'd offer you a ride home," I say, "but I have some work stuff to take care of tonight. And it's probably best if Lucas and I don't cross paths."

Vanessa nods. "I understand. I can get an Uber."

"No way!" Marlene interrupts. "Vanessa, you're riding with me. Hop in."

I watch as these two women, an unlikely friendship now taking shape between them, get into Marlene's stick-shift Passat and putter off into the night.

Then I go over to my car and hand the valet a twenty-dollar tip. But before I get behind the wheel, I walk behind the trunk and give the top a firm slap.

From the inside come frantic, muffled cries for help.

Angus, the white supremacist piece of human garbage I tackled earlier today, has been tied up in there this whole time.

I can barely suppress a smile as I quietly say, "Let's go for a little ride."

CHAPTER 62

I PULL onto St. Charles Avenue, a wide thoroughfare with two sets of streetcar tracks running down the middle. My destination is northeast, but I'm heading southwest.

Oops. Guess I'll have to make a U-turn.

I give the wheel a sharp twist. My car jumps the median, rumbles across the metal tracks, then back onto the street in the opposite direction.

With each bump, the trunk's contents rattle and thud.

"Sorry, Angus," I call, knowing full well he can't hear me. "My bad."

Once I pick up speed, I start tapping the brakes every now and then to make my car jerk and lurch—and make Angus toss and turn. My goal isn't to hurt the bastard. I just want him to feel afraid. Confused. Helpless. All the awful emotions he made Vanessa experience just a few hours ago.

Except in his case, there's nobody coming to save him.

After a few blocks, I roll down the windows. It's stuffy in the car. I can only imagine how uncomfortable it is in the trunk.

I flip on the radio and tune it to my favorite station:

90.7 WWOZ, all jazz, all the time. A scratchy, virtuoso trumpet solo blares. I recognize the song right away as the famous "Dippermouth Blues," recorded by the man himself: Satchmo, Pops—the Big Easy's own Louis Armstrong. I can't help but nod my head and drum my fingers along to the lively beat. They say one reason jazz was born in New Orleans is because it was the only place in the world where slaves were allowed to own drums. It's testament to their creativity and spirit that out of such an awful institution came something so infectiously good.

I merge eastbound onto the Pontchartrain Expressway. I'm heading out of the city, so traffic is pretty light. This gives me ample ability to jerk the wheel and swerve sharply between all four lanes.

"How ya doing back there, Angus?"

Soon I'm cruising over the Crescent City Connection, the massive steel bridge that spans this bend of the Mississippi. To my left, the downtown New Orleans skyline twinkles beautifully against the hazy night sky.

I exit the expressway in a part of the city known as Algiers. The area has high rates of gang and gun violence, but it looks quaint and feels suburban, almost like a small town. It's also where many Carnival krewes have their "dens," the giant warehouses where members build and store their outlandish floats.

If my theory about the upcoming attack is right, some of those floats could be carrying bombs as well as beads. That makes me shiver, that somewhere in one of those warehouses, at this very minute, the components of a bomb are being carefully assembled to be placed in a tractor or a float.

But there's still that nagging question: Is it a terrorist

attack to cause random death, fear, and destruction...or could it still be a family affair among the Needhams?

I just don't know.

But I'm hoping my frightened cargo back there might just help me find out.

I turn onto Winston Street and get in line with a few other idling cars. We're about to cross the Mississippi River again—but there isn't a bridge in sight.

"How many passengers ya got?" asks the ticket-taker with a snap of her gum.

"Just me, thanks," I answer, handing her three dollars for the toll.

She waves me forward, and I drive onto a massive, red-and-white, open-air ferry. I ease into a parking spot behind a silver Ford Explorer with a bumper sticker that reads KEEP N'AWLINS FUNKY. Within a few minutes, we're moving. I check my phone, see no voicemails, no texts, not much of anything. But I spare a few moments to send a text before stepping out of my car.

If you've ever sat inside a car that's on a boat, you know it's a strange feeling. It makes me a little nauseated.

It must be even worse inside a claustrophobic trunk.

And I'm depending on that.

After a short ride, I'm back on dry land in a community called Chalmette. Driving through, I pass gritty industrial sites and a massive oil refinery. When the roads start getting gravelly, when it feels like I've gone too far, that's when I know I'm getting close.

I turn onto Bartolo Street heading north, and take it as far as it goes. I finally stop—on a small concrete bridge spanning the Florida Canal, a man-made industrial waterway. All around me is vast, dark marsh.

I kill the engine, which also kills that sweet jazz. I

get out, draw my Smith & Wesson, walk around to the trunk, and pop it open.

Angus is inside, curled up in the fetal position.

He immediately starts twisting and writhing, but his wrists and ankles are bound with duct tape. He tries to scream, but his mouth is gagged with a red bandana.

"Let's go."

Keeping my pistol trained on him, I haul him out and drag him over to the edge of the bridge. I shove him forward onto the railing, so his hands and head dangle over the edge. Staring into the inky-black abyss of the canal, he gurgles out in terror from behind the gag.

Back when I was a cop, I interrogated hundreds of suspects. In all kinds of places, using all kinds of techniques. But never, ever anything like this.

"Make all the noise you want," I say. "Nobody around for miles. It's just you and me out here, Angus. And the crickets. And...the *gators*."

CHAPTER 63

I PLACE the cold steel barrel of my pistol against the back of his head.

His muffled cries of terror turn frantic.

"What happens next is up to you," I say. "Who hired you to go after Vanessa? What's happening on Mardi Gras? How's it all connected? Tell me!"

To my surprise, Angus vigorously shakes his head. He seems to grunt "no," followed by what sounds like a string of profanities. Unbelievable!

"If you're willing to die to protect some terrorist scum, your life is even more worthless than I thought," I say. "But okay. If that's the way you want it…"

I press my gun harder into his skull. I cock the hammer, stand to one side so I can see his miserable face.

He scrunches his beady eyes shut. My index finger is twitching like a live wire. A few pounds of trigger pressure are all it would take to wipe this asshole from the face of the earth. It would be so easy. So satisfying. I could probably get away with it, too.

But no. I'm better than that. And no one deserves to die in cold blood. Especially not someone who might still turn out to be helpful.

I pull the pistol away, carefully lower the hammer back down, and then jam my gun back into the waist of my jeans. I yank him off the ledge, lower him into a seated position on the ground, and untie the bandana around his mouth. He looks up at me, stunned and speechless. Relieved to still be alive. But even more afraid of what I might do next...I hope.

I pull something from my pocket. It makes him flinch—but it's just the cigarette I took from Vanessa earlier, and the Bic lighter I used at the gas station.

"Smoke?"

Nervously, he accepts. I light it for him and he takes a few anxious drags, like he's expecting the thing to explode in his face.

But gradually, he starts to relax. And it looks like he's lowering his guard.

"Look, Angus—if that's even your real name—you seem like a smart enough fellow," I start. "Who just got caught up with some bad dudes. Tell me what happened. The more you share, the more I can help you."

He holds his cigarette awkwardly in his bound hands. He stares at it, sullen. The glow casts an eerie shadow over his ropey, tattooed arms.

"Thing is," he says, "I *ain't* that smart. That's why they kicked my ass out. Instead of bein' part of the action, they got me chasin' down some poor lady."

My body tenses with anticipation. This could be a huge breakthrough...*could* being the operative word.

"*Who* kicked you out? *What* action?"

"Few months ago, word started spreadin'," he says. "Online, mostly. Message boards and the like, the ones you need a password to access. Somebody high up in the Brotherhood"—that would be the *Aryan* Brotherhood—"needed help. They were plannin' something so big and so bad against that shithole of humanity known as Mardi Gras. It would scare away all the damn monkeys and mongrels invadin' our city, once and for all. Make it ours again."

"What was it?" I ask.

"Never could figure out all the details," he says. "But at one point, they were lookin' for folks who knew explosives. That's how I got involved. I served three tours in Iraq and Afghanistan. Saw plenty of roadside bombs blow up my buddies."

"You were in the Army?"

He takes a sullen drag. "For a bit."

"What do you mean, a bit?"

He lets out a cloud of smoke. "Made it through Basic, was gettin' ready for additional infantry trainin', and then I got kicked out. All 'cause I got in a couple of fights, and they didn't like my…whaddaya call it. Psych profile. But that's okay, I got work, soon enough."

"An overseas security company?"

He nods. "That's right. They didn't care if I got into fights with some mud folks in the service, or if my psych profile wasn't a hundred percent. They just needed someone who knew how to shoot…and who could learn 'bout settin' explosives. Which took a while. And then I thought I could figure out how to make 'em myself."

He shows me the chemical burns on his hands that I noticed earlier.

"Guess I wasn't a fast learner."

"Who was in charge of the group?" I demand. "Who was calling the shots?"

"That's the thing. It was like everybody was gettin' their orders separate. We only knew our little piece of the puzzle. And the couple times we'd meet up—at different abandoned houses all over the city—the team looked like the goddamn United Nations! There were always a few ragheads there. Couple wetbacks, too. I hated it. But like they say, the enemy of my enemy is my friend."

"The bomb-making supplies you mentioned— where did they come from?" I ask. "Who was paying for all this?"

He shrugs. "Rumor is, some rich restaurant guy, sympathetic to the cause."

Holy shit. David Needham might be a paranoid asshole, all right. But is he really a closeted white nationalist?

"Then what?"

"They finally brought in some new dudes who knew bombs," he says, bringing up his cigarette for another puff. "So I got kicked to the curb. Until, that is, they needed some people to go after that girl. I didn't know who she was, or why they wanted her, but I figured it was all part of the plan."

He takes a long drag on his cigarette, then tosses it over the bridge into the murky canal below. I bite my lip in frustration. He's clearly just a tiny cog in a terrible machine. He doesn't know shit. He's not just a dumb racist. He's a pawn.

"So what happens now?" he asks. "Do I get to go home?"

I have to laugh at this man's stupidity. I'm about to answer in the negative when I see something off in the distance that instantly shatters my laughing mood.

CHAPTER 64

IN THE distance, a flurry of red and blue lights churns up the starless sky.

Shit. A caravan of cops. Speeding our way fast.

So much for taking things slow with Angus.

"You need to tell me more," I insist. "Details about the attack. Specifics. And you need to tell me *now.*"

"It's like I said, man. I already told you everything I—"

"Bullshit!" I yell. "How many floats and tractors are they using? What part of the city are they hitting? Which parade? When?"

He chews on his lip. For a second I get the feeling he's having a change of heart and wants to help me out. Maybe I'm just asking the wrong questions.

"Give me some names, then," I say, nearly pleading. "Let's start there. Who else was part of the team?"

"The Aryan Brothers came from other chapters. From all different parts of the state. I only knew 'em by their war names."

"You said there were other people, too. What about them?"

He hocks a wad of saliva over the railing into the inky canal below.

"You mean the Mexicans and A-rabs? No idea. I don't talk to animals. There was even a goddamn Russian if you can believe it. And they even got these smarty scientist types — smarter than *you,* cop, you can be sure."

Fury overtakes me. I reach down and grab this asshole by his sweaty, bloodstained tank top, tug at him hard.

"Here's the deal, shithead," I growl. "At a minimum, you're looking at aggravated assault and conspiracy to commit terrorism. That's thirty-five to life, no parole. See those cops heading this way? They're not coming to help you. But maybe I can — if you help *me.* I know some good lawyers in this city. And some flexible judges. Get what I'm saying? So unless you want to die inside a supermax, I'm the only hope you've got."

Apparently, my words finally get through to him.

"Holy Cross," Angus mutters.

"What does that mean?" I demand. "Some kind of code? Religious thing?"

"Holy Cross the *place,*" he says, almost whining. "It's where all of us were supposed to meet up tonight. Some shack on the corner of Dauphine and Flood."

A late-night gathering. In a rough part of town. Inside a vacant home.

Sure sounds like a sleeper cell's latest safe house.

And there's a damn good chance they're meeting there right now!

I push Angus to the ground and race back to my car.

Holy Cross is a neighborhood in the Lower Ninth Ward. Only six or seven miles from here. If I'm lucky — yeah, I know, not likely — I can get there in fifteen minutes, tops.

I yank on the handle and fling open the door —

when I'm instantly blinded by the two-thousand-lumen blaze of a police spotlight.

I hear tires screeching to a stop, doors popping open, feet hitting the ground.

"FBI!" comes a shout. "Freeze! Show me your goddamn hands!"

CHAPTER 65

I CAN be a cocky son of a bitch. But I'm no fool.

I stop and thrust my "goddamn hands" high into the air.

Then I yell back at the feds, "You're ten minutes early!"

No response from the assembled lawmen. But my eyes are starting to get used to the harsh spotlight. This must be what it's like to be a rock star on stage. There are five black SUVs parked in a rough semicircle at the foot of the narrow bridge. And a ridiculous number of federal agents surrounding me.

One of them is Special Agent Marcus Morgan. He's hunched over, his shoulders stooped. His face can be described with three simple words: tired as shit.

When he sees Angus bound with duct tape and slumped on the ground, his droopy eyes widen into saucers.

"Jesus Christ, Rooney," he says. "You texted my office saying you were *questioning* a suspect. Not beating one to a bloody—"

"Get an assault team over to Holy Cross!" I interrupt. "Now! SWAT, air support, bomb squad, hazmat.

Angus here just gave up tonight's safe house. It's at the corner of Dauphine and Flood."

I don't expect Morgan to start jumping for joy. But I thought he'd do more than just stand there, rubbing his temples and scratching the stubble on his cheeks.

"Did he now?" he asks. "No kidding." Then he calls out to the others, "Hey, everybody, did you hear that? Inspector Wolfgang Puck just saved the day."

His insult rolls right off me. But his sarcasm makes me livid.

"You think this is funny?" I yell at him. "This is the key to stopping the Mardi Gras attack!"

He sighs and twists his head back and forth, like he's trying to loosen muscles and tendons twisted tight from staying up night after night.

"Rooney, listen to yourself," he says, his voice eerily calm. "You tortured a goddamn Nazi into coughing up some half-baked lie. I'm not sending in the cavalry for *that*. Not when it contradicts my own intelligence. And not when my resources are already stretched so god-damn thin."

I can't believe what he's saying. I look over at Angus. At least six agents are surrounding him, restraining him, frisking him, slicing off the duct tape around his wrists and snapping on cuffs. Another six are standing sentry beside Morgan.

"But you'd bring a small army," I ask, "to make one little arrest?"

Morgan replies, "*Two* arrests."

I'm flooded with the warmth of relief. "Thank God!" I exclaim.

When I texted the FBI about my one-on-one with Angus tonight, I also told them everything I'd learned about David Needham. I'm ecstatic Morgan actually paid attention.

"Has that rich bastard said anything yet?" I ask. "Can I get a shot at him? I'm going to guess he lawyered up pretty fast, but—"

"No, you don't get it," he says. "Caleb James Rooney...*you're* under arrest. For obstructing a federal criminal investigation."

Wait. Hang on. Did he just say...

The six other agents on either side of him start to approach me.

Instinctively, I step backward. "I...I'm *what*?!"

He says simply, "You have the right to remain silent."

"Is this a joke? I haven't *obstructed* your investigation. Shit, I did it all *for* you!"

But he continues intoning the Miranda as solemnly as a monk.

"Anything you say can and will be used against you."

His agents keep advancing on me. I see one of them take out a pair of handcuffs, its silver metal glinting in the glare of the spotlight.

"Sir, please turn around," the agent says, "and put your hands behind your back."

No...*no!* This is bullshit of the highest order. Mardi Gras starts tomorrow. I'm closer than ever to bringing Needham to his knees and his sick conspiracy to a close. Like hell am I going to let these suits stop me now.

Which gives me an idea.

Maybe I can bring them *with* me.

"Sir," the agent repeats, louder, "I said turn around and place your hands—"

"All right, fine," I say. And slowly, I obey.

As I do, I look back at my car. I'm only a few feet

from it. The door is ajar. The dome light is on. Since the keys are still dangling from the ignition, a chime is sounding.

I lunge for the vehicle. I dive inside, slam the door behind me, and lock it, all in a single swift move.

Outside I hear muffled, chaotic yelling—drowned out when I start the engine.

Immediately I shift into Drive and stomp on the pedal. The agents scurry out of the way like a flock of startled birds as gravel spews beneath my tires.

Then I shift into Reverse, cut the wheel sharply, and jam the gas even harder.

I roar backward—up and over the arched, narrow bridge. I swerve and scrape against the railing—once, twice—until I get control and straighten out.

As soon as I've crossed the canal, I make a sloppy J-turn. Then I shift back into Drive and tear out of there. Soon I'm speeding along the potholed service road parallel to the waterway, back in the direction I came.

I'm almost giddy with excitement. But after a couple blocks, that feeling starts to fade. Something's wrong.

I slow down a bit and listen. I don't hear any sirens.

I glance in my rearview. I don't see any SUVs.

Seriously?

I was banking on the agents coming after me! My plan was to lead them on a high-speed chase—right to the safe house's doorstep. What the hell just happened?

Maybe Morgan was bluffing about my arrest. Or maybe he didn't think it was worth the effort to go after me, with his resources stretched so thin. I don't know whether to be relieved that he called off the pursuit…or terrified to be on my own.

Screw it. I've made it this far by myself. If Angus

was telling the truth—and I sincerely believe that he was—I'm hitting that safe house.

Apparently, with no support. No backup.

Which means no mistakes.

And no second chances.

CHAPTER 66

FLOOD STREET. Not the smartest name for a road in New Orleans. Like having an "Earthquake Avenue" in San Francisco. Or a "Tornado Boulevard" in Kansas.

But based on Angus's tip, that's where I am. And I've made it here in just thirteen minutes.

I'm still a little unsettled that the feds aren't on my tail. And I'm *really* starting to wish somebody had my back as I drive through this eerily quiet neighborhood. Earlier I tried calling my old boss Cunningham, but my calls go straight to voicemail, and I briefly considered dialing 911 for an NOPD response, but I can't stand the thought of wasted minutes explaining to a dispatcher what I had learned and what was going on.

Like most of the Lower Ninth Ward, Katrina beat Holy Cross to shit. Its namesake—the old Holy Cross School building, built in 1879—was so damaged by the flooding it had to be razed. All these years later, the site is still empty lot. However, the neighborhood's other architectural landmark, its famous Doullut "steamboat houses," a pair of homes that look like old ships, are still standing proudly near the river.

Many of the other homes I drive past, though, aren't

doing that well at all. Some are freshly painted and well maintained, with manicured lawns and glowing porch lights. Others look like crumbling mausoleums, ramshackle and dark.

When I cross Burgundy Street, I tap the brakes. Dauphine Street is just up ahead. The safe house should be around that intersection.

I'm not sure I'll know it when I spot it. I'm not sure what to expect might be inside, either. Maybe a couple of guys just sitting around, talking strategy. Or maybe a couple dozen of them, loading cartridges into magazines. Strapping on body armor. Building bombs.

I take a few deep breaths and scan the sleepy block.

There's nobody out on the sidewalk this late, let alone a stream of folks coming or going from one specific house. I don't see any obvious clusters of parked cars, either. Or any vehicles I recognize, like that maroon Jeep from earlier.

Nearing Dauphine Street now, I do spot two darkened, derelict homes right on the corner. Either one of them could be the place.

One is pretty small, with peeling paint the color of lemon meringue and an overgrown front yard. But in the driveway is a freestanding basketball hoop...with a fresh white net hanging from its rusty rim. That's all the proof I need that someone calls that place home.

The second house is a little bigger, with boarded up windows and a section of roof sagging like a collapsed soufflé. It has a detached garage in back, too, just like the safe house in St. Roch did. This one looks big enough for *two* tractors.

I make a left onto Dauphine to get a look at the vacant building from the side.

Seeping through cracks in one of the boarded-up windows, I glimpse a faint purple glow coming from inside.

A cold tremor runs through my body, head to toe.

Someone's in there.

CHAPTER 67

I PULL over down the block and cut the engine.

Keeping my palm on the grip of my pistol, tucked into my jeans, I crouch low and creep back toward the vacant house.

Here we go.

I tiptoe across the crackly dried brown lawn and up to the window with the light inside. I lean in and try to squint through the cracks.

But I can't see shit.

So I put my ear up to it.

And hear some muffled voices.

My pulse practically doubles as I slowly back away from the window and move around the rear of the house now.

I'm looking for the best way to make a stealth entry, but I don't see any side doors. Guess I only have one option.

When I reach the front porch, I hurry up its rickety wooden steps and lean my back against the wall next to the door—which I see is slightly ajar.

I draw my pistol. Keep it pointed at the ground. And try to steady my nerves.

I've made tactical entries like this a million times

before. But always as part of a team. Usually wearing a Kevlar vest. And *never* with stakes this high.

I squeeze my eyes shut for a moment to silence those noisy thoughts. Before they can return, I nudge the door open a few more inches and steal a peek inside.

The entryway looks clear. No suspects. No trip wires or cameras, either.

Just a hint of that indigo light emanating from somewhere farther inside.

Raising my gun, I push the door open all the way and "slice the pie"—a police technique for spinning while entering a hostile space to maximize cover and visibility.

The moment I step inside, a harsh stench burns my nostrils.

It's not mold or drugs or a rotting body, the stuff you'd expect to find inside a vacant home. It's some kind of industrial-strength chemicals. God only knows what for.

Keeping my sidearm aimed high and my senses sharp, I pad down the dark, claustrophobically narrow hallway. With every step, the wood floor creaks and groans.

I pass by what was once the living room. Empty.

The dining room. Empty.

I round a corner and reach the master bedroom. Empty.

But I can see where the purple light is coming from: the kitchen.

I can hear those garbled voices, too. Sounds like they're speaking…Spanish?

I edge closer. Closer. *Closer*. Until I'm standing right by the kitchen doorway.

I brace myself. I slice the pie again.

"Police!" I yell. "Don't move!"

I'm gut-struck by what I see.

Nothing and nobody.

Huh?

The whole kitchen has a ghostly violet hue—thanks to a portable camping lantern with a tinted bulb resting on one of the counters.

And those Spanish-speakers, it turns out, are just voices from a radio call-in show, wafting from a cheap plastic boom box nearby.

I moan with rage *and* despair. Deep and guttural.

This place *was* the safe house! Something *was* going on in here!

But *what*?

I glance around the bizarre scene, scanning for any clues.

I realize my fingernails and the threads in my clothes are glowing white, which tells me the tinted bulb is probably a UV black light.

But why? I thought these bastards were building a bomb, not a nightclub.

And how come they just left all this shit in here? Did they rush out in a hurry and forget it? Or was it intentional, some kind of calling card, a cryptic message for whoever found it?

None of it makes any sense.

Any goddamn sense at all.

In a fit of fury, I sweep the radio off the counter and stomp on it. It shatters into pieces, making the voices sound garbled and distorted. I hit it again with my foot and the voices stop.

My head starts to throb. My knees begin to wobble.

I sink to the filthy linoleum floor. Drowning in helplessness and desperation.

My investigation just hit another dead end.
The trail has run bone-dry.
I can't move. I can't think. I can't even stand.
I've got nothing.
Nothing at all.
And Mardi Gras is just hours away.

CHAPTER 68

"SORRY, SIR, we're closed."

The valet is waving his hands at me as I step out of my car.

I'm parked in front of Petite Amie, the Garden District saloon-turned-bistro owned by Billy Needham, David's cousin. He's the guy who comped me that incredible meal a week ago.

He's also the one who told me about all the strife and discord tearing his family apart. About David's paranoia. His threats of violence.

Billy's the reason I tumbled down this rabbit hole in the first place. Coming here tonight is a Hail Mary, but maybe he can help me claw my way out.

"That's okay," I say to the valet. "I'm not here to eat."

I approach the restaurant's glass façade, cup my hands around my eyes and peer inside. The ornate chandeliers and the house lights are on. The wait staff, typically prim and proper in front of diners, are chatting casually with one another as they sweep the floors and strip the tables.

I give the locked door a few knocks to get the attention of a busboy stacking chairs nearby. He glances at me, then ignores me. I knock again. Harder.

"Hey!" I call through the glass. "You. Yeah, you. Listen, I gotta talk to your boss. Tell Billy Caleb Rooney's outside. It's urgent. As in, *life or death* urgent."

The busboy's indifference morphs into concern. He stops stacking chairs, hesitates, then steps away and walks through the dining room toward the kitchen.

Seconds turn to minutes. As I wait, I think. About the winding path that brought me to this desperate moment. And about what exactly I'm going to say to Billy.

How the hell do you tell a man you barely know that, thanks to him, you've come to believe his cousin is a terrorist?

Here he comes, emerging from the kitchen, wiping his hands on his apron. As Billy unlocks the door and lets me in, his face is a mask of worry.

"Caleb," he says. "Hi. Is everything all right?"

"Hey, Billy. Why don't we have a drink. Because it's not. Not by a mile."

From the foyer showing the celebrity grip-and-grin pictures and his personal flying photographs, he ushers me over to his restaurant's shiny mahogany bar. As I take a seat, he steps around behind it.

"I already cut my bartender for the night," he says. "What can I get you? I'm not much of a mixologist, but I can make a mean Ramos gin fizz if you're in the mood for—"

"Just the house bourbon. A double. You'll probably want one for yourself, too."

He pours our booze and slides onto a stool beside me. He holds up his glass to clink, but I keep mine on the bar. I swirl it, searching for words in the amber liquid.

"When's the last time you talked to David?" I ask.

He scrunches his brow.

"My cousin?" he asks. "I don't know. A couple weeks ago, I guess. Why?"

I say, "I don't get the sense you two are very close. How well do you really know him? And do you have any idea what he's really capable of?"

"I'm not sure I'm following," he says, looking puzzled.

I take my first bracing sip of bourbon, the liquid sharp and hot on my tongue.

"After you and I spoke the other day, I started doing some digging," I say. "Into your family and its troubles. I spoke to Emily up at her horse farm. I pored over your company's finances. It kept leading me back to David. All of it."

"*What* kept leading back to David?" he asks.

"I was working off a good tip. That a terrorist cell was looking to strike on Mardi Gras."

Now I've got his attention, 100 percent. "Oh, my God…"

"I wanted to find out who was behind it," I say. "What they were planning. Where their money was coming from. Turns out…"

I swallow another gulp of bourbon.

"It's a complex web that I still don't fully understand," I say. "They've got multiple shell companies to hide their cash. Islamic extremists working with white supremacists. I don't get it. I've barely scratched the surface…"

I take the crumpled photograph of David and Farzat out of my pocket and set it down on the wooden bar top.

"…but your cousin keeps popping up at the center of it, again and again."

He blanches. He picks up the photo like it might bite him and looks at it closely.

"This is one of the bad guys?" he asks.

"*Was*. A radicalized Islamist who was recently tortured and killed. David was secretly funneling money to him through a crooked nonprofit."

He's gently shaking his head in disbelief.

"This…this is…insane!" he says. "Have you confronted David about all this?"

"Plenty of times," I say. "But he's a slippery son of a bitch. And that team of Israeli bodyguards he's got doesn't make him an easy person to get to."

"Tell me about it," he says. "Those guys are nuts. I took David hunting about a year ago on some land I own up in Bossier Parish? A few of them tagged along. They make the Secret Service look like a troop of Girl Scouts. They were on high alert, always suspicious, scanning the area, like they couldn't stand having anyone armed next to their client."

I nod. "I'm worried they're part of the plot, too. I just don't know. And the police, the FBI—I've told 'em everything, but no one's doing shit."

Now it's Billy's turn to sip his drink, though a desperate gulp would probably be more accurate.

"I…I can't believe what I'm hearing, Caleb," he says. "But I do believe *you*. David always seemed a little eccentric. Paranoid. Intense. I had no idea he was…a monster."

He rests a shaky hand on my shoulder.

"If there's anything I can do, anything at all…"

I say, "At this point, I don't know what *any* of us can do. Except listen. If you do talk to him…if he says anything suspicious, anything out of the ordinary…I need you to let me know. Okay? Let the cops and feds know, too."

"Of course," he says. "Absolutely."

He reaches into his apron's pocket and takes out a business card and pen. He scribbles something on the back and hands it to me.

"And let me know, too," he says. "If you learn or need anything more. That's my number. Call anytime, day or night. Jesus...you know, hearing that, it tempts me just to close up shop tomorrow and take up my Cessna, get away from it all. It's amazing how clean and safe everything looks when you're ten thousand feet up. But now..."

He wipes at his mahogany bar with his fingers, like he was trying to always remember the touch of this polished and safe wood.

"But I won't run, and I won't fly away," he says firmly. "But on the other hand, before you came in, I didn't think I'd be getting much sleep tonight anyway. Now I *know* I won't."

I take his card with one hand. With the other, I toss back the rest of my bourbon.

"Billy," I say, "that makes two of us."

CHAPTER 69

I STEP out of the restaurant and into the warm, peaceful night. All around me, a gentle breeze is whispering through the trees, many of them draped with colorful streamers and beads.

But inside of me, a storm is raging.

I did everything I could—and damnit, it still wasn't enough. To stop David. To disrupt his plot. To convince the FBI. To protect my city.

And now it might be too late.

I'm practically shaking with rage as I walk back to my car. A slideshow of gruesome images starts flashing through my head. Smoke. Blood. Crying. Screaming. The unknown horrors that tomorrow's attack could bring.

I squeeze my eyes shut, willing the images to go away. No luck.

The rest of my body is aching from exhaustion and stress. It's craving sleep more than oxygen. I should go home. Go to bed. Before I go crazy.

But I can't. Not yet.

I might not be able to save everybody. I'm starting to accept that fact.

But I *can* still warn them.

Especially the people who mean the most to me.

I pull onto the street heading north, then turn right onto St. Charles Avenue. Cars are flowing smoothly tonight, but tomorrow, the only traffic allowed on this road will be floats and the tractors pulling them. Driving along this section of the parade route feels creepy. Ominous. I'm visiting the scene of a crime— before it happens.

I don't stay on St. Charles for long. After a few blocks, I've entered the Lower Garden District. I turn right and wend my way through the neighborhood's narrow, leafy streets. I stop in front of a terraced town house, beige with lavender shutters.

It belongs to Vanessa and Lucas.

I cut the engine. My dashboard clock blinks from 11:46 to 11:47.

Which gives me pause.

Am I really going to show up on her doorstep like this, this late at night, when her buffoon of a husband is probably there, too? Is this really the smartest move?

I exhale. I drum my fingers on my steering wheel. I shut my eyes again.

Before I can change my mind, I get out of my car and walk up the path.

I ring the doorbell, wait, ring it again. A third time.

The house looks dark inside. Maybe they're not home?

Then a second-floor light flips on. The bedroom, as I fondly recall.

I hear footsteps creaking down the stairs. Locks and bolts being turned.

The door swings open.

Lucas is standing there, wearing nothing but a pair of gray boxer shorts and a bleary-eyed, indignant look.

"Rooney...?" he asks. "What the hell do you think—"

"Is Vanessa here?" I ask without hesitation. "I gotta talk to her."

He tries to puff up his chest to look intimidating, but he only looks pathetic.

"Now? It's practically midnight! She's asleep. My *wife* is *asleep*. So unless you—"

"It's urgent," I say. "Sorry."

I take a step forward into the house and give him a firm shove out of my way. He nearly topples sideways into a blue-and-white vase on the small entry table near the door.

"Hey! Don't you dare come inside my—"

"Vanessa!" I call. "Vanessa? Wake up!"

"Caleb?"

I follow her wispy voice to the top of the stairs. She's wearing a knee-length plain white T-shirt, her hair in a messy bun. She scurries down to me, frightened.

"What's going on?" she asks, worried. "Is everything all right?"

"No!" he interrupts. "Everything is definitely *not* all—"

"Would you shut the hell up for one second?" I demand.

Then I turn back to her, softening my tone.

"Listen to me," I say, the words tumbling out. "I have to tell you something. And I wouldn't have come if it weren't important—and if I...if I didn't care about you."

I grip her shoulders. Partly to calm her, partly to steady myself.

"You need to leave the city," I say. "As soon as you can. Promise me, okay?"

"What?" she asks, wiping at her sleepy eyes. "Why?"

"Something's going to happen tomorrow. And, and…"

"And what?" she says, now coming more fully awake. "What kind of thing—"

"I've been working a case. Terrorism. Someone's plotting an attack on Mardi Gras."

In shock, she covers her face with her hands.

"Oh, my God," she whispers. "What kind of attack?"

"Maybe a bombing," I say. "Or a nerve agent. There might be snipers on rooftops. Or some kind of rampage. Damnit, I don't know! I don't know when, either. Or where. So what I'm saying is, you have to leave. You can't be anywhere near this thing when—"

"Lucas!" she yells. "No!"

CHAPTER 70

OUT OF the corner of my eye I see Lucas coming up behind me.

Actually, I see his *reflection* — in the rectangular, floor-level mirror built into the wall of the entryway.

It's not an uncommon feature in this kind of old, fancy New Orleans home. High-society ladies once used it to make sure their ankles and hoop skirts weren't showing before they stepped out on the town.

Tonight, this mirror designed for fashion is now being used both tactically *and* defensively.

I glimpse him, his face twisted with anger, holding the blue-and-white porcelain vase that was resting on the entry table. In what feels like slow motion, I watch him get closer. Raise the vase. Lunge at me.

Timing it just right, I duck and spin around. I weave like a boxer to avoid the blow. Then I grab his wrists and shove him hard against the wall. The vase slips to the floor and shatters. He grunts. Whimpers. Crumples to the floor.

"You sad, sad little man," I say with a shake of my head.

"Me?" he tries to protest. "You…you're the one… messing around with my wife!"

I take a step toward him, towering over him.

I've put up with his bullshit long enough.

"Wife? She's your *prisoner*. You've been controlling her for years. And everyone here knows it."

"What the hell are you talking about?" he demands, scurrying back, still sitting on the entryway floor.

But he's just playing dumb. Between the rumors that Gordon dug up and everything I've learned from Vanessa — her scars, her sobriety, her distress — I've put all the pieces together.

It's time the truth came out.

"Vanessa was a waitress in one of your restaurants the first time you met her," I say. "Barely out of high school. Practically still a girl. You pursued her, for months. She turned you down. Again and again. But you just wouldn't accept it. You started getting angry. Desperate. Doing a little digging. And that's when you found out about her *condition* — and saw your chance."

His stony façade begins to shift.

To that of a guilty suspect, realizing he's in a corner.

He looks ridiculous, defeated, no longer dressed in fine clothes, no longer glowing from a man-made tan. He looks flabby, out of shape, pitiful.

"You learned your beautiful new employee had chronic cirrhosis of the liver," I go on. "Since childhood. She needed a transplant, a lifetime of expensive medication. It would cost this poor girl a small fortune that you knew she didn't have. So you offered to step in and cover it. Pay for everything. Even pay for a college education as your newlywed. But your actual price was even higher."

Behind me, I hear Vanessa stifle a sob. Lucas grows incensed.

"I saw a woman in need," he nearly shouts. "I gave her some help!"

"You gave her a *pre-nup,* you piece of shit," I shoot back. "That says if she leaves you, she gets nothing. Except bills she can't pay, treatment she can't afford. She doesn't love you, Lucas. She's *shackled* to you. A divorce would cost her her *life*."

His eyes start to well up with distress and humiliation. For once, he doesn't have a bitter comeback. He simply hangs his head. "I'm so sorry," he mumbles, sniffling and wiping away a tear. "I'll set things right. I...I'm so ashamed."

I turn back to Vanessa, who is blotting her own eyes. "So?" I say softly. "Yes or no? Are you going to leave?"

"Leave the city? Or leave...?"

"Both," I reply.

I hold out my hand.

Praying she reaches out and takes it.

CHAPTER 71

I'M WOKEN up by a faint buzz from my phone. In the pitch black of this strange bedroom, I grope for it, groggy and still half-asleep.

I find my phone and check the screen. A text.

10-19. ONE HOUR.

It was sent from a blocked number.

I sit up in bed. Rubbing my eyes. I read it again, trying to make sense of it.

"10-19" is police radio code for "return to station." One hour from now would be about 6 a.m.

But what the hell does it *mean*?

Is it a joke? A mistake? A trap? Who sent it to me? Why now?

It *could* be an old friend inside the NOPD who wants to share a tip on his turf. Maybe even Cunningham.

Or maybe it's Morgan, trying to lure me out of hiding so he can arrest me for real.

Whatever it is, I have to give the sender credit. My curiosity is piqued.

Trap or not, I have to learn more. Today is Mardi Gras, and I can't risk not responding.

I slip out of bed and into the pair of jeans and wrinkled black T-shirt lying nearby on the floor. I try to be as quiet as I can. But apparently, not quiet enough.

"Where are you going?"

Vanessa stirs awake under the covers. Even in the bedroom's darkness, I can see her worried face.

"Nowhere. Won't be gone long. Go back to sleep."

But she grasps my hand, pulls me down beside her.

"Not fair," she says. "No more secrets between us. No more lies. I thought that's what we promised each other, didn't we?"

I nod. We made that vow only hours ago, on the drive from her house to this place.

"I'm following up a possible new lead," I say. "At police headquarters. That's where I'm going and that's all I know. I swear."

She stares at me for a moment. Then gently touches my cheek.

"Just be careful, okay? If something happened to you, Caleb…"

She trails off. Swallows hard.

"I will," I answer. "Tonight. Tomorrow. Always."

We share a brief kiss. Then I rise from the bed. I take my Smith & Wesson from the top of the nightstand. Tuck it into my jeans.

"Vanessa, I can't stand thinking of something happening to you," I say. "Please reconsider…please leave the city. It's not safe here."

"Are you staying?" she asks.

"You know I am."

She burrows herself back into the sheets. "Then I know I'll be safe, Caleb. Always."

And so I leave.

The drive at this hour from this little house to the police station should only take around ten minutes.

Since I've got about fifty more to kill, I make a pit stop into this stranger's kitchen, and spend a few minutes doing a food-related recon. Not bad.

This home doesn't belong to me. It's owned by my PI friend, Gordon Andrews. He uses it as a secret spot to meet with clients who don't want to be seen in public or his office with him, or who need a safe place to hide out during a crisis. A call to him once I left with Vanessa led him to offering this home to me, as long as I wanted, which was probably going to be as long as the FBI was pissed at me.

He's as much of a foodie as I am, and though he leans to the, er, alcoholic side of "food and beverage," he's outdone himself with what he has in the larder.

I fire up the stove and boil a fresh pot of savory grits. Once they're simmering, I drown them in heavy cream, garlic butter, and aged Parmesan cheese.

Meanwhile, I whisk a few eggs with chunks of smoked andouille sausage and diced green pepper, and make a tasty Cajun-style scramble.

When both dishes are done, I plate them, add a parsley sprig garnish, and stick them in the warming drawer of the oven along with a scribbled Post-it to try to lighten the mood:

Dear Vanessa, Eat me.

I don't have much of an appetite this morning, but I force down a couple bites of a toasted baguette smeared with creole tomato-basil jam. I chase it with some coffee with chicory. Then, at a quarter to six, I hit the road.

The streets, as I expected, are practically deserted. Only a smattering of city sanitation workers are out, sweeping up the mounds of beads, empty cups, and other debris clogging the sidewalks and gutters. It's the calm before the storm.

I park on Gravier Street, alongside the granite fortress that used to be my second home. I trudge up the stone steps. I enter the glass-walled lobby.

I look around, not sure who—or what—I'm expecting. I see a few third-shift officers ambling through. And a couple civilians in the waiting area, many in flamboyant costumes, all of them passed out drunk.

I check my watch. It's a few minutes before six. *Now what?*

I wait. I fidget. I twiddle my thumbs. I rub my temples.

Just as I'm starting to wonder if this whole thing was a bust, I hear a hoarse voice call to me: "Rooney. Good. You made it."

CHAPTER 72

CUNNINGHAM SLOWLY walks along the corridor before the empty sergeant's desk. His clothes are stained, rumpled, and his weary eyes look like they're about to shut from exhaustion in mid-step. A couple of cops I've met on the force have served in Afghanistan or Iraq prior to joining the NOPD, and they've mentioned the look a soldier gets after hours of threats and combat, with no relief in sight: the thousand-yard stare.

He has that haunted look.

"Come on back," he says, voice weary. "We're about to get started."

My former boss turns and shuffles down the building's central corridor. I follow and wait a few seconds for some kind of explanation. It doesn't come.

So I ask: "Chief, what's going on?"

Cunningham starts to reply and then a coughing fit chokes his voice for a moment. Then he clears his throat and says, "Don't say 'I told ya so,' but I really wish I'd listened to you. Wish I'd given you more resources. Wish I hadn't caved to all the politics. Wish I'd pushed back harder when the Federal Bureau of *Ignorance* shoved us locals aside."

I take zero satisfaction in his words. I didn't agree to

help him because of pride—or out of spite. I wanted to serve my city. Do the right thing.

"You were under a lot of pressure, Chief. I get it."

He shrugs.

"Well, now the feds are trying to play nice. Probably 'cause they don't have shit. I think they're as scared about this whole thing as we are."

We reach the main bank of elevators. But we don't stop. I assumed we were going up to his fourth-floor office. Guess not. So where *are* we going?

"You've been doing some first-rate work, Rooney—blindfolded and hog-tied as you were," he says. "You've more than earned a spot at this table. The least I can do is offer you a seat."

I don't have a clue what "table" or "seat" Cunningham is talking about. I'm about to ask when we round a corner.

I see a uniformed officer standing outside the door of the first-floor briefing room.

The same room where the department's Use of Force Review Board hung me out to dry on my last day as a cop.

Seeing us approaching, the officer nods at Cunningham and opens the door.

Inside, the mood is somber. Tense. Like a wake without a casket.

Dozens of law enforcement officials of every stripe are milling around the spacious auditorium, making worried small talk.

A number of them are NOPD bigwigs. Like Superintendent Robert Fontaine, the white-mustachioed head of the entire force. I also recognize a couple deputy superintendents, whose departments include the bomb squad, the K9 unit, and the NOPD's tactical platoons—a.k.a., New Orleans SWAT.

I see plenty of folks I *don't* recognize, too. Some are in suits. Some wear black blazers with "New Orleans Fire Department" patches on the shoulder. Others are dressed in Louisiana State Police and Orleans Parish Sheriff's Office uniforms.

I slowly begin to realize what I've just walked into.

A high-level, inter-agency, emergency security briefing.

"Is this some kind of goddamn *joke?*" a familiar voice cries out.

Agent Morgan—jacket off, sleeves rolled up, tie loose—is standing on stage beside a giant map of the city. He's glaring at me, his jaw halfway to his knees.

"Your pathetic *investigation* is the goddamn joke," I fire back.

"Enough!" Cunningham yells. "Jesus Christ, let's everybody cut the schoolyard shit and focus, all right?"

I take a seat and settle in—for the most *unsettling* ninety minutes of my life.

Agent Morgan glares at me one more time, and then his team proceed to walk us through, in meticulous detail, how the FBI plans to protect the roughly one million people expected to fill the streets for the day-long, city-wide extravaganza.

Morgan is doing his best to project a sense of calm and confidence. But it's obvious that Cunningham was right.

The feds are clueless. And scared shitless. Just like the rest of us.

In addition to setting up a dedicated inter-agency communication hotline, Morgan explains that seventy-five extra federal agents flew in from DC to assist. They'll be posted up and down the parade routes, both in uniform and plain clothes.

Infrared CCTV cameras have been temporarily installed around the French Quarter and surrounding areas. The footage will be fed, in real-time, through a state-of-the-art piece of facial recognition software developed by the NSA, known as EnVision.

Tactical drones—civilian versions of the kind used by American soldiers in Afghanistan and Iraq—will also be deployed to provide additional eyes in the sky.

Morgan's voice has grown hoarse by the time he shares the final, and most chilling, component of the FBI's security plan.

Eleven highly-sensitive "particle detectors" have also been installed around the city, on loan from Homeland Security. About the size of a loaf of bread, they're designed to detect airborne radioactive particles.

Just in case—*God help us*—the terrorists are planning to set off a "dirty bomb."

"Agent Morgan?" I interrupt, shooting to my feet. "Hang on. You're really telling us there could be a goddamn *nuke* here in New Orleans? That—that's madness!"

The audience grumbles in agreement. Morgan narrows his gaze at me.

"What I'm telling you is, there's a chance. Slim, but real. And I'd rather us be overcautious than underprepared. Any other questions before we move on?"

I think, *that's it?*

That's all there is?

"Hold on," I cry out. "That's it? Morgan"—and I deliberately leave his title out as an insult—"you owe the folks in this room and the citizens of New Orleans the truth."

"Look, Rooney, there's no time—"

"Time? You've been wasting time! For Christ's sake,

what about Ibrahim Farzat, the Syrian refugee who was tortured to death? Who was with an Islamic-based charity group that's a cover for a terrorist organization? An organization supported by a local businessman? Hell, yesterday I caught an Aryan Brotherhood member involved in the plot and practically dropped him in your useless lap!"

Morgan looks both exhausted and infuriated, and before I can announce David Needham's connection, Superintendent Fontaine steps up next to Morgan like a baseball manager protecting his star pitcher.

"Rooney, that's it," he bellows. "You shouldn't be here, not at all, despite what your former boss says."

"But I—"

Fontaine holds up a hand, like a traffic cop trying to stop an out-of-control vehicle—*me!*—coming his way. "Special Agent Morgan has kept us all briefed on their investigation, including the little bits of confusion and misdirection you've come up with…which hasn't been corroborated or found to have any merit. So before you slander a prominent member of our business community and waste additional time, I suggest you sit down and keep your mouth shut."

There's a murmur of disapproval from my former comrades-in-arms, and I feel a savage sense of contentment that at least *they're* backing me up.

Fontaine adds, "Anything else…Rooney?"

"More of a suggestion," I say grimly, sitting down. "Maybe we should move this briefing to a church. It's going to take a miracle to get us through Mardi Gras without blood in the streets."

CHAPTER 73

"HURRY UP on those waddles! And gimme more crunchies, quacks, and meows!"

I do my best to obey Marlene and pick up the pace. But hunched over the sizzling-hot stove, I'm already working faster than I ever have in my life.

My knife and spatula are a blur as I whip up sautéed gator sausages, fried shrimp po'boys, seared duck breast, and our ridiculously popular blackened catfish sandwiches. I slide them across the counter conveyor belt–style, nonstop, one after the other.

"You heard the woman, Caleb," a fresh voice says. "Quit slacking off."

I feel a friendly elbow to the ribs from Killer Chef's newest employee: an accomplished fine-dining restaurant manager with many years of experience and impeccable credentials, who was looking to make a mid-career change.

Yep, you got it right. Vanessa.

Wearing a Killer Chef T-shirt cinched at the waist and a red bandana tied around her hair, she's wrapping sandwiches in wax paper, bundling them with napkins, and helping hand them out to the hordes of hungry revelers swarming our truck. Her early years as a waitress are paying off: She's managing the lunchtime madness like a pro.

"Is that any way to talk to your new boss?" I ask her with a smile.

"Uh-oh, is my new boss going to have to…*punish* me?"

Marlene calls out, "Hey, you two, save the flirting for your own time, wouldja?"

I put my head down and get back to work. I'm grateful to have these two amazing women by my side—even though I'd begged them both not to be here.

I pleaded with Vanessa and Marlene to leave the city before Mardi Gras or at least stay home, safe and out of the way. I told them the risks they'd be facing, the danger they'd be putting themselves in. Vanessa just repeated what she had said earlier: if I was staying, so was she. And she showed up this morning to work the brunch shift and join our Killer Chef team.

As for my ex-wife, Marlene just laughed in my face.

"Let 'em blow me up," she said. "What do I care?"

Dark humor. Typical. But then she shook her head and grew serious.

"No," she said. "No goddamn way am I staying home. It takes more than a couple of crazy assholes to scare me off, especially on our busiest day of the year. Killer Chef is going to be feeding folks on Mardi Gras, Caleb, whether you like it or not."

God bless her. I couldn't say no.

I take a break from my frenzied cooking for a few seconds to wipe my brow, pop a fiery jalapeño down my throat, and steal a glance out the service window.

We're parked on Bienville Street, in the heart of the

French Quarter, just a few blocks away from the parade route along Canal. With live jazz blaring from every direction, the scene is a mix of total debauchery and utter joy.

Thousands of people have jammed the narrow streets wearing colorful, crazy costumes. Beads swinging from their necks, boozy beverages sloshing in their hands, they're dancing, clapping, singing, laughing—having the time of their lives.

The energy is electric. The city is pulsing with life.

Mardi Gras in New Orleans is the greatest damn party on earth, hands-down. And if this were any other year, I'd be joining in the fun. Sipping a fluorescent hurricane while I worked, to get a little buzz going. Grooving along with the music. Feeding my dear customers, either old-timers or lucky tourists tasting my special food for the very first time.

But today, I'm tenser than a guitar string. I feel jumpy. Nervous. On edge.

I've been trying to put on a brave face. For Vanessa, for Marlene, for our happy customers crowding in front of our service window. Trying to force the bad thoughts out of my head by focusing on my food.

But it's just for show.

All I can think about is David Needham and his attack. And the utter ignorance and incompetence of Special Agent Morgan and NOPD Superintendent Fontaine.

It's barely noon; the day is just getting started. Anything could still happen. Anywhere. To anyone. At any moment.

"You okay, Caleb?" Vanessa asks, resting a hand on my shoulder. "You look—"

"Yeah. I...yeah, I'm fine. I need a little air."

Without waiting for a snarky comeback from Marlene, I hang up my apron. I check that my pistol is still tucked into my belt. And I hustle out of the truck.

I just couldn't stay cooped up in there any longer.

Not when the fate of my city is hanging by a colorful thread.

CHAPTER 74

MUNCHING NERVOUSLY on my jalapeños, I make my way into the teeming crowds.

I turn and head north on Bienville. The noise and music are getting louder. The mobs are getting even wilder. The partying even more super-extreme.

I pass people wearing flashy wigs. Funky hats. Flowing capes.

Dressed in togas. In Saints jerseys. In drag.

I see people break dancing. Making out. Throwing up.

Men and women, young and old, of every race and creed on earth, all united by a love of drink and song and life.

All packed together like sardines, flesh pressed against drunken flesh.

Good God, I think. *This is a tinderbox just waiting to explode.*

Anybody around me could be hiding a weapon or suicide vest under their costume—and no one would have any idea.

I hook a left onto Bourbon Street, ground zero for Mardi Gras.

At least I try to. The two short blocks from here to Canal Street look like one gigantic mosh pit. It's a sea of purple, green, and gold, with people jammed together so tightly, they can barely move.

But I'm not turning back. I nudge folks aside and start weaving my way through, toward the parade.

In the distance, I begin to make out some passing floats—most pulled by big-wheeled tractors like the kind in the St. Roch safe house garage.

Again, why in hell were Agent Morgan and Supervisor Fontaine being so stubborn in pooh-poohing the evidence I've uncovered? Is it because of the way I left the NOPD? Because I'm "just" a chef now?

Each of the slow-moving, grumbling floats is a giant, multi-leveled, elaborately decorated creation that could easily be packed with hundreds of pounds of explosives, stuffed with a deadly mix of screws, nails, and other scrap metal.

And each float is carrying a dozen or so crazy-costumed performers, hurling beads and trinkets at the exuberant crowds.

The performers are all wearing masks, too. It's actually illegal in New Orleans to ride a float without one. That strange law is a holdover from a different time, meant to encourage people to let loose on Mardi Gras by covering their faces.

Today, it just makes it easier for terrorists to hide their identities.

I finally reach the sidewalk along Canal Street and get my best view of the parade yet. I take out the pair of collapsible field binoculars I brought with me and start inspecting every tractor, float, and character that passes by.

I scan the crowds, too. As many of them as I can.

I even give a once-over to the NOPD cops dotted along the street, just in case.

So far, nothing suspicious.

True, I don't know what I'm looking for.

But I'll know it when I see it.

Minutes go by. Nothing.

More minutes pass. Still nothing.

The binoculars are getting damp in my clammy hands.

I can feel my heart beating a little bit faster, my breath getting shallow.

My cop instincts are kicking in.

But why? What for?

I see something yellow up ahead, and then something else. And again.

Three guys, wearing the colors of the Franklin Avenue Soldiers, taking a break from dealing drugs and shooting their rivals to enjoy the day. *Oh, great,* I think. With everything that's going on, do I need to hide now from these revenge-minded gangbangers?

I almost feel like going up to them and saying, "Take a number, fellas!" when the crowd surges, surrounds them, and then they disappear.

Good.

Suddenly, I feel a hard shove from behind. My binoculars slip from my grip and clatter to the sidewalk.

"Ohhhh, shit, sorry," says a bottle-blonde in skintight jeans and a stained Saints T-shirt who just stumbled into me and spilled her beer on my jeans. "I'm a little trunk. I mean, *drunk,*" she giggles.

"It's okay," I answer, picking up my binoculars and giving my wet pants a pat. "Don't worry about it. Happy Mardi…"

I jump as something starts vibrating in my pocket.

My phone, set on vibrate. With all the music, shouting, and tractor noise, there's no way I would have heard it ringing.

I turn from the drunk woman and look at the screen.

My PI friend, Gordon Andrews.

I shove a finger into my left ear, bring the phone up to my right.

"Hello!" I shout.

"…him."

"What? Gordon, I can't hear you!"

I close my eyes, trying to focus on what he's saying.

The message comes in clearer this time as he shouts at me. "I said, I found him! On Bourbon, between Canal and Iberville."

Less than fifty feet away from where I'm standing among the happy chaos.

"How? Did you hack his phone?"

Even among the horns and music, I hear him laugh. "The narcissistic son of a bitch just posted a selfie on Facebook. Go, Caleb, go!"

I slide the phone back into my pocket, push and shove, and—

I don't believe it. But there he is.

David Needham.

Standing in the crowd about thirty feet away, right where Gordon told me he'd be.

Flanked by two Israeli bodyguards.

Watching the parade with the icy smile of a shark about to attack.

CHAPTER 75

THE SIGHT of Needham makes my fists clench—
and my mind race.

What the hell is he doing here?

Maybe he's come to direct the attack from the
ground, like a general.

Or maybe he wants to watch the carnage in person.
Like a psychopath.

Doesn't matter. If I can get to him, maybe I can still
stop him.

Maybe it's not too late after all.

I start elbowing my way through the rowdy horde
of spectators standing between us. Despite all the commotion, I'm still careful not to draw too much attention
to myself. Like a hummingbird flying through a hurricane, I get shoved and jostled with every step. But I
keep going, gaze fixed on Needham like a spotlight.

I'm just a few yards away from him and his two
bodyguards when I see him check his Rolex. He shuts
his eyes. Then takes out his phone.

No! He could be about to call in the attack, or
remote-detonate a bomb himself.

I have to make my move. *Now.*

I pick up my pace and start to charge toward him

from behind. I'm practically shoving people out of my way as I go.

Just as his bodyguards realize I'm closing in, I lunge at one and stomp the back of his kneecap, hard. His leg buckles; he collapses to the sidewalk.

"Rooney?" Needham exclaims, flinching in horror. "What the hell do you think—"

Before his second bodyguard can intervene, I head-butt Needham in the nose.

Then I swat his phone out of his hand, sending it skittering to the ground. It disappears somewhere beneath the feet of the boisterous crowd.

Whipping out my pistol, I grab Needham by his collar. Step in close so no one else can see. And jam the hard steel of my gun into his belly.

"Tell your men to back off or I shoot!" I shout into his ear. "Tell them!"

His face has turned as white as vanilla buttercream frosting. His nose is a spigot of blood, oozing down his upper lip. With a nervous flick of his chin, he signals to his second bodyguard to stand down.

"Now call off the attack, you piece of shit!" I shout again. "Give me the details and call it off!"

"Attack?" he says, puzzled. "What attack? What are you talking a—"

I dig my pistol deeper into his gut.

"I know about everything, David," I say. "The threats you've been making. Your hit squad of ex-Mossad thugs. I know about the money you've been giving to Islamic radicals. I even found a goddamn picture of you mugging with a murdered terrorist!"

"I, I, I," he stammers. "I can explain. Honest to Christ…"

"Bullshit!" I say, my voice loud, the hand holding my

pistol firm. "Lies! That's all I've ever gotten from you. It stops right now."

"Okay...fine...just calm down," he pleads.

I feel his body trembling, hear his jagged breathing. His bodyguards are still watching me with sharp, experienced eyes.

"Do I run my mouth sometimes?" he says. "Sure. But I wouldn't hurt a fly. Ask my line cooks: I don't even have the stomach to marinate raw meat. And yes, of course I'm going to have top-notch personal security. I run a restaurant group worth over sixty million—"

"What about Crescent Care?" I demand. "What about Farzat? You lied to me!"

"Because I was ashamed!" he cries out. "My cousin told me about the group. I thought they were a legitimate organization! I even catered some of their events! Ibrahim and I became friends. When I heard about his death, about all the rumors, I was horrified. I had no idea who he really was—or where my money might have been going. If he or anybody else were planning something, I don't know anything about it, I swear!"

I hold his gaze for a few seconds, boring into his beady eyes. It's not easy to get a read on this bastard, especially with all the music and cheering around us.

But something inside of me...*tells me he's finally being honest*.

His admission feels genuine, his explanation reasonable, his terror real.

I remember Billy telling me something similar about Emily. How she convinced all of them to invest in that socially progressive café on Freret Street—the place that gave Farzat his first job in America and helped him resettle here.

Emily. Oh, my God.

Is *she* the Needham I should have been focusing on this whole time?

But then why would she have given me total access to her family company's finances? And why would she admit the FBI was trying to get a warrant for them?

Unless...it was all misdirection? My mind reels at the possibility.

Unless she *wanted* me to link David with Farzat to take the heat off of herself.

Unless she's been hiding right in front of me this whole time.

"When did you last talk to her?" I ask, tightening my grip on Needham's collar. "Where the hell is she now? Tell me!"

"When did I talk to whom?" he says, eyes wide, his upper lip covered with blood from his broken nose.

"Emily, damnit! Your cousin who tricked you into funding terrorists!"

Needham crinkles his bloodied face.

"We had dinner a few nights ago. She's in the city for Mardi Gras. But it was *Billy* who told me about Crescent Care. He and I...we haven't spoken in months."

CHAPTER 76

BILLY. *BILLY*.

The name rings inside my head like a death knell.

I try to think back to the first time I sat down with him. He was so friendly that night. Maybe too friendly. The lavish comped meal, the bottomless wine. He was so helpful, too. So honest.

Was it all a ploy?

He was quick to confirm rumors of discord within his family's empire—then even quicker to direct my attention to David, who he said was dangerous and unhinged.

He was the first one to get me curious about the Needhams' finances—by saying how juicy they were. If he'd misled David into giving money to an extremist group, he'd know I would eventually discover that—and his cousin would look even guiltier.

He even admitted to having a personal connection to Farzat—as an investor in the café where he worked!

Billy. Billy. It's all starting to make sense.

I bark at Needham, "Don't go anywhere!" as I let go of his shirt and slip my handgun back into my jeans.

Then I grope my pockets, looking for the business

card Billy gave me. The one with his number scrawled on the back.

I find it, still in my pocket from last night. I take out my phone and frantically dial.

"Who are you calling?" David asks with dread. "What's going on? Do you think my cousin could be—"

"Shut up!" I snap, and cup my free hand over my exposed ear.

Conditions are already bad for making a call, and they're only getting worse. A marching band is rounding the corner a few blocks away. They're blaring "When the Saints Go Marching In" and the crowd is starting to joyously sing along.

"Oh when the saints…"

"Come on, come on," I whisper as the line rings and rings. "Answer, answer!"

"…go marching in…"

If Billy's the one behind the attack, of course he's not going to come out and admit it over the phone. I know that. But if I can get him talking, or figure out his location, or convince him to meet up, or trick him into spilling some clue…

"Hi, you've reached Billy Needham, please leave me a message."

"Billy, it's Caleb Rooney!" I shout, raising my voice over the cacophony around me. "Call me back as soon as you get this. It's about…your cousin. It's urgent!"

"Oh when the saints…"

I hang up and stare at his business card. Then I crumple it in my fist.

I look back over at David, who's helping his injured bodyguard to his feet.

Then I look out at the street, at the parade reaching its grand finale.

"…go marching in…"

Here comes the dazzling marching band, wearing flamboyant pink and gold uniforms, high-stepping and twirling their instruments.

Behind them, a massive float, decorated as the Roman Coliseum, carrying a team of masked gladiators flinging beads and toys high into the air.

"Oh lord, I want…to be…in that number…"

Lastly, I scan the crowd. Men, women, children. So many children. Lining the metal police barricades along Canal Street, clapping and singing their hearts out.

"Oh when the saints go marching in!"

On this beautiful day, the city is pulsing with happiness. Life. Joy.

But my own pulse is creeping upward.

My stomach is cramping with fear.

My hands are damp, clammy.

I pray that I'm wrong…but I'm terrified that I'm right.

The attack is about to begin.

CHAPTER 77

SECONDS LATER, a series of explosions pounds through the heart of the French Quarter, just a block or so away from where I'm standing.

WHAM! WHAM! WHAM!

Instinctively, I hunch over and shield my face against the shock waves that ripple outward in all directions.

The marching band abruptly stops playing, the tune whining down to silence, the members lowering their instruments, looking around in confusion.

The parade grinds to a halt, with one tractor colliding into the rear of one of the large floats, this one displaying a Superdome with giant Saints players holding their arms up in triumph.

And the crowd's cheers of delight turn to screams of fear and terror, as they start charging away from the noise, and just beyond them, three billowing clouds of gray-black smoke float high into the clear blue sky. I can only darkly imagine the carnage that must be down there, just a block away.

This is the stuff of nightmares, come to life.

The dozens of uniformed cops posted up and down the sidewalks are bravely springing into action. Barking orders, shouting commands, gesturing manically, straining to keep some semblance of order, as people race, bump into one another, trip and fall down, trampling one another underfoot.

My pistol is still in my hand and I feel utterly useless. Failure.

I failed, the NOPD failed, the FBI failed.

And Billy has succeeded.

I flatten myself against a brick wall as the crowds surge by. Pushing. Shoving. Shouting. Crying. Mass hysteria begins to unfold as thousands of terrified spectators desperately try to flee. Many have their phones out, snapping pictures or recording videos as they go. But most don't dare look back. Or slow down for one second.

As for myself, I get shoved left and right. Shouldered. Rammed into. Even as flat as I am against the warm brick wall.

I'm nearly trampled in the mad stampede—*because I'm not going anywhere.*

Instead of joining the flow of evacuees, I'm battling against the current, struggling with all my strength to hold my ground.

The reason is simple.

As awful as these three initial explosions seem to be, Billy's plot was too elaborate, too expensive, too *expansive,* to be just three bombs.

I'm sure of it. I'd bet my life on it.

I have a terrible feeling that this is only the beginning.

CHAPTER 78

I GRIP the handle of my pistol, ready to shoot. Crouching low, I scan the chaotic scene.

Gotta stay cool, I tell myself. *Eyes open. Stay alert. Trust your training.*

If there's another concealed explosive device somewhere in the vicinity, I know I won't be able to spot it. Everywhere I look, there are hundreds of hiding places. Trash cans, discarded backpacks, overturned coolers. And there's no time and no resources to search these hiding places.

But I *might* be able to pick out a *human* threat.

I take a deep breath, an attempt to stem the adrenaline rush that's making my body tremble.

Then I start searching for anyone who looks out of place.

Anyone acting suspiciously calm.

Anyone not in uniform carrying a gun of his own.

And anyone I recognize. Like one of the monsters who terrorized Vanessa. Or anyone who showed up at that scrapyard meeting.

Or of course, Billy Needham himself.

Seconds tick by. Nothing.

The air begins to take on the bitter smell of a cocktail

of gunpowder, smoke, and the stench of human fear. Sirens wail in the distance.

I can feel something coming, but there's still no sign of what it might be.

Another bomb? A sniper? A chemical attack?

I stay low. Knees bent. Head on a swivel.

Scanning. Scanning.

Until…I *hear* it.

The revving of an engine. As loud as an Indy stock car.

What the hell?

My eyes focus on the source.

It's not a race car at all.

It's the big-wheeled *tractor* that was pulling the Roman Coliseum float.

It's idling in the middle of the street, belching a plume of black exhaust.

The tractor has been modified. It has a bigger-than-normal vertical muffler. An additional fuel tank. And an expanded metal grille, lined with horizontal spikes jutting out like a torture device from the Middle Ages.

I take a few steps and realize the tractor is no longer hooked up to its float.

And its driver—a gladiator wearing a costume of body armor, a metal helmet, and a pair of sunglasses with one red lens and one green—is settling back into the driver's seat.

And buckling his seat belt.

My mind races, piecing everything together. It all makes terrifying sense.

The tractors in the safe houses weren't being packed with explosives.

They were being taken apart and put back together.

Customized with powerful after-market engines.

Fitted with police-style tactical bumpers. Modified to carry out a European-style vehicle attack here in the US, to cause the maximum amount of damage to people in the shortest amount of time. London, Nice, Barcelona… and now, New Orleans.

Panic surges through my body as the driver engages the clutch and puts the tractor into Drive, and without the weight of the float behind it, it quickly roars ahead, chasing after the fleeing partygoers.

CHAPTER 79

I LIFT my pistol.

Aim.

Fire.

POP!

The driver flinches from my gunshot—damnit, I'm sure I hit the bastard!—but he keeps on driving, and the cursed thing roars by me, getting way too close to the throngs of fleeing people.

Lowering my pistol, I start running, desperate to line up a better shot, the tractor moving away from me.

But I can't get there soon enough to stop the madness.

The helmeted driver cuts the wheel sharply and plows straight through the metal police barricades, as easily as if they were made of Styrofoam.

The tractor keeps going, barreling right into the crowd. Zigzagging wildly. Wounding people with its spiked grille. Tossing them aside from its massive wheels.

More screams pierce the air and there's another roar, and I look behind, seeing another souped-up tractor emerge from the chaos, the one hauling the Superdome float, and never in my life have I felt so helpless, so alone, as this float roars up, like it's providing backup to its blood-spilling partner.

I can get a better shot here, and I whirl and lift my pistol in the approved two-handed grip, when—

The tractor halts.

The driver leaps from the raised seat.

The float—

It falls apart, pieces dropping to both sides, large plywood and papier-mâché pieces tumbling to the still-crowded streets, and—

Armed men emerge from it, where they had been hiding all the while.

Good God!

I'm heavily outgunned, overwhelmed by the force that's spilling out from the disassembled float, and I can just imagine the carnage that's about to erupt, all of these men in black battle rattle, holding automatic rifles in hand, lowering them, and I know in seconds I'm going to witness a bloody massacre.

And there's nothing I can do to stop it.

But I can at least make them pay a price.

I take aim and—

"Rooney!" comes a shout. "Don't shoot, you moron!"

Then I look closer at the armed men jumping off the float.

Bright-yellow NOPD letters are on their backs.

And a near figure comes to me, stripping away a black balaclava from his sweaty face.

It's Cunningham.

"What a goddamn shit-show, right?" he yells.

CHAPTER 80

BEFORE I can reply, two other members of the police department's tactical force run by him, and start shooting with their M4 automatic rifles at the driver on the first float. The driver arches his back and then collapses, and the tractor roars backward, until it hits a hydrant, letting loose a geyser of water.

I join the other two cops as we run to the tractor, and damnit to hell, the driver swivels in his seat, draws out a pistol and—

I fire once, twice, and catch him in the head.

This time he slumps down for good.

Body armor. If there are others out there like him, it's going to be a long, bloody mess to take them down.

I turn. Cunningham is urgently talking into a radio. I say, "How many dead from the bombs?"

"What bombs?" he asks.

"Jesus, Chief, I heard the goddamn things!"

He shakes his head. "They weren't bombs. They were concussion grenades! Meant to scare the crowds and move them into a kill zone...which is probably down the block."

I see more of the tactical cops racing along the sidewalks, and two of them are also providing first aid to the revelers caught by the heavily armored and spiked tractor. Water continues to spout and flow from the shattered hydrant.

"Does Morgan know you're here?"

Despite the chaos, the shouts, the sound of sirens, and the exhaustion on Cunningham's face, he grins. "Not yet, but I sent the son of a bitch a memo. Via snail mail. He'll probably get it next week. Hey, Rooney, love to chat and catch up, but we got work to do."

Then he trots off, speaking again into the radio microphone.

Even with the injured and the possible dead around me, I feel better than I have in a long while: at least my folks in the NOPD weren't going to stand by, weren't going to ignore the threats.

I only pray they're not too late.

Then I hear more gunfire, and race to the sound.

CHAPTER 81

THE SOUNDS of the gunfire aren't the measured, paced reports of police returning fire.

It's the fast *rat-a-tat-tat-tat* of someone firing at full auto, trying to cause as many casualties as possible in a short time.

Jesus Christ, the French Quarter is turning into a war zone!

I scurry over to the nearest abandoned float and slam my back against it for cover. After catching my breath, I peek around the side and steal a glance down the street.

More shouts, more screams, more gunfire.

Clusters of people are still frantically running in every direction, and there's a haze of gun smoke in the air. There's lots of panic but I practically weep with pride at what else I'm seeing:

A New Orleans EMS ambulance pulled up onto the sidewalk, the rear doors wide open, the two EMS personnel—both women—frantically working on two figures stretched out on the street, ignoring the sounds of the gunfire.

An older African American, standing at the open door of her souvenir shop, waving in people running by so they can take shelter.

A husband and wife team, it looks like, performing CPR on a heavyset man clad in a T-shirt and shorts.

My Crescent City is still alive, unbowed, and standing strong.

And some of us are fighting back.

I get up from my shelter, stay close to the buildings, stop at a corner where an NOPD officer is on her knees, hat gone, peeking around the corner. I race up to her and say, "I'm on the job! What's the situation?"

She looks up at me, Hispanic, late twenties, tear marks down her cheeks, but anger and defiance in her brown eyes.

"We've got a shooter down there, but I can't see who it is," she says.

I sneak a peek and hear the rapid automatic fire of the shooter, but I see what she means: there are still knots of people down the street, fleeing or running into the buildings. More sirens sound and I know the wise thing is to wait for backup, but whoever said I was wise?

"Hang tight," I say. "I'm taking a run."

She says something but I can't hear her, and I run down Canal Street, using everything I pass for cover: a mailbox, shrubs, even the skinny palm trees lining the streetcar tracks. Anything is better than nothing.

Along the way I see a college student crumpled on the street, his Tulane T-shirt stained with blood, pass piles of beads, Solo cups, sneakers, and flip-flops, and as I near Bourbon Street, I crouch behind a bus shelter—and finally get a chilling glimpse of the shooter.

Marching through the intersection, he's calmly moving along, spraying bullets in long bursts in every direction at the fleeing crowds, as casually as a gardener watering a bed of roses.

He's wearing a colorful costume—a court jester— and a masquerade mask with a giant hooked nose, disguised like the tractor driver I had dropped a few minutes earlier.

His weapon looks small, compact. An Uzi, perhaps, or a civilian version of the HK MP5. Something light and nimble. Easy to conceal under a billowy costume, and still packs one hell of a punch.

The strategy comes to view.

Shoot for a few minutes, hide the weapon, join the scurrying crowds, and then stop, take the weapon out.

Fire, kill, repeat.

Steeling myself, I creep even closer to him as he keeps on shooting.

Closer. *Closer*.

Barely a few dozen yards away from him now, I duck down behind a trash can and hold my breath.

I'm not counting his rounds. I have no clue how many his magazine holds. But I'm going to guess—no, *pray*—he'll have to reload soon.

After a few more spurts of gunfire, he does.

As soon as the gunman pops out his magazine, I spring up from behind the trash can.

I aim and squeeze the trigger three times, steady and controlled.

POP! POP! POP!

My first shot nails him in the thigh, knocking him off balance.

My second shot misses him entirely.

But my third shot strikes his neck. Blood spurts. He goes down hard.

I cross the street and approach the gunman with caution, my sidearm aimed and ready to fire, just in case he's still alive.

But by the time I'm standing over him, I see he's not moving at all. His head is surrounded by a puddle of blood. His weapon dangles limply in his arms.

I kick it away anyway—down into the sewer, where a civilian or child or another bad guy can't pick it up. Old police habit.

Then I squat down beside him—and give his chest a few hard raps with my knuckles. I'm not checking his pulse. I'm seeing if he's wearing body armor like the tractor driver.

Shit. Just what I was afraid of.

He is.

Body armor, automatic weapon...I was lucky with a head shot.

But how lucky will me and other cops be again? Especially if the bastards are wearing Mardi Gras costumes, blending in, shooting, and then hiding their weapon to pop up a block later to start killing again.

I'm about to stand—when I notice the dead jester is wearing sunglasses over his masquerade mask—one red lens, one green.

Just like the first tractor driver.

Odd. No way it's a coincidence. Is this a way for the attackers to identify one another in the melee? Or something else?

I lift them off the shooter's face and place them up to my eyes.

They feel like some kind of tactical, vision-enhancing 3D glasses. Everything I see looks just a little crisper.

But then I glance down at the gunman—and see something even wilder.

His jester costume looks practically *luminescent*.

Like it was sprayed with some kind of fluorescent paint, but a kind only visible with these special polarized shades—and maybe under a black light, too, like the one I found inside that safe house!

It makes bloody sense, to be able to quickly ID your fellow shooters, your fellow terrorists, among the screaming crowds, so you don't accidentally kill one of your own, while killing so many innocents.

A good strategy.

Which I'm going to use against the bastards.

CHAPTER 82

I STUFF the sunglasses into my pocket and scramble off the street. I take cover in the closest spot I can find, the doorway of a tacky souvenir shop.

Inside, it's eerily quiet. Rack after rack of T-shirts, keychains, and other trinkets have been toppled over in the chaos, as if a tornado had passed right through.

But outside, in the distance, I hear more screaming, more gunfire.

I also hear raging sirens. And two Black Hawk helicopters are circling overhead.

Thank God! The FBI is finally mobilizing a tactical response to this mayhem, joining up with my NOPD. I don't know what the hell is taking so long. By my count, the first blast went off almost eight excruciating minutes ago.

But in a situation like this? That's an eternity.

I take out my phone and, no surprise, I get no signal. For years politicians have been talking about increasing redundancy in cell tower coverage, because during a terrorist attack, all service would be overwhelmed.

Those plans went right on top of the pre-Katrina plan to repair and strengthen our vulnerable levees.

I put the phone back. I've caught my breath.

I've got my pistol, two spare magazines, and evidence of how the terrorists are identifying themselves.

Time to haul ass away from this place of safety and get the job done.

I run back out to the streets, down Bourbon Street, looking for NOPD members, EMS, firefighters, anyone with a working radio, because I've got to get the word out.

The street is eerily empty, with piles of trash, empty cups, strings of tangled beads, more sneakers and flip-flops. There are also drying pools of blood and discarded bandage wrappers, but no people, though I do see some scared folks, huddled in the now-quiet bars and stores, looking out with fear and hope that someone will come riding to the rescue.

I trot down the street, weapon out, waiting for something, anything, and wishing right now that I was wearing my NOPD blazer or at least my detective's shield, bouncing on a chain around my neck, because it sure would be damnably ironic if a SWAT sniper taking position saw me and took me down.

Yeah, real ironic.

As I reach Conti Street, I hear a commotion around the corner. A crowd of civilians, in total panic, are rushing in my direction.

One of them, a middle-aged woman, a crying toddler in her arms and blood dripping from her ear, shouts, "Somebody's shootin' back there! Run!"

The crowd blows past me—but I don't move an inch.

I whip out those two-toned sunglasses. Put them on. Look at the pack.

Sure enough, toward the rear of the group is a man

wearing a blue and purple samurai warrior costume…
whose torso is mottled with that iridescent paint.

The costumed son of a bitch's hands are empty, but
that could change in an instant, and he could start
hammering bullets into the back of the unarmed and
frightened civilians running past me.

"Hey, sensei!" I yell. "Police! Don't move!"

The man in the samurai suit glances back at me.

He's wearing a pair of red-green sunglasses, too. He
does a double take when he sees me aiming at him—
and realizes he's caught.

So he reaches into the folds of his costume and starts
to pull out what looks like an HK MP5, and without
hesitation, I fire three rapid shots.

POP! POP! POP!

The man grunts and collapses to the ground.

The rest of the civilians disappear around the corner
of the block, terrified—but all of them are *alive*.

"Show me your hands!" I shout at the assailant as I
move in closer.

He's writhing in pain, struggling to sit up. I
definitely landed a shot or two, but I guess the real
body armor under his fake samurai battle garb did
its job.

"Hands, hands!" I repeat.

But he doesn't obey. He tries to lift his weapon.

So I fire mine again. Twice. Emptying the magazine
until the slide of my pistol snaps back and doesn't slide
forward, meaning I'm out of ammunition.

Both bullets strike the gunman's head, sending a
reddish-pink mist into the air.

He slumps back down. Dead.

I rush over and pick up his rifle and sling it over
my shoulder. Yes, it's an MP5, all right, with two

spare magazines taped to the one in use. Very professional.

Now I'm better armed.

Which doesn't mean a goddamn thing.

I resume my run.

CHAPTER 83

INFORMATION. THAT'S what counts now, that's what's important, not what firepower I now possess.

I know how to spot any assailants still lurking among civilians. How to pick out the bad guys from the good and neutralize any remaining threats.

I've cracked the terrorists' code, but I can't assume the NOPD or FBI have done the same. And my phone is useless with the overwhelmed cell towers, and damnit to hell, I still don't see anyone in the area that has a radio I can use.

Never a cop around when you need one, I murmur.

I keep on trotting, the MP5 bouncing around on my shoulder, and I try my phone again. From the Contacts list I dial the emergency inter-agency hotline Special Agent Morgan gave out at the security briefing. I hold the phone to my ear and listen.

The line beeps. Once. Twice.

A recorded announcement tells me that my call cannot be completed at this time.

No shit, I think.

I hang up and try again. Then again. Again.

On the fourth try, the call goes through. The hotline starts to ring.

I brake to a halt.

Success!

And ring. And ring.

I count ten rings and still no answer. No voicemail, either. Nothing.

I curse Morgan's name and incompetence and stuff my phone back into my pocket.

Now what?

I think back to the briefing Morgan gave us. To all the security measures he said the feds were putting in place. The aerial drones. The nuclear particle detectors. The infrared cameras monitored by a dedicated team of specialists.

Cameras.

I look up and down the sidewalk for something that—in this part of town—shouldn't be hard to find: a folding chalkboard sign sitting in front of a restaurant or bar.

I spot one. A few doors away. Outside a quaint French Quarter watering hole called Dupré's, advertising their three-for-one Mardi Gras drink specials all week long.

I rush over. Hurriedly wipe the board clean with my sleeve. I don't have any chalk—so a stray white pebble off the sidewalk will have to do.

In big capital letters, I scratch out:

AGENT MORGAN!!!

USE RED-GREEN LENSED EYEGLASSES

TO I.D. HIDDEN SHOOTERS!!!

Then I look up, searching the awnings, rafters, and lampposts for one of those just-installed special cameras. Bourbon and Conti is an important intersection. There has to be one somewhere!

Over there. On the underside of a second-story terrace.

A small, sleek, black lens with a wireless antenna, bolted to the building with new, shiny silver screws.

I pick up the chalkboard sign and rush over. I hold it up, wave it around, pointing and gesturing like a meth addict needing a fix. I feel a little crazy, but that's the point. There probably aren't a lot of other folks dancing a jig in the middle of a terrorist attack. If the FBI really has a team of agents watching these cameras, they should notice me straight away.

I just hope they take me seriously. Read my message. Take *it* seriously. Then pass it along to the folks in charge.

After thirty seconds or so, I start to hear more gunfire nearby. So I drop the sign, take cover, pull out my cell again, and dial Cunningham to try to warn *him* and the NOPD about the sunglasses and secret shooters, too.

Damnit! The call won't go through. I try twice more. Still no luck.

Then, my phone starts ringing. Weirdly, I'm getting an *incoming* call.

A local 504 area code, but I don't recognize the number.

Maybe it's the FBI. Maybe an analyst saw my sign. Maybe it worked!

Breathlessly, I answer.

A man's voice, cool as ice, says: *"Hello, Detective. It's Billy. You rang?"*

CHAPTER 84

THE SOUND of that monster's voice snatches my breath away.

I'm on the line with the mastermind of the deadliest terror attack in New Orleans history, which is still raging all around me.

But does he *know* I know that?

He has to. Why else would he be calling? Just to toy with me?

"Hey, Billy," I answer, as calmly as I can. "Where are you? Somewhere safe, I hope. I'm sure you've seen the news. The French Quarter is an absolute—"

He snickers.

"That was some pretty convincing acting," he says, voice calm and steady. "Really. Of course I've seen the news. I've also seen things…*live*."

That last word nearly causes me to jump. I glance around with sudden paranoia. Does he have cameras of his own installed in the French Quarter? *Is he watching me right now?*

"And I have to say, I'm impressed with you, Caleb," he says. "You came awfully close to figuring it all out. To stopping me. You didn't, as you can see. But you did screw up a lot of my plans for today."

Furious, I grip the phone tighter and say, "Really? That's the best news I've heard all day. Let's get together and you can tell me personally how I screwed up your plans, and I'll screw my Smith & Wesson into your worthless mouth and pull the goddamn trigger!"

He laughs. "Oh, I'm sure we'll meet, but not right now. You screwed up some of my plans, but not all of them. We've just begun. Honest."

"What else is going on? Billy, come on, tell me!"

Another laugh. "And spoil my fun? Really?"

Jesus Christ.

"Why?" I shout. "Why would you do this? Why in God's name would you bomb, ram, shoot up your hometown?"

And like the sociopath he is—carefully hidden over the years—he's got his sermon all ready.

"Because I *love* my hometown, Caleb," he says, voice strong and determined. "For years I've been watching this city slip lower and lower. Its culture and character worn away by outsiders. The fabric of its society ripped apart. Someone had to stand up, unite us all, and fight back!"

"By killing innocent people?"

"No, by purging our city of the outsiders who come in here and suck away what's right and noble of New Orleans," he says. "C'mon, Caleb, as a cop, you've seen what the outsiders have done to our city. They take away our food, our culture, our music, and what do we get in return? Dirty money...and when the time comes when we need real help, like Katrina, we're treated like an old hooker who's overstayed her welcome."

I squeeze my eyes shut. I'm just a cop, not a shrink. But somehow, I've got to stop him...or at least delay him. My heart is thudding so hard that it nearly hurts my chest, and I realize that right now, in these very seconds, I have the possibility of stopping any more carnage, to halt whatever it is that Billy is planning to do next.

I take a breath. Swallow my anger, my pride, my cop mind.

"Billy…you know, I've never thought of it that way. I hate to admit it, but…please, tell me more. Tell me what else is coming."

Another laugh. "A few seconds ago you were promising to blow my head off. And now you want me to believe you're a convert? Not bad, but Caleb, please, don't insult my intelligence."

"Billy…"

After a pause, he asks, "Just before I go, consider this, you greasy spoon line cook. Have you ever lost something dear to *you*, Caleb? A job, maybe? A business? What about…a person? Maybe *two*?"

My mouth turns dry as sandpaper. My pulse soars.

Did this son of a bitch just threaten Marlene and Vanessa?

"Billy, what the hell did you just say to me?" I shout back. "Are you still there?"

Another laugh.

"The sky's the limit, Caleb," he says. "Remember that."

Then he hangs up.

CHAPTER 85

MY FEET jackhammer the pavement.

My arms pump like pistons.

My throat and lungs are blazing.

The MP5 threatens to shatter my shoulder from all the bouncing around.

The distance from here to where Killer Chef is parked is only about a third of a mile.

But right now, it feels like light-years.

I tried phoning Marlene and Vanessa multiple times as soon as Billy hung up on me. No luck. The calls never went through.

I tried texting them. Warning them. *Imploring* them to find shelter and stay safe, wherever they were. But the messages never went through.

I have no idea where they are.

Or…God, if they're even still alive.

And Billy could very well be bluffing. Trying to distract me, throw me off his trail.

But I've seen what he's capable of. If he really does have something planned against the two most important people in my life, I need to protect them.

I can't take any chances.

I have to find them. Save them.

And the food truck is the best place to start looking.

I still have so many damn questions. What are Billy's true motives? What's his end game? Why does he carry so much vitriol, so much pain?

Most of all, what other horrors does he still have tucked up his sleeve?

But that can wait.

Sprinting through the deserted streets of the French Quarter, all I can think about are the two I hold dearest.

But I see and hear some encouraging signs, like the first green colors of spring.

More helicopters overhead.

National Guard Humvees roaring by.

State police and NOPD cruisers screaming in the distance as well.

And I'm hearing the flat, sharp *crack!* of rifle fire in the distance, from what seems to be upper stories.

Not the rapid fire from automatic machine guns, but the carefully aimed and discharged .308 bolt-action rifle rounds, the ones used by SWAT team snipers.

Meaning my message did get through, and the good guys—now able to identify the bad guys—are taking them out, one by one, even with their body armor.

Finally, I round the corner onto Bienville Street.

I see Killer Chef parked just up the block, right where I left it.

I start shouting, "Vanessa? Marlene? I'm back! You guys all right?"

No response.

I race up to the truck—and see it's boarded up tight.

The service windows are shut, the metal security grating closed and latched. I can hear the generator running, so they're either hiding inside…or left in a hurry.

I bang on the truck's side—hard—as the sound of nearby sirens gets louder.

"Marlene?" I yell. "Vanessa?"

Still no reply.

With a Black Hawk helicopter hovering overhead, I go around to the back.

The truck's rear doors are shut and locked, too. And of course I left my keys inside when I left.

All I can do is *pound* on the doors. Frantically. Desperately. Feverishly.

"Vanessa, Marlene, open up! It's Caleb! Please!"

After a few more painful, futile seconds of this, I frantically look around. I had the crazy thought of shooting off the lock, but that only works in Hollywood. Chances are, it wouldn't work, or the ricochet could wound or kill me.

There.

Part of a shattered metal police barricade. I wrestle off a length of pipe-shaped metal, about two feet long, and go back to the rear of the truck.

I start hammering the handle.

Again and again. With all my focus and might.

It takes a solid ninety seconds, but at last the handle snaps.

I pry it off and push open the doors.

"Vanessa, Marlene, are you—"

A gunshot rocks the inside of the truck.

Buckshot sails over my head, missing me by mere inches.

I yell and duck back, and then I look in, past the gray cloud of gun smoke.

They are together on the floor at the far side of the truck. Marlene is wielding a shotgun—one I recognize, one she long ago insisted we hide behind the freezer, "just in case." I told her it was a stupid and dangerous idea. I forbid keeping any weapons inside our truck. Thank God she didn't listen to me.

"You scared the living shit out of us, Caleb!" she calls out. "Damnit, are you okay?"

I slowly step up and in, looking at the damage the shot caused.

"Marlene, really, I know you've threatened to kill me before but…"

Her expression darkens and I add, "Honest, I'm okay. But didn't you hear me yelling and banging on the door?"

They get up off the floor, and Marlene makes a point of shoving the shotgun away and says, "We heard something out there, but we thought it was some crazy man."

Vanessa smiles. "Guess we were pretty close, right?"

I burst out laughing. They join in. Uncontrollably.

Our laughter turns to tears of relief and joy as I go over to these two extraordinary women. I embrace them both, pulling them in and squeezing them tight.

We exchange no words. Just deep, heaving breaths. Overwhelmed with relief.

We're all together. Alive.

CHAPTER 86

THE SUNSET that evening is heartbreakingly beautiful, even though we only see it through a crack in our windows. The sky is on fire with a deep, luscious crimson.

A fitting end to the day.

The bloodiest one in New Orleans history since the War of 1812, although I feel it could have been much, much worse.

Vanessa, Marlene, and I stay inside our truck, even though there's still the strong odor of burnt gunpowder from the shotgun blast that nearly took off my head. Sirens are still sounding nearby and Black Hawk helicopters are roaring overhead, and I desperately work my phone to sound the alarm about Billy, placing call after call to Cunningham and the FBI's hotline.

None of them ever go through. I managed to leave three messages on Cunningham's voicemail, but he never calls back.

Eventually Vanessa says, "Hey, looks like the cavalry has arrived, Caleb."

I peer out through a crack between our windows and feel much better. Two National Guard Humvees towing trailers have pulled up, and armed troops are tumbling out, going to the trailers, pulling out wood and metal barricades.

Vanessa says, "What do you think?"

"I think it's time to get out of here," I say, "but we've got to be careful…those guys are probably nervous as hell."

I leave the HK MP5 behind and stick my pistol in my rear waistband of my jeans. I open the door and yell out, "Hey, National Guard, coming out! We're coming out!"

The three of us slowly step out of the truck, hands up, and a sergeant and trooper come over and say, "No civilians allowed here, sorry. Get moving…the city's under martial law and the French Quarter is being evacuated of all civvies."

Marlene is somber and quiet, definitely not her usual self. "How…how bad is it?"

"Shit, ma'am," the trooper says, an African-American private who looks angry and determined. "Dunno about that, but at least the shooting's died down. Look, you gotta get walking."

Vanessa says, "Can we drive our truck?"

The sergeant—an older Hispanic woman—says, "I'll be, the famous 'Killer Chef'…no can do, sorry. No civilian traffic allowed."

I say, "Sergeant, I'm former NOPD. I've got vital information about the attack…can I borrow your radio equipment?"

The private laughs. "Yeah, if any of it was working. Seems like we got the wrong frequency crystals for our radio gear. Your government at work."

The three of us walk gingerly along the nearly deserted streets, passing through two checkpoints manned by the state police—luckily, we weren't searched, because I would have had a hard time explaining my hidden pistol—and we get to my home in Tremé. At this point, it's as safe a place to be as anywhere else.

In other words, not that safe at all.

The streets are alive with moving traffic, none of it civilian. Fire trucks and EMS ambulances. Cruisers and unmarked vehicles. Additional National Guard Humvees and trucks. There's a haze of smoke and a feeling of fear as the three of us keep up a steady pace.

I've lived in New Orleans my whole life. I've lived through riots. Through Hurricane Katrina.

I've never seen anything like this.

And if Billy was telling the truth, there's more to come.

As calm as it now looks, that thought nearly freezes me with fear.

"You brought your keys, right?" Vanessa asks as we finally shuffle up the path to my town house. "Or are you going to have to bash this doorknob off, too?"

She smiles and touches my shoulder. It's the tiniest gesture, but it means the world, after the day we've all had.

"If y'all are going to be this lovey-dovey," Marlene says, "I'm gonna sleep in the hammock in the backyard. I've been through enough hell today."

After I get the door open we head straight for the living room and all collapse on the sofa.

"Should we put on the news?" Vanessa asks, arching her back in exhaustion. "See what they're saying?"

Marlene springs to her feet. But she strides over to my bar cart, not the TV.

"I've got a more important question," she says. "What's everybody drinking?"

As she fixes us some well-deserved old-fashioneds using my finest bottle of twenty-year Lagavulin Scotch, I flip on the television.

Coverage of the attack is on every channel. Reporters describing the action, dramatically waving their arms, pointing to crumpled floats and tractors behind police barricades. Blurry phone footage showing the screaming crowds, and one showing somebody in a harlequin costume, calmly walking along, shooting, until he in turn falls back when shot. Various witnesses—tourists, cops, residents—saying what they saw, with tears in their eyes and shaking voices. Talking heads drawing comparisons to the Boston Marathon bombing, the Las Vegas shooting, September 11th.

I can't stomach this. Not now. Not yet. Maybe not ever.

"Anyone care if I turn this shit off?" I ask.

I reach for the remote without waiting for an answer—just as my phone rings.

I check the screen. It's another 504 number I don't recognize.

Holy shit. Is it Billy again?

I answer nervously—then exhale.

"Rooney, it's Cunningham," comes his tired voice. "Where are you? You okay?"

"Hey, Chief. I'm hanging in there. I just got home. Did you get my—"

"That's why I'm calling," he says. "How soon can you get to Pontchartrain Park? I'm with Morgan and his team of all-star rejects. We want you down here. Now."

"It might take some time, with all the roadblocks," I say.

"No worries," he says. "A cruiser will come by and pick you up."

CHAPTER 87

THE ALFRED J. LeMont Federal Building, home to the FBI's New Orleans Field Office, is an ugly concrete tower tucked away on the outskirts of town near the shores of Lake Pontchartrain.

Over the years, I've worked a few other joint cases with the Feds, but I've never stepped inside their facility. It's not that I didn't want to. I was never invited. Until now.

It's a monument to law and order, of peace and progress, but my mood sours the moment I step inside, when I see Special Agent Morgan standing outside of a conference room, talking to a woman wearing a Homeland Security windbreaker.

"Morgan!" I yell. "You son of a bitch, this is all your fault! You idiot! Moron! I fucking gave you everything on a goddamn silver platter, and you let the attack happen!"

Morgan, eyes blazing with anger and fury, says, "What silver platter, Rooney? Huh? What goddamn platter? You focused on a poor Syrian dishwasher. You gave us a nearly illiterate Aryan Brotherhood goon who knew nothing we didn't already know...you were obsessed about David Needham...the wrong Needham! We had hundreds of tips! Hundreds! And DC kept on promising to help us with some back-channel nonsense…which never panned out."

"You could have done more!"

"We all could have done more…all of us…and for Christ's sake, what was I supposed to do? Drop everything and focus on you…a fry cook? A disgraced police detective?"

He storms off into the conference room, and one by one, others follow him in—state police, Homeland Security, more FBI, NOPD, and Cunningham, who nods at me to join him.

I feel like going back home to Vanessa and, yes, even Marlene.

But I steel myself and go in.

By the time I'm able to get into the crowded room, I stand in the corner, along with others who don't have the juice to sit around the conference room table. I only recognize about a quarter of the attendees—local, state, parish—and Morgan goes through a detailed report of how they're trying to track down Billy Needham. Photographs are all over the television and internet. Wiretaps have been placed on his business and home phones…*as if,* I think. His credit cards have been flagged to announce any activity. Every employee who either currently works or has worked for Billy is being interrogated. All of his properties have been raided, and are under surveillance.

All good work, but still, too late.

We were all too late.

A brief pause and I call out, "Casualties. What's the number on casualties?"

The air grows still and Morgan looks down, and then a burly tactical NOPD officer—still in black jumpsuit and battle rattle—pushes forward to the conference room table and says, "Well, this is what I've got." He unfolds a sheet of paper and says, "Hard to believe, but number of deaths is under twenty."

A murmur of voices, and the officer—his nametag says DUBUS—says, "And some of those are from being trampled. Wounded is about fifty or sixty, but shit, guys, it could have been worse, much, much worse."

Dubus folds up the paper. "Luckily we got intel about the red and green glasses. Once my shooters got prepped, we shot the bastards every time they appeared, like gophers popping up from their burrows. So thanks to whoever got that intel out."

I keep quiet.

So does Morgan.

The meeting breaks down with lots of arguing, more talking, and I try to slip out, and Cunningham grabs my arm.

"Need your help."

I say, "You got it, Chief."

CHAPTER 88

CUNNINGHAM AND I do a "walk and talk" as we go deeper into the concrete bowels of the LeMont Federal Building, and he gives me a debrief of the terrorists that were seized and arrested once the shooting stopped.

"Damnit, Rooney, the only thing they've got in common, is that they've got nothin' in common!" he says as we clatter down a concrete and metal stairway.

He gives me the intel:

Five in custody. Two tractor drivers, three gunmen.

That's five accomplices to terrorism.

Five potential cooperating witnesses.

Five possible leads on Billy.

All of the suspects are men. All were arrested carrying illegal weapons and wearing costumes speckled with UV-reflective paint.

"But that's where it ends," Cunningham complains. "There's no connecting thread."

They range in age from twenty-four to fifty-seven. Two are young and white. One is middle-aged and black. One is Pakistani American. One was born in Indonesia.

They have different income levels. Different education levels.

Different marital statuses. Different immigration statuses.

Some have criminal records a mile long. Others have never had a parking ticket.

One posts on white supremacist message boards. Another has ties to radical Islam. A third is a lapsed Buddhist.

"What are they saying?" I ask.

"Not a damn thing," he says. "They just spar, laugh, and keep on wastin' our time. Like they've been trained to string us along. But none of them have lawyered up. Can you figure that? Nobody."

"So why do you need me?"

He opens a heavy metal door marked with black numbers and nothing else.

"One of them is a local," he says. "Some guy who's worked off and on in some kitchens in the city. I'm hoping that…"

"I can get him to talk."

Cunningham nods as we enter a room looking into a small interrogation cell, via a two-way mirror. Inside the room is a table, and a middle-aged, beefy African-American male, who smiles and says, "How many times I gotta say it? I'm not talkin' to y'all. No, sir."

His FBI interrogator, a linebacker of a man with salt-and-pepper hair and a gruff New Jersey accent, looks like he's about to jump over the table and wring his neck.

"How many times do I have to *ask*, Mr. Broussard: What can I do to change your mind?"

The suspect shrugs. "Nothing. Y'all are outsiders. Simple as that."

Outsiders.

"Who's the guy?"

The room is filled with NOPD brass and FBI agents, and Cunningham manages to wrestle a sheaf of papers from a desk, and he says, "Reginald Broussard, age forty-nine, currently unemployed, worked in a number of restaurants including—"

I hold up a hand. Look through the two-way mirror. Outsiders.

Reginald is smiling like he has all the time in the world.

I ask, "Was he a gunman or tractor driver?"

"Driver," Cunningham says.

"He kill anybody?"

Cunningham shakes his head. "Nope, lucky us, lucky city. For some reason, his tractor stalled out right after the concussion grenades went off. When he got it started, he started after the crowd but the krewe behind him didn't like what they saw. So a bunch of macho guys dressed like mermaids swarmed over him and took him down before he could do any real damage."

"Tell me about his marital status."

"Single."

"Family?" I ask.

He flips through a few more sheets of paper. "A sister who lives in the city, works as a nurse at Tulane. A niece he dotes on, Melissa. Whatever money he's earned has gone into a college fund for the little girl. She's ten."

Cunningham looks up. "Is that helpful?"

"More than you think," I say.

CHAPTER 89

THIRTY MINUTES later and after some heated discussion from the observation room, Cunningham opens the interrogation door, and the frustrated FBI agent storms out. I slide in, holding a slim folder in my hands.

"Hey there, Reggie," I say. "Can I call you Reggie? I'm Caleb."

I take a seat opposite Broussard and flash a friendly grin. That's not an easy task when you're staring down a domestic terrorist, even if he isn't directly responsible for killing anyone. But it's what I've got to do. I've interrogated lots of suspects over the years in holding cells like this one. Angry men who shot and killed their girlfriends. Overwhelmed women who beat their children. Twisted fellows who took depraved pleasure in stalking and assaulting women.

But none were part of a terrorist team or plot, which still might not be finished.

He just glares at me. Wary.

"First things first," I say. "Why don't we get you out of those cuffs?"

Now he's *really* thrown.

Knowing I'm being watched, I turn and look at the

two-way mirror, wordlessly imploring Cunningham to send someone in here with a key.

"I can see exactly what you're trying to do," he says, grinning. "Classic good cop, bad cop shit. Next you're gonna offer me some water and a snack. You're trying to buddy up to me to get me to talk. Well, it ain't gonna work."

I shrug. "That's pretty smart of you, Reggie. But I've got a surprise for you. I'm not a cop."

"You a lawyer, then?" he asks. "A public defender?"

"No on both counts," I say. "I'm just doing a favor for a friend of mine on the force. A local, like you…like me. Nowadays I work as a chef."

He looks skeptical. "For real?"

"Oh, yeah, for real," I say. "I spent some time at Brennan's, Commander's Palace, Gautreau's…you learn from the best, right?"

He says, "Where you working now?"

"Got my own food truck," I say. "Move it around, place to place, it's called Killer—"

"Chef!" he exclaims. "You're the dude that runs that food truck, yeah, I know about you." He then looks over at the two-way mirror. "Then why are you here, talkin' to me, man?"

"Like I said, doing a favor for an old friend," I say.

The door opens and a slim, angry-looking FBI agent comes in, and without a word, unlocks Broussard's cuffs and walks out, slamming the door behind him. Broussard rubs his wrists and sighs.

"That feels good, thanks," he says. "So what's the favor you're doing?"

"Just trying to help him and the FBI figure out what went on this morning, but let me tell you, just between you and me, those outsiders don't know shit."

There's a slight smile on his face, but he doesn't let his guard down.

"Hey, settle a bet for me," I say. "Who makes the best gumbo in Plaquemines Parish? I have a buddy who says Talbot's. But I swear by Mama Gerry's."

His eyes light up at the question, as I thought they might.

"That's like picking a favorite child. Can't be done. How'd you know I——"

"I could tell you're from around there by your accent," I say, still trying to keep my voice relaxed, casual. "I always know a fellow Louisiana son when I see one. Gotta stick together. We're a special breed down here."

"You got that right."

"That's what all these suits don't understand," I say, wanting to focus on this kind-looking man before me, not wanting to think of his part in what I witnessed this morning. The blood. The screams. The crumpled bodies.

I go on. "They show up, thinking they know everything. But all they do is make a mess. If you ask me, that's what's *really* going to destroy our city. Not hurricanes. But *people*. From the *outside*. Who don't belong here."

He bobs his head. "Amen to that, brother. Amen to that."

"Now, I can see why that makes you angry, Reggie," I say. "Truth is, it pisses me off, too. When outsiders come in, try to charm us, try to steal away what's special about the Big Easy. I can understand this. But…"

I pause, take a moment to scratch at the back of my head, like I'm trying to figure out the crossword puzzle in that day's *New York Times*. "But what I can't understand is, how you could fall under the spell of a man like Billy Needham."

I watch his reaction closely. He doesn't admit to anything. But he doesn't deny it, either.

Progress.

Oh, so slight, but I know I'm making progress.

"You used to work at a seafood plant out in Buras," I say. "Isn't that right? Until a new investor stepped in two years ago, laid off a bunch of folks. Especially the old-timers. That must have hurt real bad, Reggie. But do you know *who* that investor was?"

He smiles wider, but it's an uneasy smile. "Oh, c'mon, man, Mr. Needham had nothing to do with that. He loves this city, and he cares about us folks. You're bullshitting me!"

"Reggie, please, you of all people…Billy Needham says he loves this city, and loves folks like you, but when it comes to business, the bucks come first. He was behind that buyout. Wait a bit longer, I'll get you copies of the purchase and sales agreements. His signature is right at the bottom of them. He betrayed you, your friends, and your coworkers. And when it came time to use you and others, he didn't hesitate, not for a moment."

The smile has faded. I press on.

"You were one of the tractor drivers," I say. "But something happened. The tractor stalled out, maybe you got blocked, maybe…maybe you had a change of heart. You saw all those scared tourists, the folks running away, and you couldn't do it. You couldn't do what Billy asked you to do, to drive into a crowd and kill a lot of innocents."

He says again, "You're bullshitting me. I…I was going to do it, and then I got jumped by that krewe behind me. That was the plan. I just didn't get it done."

I reach for the folder, slowly slide it in front of me. "Billy, you know what they say about plans. That's how you make God laugh. You say you're making plans. So what did you plan for your sister, Grace, and her daughter, Melissa?"

He freezes, staring at the folder. "Don't you dare," he says, his voice a near whisper. "Don't you dare."

I slowly shake my head. "You warned them, didn't you? Stay away from the French Quarter today. Don't go to the parades. Stay home. But you know how kids are...they don't listen. They promise one thing, and they sneak away, and they hope they don't get caught. But sometimes they do..."

I open the folder and rotate it so Reggie can see what's inside: a color NOPD crime-scene photo, showing a narrow street, strewn with debris from beads to flowers to empty bottles, and in the foreground, a small, yellow-blanket-covered figure with plastic numbered evidence triangles scattered around it.

He doesn't say a word, but breathes out a low, keening moan. I close the folder.

"Billy used you," I say. "Used you and the others, and we're trying to find him, Reggie. Before he can use others. Before he can kill others...like your niece."

More low moaning.

"Reggie, where is he?"

Moaning.

"Reggie...please...help us. Where is he?"

Tears are running down his cheeks, he's shaking his head, and he says, "I don't know, I don't know, honest..."

"Reggie, the police"—I make sure to leave the FBI

out of it—"they've looked at his restaurants, his warehouse, his home…there must be someplace else. Am I right? Someplace they don't know about?"

He nods his head. "Melissa…Melissa…"

I reach over, gently touch the back of his hand. "It's too late for Melissa. I'm sorry, Reggie. But you can help save others. You didn't hurt anyone, you were just caught up in something…now's your chance to make it right."

The sobs start but he says, "There's a place…near Shreveport…some old hunting camp…that's where we practiced…that's where we planned it…"

"In Bossier Parish, right?" I ask, remembering what Billy had told me about shooting there with his cousin David a year ago.

Slippery bastard, I think, pointing to his cousin as a possible suspect…

He nods. "Billy stayed there, in a little bunkhouse… lectured to us at night about what we had to do to save New Orleans…"

He lowers his head. "Oh, sweet Jesus, please forgive me."

I get up and walk out, taking the folder with me.

CHAPTER 90

THE OBSERVATION room is much more crowded than it was when I first left, but Cunningham is the first person I recognize, and I shove the folder back to him.

I say, "That little Jane Doe still not identified?"

His face is struggling with lots of emotions. "Not yet, but we'll find out who her family is...God, Caleb."

"God wasn't in that room," I say. "Just a lot of guilt. I just hope her family forgives us for what we did to her, using her body like that. Did you hear what he said, about that hunting camp?"

A different voice says, "Got it, ID'd it, and we're preparing an assault team right now to drop in."

I burn again with resentment and anger as Special Agent Morgan shoves his way forward.

"Wait a sec," I say. "You should have known about Billy's hunting camp in Bossier Parish. I thought you clowns had already searched all of his properties?"

Morgan looks pissed. Big deal. He says, "We were fooled. That place wasn't in his most recent listings...he donated the land and property to the Nature Conservancy three years back. It was a mistake."

Cunningham is right next to me, like he wants to make sure I don't take a swing at the arrogant FBI man.

"Yeah, you guys are experts at this," I say. "Making mistakes, getting people killed...when do we leave?"

"'We'?" Morgan asks, still looking pissed. "What do you mean, 'we'?"

"Don't screw with me," I say, raising my voice so that others in this crowded room look at me. "You guys are hitting that cabin, I'm coming along."

Morgan squeezes his lips together and says, "Chief Cunningham?"

"Right here."

"Is this man a law enforcement official in your city?"

"No."

In a sharp, sneering tone, Morgan says, "Sorry, Rooney. This raid's going off within fifteen minutes, and we don't plan to have it catered. Get the hell out of my way."

I try to hit him, but Cunningham and others hold me back.

CHAPTER 91

SOME MINUTES later Cunningham is escorting me back out of the LeMont Federal Building and I say bitterly, "Why are you here? Aren't you going out with the feds?"

With a weary sigh he says, "I hate helicopters. Let the feds have the glory. And I'm dead tired, Caleb. I mean, you try riding in secret in a Mardi Gras float, all bent over, not able to move, breathing in diesel fumes…"

We get to the doors and there are flashes of lightning in the darkness. Camera crews, reporters, and others are clustered outside.

Cunningham says, "Don't scream at me when I say this, but Morgan isn't totally to blame."

"The hell he isn't!"

My former boss taps my elbow. "Remember when I first briefed you on this, back when you were outside, washing your truck? I said that a lot of high-level meetings were going on, both here and in DC? That there were international security implications? Well, yeah, I found out from one of the local FBI agents…DC screwed Morgan over, and good."

"How?"

He rubs his face for a second. "Yeah, there were international implications, all right. The boys at the Hoover building got contacted by the FSB."

"Who?"

"The FSB," he says. "The Russian spy agency that replaced the KGB. Somehow they got wind of the investigation going on down here, and they told the FBI that they had some good intel they were going to pass on. Just be patient, the Russians said, we'll help you out."

I say, "The Russians didn't have anything."

"Not a goddamn thing," he says. "Morgan's superiors didn't want him to go full-out in his investigation…they wanted to wait for the Russians to step in, help us break up the plot, get great headlines about a reset in the American-Russian relationship, all that good shit. So Morgan was held back, and yesterday, Ivan called the feds and said, oops, our bad, we can't help."

I feel worn, tired, and betrayed. All of the dead and wounded out there…it could have been prevented. If I hadn't focused on the wrong Needham. If Morgan had shown a stiffer spine. If my old bosses had flipped off the FBI and told them that they would handle it…

Lots of ifs.

Cunningham gently slaps me on my back. "By the way, Caleb. The review board found that your use of force was justified and cleared your name. With everything going on, I forgot to tell you. It's not too late, if you want to come back to the force…"

His voice fades as I try to grasp what he's saying, but I'm indifferent to the news. On top of everything else, it just doesn't seem that important. But a tiny part of me is glad that I've been vindicated.

"Go home, Caleb," he says. "Go home. I'll let you know when the feds grab Needham's ass. If we're lucky, Billy will try to escape while they're taking him in...from a Black Hawk helicopter at five thousand feet."

I work my way through the crowds outside of the building, wondering how I'm going to get home, when a woman's voice says, shyly, "Mr. Rooney, please, may I have a word? Mr. Rooney? Please?"

I turn and stand, shocked.

It's Rima Farzat, the widow of Ibrahim Farzat, the Syrian refugee dishwasher I had been chasing and who had died a gruesome, tortured death.

She is dressed modestly as before—black slacks and blouse, veil covering her head—but she seems exhausted, shrunken.

"Yes, Mrs. Farzat," I say, stepping away some from the crowd of watchers and reporters, remembering our last angry meeting that ended with her attacking me with pepper spray.

She looks around and says in a low voice, hard to hear, "I...I owe you an apology. I am sorry for what I did to you."

I place my hand over my heart. "Please, Mrs. Farzat, you don't need to apologize. I'm the one who is sorry. I'm sorry for acting so arrogant toward you, especially when you were grieving. I should not have done that."

She nods, bites her lower lip. "I...I am not the only one who should apologize to you. My great-uncle, Saleel el-Sharif, from Crescent Care...he..."

I nod. The man who tried to tear me apart with shotgun shells when I was trying to get information about her husband.

"He was trying to protect you, am I right?" I ask.

She nods. I think of her, and of poor Ibrahim's body, and the violent reaction of her great-uncle, and I can almost hear the thud as the pieces fall into place.

"Your husband…he was murdered by Billy Needham and his killers, am I right?"

She doesn't say a word, but her sad eyes tell me everything I need to know. I go on. "And he was killed because Billy found out that your husband was an informant. For the FBI, am I right?"

She folds her arms, nods bitterly. "Ibrahim…he wasn't a very good husband. But he was trying to become a better man, here, in America. He found out about this man Needham, and his plotting, and he went to the FBI. I told him no, over and over again. Why should he risk his life for this country after it spends such a long time holding us up with interviews and background checks…that welcomes us here with hate and suspicion? What did he owe America after how he was treated?"

Another piece of the puzzle now falls into place. When the Farzats were first noticed and investigated by the NOPD, we passed on information to Homeland Security, who told us the family had been thoroughly vetted and weren't considered a terrorist threat.

Of course they weren't a threat. Ibrahim was working for *us*—was one of the good guys. And Crescent Care, I've come to believe, really was an honest charity. It just found itself tangled up with some less-than-honest guys.

Rima sighs. "But my husband was stubborn. He said with all its faults, this country was a good place, and he would help to make it an even better place…and for his troubles…he was murdered. Brutally murdered."

I say, "And when I came up to you…"

"I didn't know what to think. Were you FBI, sniffing around? Were you part of that Needham man's gang, looking to harm me? So I described you to my great-uncle, and when you showed up…"

"He thought he was protecting you," I say.

"Yes, and now, he is in hiding. Afraid you will have him arrested."

Out over the dark and flat waters of Lake Pontchartrain comes the *flicker-flicker* of lightning tearing through the thick gray shapes.

I say, "Tell him I am sorry, as well, and tell him he is safe from me."

The grumble of thunder reaches us. Rima laughs bitterly.

"Safe? Will we ever be safe?"

I wish I knew the answer.

I really do.

CHAPTER 92

I CATCH a cab back to my home in Tremé, and find Vanessa sleeping on the couch, and no Marlene. The television is set to Turner Classic Movies, an old black-and-white film featuring Spencer Tracy and Katharine Hepburn, and I look down at her sweet sleeping face.

Most times I've seen her in these past several days, that perfect face with the blond hair has been scared, angry, or frustrated. But now, even after surviving leaving her abusive husband and a terrorist attack, she is sleeping with the bliss of happiness and love.

I want to stand and just watch her, but instead, I go into the kitchen and get to work.

She wakes up just as I'm plating our meal for the evening: omelets made with diced mushrooms, smoked bacon pieces, Gruyere, and sharp cheddar, complemented by split baguettes heated on a griddle and dripping with butter, and French-press coffee and freshly squeezed orange juice.

She sits across from me and takes a bite, rolls her eyes in pleasure. "My dear Caleb…if you keep on cooking like this for me, you'll need to roll me out the door."

Maybe it's the look of pleasure on her face, or the raw

delight in being alive and with this beautiful woman on this cloudy and ill-fated day, but without hesitation I say, "I'll cook for you as long as you wish…forever, if you'd let me."

She blushes and looks down at her plate, and in a small voice, says, "I would like that, Caleb. Very, very much."

We eat in silence for a few more moments, and she says, "What's the news about Billy Needham?"

"There's a new lead that the FBI and the NOPD are chasing down," I say. "A hunting camp in Shreveport where he worked with others in plotting the attack. The FBI had missed that camp in their initial search, and right now…they're probably swooping down in helicopters to grab him."

"Mmm," she says. "After all you've done, I'd think you would want to be there, when he gets captured."

"I had more important things to do."

She gives me a teasing, erotic look. "Like what?"

"Capturing you."

She leans over, grasps my hand. "Caleb."

"Yes?"

"Can this meal be reheated?"

My chef brain says absolutely not, that it won't be the same.

But the smarter part of my brain wrestles control.

"Absolutely," I say, standing up and leading her to my bedroom.

We start with a slow walk.

And end in a fast run, laughing and tumbling into my bed.

Correction.

Our bed.

*   *   *

Humming wakes me up.

Loud, insistent humming.

I roll over from the sleeping form of my Vanessa, check my nightstand. It's been two hours since I got home, and it's raining hard outside, with low grumbles of thunder and flashes of light piercing through the night.

I grab the source of the humming: my phone, set on vibrate.

I open the text, and this time, there's no confusion or hidden secret about who's contacting me.

It's Cunningham.

It's short and to the depressing point.

PROPERTY RAIDED. NO JOY. BILLY STILL AMONG THE MISSING.

I put the phone down, and try to fall asleep, but for long hours, I just stare up at the ceiling.

CHAPTER 93

THE NEXT two days pass in a tired, depressing, and wet grind. The rain that started just after I left the LeMont Federal Building kept on falling, and on the third day, it's supposed to be sunny and cloud-free, just in time for a city-wide memorial service to commemorate our bloody Mardi Gras.

I think that's a spectacularly bad idea, but since I'm no longer on the force, who cares what food truck chef thinks? But the police, the mayor, and—I'm sure—the Chamber of Commerce want to reassure everyone that New Orleans is still here, standing strong, and so a service has been set for 9 a.m. at the Fair Grounds Race Course, the largest open area in the Big Easy—and home to our annual Jazz and Heritage Festival—and along with the governor, two senators, several congressmen, and the vice president, the place is expected to be overflowing with locals and tourists, all wanting to celebrate New Orleans' survival.

But in the rain-filled two days before the scheduled celebration, I sleep the sleep of the bone-tired exhausted. I spend lots of hours just talking to Vanessa, learning more about her and her health, discussing her treatment options and helping her strategize a financial plan now that she's finally free from Lucas's clutches, their prenup legally dissolved, after she threatened to go to the press about his abusive behavior and ruin his reputation, his businesses, and his life.

I even spend a rainy afternoon going through my damaged food truck. There are furrows and buckshot holes in the top and in the door, from when Marlene almost blasted my head off with that shotgun. We stare at it for a few minutes, while Vanessa is up front, wiping down an already clean counter.

Rain batters the roof and I shake my head. "Mar, just a foot or so lower, you'd have a hell of a cleaning job to take care of. My blood and brains all over the place."

Marlene just grins. "Maybe blood, but not too much brains." She traces the scarred metal with her fingers. "Shouldn't take too long to repair this time, don't you think?"

It comes to me.

"No," I say. "We're not going to repair it."

"What?"

I touch the damaged metal as well. "No, we're going to leave it. As a permanent reminder of what you and Vanessa went through—what all of us went through—and how we'll never forget."

Marlene nods. "Aren't you full of all these philosophical surprises."

Vanessa calls out, "Hey, who do you think's been teaching him about philosophy?"

Marlene just shakes her head in amazement. "You two...get a room, okay? Or at least let me get out of here and leave you two be."

The night before the memorial service Vanessa and I eat at the famed Dooky Chase's Restaurant, and then go home and tumble into bed. Before falling asleep, she asks, "Do you plan on going to tomorrow's service?"

"No," I say, my head sinking into the pillow and my spirit sinking into sleep. "Too many people, too crowded, I'll be just as happy watching it on TV."

"But watching it on TV won't be the same," she gently protests, stroking my hair.

"I don't care."

She says something in reply but by then, I'm asleep.

I wake up and realize I'm alone.

The house is empty.

But I smell something delightful.

Fresh-brewed coffee.

I roll out of bed, yawning, check the time.

It's just past 7 a.m., and in the kitchen, there's a fresh pot of coffee.

And a handwritten note.

Hey, sleepyhead…

Since you want to slack off, Marlene and I are taking the truck to the Fair Grounds to join the morning celebration and sell some breakfast.

Watch things on TV if you want, but you're welcome to join us.

And then, the best part of the note.

Love, always,

Vanessa

I pour myself a cup of coffee.

Love, indeed.

I go to my living room, plant myself on the couch, and switch on the TV. I spin through all of the news channels—like most everyone here in Crescent City, I'm sick of the 24/7 news coverage of the Mardi Gras attacks—and then I go to Turner Classic Movies, but at this moment, they're between movies and are running old black-and-white serials, which I find boring.

Finally, I settle on a weather channel, and see a perky blonde outlining the day's forecast, which is a relief from the past three days of wind and storms.

I half-listen to her little morning spiel, wondering if I should crawl back into bed, or should I do the grown-up thing and join Marlene and Vanessa, and that's when it happens.

"…and it'll be what they call CAVU for the vice president when his official aircraft lands at Naval Air Station Joint Reserve Base New Orleans in less than two hours."

I sit still.

CAVU.

Why has that phrase struck me so hard?

I feel my old cop senses tingling, like the moment you get a tiny bit of forensic evidence that will break everything open and cast a wide spotlight, illuminating what has happened, and what might yet happen.

CAVU.

In aircraft pilot terms, CAVU means "Ceiling And Visibility Unlimited"…in other words, a perfect flying day.

Billy Needham's voice comes to me:

We've just begun. Honest.

And a few moments later:

The sky's the limit.

It hits me like a sledgehammer blow to my stomach.

The attacks a few days ago…just the opening act.

To get attention. Publicity. Lots of attention.

Now, the news media, the politicians, and nearly

sixty-five thousand innocents will be gathering in a wide, open, and vulnerable park...

With Billy Needham, private pilot with lots of resources, waiting to strike again. *The sky's the limit.*

I jump off the couch so fast I drop my coffee to the tiled floor, shattering the mug.

CHAPTER 94

NEARLY AN hour of white-knuckled driving later, I've reached my destination.

The horse farm of Emily Needham Beaudette.

Billy's half-sister.

And home to wide and flat acres of grassland.

God, how could I have been so stupid?

The FBI, NOPD, the state police, Homeland Security, and everybody else have been raiding and observing any properties belonging to Billy Needham and whatever shell companies he owns.

But would they go here, a hundred miles away from New Orleans, to a horse farm belonging to his sister? Doubtful.

And if he is planning a spectacular attack from the air, he would need an airstrip and hangar.

But knowing what I know from my police experience, the airspace around New Orleans is going to be closed and tightly monitored.

In the minutes of speeding up here, I've called and texted Cunningham, Vanessa, and Marlene, telling them what I feared, telling them to contact the police and for God's sake, stay away from the Fair Grounds Race Course today.

Hell, I even tried to contact Special Agent Morgan, but nothing seemed to go through.

I have no confidence that any of my warnings have gone through. Marlene and Vanessa will be so busy with breakfast that they might not check their phones, and Cunningham and Morgan take turns ignoring me.

But I'm confident of one thing for sure.

That I'm absolutely, 100 percent right that an attack is coming, and it's coming from a horse farm owned by Billy Needham's sister.

There.

Up ahead.

The narrow country road marked PRIVATE. I brake, the car's end nearly fishtailing, and I swerve onto the gravel path, slamming on the accelerator again. The gravel road is in fine shape but I still bounce up and down as I roar down it, glancing anxiously up into the clear and inviting blue sky.

There.

The mansion and its stables and perfect flat green fields—perfect for an aircraft to use!—are up ahead, as is the large metal gate. The impressive metal barrier grows into view as I get closer, and I think, *Pure Hollywood, but I'll drive through there if I have to*—

And I see someone has already beaten me to it.

The gates are slowly swaying back and forth, and there is twisted metal and a broken lock mechanism, and I go through as well, the gates scraping at the side of the car as I burst through into the private yards.

The mansion is to the left, the nearest large barn is to the right, and parked up ahead is—

A silver Audi!

Just like the one I saw going into the junkyard that night, when I was following poor Ibrahim Farzat.

Billy Needham.

Has to be.

I slow down and pull in next to the Audi, step out, overdressed for this fine morning, but I don't care. My 9mm Smith & Wesson M&P is in my hand, with four spare magazines in my jacket pocket.

I look around as I go up to the front porch.

The place is empty.

No horses practicing out in the fields, no stable hands or other workers moving around on the grounds.

The stillness and emptiness of the place makes my scalp tingle.

I go up to the front door, and it's open.

I peer in.

A luxurious sitting room beyond the small foyer. Antique furniture, heavy wooden tables, crystal chandelier, Oriental carpets, and leather-bound books snugly placed into bookshelves.

I step in.

A figure is sitting on the couch.

I take a breath.

It's Emily, dressed in heavy riding boots with silver spurs, tan riding jodhpurs, and a fine white blouse with lace around the neck and sleeves.

"Ms. Beaudette?"

I step closer.

Her head is tilted back, and I see the black scorch mark of a bullet wound in the middle of her forehead, just above her wide-open, stunned eyes.

CHAPTER 95

I TAKE another step closer when a quiet voice behind me says, "Hell of a sight, eh?"

I whirl and bring up my pistol and Billy Needham casually makes an appearance, like he was coming in from the other side of the house, hoping to see a table set before him with his breakfast. He doesn't even spare a glance at me, my pistol, or his dead sister as he walks past, carrying a small leather case and some folded maps and charts in his hands. He goes by me and sits at the table, spreads out the papers, and glances at them. He has on heavy khaki slacks, a blue button-down shirt, and a leather jacket. Aviator-style sunglasses dangle from a cord around his neck.

I step right up to him, pointing my pistol.

"Billy..."

He looks up. "What? 'Freeze'? 'Don't move'? 'You're under arrest'?" He grins. "Oh, yeah. Not a cop anymore, are you? And not much of a chef, either. Go away, Caleb, I've got work to do."

"You...your sister..."

He looks over to Emily. "Ah, poor dear. Among the mongrels, idiots, and thieves that make up the Needham clan, she, at least, treated me well. Listened to me.

Gently argued with me. And protected me, even when you were up here, sniffing around. It only went sideways when she threatened to call you with the truth. Good Lord, Rooney, why the hell couldn't you leave everything alone?"

I'm inches away from placing the muzzle of my pistol against his temple. "Because I won't let you go on! I won't let you kill thousands of innocents! You and your—"

Billy is as calm as the sociopath he is as he looks at the maps and charts and says, "Oh, blah blah blah. Who mourns for the dead of Berlin? Eh? Tens of thousands of innocents killed when Berlin fell to the Russians, and now, Berlin is a clean, free, and safe city. Those innocents had to die for the greater good. And when I'm done, New Orleans will go back to its roots, back to the real community, without the tacky tourists, the developers, the ones who steal our culture, our—"

I jam the gun in his chest and say, "Billy, get your hands up, and stand up. Now!"

He raises his head, gives me a look like he's finally realizing I'm standing there aiming a pistol at him, and softly says, "Oh, Rooney, I'm afraid I can't do that."

His hand goes back into the small leather bag and before I can even react, he pulls out a revolver and shoots me square in the chest.

CHAPTER 96

MY CHEST feels like an elephant has stood on it with all four legs, like some deranged circus act, and I flicker my eyes open.

Oh shit, does it hurt.

I'm flat on the finely carpeted floor of Emily's sitting room, trying to take a breath, failing.

Distantly I hear Billy rustling some papers and muttering to himself, and then footsteps and the slam of the door closing behind him.

I close my eyes. So tempting just to keep my eyes closed, let the inviting darkness come forth and take me away, and let somebody else take care of things.

The police tried to screw me, the FBI wouldn't listen to me…so to hell with them all.

And then it comes to me, saves me right there.

Vanessa.

She and Marlene…they're at the Fair Grounds.

Right now.

With tens of thousands of others.

I grind out the words, "Man up, Rooney. Get moving."

I push myself up from the floor, breathing hard, flopping back against the same couch where Emily's body is resting.

I paw at my jacket and shirt, tear it open, revealing—

The Kevlar vest I'm wearing. Good enough for the terrorists, good enough for me.

I rub at the deep dimple where the round hit me— probably a .357 Magnum round—and there's broken bones, bruises, and maybe even a shattered sternum under there.

I breathe in, nearly faint from the pain. I still have the fractured rib from when Ty Grant attacked me, which isn't helping anything.

God!

I'm on my feet.

I glance down.

There.

I pick up my pistol, nearly passing out again.

I stumble toward the door, like one of the many drunks I've seen in my life, traipsing through the happy streets of New Orleans.

Outside.

The Audi is gone.

My Impala is there.

I go down the steps, nearly falling. Step closer to my car.

I hear the slight sound of an engine, look way off to the distance where two other low stables squat, and see the tiny shape of the Audi come to a halt.

There.

I go to my car.

Breathe in.

Reach in my pocket for the keys.

No keys.

Other pocket.

Still no keys.

Damnit!

What now?

The other stable is close.

I blink my eyes.

Now it seems far, far away.

I stagger toward it, forcing my legs, easing my breathing so the sharp knife points digging into my lungs ease off, and when I get into the wide barn, with the smell and sounds of the horses, I feel slightly better.

Just a bit.

Some horses poke their heads out of their stables, looking at me with equine curiosity, and I know in the movies and the TV shows, this is where the hero would gallantly leap on one of the handsome steeds and trot to the rescue.

Not this hero.

Three ATVs are parked against the wall, and overhead, on a pegboard, keys dangle free.

In less than a minute, I'm on a black, mud-splattered ATV, racing out to the pastures, hoping that I'm not too late. There were dozens of employees last time I was here, but today the place is empty—did Emily give everyone the day off to go to the memorial service?

Out on the wide pastures, I spot the two flagpoles I had seen on my first visit here, but they're no longer empty.

They now have bright-orange windsocks flapping from them, letting pilots see the wind direction.

The slight bumps and ruts spear pain into my chest, again and again.

I grit my teeth, and then scream in pain, over and over.

Up ahead, doors begin sliding open at the two low buildings.

Airplanes appear, engines roaring with devilish power, propellers spinning, and one, two, three, and then four emerge.

Two from each building.

Oh, God, I'm going to fail again.

CHAPTER 97

THE FOUR single-engine aircraft—Cessna 172s, it looks like—line up one behind another, like some horrible parade, ready to rain down death and destruction once they get airborne.

Each is carrying two metal cylinders—one under each wing—and I'm sure the cockpit and storage area in each plane is packed with explosives, shrapnel, and who knows what kind of chemical weaponry…God, almost everything and anything to tear through the crowds and kill and maim as many as possible.

Words from Cunningham come back to me:

"…*the thing is, terrorist bastards are always one step ahead, weaponizing stuff that's usually innocuous.*"

Like private aircraft.

Single-engine Cessnas or Piper Cubs.

Who would ever think?

Would ever consider?

Ever plan?

Billy Needham, that's who.

I speed along, parallel to the four aircraft, and a hint of hope appears. They're moving slowly, moving into position, and I'm managing to maintain pace near them.

Up ahead I see the grass is a different color, almost…rectangular in shape, and that's where they're headed. That's the homemade airstrip. That's what they're going to use, and in my mind's eye, it all comes together, one Cessna after another taking off, flying low to avoid detection, heading for the Fair Grounds, each aircraft coming in north, south, east, and west, and

Dropping into the open, screaming, running crowds.

Sharp metal wings cutting in.

Spinning propellers turning the Fair Grounds into a charnel house.

Explosions ripping through the once-happy and joyous place.

Shrapnel scything through, cutting down the crowds, dismembering, slicing, disemboweling, and then, blasts of flame and smoke…

With the pain, I almost feel like vomiting with the certainty of what's going to happen next.

I feel a difference in the ground, and now I'm on the airfield, and I speed away, going away from the aircraft.

A gamble.

Oh man, a gamble, but that's what my life and New Orleans is based on.

Gambling that a city can live and grow among the swamps and mangroves, and that the people from all different stations and walks of life can grow and thrive and love there.

Vanessa, I think.

Vanessa.

Finally breaking away from her abusive husband, finding a new life, a new love, finding happiness after such a long time…

And to die within the next few minutes?

No!

I spin the ATV around, facing the aircraft.

One following another following the other...

The lead aircraft increases its speed.

Starts coming in my direction.

I crank the throttle wide, speeding down the grassy strip.

Aiming right at the propeller.

Going faster.

We're coming at each other.

The propeller a blur. The Cessna bouncing along on its three tires.

Bouncing.

Starting to gain altitude.

Starting to fly off.

With its three accomplices lining up right behind it.

I lean down, hoping with head and torso flat against the ATV that I can reduce the wind drag, gain just a bit more speed, that's all I need, just a bit more speed....

I leap off, crying out as I hit the ground, and I force myself to look at what happens next, like a movie slowing down, frame-by-frame, and—

The ATV roars ahead, going straight to the spinning propeller, and it—

—misses.

Slides under the wing without striking a damn thing, and—

"No!" I scream, and the ATV, with no driver and buffeted by the propeller wash, flips over, again and again, smashing into the elevators on the tail of the airplane.

The lead Cessna makes a sharp, digging turn, the propeller striking the grass and pasture, and it tilts and—

The second Cessna crashes into the first.

The third makes a sudden swerve but it doesn't move in time, and collides with the second aircraft.

The fourth tries to avoid the pileup, the tangle of wings, tires, fuselage, and breaking propellers before it, and it starts to fly up and over the tangled mess, when a roaring, blasting, fiery explosion blows it to pieces.

CHAPTER 98

I WAIT a couple of minutes before I get up, and then I limp and stumble my way to the burning and scattered piles of wrecked aircraft. As I get closer, the stench of petroleum assaults me, and I know I guessed right: each aircraft was carrying chemicals—something to burn the already bleeding and shattered survivors of the Fair Grounds.

Then I spot the shrapnel, the screws, bolts, and nails, scattered all over the runway, ready to—

Ready to—

I stop, lean over, and vomit, again and again…like a rookie cop, looking at his first dead body.

Then I get up, start walking again, wanting to see a dead Billy, and his dead comrades. I can see Billy going through with this, his deranged thoughts and fantasies, but whom did he convince to join him? Who would these men have been? And more importantly…do they have allies out there, waiting for—God forbid it—a third attack?

I get to the crumpled cabin of one of the Cessnas, and lean down, peering through the shattered windshield, at the crumpled seat and broken instrument panel, and—

There's nobody there.

Nobody!

There are controls there, and a laptop computer, and a broken system of cables and pulleys, and it comes to me.

This wasn't a suicide mission.

This was an out-and-out kill mission, using these Cessnas as huge, weapons-filled drones.

No wonder one of the hangars had a large radio antenna behind it.

That's how they were controlled.

Angus, back when I had interrogated him at the bridge.

And they even got these smarty scientist types, smarter than you, cop, you can be sure.

This wasn't a suicide mission, then.

Meaning…

I whip around, look to the two open hangars, and there—

Is the Audi, speeding away.

Escaping.

Billy getting away with it.

I could yell, scream, shout, but I instantly react with my cop instincts.

I throw myself to the petroleum-stained grass, pull out my pistol, start shooting.

Not like the movies or TV, with rapid-fire shots.

The odds are against me.

I force myself to relax, to focus, and most of all, to aim.

I fire one shot.

Another.

Another.

With each second the Audi is getting farther away

from me, closer and closer to final escape, and I can't let that happen.

It's all up to me.

Another shot.

Another.

I lead the Audi, like a duck hunter aiming ahead of his prey, and I keep on shooting, not aiming for the tires, or the gas tank, but for the windows.

I mean to kill the son of a bitch.

I shoot again.

Then…

The Audi slows down.

Sways back and forth, back and forth.

Slows some more.

I get up, shaking, legs quivering, my hammered chest feeling like the bones there are about to impale my heart and cause me to bleed out near the burning wreckage, and I don't care.

I'm beyond caring.

I start my long walk to the still Audi.

Once again, a gamble has paid off for my beloved Big Easy, its people, and most of all, my Vanessa.

Vanessa.

It feels like half the morning has passed before I get to the car. The engine is still running but the windshield and side windows are pockmarked with bullet holes.

I tug the driver's door open and Billy slides out.

It looks like one of my rounds got him in the shoulder.

There's lots of blood on him, and the seat.

He tumbles to the ground.

His eyes open.

He's still alive.

I kneel next to him.

He's talking to me, cursing me, promising vengeance, a violent death.

I shove the end of my pistol into his mouth.

His eyes widen; he tries to scream with the cold metal in his mouth.

I lean over so he can hear me.

"Remember the other day when I said I'd screw my pistol into your worthless mouth and pull the trigger?"

I push it in farther. "It was you who sent people to attack Marlene! To trash my truck!"

His eyes are wide and he's trying to talk, but I don't take the gun out. I don't care what he has to say. "It was you who sent those Nazis after Vanessa! Why? To get to me? Are you the one who told Lucas Dodd about me and Vanessa, too?"

He's coughing and gagging, trying to explain himself, but there's nothing he can say. And I can tell from his desperate expression that all my accusations are true. "Sixty-five thousand people! You were going to murder sixty-five thousand people!"

His good arm lifts up, tries to push me away, but he can't do it. He's too feeble and I'm too determined.

"Sixty-five thousand! And those innocent people— innocent *children!*—killed in the parade! You animal!"

Then I pull the pistol free.

He coughs, chokes.

The end of the muzzle is wet with his bloody spit.

"Go to hell, Billy," I say. "But it won't be today… because each bullet in my pistol is worth about fifty cents, much more than you'll ever be."

Then I sit back and wait.

CHAPTER 99

"GIMME FIVE scoops, three quacks, six waddles, two meows, and nine shakes!"

I'm hunched over the flaming-hot stove, soaked head to toe in sweat.

I'm scarfing an endless stream of jalapeños, so many that I'm getting heartburn.

Or maybe it's my healing sternum and three ribs, still aching after the Kevlar vest stopped the round from Billy Needham's .357 Magnum.

I'm scooping grits, charring sausages, toasting baguettes, searing duck breasts, sautéing shrimp, blackening catfish, and deep-frying dough strips like a maniac, working furiously to fill the orders my ex-wife is barking at me.

I've never been happier in my life.

It's been two weeks since Mardi Gras, and things here in the greatest city in the world are back to normal, or whatever passes as normal in this wonderful, crazy metropolis. The news media coverage has dwindled away, Billy Needham is no longer mentioned on the front page, and the breathless stories about the "miracle of New Orleans"—the multiple crashes of the deadly aircraft drones on Emily Beaudette's estate—have been replaced by stories about the upcoming NFL draft and what it means for our Saints.

And there's been a few other miracles as well, like the one I keep on glancing at as I hurry to keep up with Marlene's insistent and barking voice.

Across the street, sitting on a low concrete wall, are about a dozen white guys, dressed in yellow T-shirts, pants, or hoodies.

Members of the Franklin Avenue Soldiers.

But today they're not waiting to gun for me.

They're chowing down on my food. After I saved the city, I guess the Franklin Avenue gang was so appreciative they decided not to murder me.

Yeah, miracles indeed.

I've been interviewed, re-interviewed, and told that I can expect additional *official* interviews in the future from various government agencies and congressional panels. The *Times-Picayune* has been all over the story since the first responders came to Emily's estate, and among the stories they've broken include the promotion of Cunningham, some unexpected retirements from the upper NOPD brass, and a small blurb about a high-ranking FBI official named Morgan who's been tasked a new and important assignment.

As head of the FBI field office in Butte, Montana.

The line is long and I know we're about to run out of food, but I don't care. We're alive, we're well, and Marlene being Marlene, she's also found a way to make an extra buck from all that's happened: colorful T-shirts that show a drawing of the Killer Chef truck, with a shotgun blast exiting the rear door, a caricature of me running away, and the caption: I HAD A BLAST AT KILLER CHEF!

Then I hear a voice yelling from outside, "Hey, this

place stinks! It discriminates against the less-abled! I'm going to sue, just you see!"

I walk over from the stove and fryer, look through the service window, and smile.

"Gordon, I'll be right down!"

Marlene says, "Make it quick, damnit, that line's not getting any shorter!"

I step out from the rear of the truck—where a new sign says, DON'T KNOCK IF YOU'RE NOT GOING TO PAY, an attempt to thin out the autograph seekers and reporters—and race over to see my friend Gordon Andrews, the skilled PI who had helped me and New Orleans so much in my investigation. Along the side of the truck, near the posted menus, are scores of cards, handwritten notes, and even drawings from school children, all carrying the same message:

Thank you for saving New Orleans.

I didn't want to post them outside the truck, but Marlene overruled me, as she usually does. "Think of the publicity and foot traffic, you silly man," she said.

Gordon's a middle-aged, gray-bearded man of true elegance and class, wearing a baby-blue seersucker suit and red bowtie, and as I approach, he expertly maneuvers his electric wheelchair around to face me.

He's been in that chair for twelve years, ever since a man he was tailing as part of a case got rattled and shot him, severing Gordon's spine and permanently paralyzing him. But his sense of humor, his smarts, and his connections all across New Orleans remain as sharp as ever.

I grasp his hand and say, "Gordon, again, thanks for helping me out. It made the biggest difference."

He gives my hand a strong squeeze and says in his cultured voice, "Well, old friend, if that's what you think, I'll drop my threats…if in addition I receive an extra-large serving of your famed waddle."

"Of course," I say, "and it'll be on the house."

His smile is as cheery as ever. "I have no doubt…but Caleb?"

"Yes?"

"Before you scamper back and start cooking and ignoring Marlene's insults, I need to ask you this: what's next?"

"What do you mean?"

He swivels his chair around, looks at the line of hungry customers stretching away, many leaning left or right to take selfies in front of my truck. He says, "Oh, you have quite the business here, friend. But suppose Marlene decides she's had enough? Or your feet and joints start aching too much? Or your lungs start acting up because of all the smoke and grease you inhale?"

Marlene leans out the window, gives me a sharp glare that says, *Get your ass back in here and get to work!*

"I'll figure it out then, I guess," I say. "I don't think any kind of official police work is going to be in my future…I burned a lot of bridges, insulted too many higher-ups along the way."

"And also along the way, you saved hundreds—if not thousands—of lives," Gordon says. "Here." He passes me a manila envelope from a pouch on his wheelchair.

"What's this?" I ask.

"Your future, if you want it," he says. "The application for becoming a licensed private investigator in the great state of Louisiana. It's not a cakewalk, Caleb. There's an intensive forty-hour course, followed by a rigorous exam. And if you pass, congratulations, you have to work for a sponsoring agency for six months before taking on any of your own cases."

I gingerly hold the envelope. It should feel heavy with all of the paperwork inside, but instead it feels as light as a feather.

"You think I have what it takes to be a private investigator?" I ask.

"After the events of the past few weeks, I do," he says. "And so do many others. I've gotten numerous phone calls, inquiring if you were available to help in some…complex cases. And Caleb, I'd be honored to be your sponsor when the time comes."

I nod. "I'll think about it."

"I know you will," he says, smiling. "In the meantime, how long are you going to make a poor cripple like me wait for some food?"

"Not long, I promise," I say, turning, and instantly realizing I've just uttered a lie to my old friend.

Because Vanessa is standing at the rear of Killer Chef.

I go up to her and she nearly leaps into my arms, hugging and kissing me, and I hug and kiss her back.

"Hold on," I say, laughing. "I must stink of sweat and grease."

She kisses me again. "And you think I care?"

We break apart, but not too far apart. My chest is hurting after that hug, and I couldn't care less.

"I'm hoping you don't," I say.

Wearing jeans and a white blouse, she looks positively angelic. Her blond hair looks like spun gold, her simple clothes can't hide her curvy body, and her smile is the true expression of someone who has stepped onto a new path of life and love.

"Lucky for you, you're correct, Mr. Rooney," she

says. "I know you're busy, but do you have time for one of our famous walks?"

"I'll make the time," I say, tearing off my apron. I open the rear door and shout in, "Mar, I'll be gone for a couple of minutes! Make sure you give Gordon whatever he wants, on the house!"

I drop the apron and envelope on the truck floor and Marlene shouts back, "Make it quick or I'm coming after you with that shotgun, and this time, I won't miss!"

We start to take a quiet walk down Esplanade Avenue, a wide boulevard lined with stately, stunning old homes. Before long, our hands find each other's, our fingers intertwine.

"I never said thank you," she says. "For, you know, everything."

"That's because you didn't have to," I say.

"If it weren't for you, I'd still be trapped," she says. "Stuck in a job I hated. Married to a man I despise."

"I don't believe that for a second."

"It's true, Caleb. You didn't just save this city. You saved...*me*."

We stop walking under the shade of a gently swishing oak tree. I turn to her and slip my hands around her waist.

"You're a lot stronger than you realize, Vanessa. You deserve nothing but the best in the world. You would have found a way to get it."

She smiles at me and leans in.

"I think I already have. Scratch that. I *know* I have."

Under the spreading oak trees, we kiss and kiss, and then I hear the honking of Killer Chef's horn.

She laughs. "I see Marlene is calling you back."

"Great food and great customers can never be denied," I say.

She takes my hand, gives it a loving squeeze, and starts to gently propel me back to the place I love most.

"Come on," she says, "I'll lend a hand…if you want."

I squeeze her hand hard.

"I want," I say. "Very, very much."

RECIPES FROM THE KILLER CHEF FOOD TRUCK

Blackened Catfish Sandwich

- 1 catfish filet, about 5–6 oz.
- 1 tbsp. honey
- ¼ tsp. kosher salt
- ¼ tsp. freshly ground black pepper
- ½ tsp. cayenne pepper
- ¼ tsp. ground cardamom
- 1 tbsp. prepared horseradish
- 2 tbsp. mayonnaise
- 2 tbsp. olive oil, divided
- 1 small yellow onion, halved and thinly sliced
- 1 small green pepper, halved lengthwise, seeds removed, and sliced into thin strips
- 1 small baguette, preferably from Leidenheimer Baking Company
- 1 tsp. butter

Pat catfish dry with a paper towel. Coat with honey and season all over with salt, black pepper, cayenne pepper, and cardamom, and set aside.

In a small bowl, mix together the horseradish and mayonnaise.

Place 1 tbsp. of the olive oil in a medium sauté pan over medium heat. When oil is shimmering, add onion and green pepper and stir to coat. Cook, stirring occasionally, until onion and pepper are soft and beginning to brown slightly, about 5–7 minutes. Remove from the pan and set aside.

Raise the heat to medium-high, and add the remaining tbsp. olive oil to the sauté pan. When oil is shimmering, add the catfish and cook until spices are blackened and catfish is cooked through, about 3 minutes per side. Remove from the heat.

Split the baguette down the middle lengthwise, and melt the butter in another pan set over medium-high heat. When butter is melted and bubbling, place baguette facedown in the pan, making sure it's in contact with the butter, and toast until golden brown, about 3 minutes. Slide toasted baguette onto a plate and spread the top half with horseradish and mayonnaise mixture. Top with the catfish, onion, and peppers, and serve.

Cajun-style Scrambled Egg Po'boy

- 1 tbsp. rendered duck fat
- 1 small yellow onion, diced
- 2 extra-large eggs
- 1 tbsp. heavy cream
- ¼ tsp. kosher salt
- 1 tsp. Cajun seasoning*

---

* You can find Cajun seasoning blends in the spice aisle of any grocery store, or you can make your own by mixing

- 1 small baguette, preferably from Leidenheimer Baking Company
- 1 tsp. butter
- 2 scallions, white and green parts thinly sliced

Melt duck fat in a medium frying pan set over medium heat. When fat is shimmering, add diced onion and cook, stirring occasionally, until onion is soft and translucent, about 5 minutes.

While onion cooks, crack both eggs into a small bowl and beat with a whisk. Add cream, salt, and Cajun seasoning blend, and whisk to combine.

Add the egg mixture to the pan with the onion and lower the heat. Using a heatproof spatula or wooden spoon, gently stir and fold eggs until large curds form and the eggs are no longer runny. Remove from the heat.

Split the baguette down the middle lengthwise, and melt the butter in another pan set over medium-high heat. When butter is melted and bubbling, place baguette facedown in the pan, making sure it's in contact with the butter, and toast until golden brown, about 3 minutes. Slide toasted baguette onto a plate, fill with eggs and sliced scallions, cut into halves, and serve.

equal parts ground black pepper, garlic powder, onion powder, dried thyme and/or dried oregano, sweet paprika, and cayenne pepper.

Duck-Fat Fries

- 1 lb. russet potatoes
- 2–3 qts. rendered duck fat*
- Sea salt

Scrub potatoes thoroughly and peel if desired (though leaving some or all of the skin on is fine). Slice potatoes in half lengthwise, then cut into ¼-inch-thick strips. Soak the potato strips in cold water for one hour, then drain.

While potatoes are draining, melt duck fat in a large (at least 5-quart), heavy, high-sided pot or saucepan. Once fat is thoroughly melted, heat over medium heat until temperature reaches 325 degrees on a frying or candy thermometer. Carefully lower drained potatoes into the melted fat, working in batches if necessary so as not to drop the temperature of the fat, and cook through, about 5–7 minutes. Remove potatoes from the fat using a slotted spoon or spider, and drain on paper towels.

Potatoes should be fully cooked but not fried.

While potatoes drain again, raise the heat under the fat to medium-high, and heat until temperature reaches 375 de-

---

* You can render and save your own duck fat whenever you roast a whole duck or sear duck breasts. Tubs of rendered duck fat are also widely available at most grocery stores and online.

grees. Return the potatoes to the fat, in batches again if necessary, and fry until crispy and golden, another 2–3 minutes. Remove potatoes from the fat using a slotted spoon or spider, drain on paper towels, and sprinkle liberally with sea salt. Allow to cool slightly, and serve.

Duck fat can be stored for later use: Allow to cool thoroughly, pour through a fine mesh strainer into desired storage container, and chill in the refrigerator. Duck fat can then be stored in the freezer for up to six months.

Crab Gumbo

- ½ c. unsalted butter
- ⅔ c. all-purpose flour
- 1 tbsp. vegetable oil
- 1 lb. Andouille sausage,* sliced
- 1 large yellow onion, finely chopped
- 1 medium green pepper, seeded and finely chopped
- 3 large celery stalks, finely chopped
- 2 garlic cloves, minced
- 1 (14.5-oz.) can diced tomatoes
- 2 bay leaves
- 2 tbsp. Cajun seasoning
- 2 tsp. kosher salt, plus more to taste
- 8 c. shrimp stock (or shrimp stock and water)

* You can find Andouille sausage in most grocery stores and butcher shops, or online.

- 6 oz. dark beer
- 1 c. sliced fresh okra, or 1 c. frozen cut okra, thawed
- 1 lb. jumbo lump crabmeat
- White rice or grits
- Parsley and chopped scallions for serving

Make the roux: In a large, heavy saucepan or Dutch oven, melt the butter over medium heat. When butter is bubbling and frothy, whisk in the flour until combined. Lower the heat and continue cooking, whisking or stirring frequently, until mixture turns a deep chocolate brown, 30–40 minutes. Remove the roux from the heat, scrape into a bowl, and reserve.

In the same saucepan or Dutch oven, heat the vegetable oil over medium-high heat. Add the Andouille and cook until sausage is brown and has released some of its fat. Add the onion, green pepper, celery, and garlic, and cook until vegetables are starting to soften, 5–7 minutes. Add the reserved roux back into the pan, stir to combine with vegetables, and cook until starting to bubble. Add the tomatoes, bay leaves, Cajun seasoning, and salt, and stir everything to combine. Add the shrimp stock (or stock and water) and the beer, scraping up any brown bits of sausage off the bottom of the pan. Bring to a boil, then lower heat, cover, and simmer mixture for 1 hour.

After an hour, remove the cover, add the okra, and continue simmering, uncovered, over medium-low heat for another half hour.

Stir in the crabmeat and cook for another 5 minutes, until the meat is just cooked through. Remove the bay leaves. Serve over white rice or grits, and garnish with chopped parsley and green onions.

Savory Grits

- 3 c. water
- 1 c. stone-ground corn grits
- ½ tsp. salt
- 1 c. heavy cream, divided
- 2 tbsp. butter
- ¼ c. grated Parmesan cheese (optional)

Bring water to a boil. Add the grits and salt, reduce the heat to medium-low, and cook for 10 minutes, stirring occasionally. Most of the water should be absorbed and the grits should be thicker.

Add half of the heavy cream and continue to simmer, partially covered, stirring occasionally, for another 10 minutes. Stir in remaining heavy cream and simmer, partially covered, stirring occasionally, until all the liquid is absorbed, another 20–30 minutes.

Stir in the butter and Parmesan cheese (if desired) and serve warm.

Dirty Rice with Crawfish Boudin

- 2 tbsp. vegetable oil or bacon fat, divided
- ½ lb. pork sausage, casings removed
- ½ lb. chicken livers
- 1 medium yellow onion, chopped
- 1 small green pepper, seeded and chopped
- 2 large celery stalks, finely chopped
- 2 garlic cloves, minced
- 2 tsp. Cajun seasoning
- 1 tsp. kosher salt
- Bay leaf
- ¼ c. chicken stock or dry white wine
- 4 c. cooked white rice
- 2 tbsp. chopped parsley
- 4 links crawfish boudin*

In a large heavy saucepan or Dutch oven, heat 1 tbsp. vegetable oil or bacon fat over medium-high heat. Add the pork sausage and chicken livers and stir to break up the sausage meat. Cook until meat is starting to brown on the bottom, about 3 minutes. Add the second tbsp. of oil to the pan, and, once heated, add the onion, green pepper, celery, and garlic, and continue cooking until all the meat is browned and vegetables are soft and translucent, another 5–7 minutes. Stir in the Cajun seasoning and salt and cook until fragrant, another 1–2 minutes. Add the bay leaf and the broth or wine to the pan

---

*   You can purchase crawfish boudin online from various specialty retailers.

and cook, scraping up any brown bits on the bottom of the pan, until liquid is nearly evaporated. Stir in the rice and parsley, remove from the heat, and cover to keep warm while boudin cooks.

Crawfish boudin can be grilled or sautéed:

To grill: Place boudin links over hot, oiled grill and sear on both sides, about 3 minutes per side. Turn grill heat down to medium, close cover, and continue cooking another 5 minutes until plump and heated through.

To sauté: Fill a 12-inch frying pan with ¼ c. water and bring to a simmer. Add sausage and cook, partially covered and turning occasionally, about 10–15 minutes. Remove the sausage links to a plate and drain the water remaining in the pan. Put the pan back over medium heat, and add remaining tbsp. vegetable oil. When oil is hot, add sausage back to the pan and sear until golden brown on both sides, about 3 minutes per side.

Let sausage rest off the heat for 5 minutes and slice. Remove the bay leaf and serve sausage with dirty rice.

ABOUT THE AUTHORS

James Patterson is the world's bestselling author and most trusted storyteller. He has created many enduring fictional characters and series, including Alex Cross, the Women's Murder Club, Michael Bennett, Maximum Ride, Middle School, and I Funny. Among his notable literary collaborations are *The President Is Missing*, with President Bill Clinton, and the Max Einstein series, produced in partnership with the Albert Einstein estate. Patterson's writing career is characterized by a single mission: to prove that there is no such thing as a person who "doesn't like to read," only people who haven't found the right book. He's given over three million books to schoolkids and the military, donated more than seventy million dollars to support education, and endowed over five thousand college scholarships for teachers. The National Book Foundation recently presented Patterson with the Literarian Award for Outstanding Service to the American Literary Community, and he is also the recipient of an Edgar Award and six Emmy Awards. He lives in Florida with his family.

Max DiLallo is a novelist, playwright, and screenwriter. He lives in Los Angeles.

JAMES
PATTERSON
RECOMMENDS

JAMES PATTERSON

THE BLACK BOOK

& DAVID ELLIS

THE BLACK BOOK

I have favorites among the novels I've written. *Kiss the Girls*, *Invisible*, *1st to Die*, and *Honeymoon* are top of the list. With each, I had a good feeling when the writing was finished. I believe this book — *The Black Book* — is the best work I've done in twenty-five years.

Meet Billy Harney. The son of Chicago's chief of detectives, he was born to be a cop. There's nothing he wouldn't sacrifice for his job. Enter Amy Lentini, an assistant state's attorney hell-bent on making a name for herself — by proving Billy isn't the cop he claims to be.

A horrifying murder leads investigators to a brothel that caters to Chicago's most powerful citizens. There's plenty of evidence on the scene, but what matters most is what's missing: the madam's black book.

JAMES
PATTERSON

THE
FIRST
LADY

BRENDAN DUBOIS

THE FIRST LADY

The US government is at the forefront of everyone's mind these days and I've become incredibly fascinated by the idea that one secret can bring it all down. What if that secret is a US President's affair that results in a nightmarish outcome?

Sally Grissom, leader of the Presidential Protection Division, is summoned to a private meeting with the President and his chief of staff to discuss the disappearance of the First Lady. What at first seemed an escape to a safe haven turns into a kidnapping when a ransom note arrives along with what could be the First Lady's finger.

It's a race against the clock to collect the evidence that all leads to one troubling question: Could the kidnappers be from inside the White House?

JAMES PATTERSON

TEXAS RANGER

★

& ANDREW BOURELLE

TEXAS RANGER

So many of my detectives are dark and gritty and deal with crimes in some of our grimmest cities. That's why I'm thrilled to bring you Detective Rory Yates, my most honorable detective yet.

As a Texas Ranger, he has a code that he lives and works by. But when he comes home for a much-needed break, he walks into a crime scene where the victim is none other than his ex-wife—*and* he's the prime suspect. Yates has to risk everything in order to clear his name, and he dives into the inferno of the most twisted mind I've ever created. Can his code bring him back out alive?

JAMES PATTERSON

THE HOUSE NEXT DOOR

THE WORLD'S #1 BEST-SELLING WRITER

BIG THRILLS. SUSPENSE THAT KILLS.

THE HOUSE NEXT DOOR

The most terrifying danger is the one that lurks in plain sight; the one that is always there, but you don't notice it until it's too late. Here are three bone-chilling stories about exactly that.

In "The House Next Door," Laura Sherman is thrilled to have a new neighbor take an interest in her, but what happens when things go too far and things aren't really as they seem? In "The Killer's Wife," when six girls have gone missing, Detective McGrath will do anything to find them, even if that means getting too close with the suspect's wife. And finally, "We. Are. Not. Alone." proves that we aren't the only life in the universe, but what we didn't know is that they've been watching us...

For a complete list of books by
JAMES PATTERSON

VISIT
JamesPatterson.com

 Follow James Patterson on Facebook
@JamesPatterson

 Follow James Patterson on Twitter
@JP_Books

 Follow James Patterson on Instagram
@jamespattersonbooks